Lois Keith was the first recipient of the national Sue Napolitano Award for Disabled Writers. She edited the ground breaking anthology: *Mustn't Grumble, Writing by Disabled Women*, winner of the MIND/Allen Lane Book of the Year Award and is the author of the teenage novel, *A Different Life* and *Take Up Thy Bed and Walk: Death, Disability and Cure in Classic Fiction for Girls*, all published by The Women's Press. Lois Keith lives in London with her husband and their two daughters.

Out of Place

Lois Keith

First published in 2003 by Crocus
Crocus books are published by Commonword Ltd,
6 Mount Street, Manchester M2 5NS.

Crocus Books are distributed by Turnaround Publisher Services
Ltd, Unit 3, Olympia Trading Estate, Coburg Road,
Wood Green, London N22 6TZ.

Cover design by Ian Bobb.
Cover photography supplied from a Private Collection.

Printed by Shanleys, 16 Belvoir Street, Tonge Fold, Bolton
BL2 6BA

British Library Cataloguing-in-Publication Data. A catalogue
record for this book is available from the British Library.

For Colin, Rachel and Miriam

CONTENTS

REBECCA

London

2000

Grandma Susi and auntie Eva died at the opposite ends of the same week, grandma at the beginning and Eva at the end. Grandma was seventy-eight and auntie Eva was sixty-six.

It was two weeks after my sixteenth birthday and one week after I had finished my exams. I'd been imagining long mornings lying in bed eating chocolate biscuits, reading, watching television, talking to my friends on the phone, spending time with them in the park. I hadn't been expecting the world to fall on my head.

When grandma died on Sunday morning, mum went to bed and stayed there. She had one of her really bad headaches and all her bones ached; she needed to lie down and rest. By the time she got up again, auntie Eva and grandma were both buried or burned and the world was put back in a different place. A fixed point in my life, two separate fixed points, had gone.

It wasn't mum's fault being ill. I knew that even at the time, but I couldn't help feeling that it wasn't exactly fair. Other people's mothers would have dragged themselves up to make the phone calls, to arrange things. I loved mum more than anything but I couldn't stop myself imagining a story where people looked after me, not the other way round.

Of course, mum wasn't in bed all of the time. She got up on Monday afternoon to go to grandma's funeral with her sister Jackie who had just arrived from Israel with her daughters, the grown up cousins who were so wonderfully clever and successful at everything they did. She sat on a shiva chair with auntie Jackie, listened to the prayers with her eyes closed. She hugged me when I cried and shook hands with all grandma's friends when they wished her 'Long Life'. And just over a week later she got in a taxi with me to go to auntie Eva's, *her* aunt Eva's, funeral which was held in the Crematorium at Golders Green. But in between she was in bed, in pain, with the curtains drawn and her eyes tightly shut.

Until that week, I'd never thought about funerals. Of course I knew that when people died they got buried or cremated but I had no idea how that happened. I didn't know who made the decisions, didn't even know there were decisions to be made. People died and then there was a funeral. I'd seen pictures on the television of plumed black horses pulling a glass carriage with a shiny coffin inside and at those funerals there would be words made up in brightly coloured flowers, saying MUM or TERRY and people stood on the street watching the procession go by, but these seemed to be for East End villains or their mothers. I knew that Jewish people never got buried like that, even if they were criminals.

The little bit I did know about death, I knew because of grandma. A lot of her friends had died over the last few years and she used to like me to go with her to pay her respects and to see the friends who were still alive. I didn't mind. I liked to please people; it was one of the things I was good at.

It was the shivas we went to together anyway, not the funerals. I'd never been to one of those. Grandma didn't go to funerals; she said it wasn't traditional for women to go. She didn't like cremations; she didn't approve.

'Feh,' she would say in disgust. 'What way is that to deal with a dead person. To burn them to ashes like a piece of rubbish. I want to lie next to my Ziggy, may his beloved soul rest in peace, in a proper grave with a proper headstone. Then you can come and visit me and put a nice, clean stone on the grave. If you don't, no one else will, that's for sure.' When she began to talk like that, you knew it was best to say nothing.

Nobody asked me to make any decisions about grandma's funeral. Auntie Jackie was already visiting because grandma hadn't been well for a few weeks and she arranged it all. There weren't really any decisions to be made because Jewish people all get buried in the same way. There's no choosing of flowers or coffin handles or the music to be played. Nothing personal for the dead. Dust to dust, ashes to ashes, as grandma had been fond of saying.

'That Maxwell fella who owned all the newspapers,' she said to me once, the corner of her mouth raised in disgust. 'He paid all that money to be buried on the Mount of Olives, but they buried him in a sheet like everyone else. Rich man, poor man, it's all the same. They put him in the ground and his body rotted like everyone else's. Quicker I hope.'

She was living in a block of flats for older people, all Jewish, in the Finchley Road. There was a warden there, a rabbi who visited and lots of volunteers who organised outings and little concerts. She had a lovely flat: two bedrooms and a little kitchen and bathroom. Most of the people who lived there had come over as refugees from Germany and Austria in the 1930s just like her. The warden knew that we had no men in our family, no *Jewish* men who could arrange everything and say the prayers, so she organised it for us. All we had to do was turn up to the funeral and go back there afterwards. There was this social room on the ground floor where grandma used to go every afternoon for *Kaffee und Kuchen* and to eye up what all the other old ladies were wearing and that's where they held grandma's shiva: Monday evening after the funeral and Tuesday.

Auntie Jackie was worried that there wouldn't be the eleven men you needed to make up a minyan for the evening prayers, but in the end there was a big crowd. I suppose they must have been the sons and grandsons of grandma's friends. There always seemed to be lots of men in other people's families: plenty of fathers, brothers, uncles and nephews.

I'd hardly ever been to a synagogue in my life. I didn't believe in God. I didn't understand the words the rabbi said and the men echoed, but I liked the feeling of being there and the thought that this was the way it should be done. I liked the high, proud Hebrew words. I liked the food and the way the women served it and the glasses of whisky on the side. I liked all of the people who were there. I liked the way the unknown sons and daughters of grandma's friends kissed me and told me how proud grandma was of me. Of course I was sad that I'd never see her again, but it felt, for once, that our weird, muddled up family were all in the right place, doing the right thing.

Grandma's funeral was a long way away, right out in Bushey, a great flat place with thousands of black and white marble gravestones. I hated the fact that auntie Eva came to grandma's funeral all on her own. Auntie Jackie and the cousins, mum and I, all went in a huge hired car but she came in a taxi. It didn't seem right. She had her own car but when she drove, she could only get her little wheelchair in with her. I thought perhaps she came in a taxi because she wanted to be in the electric wheelchair so that she could get to the grave without having to ask anyone for help – it was a long, long walk from the place where we said the prayers, I was worried that it would be too far for mum.

At the shiva in the evening, auntie Eva sat on an ordinary chair next to mum and Jackie, not on the little dark wooden shiva chairs that looked like something out of an ancient nursery. Her face was still and white, and she held the prayer book very tight and sang the Kaddish in Hebrew along with the men. She ate the bread with pickled herring on it and the bread with the egg and then she went home. And four days later, she died.

The sense of her has faded much more quickly than grandma. When I think of grandma Susi I immediately see her with her big bosom and pencil thin legs and heels that were too high for someone her age, her brightly coloured suits with gold buttons, royal blue or crimson. Immaculate. Not a hair out of place, ever. Lipstick, foundation, rouge, nail varnish. And I can summon up her voice. The trace of the accent, the 'r's that came from the back of her mouth not the front, and the 'w's, that sounded like 'v's. But every time I try to capture a picture of auntie Eva, it twists away from me and changes shape so that I can't be sure what I'm looking at. I just seem to be left with the feeling of her. Just a memory of someone warm, the smell of her soap, a soft jumper, the wristwatch with the stretchy gold strap that she used to let me wear when I was young. She was someone I only thought I knew.

Skeletons in the cupboard. Later when I knew Eva's story, I couldn't believe how patient and calm she'd always been. If it had been me, I'd have been the angriest person alive. When I understood that she wasn't related to grandma, not even a cousin, I cried and asked mum why no one had told me.

'I didn't know either,' she said. 'Maybe they thought we'd love her less.' But I wouldn't have. I would have loved her more.

Auntie Eva's death was the most grown up thing that had ever happened to me, because I had to do it all on my own. The doctor who came said it was 'peaceful and painless' but how would he know? He wasn't there, no one was. Her next door neighbour saw two days worth of papers sticking out of her letter box and opened the door with her spare key. She found Eva lying in bed in a pale pink nightdress with little embroidered rosebuds on the yoke and thin satin ribbons to tie it up. Afterwards the doctor said the words 'heart attack' as if that was a good thing. But to me it sounded violent and lonely. Her heart was attacked. Gentle, solitary auntie Eva. We hadn't taken good enough care of her, nobody had.

She'd been dead for twenty-four hours when Mrs Lampeter found her; that's what they said. She called us up, next of kin, and she was crying and shouting and said she didn't know what to do, it wasn't up to her to do anything, and mum had to come over straight away. But mum couldn't. She tried to, she really did, but she couldn't.

Afterwards people, people like my friend Ellie's mum, said, 'Why didn't you call us? Why didn't you call us if your mother was ill? We would have helped.' And maybe they would have, these capable other people's mothers, but I thought I had to go on my own. I had to do it for auntie Eva and I had to do it for mum.

I got on the bus to the Elephant and Castle and then the underground. I looked at the faces of the people on the train, trying to think about nothing at all. At Euston I changed onto the other branch of the Northern Line and began to count off the stations: Mornington Crescent, Camden Town, Chalk Farm, Belsize Park, Hampstead, Golders Green, Brent Cross, Hendon Central. Everyone lived so far from each other.

It was ten minutes walk from the station and the nearer I got to auntie Eva's flat, the sicker I felt. If I managed not to step on any cracks in the pavement, I would know what to do when I got there and know what to say. If I touched every lamp post, I'd be able to look at her body.

And then, two minutes from her front door, I caved in. I couldn't deal with hysterical Mrs Lampeter; I couldn't deal with any of it. I sat down on the kerb, my heart banging out of my chest, not knowing what to do. I took the phone from my bag, the phone auntie Eva had given me for my sixteenth birthday, and stared at it, like people do in films. I couldn't ring mum; I couldn't ring my friends. I didn't even know whether you could dial 999 from a mobile phone or had to ring a different number, but I tried and miraculously someone answered and asked me what service I wanted. I didn't know. I tried to answer but my voice trembled and quivered and became that horrible choking, runny nosed, squeaky sound which is the only noise you can make when you're just about to lose it entirely. The voice at the other end remained perfectly calm and put me through to the police who told me to wait outside the house for them to arrive. Someone would come in with me they said, and they would sort out a doctor, and help me with the papers. My job was to calm myself down, go to the flat and wait for them to come.

And they did come. By the time I'd pulled myself together and walked round the block, they were there, a policeman and a policewoman. Everyone was very kind to me and surprised that I was doing it all on my own, which helped to make me feel grown up and the sort of person who could cope. They stayed with me through the long afternoon and even gave me a lift home. Mrs Lampeter stopped being hysterical and started being pleased that she was the one who'd found her, especially when the policeman told her she'd done the right thing. She made everyone cups of tea all afternoon and opened a packet of auntie Eva's biscuits. I don't drink tea, but that hardly mattered.

After about an hour, auntie Eva's doctor arrived. He said he'd seen her a few days earlier, and he wasn't surprised with what had happened. I asked if it was to do with her arthritis – she'd always had trouble walking and recently she'd been using her wheelchair nearly all the time, but the doctor said no, it was a heart condition and something like this could have happened at any time.

'She was a fine person, your aunt. I thought a lot of her. She was an unusual patient, one who always asked me how I was. You don't get many like that.' He shook his head and put her death certificate on the table on his way out.

'Do you know what sort of funeral she wanted?' the policewoman asked.

I shook my head glumly.

'Is there anybody to help you with the arrangements? Are you sure there isn't anyone you'd like to call to come over now? It could all take some time.'

'She's Jewish,' I said, hoping this would help.

Mrs Lampeter, still irritatingly hanging around in the doorway, said, 'Yes that's right. She was out of the house most Saturday mornings, all dressed up. And she had a lot of meetings round here. I think they were people from the synagogue who used to come.'

'You nosy old cow,' I thought. Then the phone rang. It was auntie Jackie from Israel. Mum had rung her, which was a brave thing to do because to say that they didn't get on is an understatement and Jackie's opinion of me was that I was okay considering, but not quite what I should be. Not that she ever said it, but she had that look above the eyebrows, the same expression grandma sometimes had when she looked at mum.

Jackie didn't know much about Eva, but she did know about religion and she knew that when Eva had moved into her own flat, she had joined a different synagogue. 'It's Progressive,' she said, as if she were telling me that Eva had joined some kind of weird cult. 'In Temple Fortune. They say their prayers in English and the men and women sit together. Just ring the synagogue, they'll tell you. Look in her things to see if you can find the number.'

'Will it be in the phone book?'

'I expect so. Is your mother going to be able to handle this one? Only I'm afraid I won't be able to come back to England for the funeral. I'll be back in a few weeks to sort out grandma's things.' I didn't bother to reply. Mum wouldn't have either if she'd been here instead of me.

There are some wonderful things about religion. Not the believing in God part, or even all the traditions and festivals, although I can see the appeal of those, especially since my family's so small and without any traditions at all. It's that religion is always so certain about what to do; it never flaps around trying to decide what to do on serious occasions. It's absolutely certain what's right and proper and it gets things organised. Two things sadly lacking round my house.

Auntie Eva had, of course, anticipated that one day we might have to make decisions for her, and we wouldn't know how to do it. She had paid up into the synagogue burial society so no one had to find the money and she'd made it clear that she wanted to be cremated. Only an hour or so after I made that first phone call to the synagogue, the hearse arrived. Her coffin was made of plain, pale wood. Dust to dust, ashes to ashes. I cried when I saw it and the policeman put his arm round my shoulders and told me I was a brave girl.

Of course there was plenty for me still to do and I travelled into new parts of London feeling resentful that I had to do it by myself and proud that I could manage it. By the end of it all, I could have taken a GCSE in death certificates, coroners, post mortems and crematoria. Mum kept ringing me to make sure she knew where I was and that I was okay and every evening she listened to what I'd achieved that day. She did everything she could do, but she wasn't well. I could see that; she could hardly lift her head off the pillow. She went through Eva's address book and rang people she'd never heard of to let them know, and she spoke to the rabbi about the arrangements for the day. None of us had known that Eva had so many friends, people who wanted to help in any way they could.

The rabbi was a woman. I didn't even know that you could have a female rabbi. She had long dark curly hair and wore a white, fringed shawl and a pretty embroidered skull cap. Then there were all the people I didn't know. There were some friends of grandma's whom I'd known all my life, the aunties and uncles who weren't really relatives, but there were also lots of people mum and I didn't know – all sorts of people, all different ages. Friends from her work even though she'd retired years ago, friends from the synagogue, and people we didn't know how she knew, not just old people. Mum and I were walking into the chapel when a man stopped us. He was small with grey wavy hair and he was wearing a navy blazer with gold buttons. He had tears in his eyes and his hands were shaking badly.

'You don't know me, but I was a very good friend of your aunt's. She was a wonderful woman, wonderful. Most people didn't recognise how good she was. I just wanted to say that and to wish you both 'Long Life'. I know that she loved you very much. We will all miss her.' His voice broke and he turned away from us.

'Who's that?' I asked mum.

'I'm not sure. I think he might have been auntie

Eva's boyfriend when she was a girl.'

At grandma's funeral, everyone except Eva had stood in a small, bleak chapel and said the Hebrew prayers: men on one side, women on the other. Nothing had been said about grandma, even though her life was so full and busy and interesting and auntie Jackie had told me it was because it wasn't the custom at traditional Jewish funerals to make it personal. At auntie Eva's, the rabbi spoke for a long time about her. A whole new person began to take shape, not the quiet, lonely, unmarried one she had seemed to be in grandma's eyes, the little cousin she had always taken care of, the one who couldn't walk very well and needed her – our protection, but a different person altogether. Someone with a whole life. A woman talked about her work, what an inspiration she had been to the other teachers in the centre where she'd worked and how they had all learned from her about the importance of independence. Another woman stood up and read a strange prayer about why we have to die, to make room for new babies in the world. Lots of people had tears in their eyes, not just the man who had spoken to us earlier. I thought about Eva with no babies of her own and myself as a baby with everyone looking after me and everything felt wrong. When the coffin drew back behind the red curtain on its invisible wheels, I suddenly heard grandma's voice, 'Ach, to burn you like a piece of rubbish' and wondered what she would have made of it all. Everyone I loved was disappearing and I hadn't even said goodbye to them. No grandma, no auntie Eva, just me and mum. I wanted to be looked after. I wanted to be the baby they had loved and fought over for attention. I wanted to be with grandma of the noisy kisses, flattery and showy presents, the hardback books with shiny pictures, the expensive decorated cardigans from Selfridges. I wanted to be in auntie Eva's calm, quiet presence where everything I did was wonderful and every mark I got in school proved what a clever girl I was. I put my head down and sobbed.

Vienna

November 1936

Maria sits by the fire, Eva on her lap. It is cold all around her, only the heat from the iron kitchen range licking around her face and her feet. Outside it is raining hard, a dark, grey day just short of freezing. Soon she will get up, wrap Eva in her blue woollen hat and mittens and the hand-me-down winter coat and walk to the end of Obere Donaustrasse to collect Susi from school. Susi is really too old to be collected but it is a habit with them and Susi's mother, Frau Rosen, encourages her to go whenever she can. Susi loves to see little Eva, her best pretend sister. In eight months there will be another baby for Maria. She knows this for certain, but is waiting for the right time to tell her husband. She has no idea when that right time might be.

Maria worries about Susi – Susi who has always been so independent. But the streets are no longer safe. Jewish children are pushed about and pelted with stones. Gangs of boys gather round children on their way home and spit insults. Holding your head up high and not caring what people think of you no longer works as a protection. These boys are followers of the Austrian Fatherland Front who wear their red-white-red ribbons and their crutched crosses. Susi knows, everybody knows, that when you see a gang wearing their white knee length socks, you have to get out of their way.

Maria's husband Johann is out now; she doesn't know where; she doesn't want to guess. The job of a caretaker is a loose one: some cleaning here, a bit of odd jobbing there. Plenty of time for him to be away as long as she stays at home. Maria is here, worrying as always.

She understands the feeling in the air but not the details. She knows that her husband goes off to meetings where he talks and plans things with other men and that when he returns he is both angry and elated. There is one man in particular whose thinking he admires very much.

She doesn't like the language he is beginning to use, but plenty of other people talk that way. Sometimes when he has had a beer or two, he begins to lecture her about the loss of the Empire or the unemployment and poverty in Vienna.

'What we need is a strong, new Austria. Look what's happening in Germany, it's terrific: new roads, whole new factories. The Volkswagen factory, it works like a dream, and the conditions for their workers – it's incredible. You don't see people begging on the street for a piece of bread like you do here. There's work there and good wages. They're not rotting away, dreaming of a past Empire. We need a bit of what they've got.'

She can see he is wearing a new face. It's not just his ideas that are changing. He's become distant. He doesn't even show his own daughter affection.

When she gave birth to Eva, he seemed proud enough, even though she knew that in his heart he longed for another son. She was a pretty little baby with light hair and round eyes like buttons. But when he looks at Eva now, Maria can see all too clearly what he feels.

Maria holds Eva close to her, buttons up her scratchy woollen leggings and waits another five minutes before she steps out into the cold. It is not nice to walk with the slush freezing over again and the wind biting into your face. In a minute she will put Eva into the deep wicker pram which Frau Rosen gave her. She remembers taking little Susi in the same carriage to the Jewish kindergarten in the Augarten park nearby. As soon as they were home, Susi would jump out of the pram and insist on walking 'all by myself' up the three flights of stairs to her flat, counting the curved stone steps: seventeen for the first floor, seventeen for the second floor until she reached home.

Maria was seventeen years old when she came to live with Sonya and Otto Rosen and little Susi. She thinks about her seven years there with pleasure, which is surprising considering how she lived in that flat: just a little bed behind a partition in the kitchen, just a bowl to wash herself in, no privacy. But it was a kind household, and space was a luxury she'd never known. Rooms doubled up: dayrooms became bedrooms, the study became the sitting room, the sewing room turned into the dining room. On Jewish festivals and family birthdays, furniture was moved around so that a big table could be opened up to seat all the guests.

Maria loved those family parties, even though it meant such a lot of work, Passover especially. For days she and Frau Rosen would clean and scrub, prepare and cook. For the Seder plate she helped make a paste of apple, wine and nuts to symbolise the mortar of the lost temple; horseradish sauce for the bitter times of the Jewish slaves under the Pharaohs; egg and salt water for life and bitter tears. Maria knew these stories from her own mother who had worked for Frau Rosen's mother. The meal itself went on for ever. Chopped liver with eggs and fried onions; a boned, stuffed fish bought whole from the fishmonger's with raisins for eyes; chicken soup with little dumplings made of matzo flour; roast poultry with potatoes and vegetables. And when it was beyond belief that anyone could possibly eat another mouthful, Maria would carry in the big silver platter with a bowl of stewed dried fruits and a mound of flourless cakes made with eggs and ground hazelnuts, and lemon tea served in long silver handled glasses.

On these special days, the table would take hours to prepare. The hand painted china had to be taken out of the top cupboard and washed and then all the silverware had to be polished. Maria would iron the special white linen table cloth, hand embroidered by her own mother, first on the board and again on the table. Maria's mother had worked for the Shapiros, Frau Sonya Rosen's own mother and father, for more years than she could remember, first as a girl in 1902 and then on and off after her marriage. She had practically brought Sonya up, what with Frau Shapiro being so busy helping with the shop in Mitteldorf. She still mended and embroidered the family linen and once a year she would come on the train to Vienna to bring it to them, just as she had always done: pillow cases and sheets beautifully wrapped in white tissue paper and tied with ribbon.

When Maria left to get married four-and-a-half years ago, Frau Rosen had to hire a new maid, a sturdy girl called Dora with a square jaw and sulky eyes. If Maria happens to pass Dora on the stairs when she is talking to one of the other maids who work in the building, she can sniff the familiar odour of hatred and envy, and it hurts her although you smell it often

30

enough in Vienna these days. The new maid smiles sweetly enough when she sees Herr Rosen or Susi coming along.

Maria misses her sixty schillings a month. It wasn't a fortune but she liked to have a little money of her own. She misses the company too, the bustle and the warmth of their family life. Some people might have thought Frau Rosen a bit neurotic, a bit of a moaner, but Maria liked to listen to her worries, and even now, she looks forward to their chats. She understands her and she loves Susi with all her heart, just as if she was her own. And she knows that Frau Rosen still confides in her, even though she is a younger woman. They discuss female things, the concerns of family life, just as her own mother confided in Maria's mother. Frau Rosen has to be more careful with Dora, the new maid. When Maria was living there, there was never a locked cupboard in the house.

Frau Rosen was very particular but she wasn't one of those women who put her feet up all day and treated the maid like a slave. In fact, she loved the housework. Every morning when she came back from doing the shopping, she liked nothing better than to tie her hair up in a scarf, pick up her dusters and search the house for dust and dirt. When Herr Rosen bought her one of those new fangled vacuum cleaners, she declared it was the best present she'd ever had, better than diamonds. But then she worried that somehow the dust was invisibly rising into the air through the hose and she worked even harder with her duster to catch it. It was Frau Rosen who taught Maria how to keep house, how to look for the best prices in the market, how to use leftovers so no one knew they were eating the same thing twice.

Susi was a fat little two year old with dark brown hair and a determined face when Maria had come to live with them. A busy, active child already making plans about how she wanted her world to be. 'So much to do, so little time,' her mother used to tease as Susi chatted away, wanting this, wanting that, arranging and re-arranging her toys, talking to invisible friends. She loved Maria straight away; they loved each other. If Herr and Frau Rosen went to a concert or to friends in the evenings or when Frau Rosen went to the smart coffee house to play bridge and drink tea and eat pastries with her friends, they would play together and Maria would teach Susi the songs her own mother had sung to her. Frau Rosen sang the songs of Schubert and Haydn, but Maria sang the folk songs and lullabies from the Austrian countryside. If Susi cried, she would make up little stories about two animals, a squirrel and a giraffe, who were great friends and went to the park and school together. The animals might quarrel but by the end of the story they had always made up.

How Susi, just past her eighth birthday, cried when she heard her beloved Maria was engaged to Johann. 'I'm going to kill him!' she declared.

'But you've never even met him,' her mother argued reasonably. 'You might like him. Maria does.'

'I'm going to shoot him with a gun.'

'You haven't got a gun,' her father pointed out.

'Well then, I'll save a lot of money and buy him a train ticket so that he can go on a long journey and never, ever, ever come back.'

Maria and Frau Rosen had to bite their lips to

stop themselves from laughing. They thought it best not to tell Susi that it was her own father who had approached the agents of the building to put in a good word for Johann, together with some money in an envelope, so that this younger man, unemployed with no qualifications, could get a job and a roof over his head. It was unusual, of course, for a job like this to go to someone so young, but where were the opportunities for a man like him in Vienna in these times? Herr Rosen did it, of course, for Maria for whom they all cared and to stop his wife and his daughter from carrying on so.

'What did you imagine, that you would keep her forever? She's twenty-three years old, pretty, affectionate. She's not a baby or an old maid, it's natural that she wants to get married.'

'Yes, but what do you think of him?' Frau Rosen asked her husband one evening.

'He doesn't seem to be a drunk or a gambler as far as I can tell.'

'Otto, be sensible for a moment. Do you think he's a good man?'

'A good man, how do I know? He's a good looking man. He seems to be willing to work for a living. He probably thinks he's cleverer than he is, but so do most of these young men. All we can hope is that he's good to Maria, and makes sure the roof doesn't leak.'

'Honestly, can't you be serious for a moment.'

'Sonya darling, don't get yourself into a state about this.' He put out his hand, guiding her onto his lap. 'You're lucky she'll only be downstairs, Susi will still see her, you'll get a new maid who will work hard and who you can fuss over. We'll give her a good send off, don't worry so much. Now come and listen to some music.'

Otto Rosen likes to think of himself as a serious man but one with a sense of humour too. After a day's work, he likes to read the newspaper or a novel by one of the great English writers. Or he likes to sit hand in hand with his wife, listening to a concert on Radio Vienna: Mozart perhaps, Beethoven or Schubert.

Tomorrow Susi is fourteen and Maria is to go upstairs to help prepare for her grown up tea party. Dora doesn't mind; she is glad not to have the extra work. Otto Rosen will leave the office a little earlier than usual, carrying the square white box marked with the name of the best bakery in Vienna. It will be full of tiny croissants and poppy seed rolls, buttered and filled with delicious smoked salmon or chopped egg. Then there will be Frau Rosen's speciality: a rich, creamy chocolate and orange cake to which Maria will add the final decorations of dark chocolate and whipped cream while Susi is at school. This year Susi has decided she wants a family party with just her best friend, Julie Kohn. Sonya Rosen, usually so inquisitive about every aspect of her daughter's life, does not ask why.

What they call the 'Mitteldorf family' will all be there for her birthday tea. Susi's beloved grandmother, Rosa Shapiro; aunt Fanny, her mother's sister; the younger brother, uncle Freddi; and Fanny's two daughters, Klara and Lori who are in their twenties. Susi is the baby of the family. Fanny, the oldest of her mother's siblings, is fifty-one, and Freddi, the baby of that generation, is thirty-three. Everyone in the family thinks of him as a big kid. He will make his jokes as usual and perform his party tricks and the family will shake their heads and laugh, despairing at his inability to grow up. Uncle Georg, Fanny's husband, won't be able to come to the party. He runs the family shop in Mitteldorf and cannot have the day off.

After the tea, everyone will do a little party piece. They all love to sing, uncle Freddi especially. Susi's big cousins Klara and Lori will probably play a duet on the violin and clarinet and aunt Fanny and Susi's mother will sing her a birthday song in their clear, bell like voices, probably Schumann or Liszt. Maybe they will persuade grandma to sing a song.

'I'm too old,' she'll protest. 'My voice is long gone.'

But after a little persuasion, 'Please grandma, please,' she usually gets up to sing a song of love and yearning in Yiddish, the language of her Polish childhood. Susi loves these songs. Grandma puts out her hands, changes the expression on her face to something full of ancient longing, and in a husky voice still strong and full of spirit, she sings a sad lullaby: sleep my baby, sleep, – *schlaf meine Yiddele, schlaf,* she sings in a voice that makes you want to cry. And then the slow refrain. *Ooh la loo la loo la loo. Ooh la loo la loo la loo. Schlaf meine Yiddele schlaff.* Sonya sings this song to Susi in German, just as in years to come, Susi will translate it into English to sing to her own daughters.

Otto loves his mother-in-law Rosa as if she were his own mother, but he doesn't really like to hear Yiddish which he thinks is a guttural, bastardised language, full of sighs and groans. He is proud of the fact that his family have been true Austrians for at least three generations. He speaks High German, the purest of languages.

Freddi has the best voice of all, a beautiful operatic baritone, classically trained. But he is a teaser; he doesn't take anything seriously. On Susi's last birthday, he sat down at the piano and began to sing Schumann's *Wanderers Nightsong,* to a poem by Goethe. *Over all the mountain tops is peace. In all the treetops you feel hardly a breath. The little birds are silent in the woods. Wait awhile: soon you too will rest.* And in the middle of this, he winked at Susi and segued effortlessly into the Amercian song *Ol'man river.* Susi laughed but the rest of the family groaned at Freddi's low taste.

*

Maria lifts Eva into the pram, where she sits staring at the world. She does not want to get into this prison and struggles to get out, crying, 'Me walk, me walk' with the intense fury of a two-and-a-half year old.

'No,' Maria says, firmly but kindly. 'It's wet and cold outside and we don't want to be late for Susi.'

She hopes that Eva is too young to understand her father's words.

'Put her in the pram when you take her out. I'm not having other people staring at her. God knows what they must think. How old is she now, nearly three? It's not normal the way she moves. What's wrong with her?' He refuses to look at his daughter as she walks, her hips rocking forward, one at a time. Left to herself, Eva moves across the room with amazing speed, swaying from side to side like a little penguin. When Johann has had a drink or two, or when he comes back from she doesn't know where, he shouts, 'It's your fault she's like that. You can't even bear a child normally.' Although how it is her fault that the baby had to be pulled out feet first like a little animal on a farm, she does not know.

*

At the door of the school Susi says goodbye to her friends and walks quickly towards them. When she sees Eva with her cheeks red from the cold she smiles for the first time that day. On the walk home she tells Maria what she will never repeat to her mother or father, trusting Maria to do the same. Today, the most hateful teacher in the school, Frau Resch, made her say the history lesson out loud. Susi had known that she would be picked, so she'd practised it all yesterday afternoon and evening until her mother came into her bedroom and made her turn out the light. But still it came out wrong. Clever Susi, who never failed to gain the Vorzugszeugnis each year, whose reports were always full of As and Bs, stuttered and was unable to recite the lesson she knew by heart.

'She grabbed my exercise book and threw it onto the floor as if it was a piece of rubbish. And she had such a horrible, hateful expression on her face.

"You think you're so clever don't you? You and the rest of the Jew girls in this school. You think you can get all the best grades and be doctors and lawyers and politicians and run the country. Well, listen to me, you Jews are in for a big surprise. You are not going to make history in this country any longer. It is Herr Hitler who is going to help the Austrian people make history from now on."

'Then she told me to pick up my book but my hand was shaking so much I could hardly do it.

"You're not so clever Susi Rosen. You can't even recite a simple history lesson. You can stay in tomorrow at break and see if you can remember it then, otherwise you won't be getting your precious As and Bs. Go back to your desk." '

Maria hopes that just listening is enough because she does not know what to say. On this freezing afternoon, Susi wears her angry tears like a badge. She will no longer let Maria wipe them away; instead she lifts Eva from the pram and twists her wildly in the air causing Maria to gasp and Eva to shout with joy. Together they run along the cinder path of the park hand in hand, along the side of the skeleton silver bushes in the bare flowerbeds, Eva shouting with joy and surprise at her unexpected freedom. And the biting wind stings the tears away and erases the cruelty of this particular day.

*

Otto Rosen lets himself into his flat, carefully carrying the savouries for Susi's birthday tea. In his pocket he has, as usual, a little extra surprise. It has been hard for him not to go into the toy shop to buy her a china doll or a book with coloured pictures but, after the argument about her clothes, he is reluctantly beginning to acknowledge that his Susi is no longer a little girl. He doesn't care to think that for a few years now she had been 'getting a shape', although he can see how sometimes the boys turn to look at her as they walk down the street together. The photograph he has in his wallet still shows her in a sailor dress with a big white collar and her hair in plaits tied with broad satin bows. How she wheedled and argued when she wanted to have it cut to the sleek bob she is wearing today.

This year Susi did not want to wear a birthday dress made by her clever mother. What she absolutely had to have, she argued, was a Tyrolean costume. *All* her friends, proud little Austrians, were wearing clothes like this.

She hears her father at the door; she runs towards him. He holds her at arm's length to take a good look. She is wearing a dark woollen dirndl skirt with red, green and amber embroidery around its hem and a little white apron, a blouse with a neat lace collar, and a red fitted jacket. She twirls round him, her skirt belling out around her, her arms spread wide.

'What do you think, Papa?'

'It's just a shame you cut off those plaits,' he teases, 'otherwise you'd look like a real country girl.'

She laughs, putting a big kiss in the middle of his forehead. His big, beautiful girl, his only child. After her long, difficult birth, the doctor had told them that there could be no more, and after a few tears they realised that they were happy with just Susi. She is enough.

'Shall we go on a little tour?' he asks. She takes his hand as usual and they walk slowly around the room her father calls his study and her mother calls the salon. They admire the things they see every day: the books; the pictures; the parquet floor; the elegant, highly polished Biedermeier furniture; the chairs covered in striped, silky fabric; the drop crystal lamp. Susi can never decide whether her favourite thing in the room is the big, red and blue Persian rug or her special painting. There are lots of framed pictures and photographs on the wall, but since she was tiny, she has loved one in particular. It is a country scene, with a dark green strip of grass, a hill of fir trees and a purple early evening sky. A farmer and his wife stand together outside their small, white house, looking towards the forest. In the foreground is their cow. It looks straight towards you with soft eyes. She doesn't know why she likes it so much, but it draws her in like a dream.

She doesn't think much of the other pictures, the still lifes full of vases and what look to her like dying fruit, and the portraits of men in frock coats and top hats or in military uniform. Her father can name all these people and proudly tells her stories about them, stories she instantly forgets. She likes the picture of her mother's family taken on Passover last year. Everyone is in their best clothes: the women wearing their jewellery with pride, the men with high collars and silk handkerchiefs in their top pockets. They are posed in front of the mother of pearl cabinet which holds the silver and best china.

'What do you think I've got for you?' her father asks her, his right hand absently playing with the corner of his neat moustache. Like a magician, he produces from his pocket a little white box. Susi recognises it immediately but cannot imagine how her father knew that this is just what she wanted. She opens the box and picks out a small white visiting card, printed in black ink. *Susi Rosen, stud. Gym., Wien II,*

Obere Donaustrasse 6, Apt 4. Perfect. She imagines exchanging them with her friends at school, maybe even giving one to Kurt at synagogue next Saturday. She imagines him smiling back as he takes it.

'Thank you my dear Fräulein,' her father says, bowing elaborately and taking a card from her. He puts it in his top pocket and kisses her hand. She laughs.

Of course, Susi loves both her parents but her father is a kind of hero to her. Her mother is a warm, passionate person whose kisses are like gunfire, rat a tat tat, and whose sudden hugs can take your breath away. But there is always the possibility of explosion. Her father is the peacemaker. His life is a calm routine. He rises every morning, dresses neatly in his dark suit and white shirt, drinks a cup of coffee and walks briskly to the barber's for his morning shave. When Susi was little it had been her great treat to go with him. It was frightening and exciting to see the barber wrap her beloved Papa in a clean, white towel, lay out his shining instruments and begin to sharpen his razor. It was magical to watch him work the soap in the steel bowl until it became a lovely white lather. She would hold her breath as Papa was lathered and shaved, his moustache carefully clipped. Then he would be massaged and patted with eau de Cologne. Sometimes the barber would put some cologne behind her own ears which tickled her and made her giggle. Afterwards they would go to their favourite café for a huge second breakfast. She would be allowed to spoon off the sugary whipped cream, as stiff as the barber's foam, from the top of his coffee.

On a normal day, Otto Rosen heads straight from the barber's to the International Bank where he is chief accountant, returning at lunch time for a big meal, cooked by his wife. After lunch, he has a little nap in his study and then back to the office for the long afternoon's work. The household can set its watch by his comings and goings. Even on a Sunday when they go on what he calls a 'walking tour' of the Vienna Woods, they usually leave and return at the same hour. He loves his solid, happy life.

Sonya Rosen's life, on the other hand, is a helter skelter of more activities than can easily be fitted into each day. She organises Susi's busy life: school six days a week, 8am to 1pm. Monday afternoons a piano lesson; Tuesday and Friday an English lesson at the home of her old teacher; Wednesday, games or swimming with the school; Thursday, singing. On Saturday morning there is school as usual and in the afternoon, Susi goes to the synagogue, as decreed by the government which requires every child to have religious instruction. It is Sonya who supervises Susi's homework, sometimes even sitting alongside her to learn for herself. And there is so much homework!

At the Gymnasium there are exams all the time, ten a year for German, eight for French and Latin, six for maths and a pupil can be called up for an oral exam whenever the teacher feels like it. Even with a maid, Sonya is hardly a lady of leisure. She looks after the house, shops, cooks, entertains, makes clothes for herself and Susi, takes the train to visit her mother and sister once a fortnight and rushes around all day long, skirts flapping, pins falling out of her hair. But as her husband comes through the door, miraculous calm descends. Blouses are smoothed and tucked back into belts, stray hair pins are put back in place, kisses and affectionate pats are given and received, delicious meals are put onto a nicely laid table and all is right with the world.

*

On the afternoon that Maria is helping with Susi's birthday party, her husband Johann crosses the Donau Canal from the 2nd District into the 9th and heads towards the cinema on Nussdorfer Strasse. It is a long, brisk walk and by the time he reaches the cinema, it is dark outside and he feels alive and fizzing with good health. A huge cardboard figure of a steel helmeted German soldier stands at the cinema doorway, his mouth screaming in wide open fury at the enemy. But it is not the war film that Johann has come to see. He has been invited to an exhibition and a special, private showing of a new, scientific film, one made for people like him who are interested in improving themselves and moving their country forward.

At the door he meets Herr Brandt, the man who has invited him. He is older than Johann, a solid, middle aged man wearing the uniform of the Tyrolean Defence Volunteers.

'Heil Österreich!' Johann addresses him with the greeting of Austria and the Fatherland Front.

'Heil Hitler!' he replies and Johann, a grown man, blushes.

In the foyer of the cinema, the exhibition *Volk und Rasse* is promoting the idea of the importance of racial purity and the evil of race defilement. There are a variety of things laid out for inspection: metal implements for measuring skull and body shapes, height and bone structure; trays of glass eyes in twenty different colours; a box marked 1 to 30, showing different shades and textures of hair. Large black and white photographs of people are displayed on stands, illustrating the Nordic ideal – the superiority of the Aryan race. One picture in particular attracts his attention. It is a perfect family: the mother sits by a lake with her little girl helping to lay out a picnic; the muscular father walks towards the water with his son at his side; the two children: fair haired, strong limbed and bright eyed.

In a glass cabinet is a book, displayed on a stand like a bronze head. In gold lettering Johann reads, *The Permission to Destroy Life Unworthy of Life,* by Alfred Hoche and Karl Binding, 1920. Herr Brandt has spoken to him about this book.

He is proud to be invited to this event. Most of the people here are not ordinary workers like him; they are people who work for the government: scientific men, even people from the university. Herr Brandt is a teacher in a secondary school. Johann knows he is not stupid. Like his wife, he comes from a poor family but he is nobody's fool. He is good with his hands; he can talk the hind legs off a donkey; he likes to read the newspapers. At school, the little he had, his teachers thought he was a clever boy, although he never seemed able to pass his exams. He loved science; he loved to cut things up and see how the parts fitted together. He would have liked to have been a doctor, but a boy like him had no chance. Boys like him don't become doctors in Vienna.

He settles into the dark. The film begins with shots of low clouds, mountains, stormy seas and fast flowing rivers. Strong men, labourers and lumberjacks struggle against the elements to the accompaniment of heavy, stirring music. The light changes. There is the courtyard of what looks like a grand palace.

A strong voice tells him, *All living things on this earth are engaged in a permanent struggle with the forces of nature. Wherever fate puts us, whatever station we must occupy, only the strong will prevail in the end. Everything in the natural world that is weak will ineluctably be destroyed. In the last few decades, mankind has sinned terribly against the laws of natural selection. We haven't just maintained life unworthy of life; we have even allowed it to multiply. The descendants of such sick people look like this!*

The screen shows people who cannot stand, or walk, who talk in riddles and cannot feed themselves. A girl tries to support her sister who cannot sit up. A child lies in a hospital bed, his legs too withered ever to walk. Strange looking adults, their features lit from below, stare out of the screen, mouths open. Physically impaired children transmute into strange, misshapen adults who become Jews with hooked noses and long buttoned coats, who become crazy looking criminals in prison uniform. The music rises to a climax.

Now there are pictures of healthy young nurses and doctors who devote their lives to these pitiful creatures. The voice talks of the expense of the care the inmates receive, the great drain on the nation's resources.

You are bearing this burden. A hereditarily ill person costs fifty thousand marks to maintain until he reaches the age of sixty. And while the more valuable sections of the population fail to reproduce, in one hundred years time, the 'valuable' will be hopelessly outnumbered by the 'unfit'.

Suddenly the mood of the film changes. A kind looking doctor sits at his table with a young couple. He explains something to them.

It is important to have one's physical constitution and hereditary health tested, so that one may discover whether the hereditary disposition of one's forebears is worth passing on. The young bride looks on admiringly. *In future, these poor creatures will no longer live alongside our healthy children. Sterilisation is a simple operation. It is a humane method to spare the nation endless misery. The Law for the Prevention of Hereditarily Diseased Progeny is the restoration of the natural order which mankind has disrupted because of a false sense of humanity.*

The film ends with uplifting music. A large group of boys and girls in immaculate uniform march towards a new future. Athletes and gymnasts are shown, troops of uniformed soldiers. A smiling Hitler appears at the 1936 Nuremberg Rally, surrounded by his people.

Johann leaves the cinema alone. What is he feeling? He cannot put a name to it. He is stirred, perhaps elated, definitely unsettled. Personally, he keeps himself very fit, just like his father who never had a day's illness. He is proud of his strong body and his strong hands. He believes in the Nordische Gedanke, the Nordic Ideal and when he looks in the mirror for his morning shave, that is what he sees. He does not look back to Franz-Josef and the old Empire; he wants a new future for his impoverished country.

Racial Hygiene, Volk und Rasse, the words run round in his head.

He walks back through the cold, dark streets in no great hurry to be home. He is thirty, it's not so old, he still feels like a young man with a future ahead of him. He thinks about his wife, his little Maria. When they met he was so proud of her with her healthy body and her quiet ways. She could have been a farmer's wife with a pack of children and a big kitchen. But who could earn a living in the country nowadays? He had dreamt, they'd both dreamt, of a big family, lots of healthy, strong children running around. But now? A shutter in his mind comes down when he thinks about children. Maria hasn't really changed, of course. He has to admit that she keeps a good home for him even in these difficult times when money seems to buy nothing. She knows how to make a little go a long way. Still, it's no good kidding himself. The truth is, he no longer sees her as his lovely country girl. When he thinks about Maria now, well, it is hard to put a word to it.

Johann enters the front door of the building and meets quite a procession coming down the stairs. Nearest the bottom is Susi carefully carrying a sleeping Eva, dropping silent kisses on her head. Next his wife carrying a metal container of leftover food and a large slice of birthday cake. Then the stately grandmother, Frau Shapiro, whose name is never mentioned by Johann's mother-in-law Hanna without many blessings and thanks for her wisdom and generosity. She is followed by her son, that big kid, Freddi who always has a terrible joke or a silly trick up his sleeve; her daughter Fanny who runs the shop in Maria's home town; the granddaughters: Klara the pretty one, twenty or so, Lori a bit older, not so good looking, neither of them married. There's the young girl Julie, the one whose father is the big shot Dr Kohn who teaches at the university, and lastly the Rosens, saying goodbye to their guests.

Johann greets them politely with a slight bow of the head for each one.

'Grüss Gott, Fräulein Susi, happy birthday. Good evening, Frau Shapiro, Herr Shapiro, Frau Stoller, Fräuleins, Frau Rosen.' And finally, giving Otto Rosen his full title, 'Grüss Gott, Herr Uberinspektor.'

And they, in turn, acknowledge him. 'Good evening Johann. Good to see you, you're looking well.'

Susi carries Eva into the flat and lays her on her bed. Without knowing exactly why, she takes her little legs and gently strokes them from thigh to ankle, tucking the feather quilt around them. The protective love she sometimes feels for this little girl almost hurts, as if no one in the world could love her this much. It doesn't seem to matter that their backgrounds are so different, or even that Susi is not the kind of girl who loves babies. She never played with dolls when she was little and her dreams are not of motherhood and children, but sometimes she just wants to pick Eva up and run away with her.

Maria can smell the beer on Johann's breath, but she doesn't mind him having a drink after a night out. He looks at Susi as she disappears through the door and turns down the corners of his mouth as if to ask, 'What's she doing here?' She does not ask him what his evening was like and says nothing about her own day. In the early days of their courtship and marriage, he happily listened to her stories about the Rosens, and would laugh or shake his head with her. She didn't expect him to feel about them as she did, but he had taken pleasure, even pride, in their achievements and she'd heard him boasting to the man who delivered the wood when Herr Rosen was promoted at the bank.

She can no longer guess what he is thinking by looking at his face. She tries to remember the last time he pulled her towards him for a hug, or even the last time they laughed together. He used to talk to her all the time, jokes and stories about his day. He talked about people in the building – what this one had said to him, what he had seen that one do, what fancy hat Frau so and so had taken to wearing, who wanted to leave their horse in the courtyard as if they were living in the country, whose son was carrying on with whose daughter. Her mother Hanna used to say that he was more like a woman than a man the way he liked to gossip. Now, at home, her husband is mostly silent.

She puts some more wood on the kitchen fire and begins to warm up the food she brought down with her. He sits in the chair, pulling off his boots, thinking about the film, the exhibition, the clever people who were there. In her head, she practises telling him about the new baby which must be due in May or June when the weather will be warm and sunny, but the words will not form clearly enough in her head. How can this be? Her mother thinks it is a woman's privilege to decide the right time to speak about a pregnancy or see a doctor. But Maria has never been one for keeping secrets, and this one worries her.

She dreads telling him because of what has gone

before. Eva is not their first born. The first baby was a son, a beautiful strong boy, named Johann after his father. Everyone said he was the spit of him – strong nose, strong chin; he even had his curly hair. Johann's birth wasn't easy exactly, but at least he came out the right way. But when he was only a few months old, their lovely boy, his father's pride and joy, had caught a brain fever and died. First the baby cried and screamed and nothing they could do consoled him. Then, he became quiet and his face went purple round the eyes like a panda bear.

Herr Rosen had called in his friend, Dr Kohn, when he saw how worried she was, and he said it could happen to any baby, rich or poor. He'd seen many cases like it. Afterwards, he said that even if the baby had lived, his little brain would have been damaged; he wouldn't have been right. But what would a mother care about this? If little Johann had lived, she would still have loved him. There wasn't a single day when she didn't think of him or pray for the protection of his soul.

'What did they say about her?' Johann's voice comes out of his thoughts. 'Eva, our daughter,' he repeats sarcastically. 'What did they say about her?' She knows what he means.

'I don't think they said anything much. I was in the kitchen most of the time, helping. They just patted her and said how much she looked like me when I was little. And Herr Shapiro played that disappearing trick with a coin that he always does and he gave the money to her. I didn't want to take it, but he insisted. He said to put it towards her dowry. You know what he's like, he's always joking.' She looks towards him nervously.

'I don't mean that. What did they say about the way she moves, her legs, the fact that she's not right?' His voice is rising, perhaps he's had more than just one beer.

'They didn't say anything. Johann, she's still a baby, she'll walk properly soon. She's just... She's just got her funny ways now. It'll come right. Please.' Her voice takes on a pleading tone.

'Come right?' The look in his eyes is something near to disgust. In his head he sees those images of healthy, marching children, and worse, he sees images of the other kind: the faceless ones who cannot walk and who look into the distance seeing nothing, hearing nothing. 'She's not right anywhere that child. She doesn't walk right, she doesn't look right, she doesn't even speak.'

'She does talk, it's just when...' She stops and starts again. It is not the moment to mention how a single look from him is enough to silence his own child.

'Frau Rosen says it's not that unusual for children to develop in different ways. She showed me how good Eva is with her hands; she gave her some little blocks to put together and she did it so nicely. And she said that if you were really worried, she's sure Herr Rosen would ask Dr Kohn to...'

'You stupid, stupid woman.' She has never heard this voice before. 'How dare you speak to that fat Jewish cow about our business.' The shock of his words causes her to turn from the kitchen stove and look at him directly. Without warning, without precedent, he lifts the back of his hand and strikes her face. The force of his blow, the complete surprise of it, causes her to stagger against the range. The hot pan on the stove falls and splatters at her feet. She is too stunned to reply.

Vienna

June 1937

Otto Rosen emerges from the barber's clean shaven and pink faced. Despite the hot day, he is, as always, immaculately dressed in a dark three piece suit. He heads towards the bank where he has worked for the last fifteen years, building up a successful career as a chartered accountant of the first rank. His bank: a job for life, a successful, international enterprise with branches all over Austria and in France, Germany and Czechoslovakia. He likes the work and the respect he receives. He likes this daily walk through the centre of Vienna.

This sense of security, of pride, of happiness even, is as transparent as the tissue paper which wraps the beautifully laundered shirt he puts on each morning. The writing has been on the wall for a long time but he has chosen not to read it. He tries to think only about what is most important in his life: his family, his home, his comfortable job at the bank, his music, his love of books, sometimes even his religion. Being Jewish may not be the most important thing in his life, but he would never deny this heritage.

He does not consciously set out to make himself ignorant. He reads the papers, he walks on the elegant wide streets of Vienna every day, he talks to other men. He knows that behind the grand buildings of the Ringstrasse with its baroque palaces, along the wide tree lined boulevards of elegant shops and coffee houses, drumming on the walls of the opera house built like an Italian palazzo, and in the cracks of the cobbles of Stephanplatz, there are, if he chooses to listen, messages of hatred and poison.

He clings to the illusion that this will pass, that Jew-hating has always been part of the Austrian way of doing things. Austria is, after all, not Germany where it is true, things are not looking too good. The speeches of Austria's politicians have always included anti-semitic remarks and slogans. A Jewish person does something which gets in the news and foul words are spoken about how the whole race is lacking in honour, how they are like the vermin in the streets, how they are taking over the country. These things are in the blood of the Hapsburg Empire.

Hitler won't last long. That's what Otto Rosen believes, what many of his friends believe; it's what Chancellor Schuschnigg himself believes. Austria will not allow itself to be taken over by the Germans. The swastikas that are appearing on the walls overnight, the people shouting Heil Hitler to each other in the street, the group of schoolboys singing the vile Horst Wessel song, there isn't much new in all this. Things aren't good it's true, but they have to get better. He's not one of these Yiddish speaking Jews from the East, with their long caftans and old fashioned ways. He's an Austrian. He continues to do his job at the bank, he continues to provide well for his family, he earns the respect he receives.

*

Sonya Rosen is at the big table, her sewing box open, putting the finishing touches to a taffeta blouse with a lace collar she has made for her mother. Susi, who is recovering from a summer cold, sits curled up on the sofa next to a side table piled high with books. She is reading *Jane Eyre*, and she can feel the chill of the

English country house and the torment Jane suffered with no loving family to guide her or keep her safe. She puts the book down because her head still hurts and takes a peep at the pile of little cards she has exchanged for her own. At the top is Kurt Kohn's, Julie's handsome older brother. Last week, Kurt walked her home and when they got to the door he gave her a kiss, not on the cheek like he had always done, but right on her lips. She had a funny feeling down below, and for one terrible minute she thought she was going to wet herself. Since then she hasn't stopped thinking about him. She kisses his name on the card, knowing how silly this is.

Thinking about Kurt is a delicious way to pass the time on a slow day like today. Tomorrow, she will go back to the important things in her life: her schoolwork and her exams of course, practising that demanding piece of Haydn on the piano, and finishing her book so that she can talk about it to Papa. Susi wants to be a serious person, not one of those silly, frivolous girls at school who think of nothing but clothes and boys. She tries to imagine putting all the things in her life into different drawers which she can open and close at will. One drawer would be for Kurt and the feeling of being kissed and the blissful prospect of future kisses, one for exams and doing well at school, and one for bullying Frau Resch and the boys in white stockings. Susi would like to shut this drawer and never open it again.

Her father is not coming home at mid-day because he is auditing the books at the factory of one of the bank's clients, so they are not going to eat their usual big lunchtime meal. Instead, Sonya Rosen makes

Susi's favourite dish: very thin noodles baked with onions, eggs and cheese. It is made in a special little painted bowl with high sides, just big enough for one person, and when it's cooked, it is turned out so that it holds its shape. The edges are brown and crispy and the inside is soft and buttery with the strong tangy taste of the cheese.

Downstairs Maria is feeding the new baby. She is two weeks old with hair that looks as though it is going to be dark and straight like her mother's. Maria is exhausted; the baby is lovely of course, but fretful, and it is all she can do to keep going. Eva is pleased with her new baby sister, but cautious. When Susi comes downstairs, she does not like it when she picks up the baby and gives her lots of kisses. 'Kisses for me,' she says.

Maria is up and about doing her usual jobs. There is food cooking on the stove and baby clothes drying on the fender. Susi would like to give her a hand but she is not sure how to offer. She hopes it is helping when she sits with both children in the old armchair and keeps the baby from crying by supporting her little head carefully with her hand as she has been shown, and singing a lullaby. Maria, passing with a pile of clothes, stops in front of them and says fondly, 'My three girls'.

Maria's bruises have long since healed and she has removed the incident from her mind. Johann is kind now, not in his old way, but he still takes care of her. There is always wood by the stove, and he helps with the heavy jobs in the house. Sometimes it is hard to buy what they need: food, clothes for Eva and the baby; everything is so expensive now. But Johann doesn't seem to be spending money on beer and he seems to have a number of jobs on the side, so they aren't starving.

Neither of them has ever mentioned the time when he spoke about Frau Rosen so viciously and lost what he most values in himself: discipline and restraint. In his mind he has never hit his wife. A man like him would never do a thing like that. He thinks of it as an accident, caused by her clumsiness. Women who are expecting sometimes get like that; they lose their balance and fall over a lot. She was working too hard, she had their own place to look after, she shouldn't have been expected to keep helping them out upstairs as well. He put a stop to that after the fall.

And that wasn't the only thing he put a stop to. He'd made up his mind that there weren't going to be any more kids with Maria. He found he felt nothing for the new baby, absolutely nothing. What was the point? There was bound to be something wrong with it. Maria didn't seem capable of bearing him a normal child. He missed it of course, the sex thing, any man would. In the beginning it had been great, fantastic, the feeling of her. He'd been with other girls before and it had been fun, but with them it had been just one, two and all over. With Maria, well, she was his wife and underneath the modesty, she had a lovely little body, fresh and sweet. There was nothing in the world like being with a woman like her, night after night, whenever you wanted. Her smooth skin, your hands on those firm little breasts, getting big slowly, getting right inside her. There was nothing in the world to beat it.

Still, discipline and order in his life, that was the

thing now; he wasn't going to risk more kids with her. If she had had the operation like German women with kids like hers, that would have been different. But how do you ask your own wife a thing like that? That's why you needed laws, he thought, and rules, so people didn't have to make their own decisions.

Johann does a lot of thinking about what is right for his country. Herr Brandt obviously thinks that he can go a long way. He believes that there is no future in the Fatherland Front and that Germany and Austria must become one. If Schuschnigg was prepared to work with Hitler that would be one thing, but otherwise he has to go. He doesn't care that the National Socialist Party is still illegal in Austria. The people he knows openly 'Heil Hitler' each other on the streets and march in their brown uniforms and swastika armbands. They all hate the Jews.

Johann is for the moment a little more cautious. Perhaps Herr Brandt is right, that there would be more chances for men like him if there were less of them in Vienna, taking all the good jobs, owning all the shops. But still, when he sees the Rosen family or old Frau Shapiro, even young Susi, he continues to be polite, nodding when he sees them, carrying out the work he is paid to do.

*

Sonya Rosen gets on the train to Mitteldorf for her fortnightly visit to her family, holding a box of pastries and the beautifully finished white taffeta blouse she has made for her mother's birthday. Despite the fact that Sonya is forty-seven years old and with a home and family of her own, the nearer the train gets to Mitteldorf, the more she feels like she is twelve years old. Her mother will fuss over her and feed her more than she wants to eat and her big sister will hug and kiss her and then look at her dress, her hat or her shoes and admire them before wondering, often aloud, how much they cost and whether they are more expensive than her own.

It's a long journey, particularly on a hot day like today. Sonya is wearing a calf-length, cream linen dress and jacket, loose fitting and low waisted. Her figure is not as slender as it was, nor her face, but she is still a pretty woman. Her thick, dark hair feels heavy at the nape of her neck. She would have loved to have it cut short like Susi, but Otto won't hear of it.

Sonya likes to be back in the family home even though her father, may his dear soul rest in peace, is no longer with them. The place has hardly changed since she was born, somehow managing to be what it always was: ancient and dark, yet still lively and full of love. Since she was small she has loved everything about the big, solid house, except the open beamed roof which always looks as if it is about to fall in. The living room is on the first floor and its big windows look out on one side to the comings and goings of the town, and on the other across miles of open countryside with its fields of flowers and grazing cattle. Inside, nothing changes: the heavy, comfortable furniture is draped with deep burgundy velvet and yellowing lace, and the walls are lined with the framed family pictures of relatives with skull caps and long buttoned up caftans.

Sonya sends Susi here every summer. There is a huge grand piano which she is allowed to play whenever she wants to, a wind up gramophone with a collection of modern American songs by Gershwin and Hammerstein, an ancient dog called Poldi, and a lazy cat who gives birth to a litter of kittens every year. The outhouse at the back of the store is always full of discarded objects just asking to be played with: an ancient tricycle, a collection of left footed rubber boots in different sizes, scraps of ribbons, buttons and bows, a torn lace collar, a striped apron with the pocket half off, bits of tape and string, brushes with most of the bristles missing.

When Sonya was a girl, she would sometimes be allowed to accompany her father when he drove the pony trap to the outlying villages, selling a huge variety of products to the farmers and their wives: pots and pans, tools, sewing kits, ribbons, buttons, work clothes, socks, underwear, aprons, hats, feathers, clothes pegs, hairbrushes, mesh boxes to keep things cool, nightdresses, scissors. She'd tried to count them once and had given up when she reached a hundred. Nowadays, these trips are rare; the people from faraway villages usually come to them.

Mitteldorf itself is a small town, a big village really, of a few thousand people. It has its own synagogue, a tiny but beautiful wooden building, and on the High Holy Days, Jewish families come in from the surrounding villages. Sonya's brother-in-law, Georg, a good man with high principles but no sense of humour, is a warden at the synagogue. He runs the shop, with the help of Fanny and their daughters. They live comfortably, with some luxuries that most people in the village don't have: a telephone, good heating, a modern bathroom.

As soon as she comes through the door, Sonya realises that something is up. She has hardly put her bags down when Fanny approaches and whispers urgently.

'Oh, I'm so glad you're here. I need you to help me speak to mother.'

'My God, what's the matter?' says Sonya, alarmed, already imagining an unknown, fatal disease.

'It's Freddi, he's married the shiksa.'

'Oh my God,' Sonya says again, clapping her hand to her mouth. 'When? He's already married? Does Mamma know? It'll kill her.'

'I know,' Fanny whispers. 'He says she makes him happy and there's nothing he could do about it.'

'Nothing he could do?' Sonya shakes her head. 'Nothing he could do? What does that mean for God's sake? Has he got her pregnant?'

'He says not. They went to the Town Hall and he married her. He says he didn't tell us because we'd only have tried to change his mind.'

The sisters stand so close together in the dark hall that they can feel their breath on each other's faces.

'Darling,' their mother calls from upstairs. 'What are you doing? Is that Sonya? Sweetheart, aren't you going to give your old mother a kiss?' The sisters part and go up the stairs into the light. In the rapid exchange of nods and looks which follow, the sisters establish that Freddi is in his room and Sonya will have a quick word with him and see how the land lies, that they will have lunch first and then, together, will break the news to their mother.

Nobody eats very much. Georg removes the enormous linen napkin tucked into his shirt and he and his daughters, Klara and Lori, move to more comfortable chairs by the window. Fanny makes the coffee to go with the exquisite pastries Sonya has brought from Vienna and their mother admires and fusses over the blouse she has received for her birthday.

Georg coughs. Freddi moves uncomfortably in his chair and makes crumbs of the pastry on his plate. Klara and Lori look on expectantly.

'Freddi, what are you doing?' his mother says, as if he were still a child. 'If you don't want to eat it, leave it alone.'

Fanny looks at Freddi who says nothing. There is no easy way to do this. She plunges in. 'Mamma, now try not to get upset. Freddi has something to tell you.'

'Don't get upset?' their mother says, clutching her hand to her heart as if a death has already been announced. 'Pte, pte.' She makes a spitting shape with her mouth to ward off the invisible evil eye. 'Tell me quickly, don't try to spare me.'

'Mother please, hear him out, it's not so terrible.' The whole family turns to Freddi who has gone pale. He has begged Fanny and then Sonya to break this to his mother, but for once they will not let him off the hook.

'Mamma darling, there's no easy way for me to say this to you.' Rosa Shapiro turns sharply towards her son and listens to his story with eyebrows already raised.

The truth is that although Freddi has the role of the youngest son, the amiable fool, the joker, he is, in fact, a mensch, a decent man. Yes, he has fallen in love with a shiksa, a non-Jewish girl, called Liesl, but she adores him with all her heart and sees him as talented, clever, funny, a man quite capable of making grown up decisions. And she's a beauty too, sweet faced with a curvaceous plump body.

Freddi has always had a lot of licence, growing up without a father. Unlike his older sisters he has had plenty of time to wander and to do what he pleases. It helped, of course, that he had such a talent. His piano teacher was a student of Artur Schnabel's and his voice teacher was sure that one day he would be performing in the best concert and operatic halls of Austria. But when he was twenty he said that wasn't the kind of music he wanted to play and none of them could do anything about it. Beethoven, Haydn, Schubert, Mozart, Brahms, that's what serious people called music. Mahler, Bruckner, Schönberg, even Johann Strauss's operetta was music. But what Freddi chose to play, nobody in the family thought of that as proper music, the kind that used his God given talent. That plinky plonk stuff was just playing around, like his silly card tricks and disappearing coins.

They have no idea that whilst living under his mother's roof and occasionally going out to the villages on selling trips for Georg, Freddi has been building up quite a reputation. He's managed to put away a sizeable sum too, enough to get him out of Austria. In the night clubs and dance halls of Vienna, Freddi plays the piano and sings songs from American musicals. His fans think he's talented and handsome. *You are my lucky star*, he croons to the pretty women, *I worship from afar.* To the dancers wrapped around each other's bodies, he shmoozes, *when a lovely thing dies, smoke gets in your eyes.*

Freddi leans over and smooths his mother's soft, puckered hand and looks into her dark eyes. She shakes her head and says nothing. She can see that her boy is happy and more than that, that it is too late to do anything about it. Marrying outside the faith is not the end of the world. She was lucky in the way the girls married and she, unlike her daughters, has seen for months that he is a man in love. She sighs, puts her hand on his and asks one question.

'Will she convert?'

'Mamma I don't know. Perhaps. I won't forget I'm Jewish, but we've got a whole new future ahead of us, we're not thinking about that now.'

'A whole future, here in Austria?' Fanny says. 'And what if you have children? Do you think a mischling will be better treated than a Jewish child?'

'We're not going to bring up any children here.' He leans over and speaks to his mother as if she is the only person in the room. 'Mamma, I didn't want to tell you this all at once, I'm a coward I know. Liesl and I are going to America.'

'America?!' snorts his brother-in-law. 'They'll let you out of Austria for sure, but why should they let you into the land of milk and honey?' He's lived here since Freddi was eight years old; he's been underestimating his brother-in-law for over twenty years.

Freddi of the flawless baritone has a work permit. In fact, he has more than a permit, he has a cast iron job. 'Mamma, I'm leaving Austria in a week's time. I'm going to be the lead singer with the Joe Green Dance Band. You remember Jo, Josef Grüssmann, the tall skinny kid?'

'You mean Josef, who used to play the violin in the concerts, the one who always had a runny nose?'

'That's the one.' Josef, who played in the little concerts organised by the Jewish community, is now the leader of one of the most successful dance bands in New York. 'He plays in the best dance halls, in Radio City, on ocean liners. He tells me we're going to be in the movies before too long.'

The whole family is silent, imagining him there.

'Mamma, there's no future in Austria. It's no good here any more. We can't go on kidding ourselves that the Nazis will stay in Germany, they're here now. You just have to look around you, there's one on every corner. People are being thrown out of their jobs. What do you think they mean when they scream "Jews perish"? Do you think it's a joke?'

'Freddi, don't scare Mamma,' Sonya says. 'It's not that bad.'

Freddi ignores her.

'Please, Mamma. I don't want to hurt you. I know it's not what you wanted, but I love Liesl. She makes me happy. Please give me your blessing.' He is crying, she is crying. Sonya and Fanny clutch their handkerchiefs. Lori and Klara hold their hands to their faces. It is a mock opera.

'Ach, for God's sake, Freddi. No one's died. It's not the end of the world.' His mother kisses him on the head and wipes his eyes as if he were a baby. 'Klara darling, go and make me some tea with lots of sugar.'

'It's not such a bad idea,' says Georg in the pause that follows. He wouldn't mind moving to America, opening a shop there. His sister's husband sold up in '33, crossed the Atlantic and started a new business. They seem to be doing well.

'So he says,' Fanny retorts. 'I hear a different story. They live in an apartment without any light to look out on, it's freezing in winter, boiling in the summer. They're poor there and the city schools are terrible, no one respects the teachers. Who knows what their children are learning?'

'Poor is what we're all going to be soon when Herr Hitler marches his way into Austria.' Georg says in a voice they have rarely heard. 'Then we'll see how our friends the gentiles treat us. We'll be turned out of our own homes.'

'Don't exaggerate Georg,' Sonya says as mildly as she can, glancing over to her mother. She repeats the words she has often heard from Otto. They have a good life here, a comfortable life. Where else could they get what they have in Austria – a beautiful home, the most elegant city in the world, the Vienna woods, wonderful holidays by the lakes, the restaurants and the music, a first class education for Susi provided by the State? They speak other languages, they know about other countries, but German is the language of their hearts and minds, it is their culture. How could they live anywhere else? Also, and this Sonya repeats with confidence, Otto has privileged information, he knows senior men in the Schuschnigg administration. They know for certain that Hitler will not last long. Civilised Austrians will never allow him across the border.

'What about Susi? Do you think life is fine for her with all she has to put up with every day?' It is quiet, plain faced Lori who has spoken, betraying a confidence. The family look at her in surprise.

'What do you mean?'

'Every day she is scared to go to school and even more scared when she gets there.' Sonya looks at her in amazement. She knows nothing of this, only that Susi is a little quieter than usual, a little more studious and careful in her ways. 'I know I shouldn't say this, I promised her I wouldn't, but it's not right for you to say wait, wait, wait, it will get better soon.' Lori tells them how going to school isn't too bad, because Kurt walks Susi and his sister Julie to school each morning and when he can he meets them in the afternoon. But when he isn't there, the gang with the white knee socks hiss at her and call her names, spit at her and chase her. Last week one of them put out his feet to trip her up and her school books fell onto the pavement. He threw her cards in the air where they scattered like confetti. She ran home, listening to them shout after her: 'Susi Rosen, filthy Yid. Stupid, dirty little kid. We know where you live.'

Quiet Lori tells them how in school, the Nazi teacher has become worse. She bullies and plagues Susi in the history lesson, and worse, she tells untrue stories to the other teachers to turn them against her, so that sometimes Susi finds it hard to remember herself as the cheerful, confident student she used to be.

Sonya feels her heart might stop. To think of Susi, her precious child, going through this alone and saying nothing. 'Why? Why doesn't she talk to her father and me?'

'Why? Because she feels she would be letting you down. Because you have such high hopes for her.' And unsaid, because you want so much to believe that everything is fine, that nothing bad can happen here.

Vienna

March 1938

Otto, Sonya and Susi sit on the burnt almond sofa in their living room, listening to Radio Vienna. Susi is on her father's knee, her arm around his neck. Her mother gets up and walks around the room, picking things up, putting them down. It is a Friday evening, the 11th of March. Sonya, unusually, has lit the Sabbath candles and said the blessing over the bread and wine.

The whole of Austria, it seems, is sitting somewhere waiting for the news. It has become an obsession. A month ago, sitting on the same sofa, listening to a concert of light music on the radio, they heard that talks were about to take place between Chancellor Schuschnigg and Hitler in the mountain retreat of Berchtesgaden. A few days later, in the *Neue Freie Presse*, Otto read a report of the speech Hitler made in the Reichstag about this meeting and took it as a good sign that Hitler only mentioned the Jewish question a few times. The conductor Bruno Walter's contract with the Vienna orchestra was renewed for a year. Surely this was grounds for hope. On the 22nd of February, whilst the Rosens and some of their friends were reassuring themselves that things were no worse than they had been for a while, and that it was inconceivable that the Austrians would ever vote for a low degenerate like Hitler, Winston Churchill in the British parliament, spoke of the tragedy of Austria and the violent pressure being put on the people of that country.

The word 'detente' is on everyone's lips but the Rosens cannot gain comfort from this.

Now, like every Jew in Austria, they wait in silence for the news. For the first time in thirty years, there is talk of a plebiscite, a referendum for Austrians over twenty-four years of age: a vote for or against unification with Germany. Twenty-four is an unusual age for a vote, but most of Austria's Nazi followers are young. In the streets of Vienna, supporters of the Fatherland Front begin to stencil images of Schuschnigg's portrait on the pavements. The huge 'yes' painted underneath seems encouraging.

Otto, listening intently, pushes his beloved Susi off his lap and sits on the edge of his chair, his fists clenched. Susi, startled, goes to stand by her mother who puts her arm around her daughter's waist. The plebiscite has been called off. Father, mother and daughter look at each other, appalled. Schuschnigg tells the country that he is no longer able to resist the brute force of the Germans and the Austrian armed forces have been instructed that, should an invasion take place, they should withdraw without resistance. His voice is strained. 'So, in this hour, I bid farewell to the people of Austria with a German word and a wish from the bottom of my heart. God Save Austria.' A German word. A German word? Otto slaps his hand down on the sofa in a gesture they have never seen before. For the first time in his life, he is beginning to understand that he is not considered to share this common German word, this Teutonic blood.

Sonya takes the face of her tall daughter and kisses her head, her cheeks, her eyes.

'My baby,' she whispers into her hair. 'How I wanted to save you from this.' The music of Haydn's *Kaiser quartett* with its melody of the national anthem sings miserably into their beautiful room.

It is the Anschluss.

Abruptly, from the hall, the phone rings and

Sonya rushes to answer it. It is Fanny, of course. Has she heard the news? What will it mean for them? Sonya doesn't know. They'll have to wait and see but one thing is for certain, they need to get money out of the bank as soon as possible. How is mother taking it? She seems to be okay. Hanna came over as soon as she heard the news to see if there was anything she could do to help the family. She is in Mamma's room now, she will help to keep her calm. Mitteldorf will be safer than Vienna, there is hardly a person in the whole town they haven't known all their lives.

In the sitting room, Susi sits with her father at the table covered with the fringed cloth. He tries to explain to her what this news will mean for them, but he is struggling.

'This will give the Nazis the go ahead to move into Vienna,' he is saying to Susi as Sonya makes her way back into the room. 'How can you be so stupid?' Sonya shouts at her husband. 'You must be the only person in Vienna who doesn't know the Nazis are already here.'

It is the first time Susi has ever seen this look on her mother's face.

The terrible moment is broken by a loud knock on the door. Dr Kohn comes in with a pale faced Kurt behind him. 'Tell them what happened,' he says to his shaken son.

'I was on Nussdorfer Strasse with a friend, we were going to the *Kino*, and we walked right into a demonstration. There were hundreds of lorries full of screaming, shouting men waving huge swastika flags over their heads.' He looks at Susi. 'They were brownshirts; some had storm trooper caps on, some had steel helmets, swastika armbands, anything they could get their hands on. And you know what they were all screaming? *Ein Volk, ein Reich, ein Führer. Judah Verreke! Jews Perish!* It took nearly twenty minutes for it to pass.' Kurt stops suddenly and the excitement on his face looks like fear.

'Where had they all been waiting?' his father asks quietly. 'They must have known all the time that this was going to happen.'

In the kitchen, Susi warms some milk for Kurt and mixes in the chocolate, conscious that Dora, the maid is staying behind her partition. Kurt, her defender and her champion is trembling and on the verge of tears and she doesn't know what to do for him. She reaches out for his hand and he holds it tightly. He leans towards her like a child waiting for a hug and she kisses him. He would have liked Susi to be his girl, to walk in the park with her, to buy her little gifts, maybe even to take her to his favourite restaurant for steak and fried potatoes and an ice cream. He tells her he is leaving Austria for good.

In the living room, his father is telling the same story. They have their passports ready, a ticket and all the documents. Norbert Kohn, his non-Jewish wife and their children, Julie and Kurt are all ready to get on the train to France and sail to America to start a new life. Their children will never have to wear the small chrome swastika of the half-Jew or see Vienna torn up with hate. Colleagues in the United States who have read his research papers on infection of the lungs are happy to write the affidavit he needs and guarantee him a job in the medical school in Chicago. He promises that when he gets there, he will do whatever he can to help Otto, his oldest friend.

'I swear on my dear wife's life...' he begins.

'Norbert, please don't,' Otto interrupts. 'You don't need to worry about me. We'll be fine. If the worst comes to the worst, my bank will get me a transfer to France or to Czechoslovakia. They have branches there. And also.' This is something they have laughed about in the past. 'We both have good records as officers in the last war. Surely that will hold good?' He grasps his dearest friend and they make promises for the future, promises they will never be able to keep.

*

Maria is about to lock the front door of the building for the night when she hears footsteps coming downstairs. The rings under her eyes are the colour of bruises. She holds the fractious baby in her arms, willing it to sleep. Even at this troubled hour, Norbert Kohn has the good manners to stop and ask after the health of her children.

'How old is the baby?' he asks, pulling the shawl back so that he can see her face. 'And your other little girl?'

Maria would like to ask him a question but she is too shy and there could hardly be a worse moment than this. What could she say anyway? Frau Rosen told her a long time ago that Herr Doktor thinks she should take Eva to see an orthopaedic doctor.

*

The next morning they wake up to a changed world.

Some perverse miracle in the night has spawned thousands of swastika armbands, balloons, flags, stencils. It is as if the whole city has been waiting for this moment. The same people wearing different faces appear on the streets dressed in crude uniforms, shouting, 'Heil Hitler' with frenzied enthusiasm. The policeman on the corner, who has greeted Otto with a polite salute every morning, now wears a swastika tunic over his green uniform. From her window, Sonya sees him beating an elderly Jewish man with an expression of berserk fury on his face. The weather is bright and sunny, the air is cold and clear, but for every Jewish family waking up on this Saturday morning, there is only anxiety and fear.

The first squadron of German bombers appears over Vienna, flying low in formation. Hundreds of Luftwaffe planes noisily circle the city and shiny new swastika badges appear like roses in people's buttonholes. That evening there is a torchlight procession of thanksgiving, and thousands of ordinary Viennese appear on the streets, shouting, waving and singing. *When Jewish blood spurts from the knife, everything will be so much better!* Around the government buildings, swastikas are hastily stitched on to the red white red flags and Nazi uniforms appear everywhere. On Saturday night it snows and the Fatherland Front slogans disappear under the cool whiteness. The marching jackboots of the SS and the roar of countless army lorries soon turn it into slush. The German Wehrmacht is taking over the city.

Vienna's leading coffee house immediately changes its name to Café Berlin. Jewish children are forced to write huge red Js on their fathers' shop windows. Men and women surge through the streets, breaking into Jewish homes, stealing and looting. This Jew-hating is a great joke to them. They drag Jewish people into the street and force them onto their hands and knees to scrub away the pro-Schuschnigg slogans. They roar with laughter: 'Isn't the Führer wonderful to create work for the Jews.' Otto and Sonya hold their breath and wait. Susi looks at her parents' faces and knows that nothing will be the same again.

On Monday evening at five o'clock, Hitler enters Vienna. Standing bolt upright in his Mercedes, he greets the roaring crowd, two hundred thousand strong, who jam the Heldenplatz. Austria, now known as the Östmark, becomes absorbed into the Third Reich.

*

Johann stands on the streets, his hands in his pockets, watching all this going on. He is comfortable on the edge of things, observing, listening. Even he is amazed by the mad, cruel frenzy of ordinary people. He shakes his head at the sight of the crazy policeman who is kicking an old Jew into the gutter. It is clear that things are going to be different from now on.

Maria is in the flat. She would like to go upstairs to see how Frau Rosen and Susi are, perhaps offer to do some shopping for them, any little thing on this terrible day. But the baby is not well again. Little Gertrude is small for her age, she is not thriving properly, she often has diarrhoea. Eva is crying to see Susi again. 'Just for a minute,' she pleads, 'just for a little minute.' She looks longingly up at the ceiling as if wishing very hard could make Susi parachute through the three floors and arrive in her kitchen.

*

Otto walks swiftly through the streets, looking straight ahead like a blinkered horse. He reaches the elegant entrance to the bank with its plate glass windows and heavy, polished wood and waits for the commissionaire to open the door for him. Since he has never had occasion to look into the face of this man, he does not notice the change in his expression, although his usual, 'Grüss Gott, Herr Uberinspektor,' is curiously muffled. Inside he approaches his desk, nodding to junior staff as he passes them, greeting his close colleague Dr Gabriel, with the familiar informal, 'Grüss dich Gott Peter.' He waits for the greeting to be returned as it has been, every day, for so many years.

Instead, Dr Gabriel, a pillar of Austrian society, clicks his heels, raises his right arm and shouts, 'Heil Hitler, Otto!'

Later that morning, he stands over Otto's desk and says as if talking to a stranger.

'I can no longer work with or accept instructions from a Jew.'

In a month's time a letter arrives at Otto Rosen's home depriving him of the right to sign on behalf of the bank, but he has long since stopped going into work.

*

Susi, Julie and Kurt walk along streets which are

surprisingly quiet. Outside the school, two large swastika flags are flying, one on the entrance gate and one in the courtyard. Susi and Julie look at each other but there is nothing to say. Kurt kisses his sister on the cheek and presses Susi's hand.

'If there's any trouble, go straight home, don't wait for me,' he says. The girls walk across the playground, close together. The friends who have greeted them every day, who swapped cards, talked about clothes, helped each other with difficult work, part like the Red Sea. Did they plan this? Did they all arrive early and instruct each other to ignore them, to act as if they were diseased? All the Jewish girls in the Gymnasium, forty or fifty, who have never before seen themselves as a separate group, huddle in one corner, their faces to the wall. In Kurt's school, the boys are gathering together to attack the Jewish students with their fists, screaming obscenities. *Saujud* – pig of a Jew, *Untermensch* – cretin. In Susi's school it is whispers and pointing, but it hurts just the same. Inside the classrooms, the teachers have been busy. In each room there is a portrait of Hitler and a swastika. In some there are posters of the Hitler Youth and 'scientific' charts: the Nordic Ideal at the top, disfigured children at the bottom and last of all, the hook nosed, black coated Jew. And in each room the desks are differently arranged. Susi, Julie and four other Jewish girls now sit at the back, a space of two rows between them and the girls in front. At the end of the day, Frau Resch is delighted to tell them that they must leave early: their presence defiles the singing of the Horst Wessel song.

Every day until the summer, Susi will sit alone

in this row. Julie leaves for America and the parents of the other Jewish girls transfer their daughters to an Orthodox school. At the end of the second week in the mid morning break, the girls, Catholic and Protestant together, form two straight lines and make Susi walk through the middle. They pull at her clothing and her school bag, chanting ugly words which Susi refuses to carry in her head. The teachers look the other way. Still she goes to school every day, studies hard and does her homework, because her father tells her that education is the one thing that nobody can take from you, that you can carry it with you wherever you go.

On the streets, the favourite outfit of the girls of the Hitler Youth is the Austrian national costume worn with white socks. In her kitchen, Susi opens the door of the green tiled stove and throws in her embroidered dirndl skirt, her pretty white blouse with the lace collar, and her red jacket, and watches as they burn. Now she is only Jewish.

Vienna

November 1938

November the 5th is Susi's sixteenth birthday. She spends it in Mitteldorf with her grandmother, aunt and cousins.

In Vienna, her mother runs from place to place. She needs to get money from the bank, she needs to get hold of the forms, passports, visas, exit permits which will get them out of the country. There is no time to sit and do nothing. Dora the maid left months ago, taking with her some of their silver and a few bits of jewellery. Sonya and Susi now do the housework and the shopping and Sonya takes in sewing to earn a little cash. There's not much call for couture work these days. She does alterations, turns linings, anything. Otto has become a teacher of sorts, not a very patient one. A group of young students come to his house; everyone wants to learn English. It is a terrible thing for him to be without a salary, without a position in life. Still, he tries to make a joke about it to his wife.

'Maybe you should give me a little housekeeping money and I'll keep house. What would you like, an omelette with or without eggs?'

Susi, no longer in school, is about to start a re-training course organised by the Jewish Cultural Centre. Perhaps she will do pattern cutting or maybe she will learn to make the pastries she has always loved to eat. Hairdressing too is an option. Any skill which she can take with her when she leaves.

In the flat on Obere Donaustrasse there is only one topic of conversation.

'What did I talk about before?' Sonya and her friends ask each other. 'Dresses, hats, the maid, where to go on holiday. How did we ever think those things were important?'

And every sentence of Otto's begins with the words: 'If only I had...'

Returning home one day, Susi opens the door to their flat and sees her father on the floor with his head in her mother's lap, crying like a baby. 'How could I have been so stupid? If only I had listened.' Sonya strokes his head and says nothing.

Leaving the country, getting out, is the thought they wake up with and the one on their minds when they go to sleep. Each night, Otto and Sonya lie side by side like marble carvings on a medieval tomb. In her bed, Susi lies alone, trying to think of nothing at all.

Everyone is scared to go out but they run from one office to another trying to get papers, visas, tickets to anywhere. The queues around the Passport Office on Prinz-Eugen-Strasse stretch for miles around the block, and every passport must be stamped with a big, red J. People queue there for days and nights in the freezing cold, and there is always the possibility that some Nazi will pull you out of the queue to go and clean their barracks. One day, Sonya is stopped by a young man in his immaculate SS uniform.

'You are not wearing a swastika badge. Come with me.' He takes her to an empty room and tells her to wash the floor. Sonya, imagining Susi coming home and finding her mother has disappeared, washes the floor cleaner than it had ever been. Half an hour later, he returns and lets her go.

To get out of the country you need a passport, a sponsor from another country who will act as a guarantor, a visa, documents from the authorities to confirm you have paid your taxes, an exit permit. Every document has to have its stamp and everything has to come together within a certain time, otherwise it all expires. Round and round the Jews of Vienna go: doctors, lawyers, professors, teachers, shop keepers, furniture makers, pastry chefs, artisans, those with no work at all. Each one queues for hours to get a particular piece of paper in their hand, then runs to another office to get a stamp from a different official who loves to keep them waiting, only to be told that the first one has now expired. And even if by some miracle all the documents come together, then where will they go?

Countries known only from the geography book, whose names exist on the smooth blues and oranges of the school globe, now appear as possible places to live: Ecuador, Argentina, Brazil, Cuba, South Africa, the Dominican Republic, Panama, Peru, Shanghai.

Shanghai, a city in China now occupied by Japan, is the only place in the world where a Jew can enter without a passport, visa or money. 'Can you imagine being a Jew in Shanghai?' Otto asks his wife in a rare, lighthearted moment. He tells them the old joke about the Chinese Jew. 'A Jewish man goes to China and meets a Chinese man who tells him that he too is a Jew. That's funny, the Chinese man says, you don't look Jewish.' Otto laughs, his brother-in-law Georg looks on appalled. Nevertheless, they say, someone will go to the shipping company to see how much a ticket for Shanghai costs.

At night, in bed, Otto says to his wife without looking at her.

'I am a European. How could I live anywhere else?'

*

Johann stands at the little mirror and watches himself as he shaves. Still a good strong face, he thinks, still a full head of hair. Soon there will be a war and he is determined to join the army, maybe see a bit of action. He imagines himself in a black uniform with silver buttons, a stiff peaked hat and long, polished boots. This is a dream of course, he knows he isn't officer class, but he wants to make a new start, he is sick of this life. A caretaker is an old man's job and the family has become a millstone around his neck. When the war comes, he'll find somewhere else for Maria and the baby to live. Then after the war, who knows?

Being a caretaker is like being a spy these days. There's always someone who wants to know what's going on in your building: who's coming in and out, anything suspicious. He was in a bit of a tricky position over the Rosens. It was good there was only one Jewish family in the house, otherwise, who knows? He wouldn't stick his neck out for them, but he wasn't going to make trouble on purpose. With a bit of luck, they'd be out of the country before too long and someone else could have their problem. Adolf Eichmann was in the Rothschild Palace right now, trying to get rid of as many of them as possible.

The Rosens keep out of his way these days. No more coming down the stairs to ask him to do this or that for them or to palm off things they don't want any more. He assumed Rosen must have lost his job, most of them had. No more Herr Uberinspektor now. You had to hand it to him in a way. He still dressed himself up in the three piece suit and the white shirt every day, made sure he'd got that decoration from the war in his lapel. One day he came down with his keys in his hand and said, 'I understand that I should leave these with you.' They'd just made a law about it, in case someone needed to investigate what the Jews had up there in their flats.

Maria would know what was going on with them; he knew that when he was out, she was up and down those stairs as if she still worked for them. He should probably put his foot down about that, it didn't look good. One thing he wouldn't have any more was their daughter coming down to their place. It wasn't right. He didn't want her snooping around, knowing his business.

*

At mid-day, Maria prepares a meal of dumplings with a few chives. Eva sits in a corner of the table, quietly turning the pages of an old picture book. Gertrude, not yet walking, plays on the floor with a pile of wooden pegs. Johann comes in and warms his hands by the kitchen range. He seems to be in a good mood today, talking about this and that, almost like in the old days. It makes her uneasy, she is more used to his silences. They eat quickly and Maria stands to clear the plates away. Johann touches her arm and she looks up surprised.

'I want to tell you,' he says, removing his hand. 'I've made an appointment for you at the hospital.'

She looks down at him. She stopped asking him to let her take the children to see the doctor some time ago and she has no idea why he has changed his mind.

'You've been looking tired for a long time and I've been thinking.'

She says nothing and waits.

'I've been thinking. You don't want any more children do you and you're not well, I can see that. It's hard enough taking care of these two.'

Maria holds her breath.

'It's just a small operation, a little routine thing. They do several every day and they advise it in cases like yours. You'll be in about a week, it'll be good for you, you'll be able to have a rest.'

'And the children?' She cannot grasp what it is he wants her to do.

'Don't worry about the children. They can go and stay with your mother for a couple of weeks.'

'Am I seeing the doctor about Eva? And the baby?'

'No, I'm thinking about you, getting you better. I've spoken to Herr Brandt about it. He thinks this is the best thing to do now. And afterwards, he'll help me find the best doctor for her.' He smiles his old smile and for a moment she is reassured.

*

Maria takes the long tram ride alone. It makes its way past the suburbs of Vienna to a large hospital laid out with flowerbeds and lawns that look like a park. The doctor she sees is kind enough.

'You will have a general anaesthetic and we will perform a tubal ligation to prevent conception. It is a straightforward procedure.'

Perhaps they think she will not understand these long words. She doesn't tell them that the way things are between her and her husband, there will be no more babies anyway.

Afterwards she sits for a week, staring out of the window at the bare trees, missing her children. It is the first time she has ever been alone like this. They bring her regular meals, good plain food, and wonder at her silence.

On the day she is ready to leave, the doctor comes to see her again. He congratulates her on satisfying the Protection of the Genetic Health of the German People.

'I would now like to do a little Hereditary Biological Survey. If you would be so kind as to answer a few simple questions about your family?' He takes a piece of paper from his desk and unscrews the top of his fat pen. 'Is there any history of illness in your family, any hereditary diseases?'

No, she doesn't think so.

'What about your husband's family?'

She knows better than to talk about Johann's business but the doctor can read her mind.

'My dear madam,' he addresses her formally. 'There is absolutely no need to worry. What you tell me is completely confidential.'

'Well,' she begins reluctantly. 'There was a cousin, I believe, he died when my husband was just a little boy.'

'Could you tell me a little more please?'

'I never met him of course, but I think he was the kind of child who couldn't learn anything. Couldn't sit up on his own, couldn't speak.' She remembers being told that he was born with a very big head, that the fluid that should have been in his spine was all captured in that head.

'Yes?' The doctor writes *Hydroencephalitis* next to the column marked *Hereditary Illness.* 'Now about your own children, how many do you have?'

'Two. Two girls.'

'And they are both thriving as they should?'

'Well the little one seems fine but she is small for her age and she often has problems with her digestion, but I think its because sometimes it's hard to get her the food she needs.'

'And the older one?'

'Well, there is a little problem with her legs.'

'Really?' He looks at her over his glasses.

'Her legs are not very straight, she has an odd way of walking although she doesn't seem to feel any pain. She is very clever and bright, she talks like a six or seven year old and she has a very good memory.'

The doctor continues to write, nodding all the time. His interest makes her feel braver.

'A doctor I met through the family I used to work for said she needed to see an orthopaedic specialist. Would that be possible?'

The doctor opposite smiles. 'Of course, my dear lady. We will send you a letter in due course.'

Two days after she returns from the hospital, Maria lies in bed feeling washed out and cold. She has not yet told Johann about her conversation with the doctor. She hears him unlock and lock again the heavy front door at the entrance to the building and then their own flat. In the kitchen she can hear him taking off his boots and trousers, washing his face and hands in the bowl of cold water. She knows what this washing has always meant but cannot believe it. Not now, not so soon.

For the first time in many months, Johann turns towards her as he climbs into bed. She lies very still with her back to him, scarcely breathing, hoping this moment will pass. He moves his hands over her nightdress and begins to rub his hands heavily over her breasts. She can feel his breath on her neck, smell the cold on his skin. For a moment, she wonders if her body will begin to warm towards him as it did in the old days when things were good between them, but instantly he is big and breathing strangely.

'No, please,' she says. 'No Johann, not yet.' But he is already turning her, pulling up her nightdress, parting her legs and he is inside her. It hurts.

'Come on, come on,' he is saying and she does not know whether he is talking to himself or to her.

When she wakes up in the morning, he is gone. In the kitchen, the stove is lit and there is hot water. Everything is neatly arranged and she can see that his clothes are packed.

*

In Mitteldorf, in the little house across the street from the general store, Eva, four years and nine months, and little Gertrude, seventeen months, are staying with their grandmother Hanna. In celebration of Susi's sixteenth birthday, Hanna makes her an excellent birthday cake with ground hazelnuts and dried cherries. She is like a squirrel, they say, storing all those ingredients. Eva stands behind grandma Hanna as the family eat the cake and drink coffee.

'Sit down Hanna,' aunt Fanny says, 'take the weight off your feet.' But no, Hanna will not sit down; it would not feel right.

Hanna has taught Eva a special song to sing for Susi. They gather round and the little girl stands stock still and sings her party piece. She stops after each verse grinning with importance at her task, and takes their laughter for applause. Susi picks her up and hugs her till she squeals. It is a moment of pleasure to be held.

'Such a shame, poor thing, and she's got such a pretty little face.' Aunt Fanny tuts and shakes her head, addressing no one in particular. Susi has grown used to hearing people talk about Eva like this. When she was younger she always thought it was because Eva was poor and had to have their cast-offs. Now she understands why the adults think she should be more pitied than loved.

The women lean forward to discuss Maria's 'troubles'. Fanny takes a sidewards look at Susi to see if she is listening and leans towards her mother.

'He's had her sterilised you know. That's why the children are with Hanna.' She pauses and lowers her voice. 'Sonya's very worried about them all. Maria's not getting on so well with the husband, Johann. I've never liked that man, I never knew why Otto trusted him. He's never seemed to care about his own children.' She nods towards little Eva who is playing with the handles of the wooden chest in the far corner of the room. 'He wants to send her away.'

'Send her away? Where is he going to send her?'

'You know, to some kind of institute where they

have handicapped children.'

'Well, maybe it would be good for her to get some treatment. You can't say she doesn't need it. What will she be like when she gets older?'

'I can't see him wanting to send her any place that will do her any good.' Fanny replies scornfully, 'I think he just wants to get rid of her.'

'What do you mean?' Rosa Shapiro asks sharply.

'I mean.' Fanny raises her voice and her eyebrows. 'Put her some place, an institution of some kind, and never have her back home.'

'Honestly Fanny, you do exaggerate,' her mother sighs. 'I'll have a word with Hanna, but I can't see what any of us can do about it.'

Susi, overhearing, understands that this is one more cruel thing in a world already filled with injustice.

*

A week after Susi's sixteenth birthday, two weeks after Johann leaves the flat and a few days after the children come back to Vienna to be with their mothers, the world falls apart in a new way.

Kristallnacht, the evening of the 9th of November. The night of broken glass. The night when Vienna forgets that it is the elegant, sophisticated capital of Europe. The sky is red with fire; every synagogue in Vienna is burned down, every window of every Jewish shop smashed, every Jewish home ransacked and looted. Jewish graves are desecrated; thousands of Jewish men are rounded up and arrested and the beards and heads of old rabbis are shaved until they bleed. In the parks, Jews are made to cut the grass with their teeth; on the streets they scrub the pavements with water laced with acid so that their hands are scorched and burning.

The word Jew is everywhere. No entrance for Jews. No sales to Jews. No Jews or dogs. Jews Keep Out. Jewish Customers Not Wanted Here. On every house, every window pane, every store. On the only remaining glass window of a shattered Jewish shop a joker writes *A Holiday in Dachau*. The Nazis have covered Otto's beautiful Vienna with this word. The six pointed Star of David has become a symbol of abuse.

Everywhere is banned: parks, cinemas, concerts, theatres, museums, libraries, public baths, all banned. Only the streets are allowed and they are hardly safe.

On the morning of the 10th of November, with the synagogues still burning while people on balconies and rooftops laugh at the flames, there is a loud knock and shouting at the door of the Rosen's flat.

'Don't answer it,' Sonya begs Otto, 'hide in the wardrobe, get out over the roof.'

'There's no point,' he says, 'they'll be back sooner or later and it will be worse.' He means worse for them. 'Get into bed and pull up the covers as if you're ill,' he tells Susi. At the door, two plain clothes Gestapo officers have come to arrest him. They give no reason.

When he is gone, Susi and her mother, equal height, cling silently together, as if to stop each other breaking into pieces.

The next day, whilst Sonya is running from one office to the next to try to get some news of her husband, Dora the maid and her trouble maker boyfriend enter their flat with a few friends and ransack it, smashing up a few things, taking what they can get their hands on. They steal jewellery, money; drink the whisky; tear up a few books. They stop only when Maria appears at the door, demanding to know what they are doing.

'Jew-lover,' they spit at her. 'They'll lock *you* up one of these days with that Untermensch brat of yours.' But they leave anyway. The last one to go, the boyfriend in the brown Storm trooper's uniform, faces Maria at the doorway and shouts in her face. 'Tell the Jew bitch, she's got to get out by the end of the week. This flat has been allocated to an Aryan family.'

Otto is not alone in the morning streets of Vienna. There are hundreds of men being marched towards the station for the train to Dachau. Some housewives out shopping and children on their way to school stop and smile as if watching a band or a parade. At the station, the Schlagkommando takes one look at the weight of Otto's overcoat and the quality of his shoes and asks him if he's not ashamed to have money when there are so many Aryans out of work. Otto, assuming this is a question which must be answered, opens his mouth to reply and receives the first beating of his life, a beating so violent that it feels as if his head has burst open. His glasses break into his left eye and it is so bloody and swollen that he cannot see.

For fourteen hours he stands silently in the crowded train. At Dachau, boys not much older than his own Susi, men old enough to be his own father are marched between the guards who trip and kick them, laughing. His clothes are removed, never to be returned, and his head and moustache are dry shaved.

He is given a prison uniform and a number, a red triangle and a yellow one to form the six pointed star.

For the first time since his barmitzvah, Otto Rosen prays to God for the safety of Sonya and Susi and his own soul. The only prayer he can remember is the first line of the Shemah. *Hear O Israel, the Lord is Our God. The Lord is One.*

*

All day Sonya runs from place to place searching for news of Otto. It is Maria who persuades Sonya Rosen that they must get ready to leave the flat and take Susi to Mitteldorf. Hanna has an old outhouse where they can store some of their things.

'But how will Otto know where we are?' Sonya Rosen asks. 'How will he find us?'

'Don't worry,' they reassure her again and again. 'He'll know where we are.'

Just as they did when they were spring cleaning or preparing the table for the Seder meal, Maria and Sonya Rosen work together in quiet sympathy. They wrap the menorah and the candlesticks which belonged to Otto's mother and some silver which was hidden behind the book-case. They choose Otto's favourite books, some of their own. They pack what they can of their clothes and carefully wrap some china and the jewellery that is left. Hanna's embroidered linen rests in its tissue paper. The pictures leave their shadows against the wall. Most of their things must be left behind; the visiting Nazi officers have already made a list of what now belongs to them. But for a handsome tip, the men agree to carry down the glass fronted cabinet and some chairs.

'Don't look back,' Sonya tells her daughter as they make their way downstairs, 'don't look back.'

*

In Mitteldorf, a week after Kristallnacht, on a freezing cold, starless night, the family lie in their own beds, all awake. Georg and Fanny talk once more of how to get out, even though there is nothing new to say. His sister in America has no money to act as guarantor; they haven't heard from Freddi. The girls, maybe they will send to England as servants, a job no English person wants to do. Rosa Shapiro lies in the huge, carved bed where she has slept alone for over twenty years. She is an old woman now; she wants no more of this world. She prays that she will die in her sleep, maybe tonight. Sonya thinks only of Otto, although to imagine where he might be and what he might be feeling is unbearable. Susi, lying next to her, pretends to sleep.

Into the dark silence, down below, there is a screech of brakes, the terrible crashing of metal against broken glass, the crack of split wood, of things falling one upon the other, the brutal sound of laughter without humour.

Everybody listens and nobody moves. The sound of heavy boots is on the stairs and suddenly their rooms are full of the heavy smell of men. Rosa, Fanny, Georg, Klara, Lori, Sonya, Susi get up from their beds and go downstairs, the men pushing them from behind. Georg, in particular, they prod and poke, hitting him around the head. In the streets and on the little square a light comes on in every house. Doors and windows are thrown open and the people they have grown up with, who played with them in the school playground when they were young, who sell them their milk and eggs and vegetables and buy goods from their shop, now stand and jeer. The open truck has crashed through the strong door of the shop and the men, still laughing, grab everything they can until it is full. With the butt of a shovel from the store, one man smashes each window in turn, leaving just one. Another takes a pot of paint and a brush from the stolen pile, and Georg is made to paint 'We Do Not Buy From Jews' on the one remaining window of his shop.

Hanna steps into the November night: modest Hanna, wearing only her nightdress, her grey hair flying loose in the freezing wind.

'How can you do this you bastards, how can you?' she cries, hurling her words at the crowd. 'They're the only decent, honest people in this whole stinking town. They've never done you any harm. God will look down from heaven and spit on the whole lot of you.'

'Shut up you stupid cow, or they'll arrest you,' a voice calls from the dark.

'I don't care, I don't want to live in this place another day. May your filthy souls rot in hell.' Hanna's voice cracks and her short, sturdy body shakes and she sways as if about to fall. It is Sonya who steps forward and puts her own wrap around Hanna's shoulders and leads her quietly inside.

Vienna

January 1939

Maria smells Johann before she sees him: the damp wool of his new uniform as he comes in from the cold night air, the cigarette smoke. She has not seen him for weeks. She remains where she is, darning a stocking for Eva at the kitchen table.

He comes in as formal as a stranger.

'I won't stay long, I'll just sit down for a moment. Don't worry about food. As a soldier in the Wehrmacht, I eat well enough. I'm sorry to surprise you like this, but it is hard to know when it is possible to leave the barracks.' Maria looks at him, handsome in his uniform, and feels uneasy. He looks her up and down without much interest. 'How are you?' he asks.

'Fine.'

There are two important things he has to say. Firstly, she has to move; obviously she cannot stay here in this flat now that he has gone. He has made arrangements for her. In two weeks time, she will move to a room in the house of his school master friend, Herr Brandt. The accommodation is good. There are two boys in the house, fourteen and sixteen and she will help Frau Brandt with the housework and so on. Maria nods and says nothing; she is ready to move from the house on Obere Donaustrasse where it is hard to remember any happy times. And she needs to be near Frau Rosen and Susi, who are living precariously in a room in the next district.

The second thing is that he has heard from the hospital. There is an appointment at a children's clinic run by the National Socialist Party and she must attend with the girl next Wednesday. Herr Brandt will accompany her if he cannot come himself.

'Are you talking about Eva?'

'Of course, what did you think?'

'Is he an orthopaedic doctor, like Dr Kohn said?'

'I should think so.' He has a new kind of confidence about him, and it is clear from the tone of his voice and the way he looks at her, that he does not want to talk. 'Let me see her now.'

'But she's asleep.'

'Get her up then.'

Reluctantly, Maria lifts Eva from her bed and puts her down gently in front of her father.

'Walk,' he says as if talking to a dog.

'But she's still half asleep, look at her.'

'Walk for your father,' he repeats.

Eva looks up at him with frightened eyes and then at her mother for reassurance. Maria tries to smile at her daughter and nods at the far end of the table. 'Go and get my knitting wool, my love,' she says gently, trying to make some sense of this to her. 'Go on, sweetheart.'

Obediently, Eva makes her own peculiar, purposeful way across the room, rocking her hips from side to side, holding on to the table as she makes her way to the end.

'As I thought,' he says grimly. 'As I thought.'

Alone in the kitchen, trying to warm herself by the fire, Maria does not understand how this has happened to her. How did she become someone who must just listen to her husband and agree, who asks no questions, even about the people she loves most in the world? She wraps her shawl tightly around her body.

*

Susi Rosen wakes up in the cramped room she shares with her mother. She looks at the pale, worn face sleeping beside her with her dark hair dull and frizzled and it is hard to remember the elegant, groomed lady who went out to play bridge in stylish dresses and hats and who was interested in the minutest details of her daughter's life. Sonya has been crying in her sleep, like a little girl needing comfort. 'Mutti, mutti, where are you?'

For the fifth night in a row, Susi has stroked her mother's outstretched arm and said, 'I'm here, mummy, I'm here, we'll be alright. Don't cry.'

It is six weeks since Sonya buried her mother in a hurried, nervous ceremony in Mitteldorf, with the wooden embers of the little synagogue still smouldering. Rosa Shapiro died alone in her marriage bed two days after Hanna had stood in the street and screamed like a woman possessed. In the morning, Lori, the oldest granddaughter opened her drawer and threw away all the medicines. Nobody spoke about it and the next day they buried Rosa next to her husband in the Jewish section of the Mitteldorf Cemetery.

In the daytime, Sonya is strong once again. Every morning she and Susi set out with a list of embassies to visit, documents to get stamped, officials to see. In the evening in their tiny cramped room in the house of a distant cousin, they share a plate of potatoes with perhaps a little sour cream and try to cheer themselves with whatever inches of progress they have made. Sonya thinks only about getting Otto released from the labour camp and finding a way to get Susi out of the country. Every official she manages to see is reminded of Otto's meritorious record as an officer in the war and of his good standing at the bank. From the Paris branch of the bank where he worked for so many years, she receives polite letters promising to do what they can in these difficult circumstances. For Susi, Sonya visits obscure Dutch charities who say they can do nothing for her unless she is baptised. The Quakers, the Christadelphians are trying their best. Perhaps she can get Susi on to a children's transport to England. Every day one of them queues outside the Kultusgemeinde, the Jewish Cultural Community Centre in the city, hoping for a chance to leave the country. If they can find a guarantor, the British Government would let Sonya come to England to be a domestic. Sonya isn't too proud to be a servant, but first she must get Otto released.

'One day we will all be together in a safe place,' she says every day to Susi. 'One day we will, you'll see.'

Maria has become indispensable. She sells a brooch or a ring for Frau Rosen. There are lots of bribes to be paid and there is no time for Sonya to shop for food. It is hard for Maria to get about with the children, she worries constantly and does not eat, but there is nothing she will not do for the Rosens.

*

On Wednesday at ten o'clock exactly, Herr Brandt knocks at Maria's door. He is a big man in his late forties with receding sandy hair. On his tweed jacket he proudly displays the badge worn only by those who can prove their blood is pure Aryan for a hundred years: the red, black and white swastika.

Maria smooths down her grey wool skirt and

straightens her stockings. Eva's hair is newly washed and the short fair curls spring sideways from her head. Maria buttons the coat which is much too tight and laces up her sturdy brown boots. Susi, who has come to look after Gertrude, waits in the other room with the door closed.

He proudly ushers Maria and the child into the back of a small black Volkswagen. Maria assumes it must be borrowed, even Herr Rosen did not own a car like this. Eva opens her eyes wide in excitement. A car! She cannot believe her luck. All the way there, she asks questions.

'What is the man doing to make us move?' 'Why is he turning that round black thing?' 'Why do those orange triangles clack out at the side when we go round a corner?'

'Hush a minute,' Maria tells the child. She needs to think about what she will say to the doctors. It is hard not to be scared of their superior faces and condescending smiles but she knows she must speak up for Eva; there may not be another chance.

'I'll carry her for you, it's quite a walk, I think.' Herr Brandt says as he parks the car in the leafy grounds of the hospital. He talks to Maria as they make their way towards a two storey white pavilion telling her about his sons and the home where she will soon be living.

In a bare room with a green, tiled floor and cream walls, all three sit silently in the waiting room, watching a secretary type notes from a long hand-written form. She stops typing and looks up.

'You can go in now,' she says, addressing no one in particular. Herr Brandt stands up with Maria and leads the way into the consulting room. Appalled, she follows him and there is nothing she can say.

The men greet each other with a clicking of heels and a Heil Hitler. The doctor is not old, but he is quite bald and his head shines under the hard white light. He wears gold rimmed spectacles and it is hard to see his eyes. He examines Eva as carefully as Maria had hoped. She undresses the child and he looks at her legs and hip joints. He weighs and measures her and watches her walk, all the time writing notes on a big printed form. Eva stands but will not look at his face. There is something about the doctor's manner that frightens her into silence. She says nothing when the cold stethoscope touches her chest and only cries when he moves her hips in such a way that it hurts her.

'It is very good that you have brought her to see me. Without boasting, I can assure you that this is an excellent clinic. The work we are doing here is entirely in line with the thinking of the Reich.'

'Do you think she needs an operation?' Maria asks shyly.

'We'll have to see, once we have her here, we'll do a full assessment. But in cases like this, it is best not to be too hopeful.'

'What do you mean?'

'Well my dear,' the doctor says evasively. 'We will have to see what possibilities there are for her future.'

'Of course,' Herr Brandt steps in with a little laugh. 'It is difficult for any mother to part with her child, but I'm sure she understands that it is the right thing to do. The child has been like this since birth and I think the mother would agree that things get worse with each year. The child is handicapped to a great degree. I think the only possibility in a case like this is to...' It is fear which makes Maria interrupt.

'This is not the child's father,' she begins quietly, and then more firmly. 'This is the first time I've ever seen him; he cannot decide what is best for her.'

Herr Brandt looks at her with raised eyebrows and then at the doctor. 'No, the father of the child is in the army. He asked me to come and represent him. Would it be possible to have a word?' He nods towards the door and the doctor follows him, leaving Maria and the child alone.

The form lies on the desk, face up. Perhaps the doctor thinks she is just a peasant who can't read. There is such a compression inside her that she feels like she is going to be sick, but she leans forward and turns the form to face her. In heavy black ink she reads the words, **Clinical Diagnosis. Prognosis. Recommendations.** And against these, in a spidery hand, the doctor has written: *Retarded since birth. Severe malformation of legs. No intelligence. Will never improve and will never provide socially valuable activities. Treatment in line with the directive of the Reich Committee.* With thumb and forefinger, Maria turns the paper back to its original position and sits waiting for their return.

On the way home, terrified and silent, Maria is aware of Herr Brandt's calm, expressionless voice talking on and on, so unlike Johann who, when he chooses to speak, is always trying to persuade and wheedle and wear you down. He tells her what an excellent doctor she has just seen, a very good man. Of course, he understands that it will be a sacrifice for her to let the child go. There is no doubt how hard she has tried to care for her, but it is very important not to be selfish in this matter. There is the expense to think of, and the trouble and the future of the country. Maria says nothing, only waits for the moment when she can get out of the prison of this car.

Susi is feeding Gertrude some potatoes mashed with a little milk, just as Maria once fed her. The moment Maria enters the flat, she can see that something is terribly wrong. In the last months, Susi has seen all the adults in her life upset and desperate, but never calm, unflappable Maria.

'What's the matter? Maria what is it?' But for a moment, she cannot speak and gasps for breath as if she has been drowning. Susi brings her a glass of water, and as her mother would do, she holds her hand and asks questions, waiting patiently for the reply.

'They're going to take her away from me. God alone knows what they'll do with her once they've got her there. It's what he's always wanted, he's always hated her. Someone's got to help me. If they take her I'll never see her again. I read what he wrote, I know what it means.'

'We won't let them, we won't let them,' is all Susi can say. 'I'll find a way, I promise.'

Maria wipes her eyes and begins to come back into the world. 'Thank you darling, you're a good girl. Don't tell your dear mother, she has more than enough to worry about.'

*

Maria is sick, the baby is sick and the new caretaker is

moving in in a week's time. Nothing is organised and there is no fire in the kitchen. Maria sits at the table, trying to get the baby to eat something.

On Sunday afternoon, Susi walks Eva along a tiny strip of grass by the banks of the Donau Canal, the only green space in Vienna which is not full of watchmen checking who is wearing the swastika badge. She would love to run with Eva along the wide cinder paths of the Augarten as they used to do together. Eva, too big by far, stands up in the battered old wicker pram with its tiny wheels, calling for her attention.

'Why is the sky so big?'

'Because it has to have room for all the clouds.'

'Why are there so many branches on the trees?'

'So that the birds have lots of room to hop about.'

And on and on, the repetition of a much loved game. 'Why are you so beautiful?' Susi asks, like her mother used to.

'Because I'm me,' Eva replies, pleased with herself.

'That's right, exactly,' Susi says looking at her bonny face. 'Because you're you.'

Crossing the bridge on their way back home, Susi bumps into a girl she has known for years.

'Hi Susi,' she says, looking curiously into the pram.

'A friend of the family,' Susi says automatically.

'Oh, I see.' The girl is grinning. 'I'm leaving,' she tells Susi proudly. 'They're registering children under eighteen for a transport for England at the Metropole Hotel. I'll be gone by the end of the week. What about you?'

Susi shakes her head.

'Well, they were still taking names when I left. You should have a go.'

Susi is only a few minutes from home. She knows that when her mother wakes up from her afternoon nap, she will be terrified to find Susi gone, just as Maria will be if she does not return with Eva. And maybe this could be the day when Papa is released and is waiting for her in their cramped room. But still, Susi turns the pram around and runs towards the centre of the city.

The queue is long but not so long as the one which always snakes around the Israelitische Kultusgemeinde. In front of her, a father with twin boys, seven or eight years old, looks at them with interest.

'Why is that big girl in a pram?' One of the boys asks his father.

'Is that your sister?' his father asks, looking at Eva's fair curls and Susi's dark bob.

Susi nods without replying.

'Are you going to register both of you?'

Susi nods again.

'What will I need in there?' she asks. 'I haven't got any papers with me.'

'That's okay,' he replies kindly. 'The authorities have made a special agreement with the British Government. They're taking children without a visa; you give them your details and they make all the arrangements.'

Susi waits, her heart pounding, as the line edges nearer and nearer to the row of desks. Fear is nothing new, she lives with it all the time, watching, waiting for something else bad to happen, knowing there is scarcely a stranger you can trust. But this is different. This might be the moment where she does not have to watch while evil people destroy everything she loves. Maybe in this moment, she can make a difference.

The list of children to leave on the next transport grows longer and longer. The queue is closed off behind her and she watches as little children with anxious parents and boys who are as big as grown men are photographed, examined and asked for their details. It seems so ordered, the gentle, efficient people at the desks asking questions, checking the facts. Each person's details must be sorted out and telephoned to England; every name must be checked and double checked as quickly as possible. Susi hopes that in all this work, this calm, ordered chaos, there is a place for one small lie about a little girl whose life is in as much danger as Susi's own. With hundreds of children leaving each week, surely there is a place for one child who walks in a funny way and whose own father does not want her to exist?

What should she tell them? That Eva is a mischling, a half Jew, a quarter, an eighth? One drop of Jewish blood would be enough to get her out. Or the truth. That she is one of the 'useless eaters' who is valued as little as Susi is in this terrible place.

Eva's pram has been left outside. Holding her tightly by her side, Susi explains to the gentle, efficient man that her father is in the labour camp at Dachau and her mother will not leave Vienna without him. She has heard that they give priority to children whose parents have been deported or taken prisoner.

'We do not have anyone who can act as

guarantor, really the Kindertransport is our only hope.'

'And the little girl?'

'She's my cousin and all her papers were burned on Kristallnacht.'

From Susi's mouth, the lie that will order the rest of their lives comes out clean as the spring air. From your mouth to God's ear, grandma Rosa used to say.

This diligent man, writing, checking, noting, has no reason to suspect that an honest faced Jewish girl, sixteen years old, would tell a lie about a little non-Jewish child with crooked legs, nearly five. They begin to take down her details.

In this odd way, uncle Freddi, who Eva will never meet, who at this very moment is sitting at a piano in a dark Manhattan bar singing, incongruously, *can't help loving this man of mine*, becomes the putative father of a child who for the next five years will be known as Eva Shapiro. Eva Shapiro, Kindertransport Identification No. 111, travelling with her older cousin, Susi Rosen, aged 16, Kindertransport No. 112 – all written with care on two white cards bearing their photographs and the legend: *Personal Particulars. Issued with the approval of His Majesty's Government in the United Kingdom.*

Susi walks through the cold night air elated and scared. She takes Eva home where the mothers are waiting, frantic and panic stricken. It takes a while for Susi to make her mother calm enough to listen to her story. Sonya's hand goes to her mouth, she pulls at her hair. She cannot stop herself.

'Susi have you gone mad? You can't possibly look after her, you'll never get away with such a lie. She needs medical treatment, they'll never let her into England.' And softer. 'She's not our family, you shouldn't have done this. It's not safe.' If only Otto was here with the right words. 'Maria, what do you think, surely you don't want her to go?'

Maria looks up at her with eyes that are barely alive.

'It's the only way.' She takes Susi's hand and clutches it fiercely. 'Thank you, thank you, you've saved her.'

'My God. Maria my dear. What will you tell them when they ask where she is? What will you tell Johann?'

'I'll tell them that someone came from the hospital and took her, because they wanted her a few days early.'

'Will he believe you?'

'I expect so,' she replies in a voice so quiet they can scarcely make out what she is saying. 'It's what he wants to hear.'

On Tuesday, a letter arrives. The transport leaves at midnight on Saturday from Westbahnhof. There are only five days to get ready and for Eva everything must be kept secret. Sonya Rosen, as always, survives by keeping busy. There is a list of things which must be bought or mended, labelled and packed: pyjamas, socks, underwear, skirts, jumpers, a warm coat, sensible shoes. Sonya sells a few more things to provide the girls with clothes that will last. If Eva is going too, and in her heart Sonya knows she must, then her clothes must be as good and strong as Susi's. She sews and packs, folding and kissing each item as she places it in the little brown suitcases. They are allowed one small case, one bag and a little money, nothing valuable.

She feels the loss of Otto more than ever; fear now eats at her soul. What advice would he give to his daughter for a life without her parents, even for a while? She knows he would talk about her education and respecting the people who are good enough to take care of her. When Sonya was sixteen she was still a girl with a big sister and a naughty baby brother. Her life was new dresses, parties, friends, family celebrations. She watches Susi, adult and composed one minute, on her lap for hugs and kisses the next, and feels her heart contract. How can she let her go to a new country where there might be no one who will love and guide her? She is sick at heart at the thought of her having responsibility for Eva. Wasn't life complicated enough? But she knows that Susi, with her clear, young person's sense of right and wrong, will not leave without her.

On Wednesday, Susi has her last day at the training centre where she has been a star pupil in the pattern cutting course. From an old suit of her mother's she has made herself a blue wool dress, neat and belted with a Peter Pan collar. She dreads the walk home. Wherever you are it is the wrong place to be, wherever you go, someone is watching. She walks towards the park with the big Ferris Wheel and turns left off Prater Strasse, into a little street and through the door of the small, dark building where they now live, up the unlit staircase. On the stairs she hears her mother's voice.

'Otto, darling, we must let her go, there's no choice.' She holds her breath outside the door waiting to hear her father speak, but he has heard her steps. He is at the door, thin, more than thin, gaunt. His head is shaved and his glasses are kept together with string.

'Feel this,' he says smiling, tears streaming down his face. He rubs her hand against the stubble on his head. 'Feel what a good shave they gave me.'

He will not talk about what happened to him. 'I have come back alive,' is all he will say. 'Thank God.' They put him on the train back to Vienna in the same way as they had taken him away, without explanation or reason. A kind stranger noticed his prison shirt and his shaved head and gave him the tram fare home. He does not speak against Susi leaving, although it is the most painful thing that has happened to him. He trusts God to take care of her. Trusting in God is a new thing for Otto Rosen. God is all there is left to trust.

On Saturday night, in the freezing darkness, Susi gets into a taxi with her parents and they drive to pick up Eva. Otto's shaved head is covered in a big Homburg hat and his shoes are polished and shiny. On the subject of Eva, he has said very little to Susi. Maria and the girls are ready for them; her eyes are dark circles and she cannot smile.

'There is a little packet in her bag,' she tells Susi. 'Nothing valuable, a photograph and a little necklace which belonged to her grandmother.'

'Maria, darling, are you sure about this? It's not too late.' Sonya feels sick with guilt, she would give anything for Eva to stay. Maria merely shakes her head and shrugs. Her heart is broken and she is beyond words.

'I know you'll take care of her,' she says to Susi. 'Your family and mine...' She stops. 'Look after her for me. Keep her with you if you can. I hope that she will be brought up like you.' She kisses Eva and holds her tight for a minute, then lifts up Gertrude to be kissed. Eva kisses her little sister; it is all an adventure to her.

The station is full of SS men, standing, watching, ready to move. The platform is full of parents and children. Sonya fusses over the girls, smiling and talking, talking all the time as if this is the most ordinary thing in the world.

'It's not for long. Once you are settled, you can help us find a way to be together. Everything will be fine.' She hugs Eva and kisses both her cheeks. 'Here is a little sandwich for you sweetheart, here is a piece of fruit. Susi will look after you, don't be scared.' Her face is as red as fire. She gives Susi one more kiss, determined that the last face she sees is her mother smiling. 'Always remember how much you are loved.'

Otto stands solemnly before his daughter. 'You have a bigger responsibility than anyone your age should have. Be honest and carry with you what you have learned. No one can take away what is in your heart and in your mind.' He puts his hand on the heads of both girls and blesses them In Hebrew. 'The Lord bless you and keep you; the Lord cause his face to shine upon you, and be gracious to you; the Lord look upon you with favour and give you peace.'

The guards push the parents away from the platform. 'Anyone making too much noise will be arrested. Get out, get away from here, you scum.' They do not want a scene when the train leaves.

The train pulls away from Vienna. Young children cry and the older girls hug them and talk to them softly. All through the night, the children travel, some sleeping, some wide awake with fear and expectation. At the border between Germany and Holland, the station is full of swastika flags. The soldiers come on, pushing the brown suitcases with the butts of their rifles, emptying bags on the floor.

'If any of you are trying to bring out valuables, the whole train will return to Vienna and then you'll be for it. We know what you Jews are like.' Eva sits as still as still can be. She must not move one little toe or one finger until the bad men have gone.

Over the border, Susi rubs her legs and toes to get rid of the pins and needles. Wonderful Dutch women fill the train with mugs of hot chocolate and sweet cake. A farmer's wife with wrinkles in the shape of a smile gives Eva a woollen doll with a knitted red dress and a blue bonnet.

'That's for you my dear, for being so brave. Are you related?' she asks Susi.

'Yes, she's my cousin.' Susi replies and feels it to be true.

The older boys break into wild songs of the Promised Land and the others join in. Through the flat morning light, the children rub their hands against the windows and look in amazement at storybook windmills and canals. The train takes them through Rotterdam and into the port of the Hook of Holland where a huge white boat with a thousand windows is waiting for them. They are on their way to England.

EVA

Harwich and Dovercourt Camp for Refugee Children

1939

The boat was very, very big. It went up and down and up and down and up and down and my tummy went up and down with it. But I wasn't sick at all, not like the other children.

Susi wouldn't let me walk on the boat because she said I would fall over. She carried me everywhere and I didn't like it. She said, 'I'm going to teach you a little bit of English.' I didn't understand what that was, English, but when Susi started talking she made me laugh because she kept opening and closing her mouth very wide and said words that weren't like real words. I tried to pull her mouth back into shape so she would talk properly and I could understand her. Then she put my hands back down and she said, 'Listen carefully Eva, I'm going to teach you something important. People will ask you what is your name and you must say, "My name is Eva." And they will ask you, how old are you? And you must answer, "I am four-and- a-half years old."'

She said, 'These words are English and these words are German.' She made me say it and I opened my mouth very wide to say the funny words. Then we played a game with these words to say them over and over again until I could remember them properly. I could say, 'I am four years old' and she could say, 'I am sixteen.'

She made a very serious, long face and she said, 'Eva, this is very important. When people see you walking they will ask you, "What's the matter?" And you must say, "I broke my leg but soon it will get better." '

I didn't understand that because my leg wasn't broken like when mummy dropped a cup on the floor and picked it up and wrapped the pieces in some paper. Susi said, 'No, not broken like that. It means you've hurt your leg.' I asked her when did I hurt it because I couldn't remember and she looked very serious again and she said, 'You must say, I fell over and broke my leg but the doctor said it will get better soon.' She made me say those words again and again and she kept saying to me, 'They will ask you about your legs and that is what you must tell them.'

Susi took me on the deck and showed me how the sea went on for ever and ever. If you went near the edge you could feel the cold water on your face. We played a game. She blew out of her mouth and made smoke come out and then I breathed out of my mouth and made smoke. Susi told me it was because it was so cold. I asked her, 'How big is the sea?'

But she said, 'Not now, darling.'

When the boat stopped there were lots and lots of stairs. A boy carried me because Susi had to carry her case and my case. I didn't like the boy, because his coat scratched my face and he smelled of sick. I could have walked by myself but Susi said no.

Outside it was very bright and cold and the smelly boy carried me a long way and I thought he was going to drop me.

The place we went to was very big and it was cold just the same as outside and everything was windows, tall, tall windows even up in the roof and the roof was so high up you could see that it went right up in the sky. Some of the children were crying but I wasn't. Susi put our two brown suitcases together in a corner of this big place and she sat down. I touched the white part that held the windows together and it was hard and so cold that it hurt my fingers. Susi spoke to me in a very little voice. She said, 'I don't want you to move now. I don't want them to see you walking so you must stand between my legs as still as you can and if they ask you, you can tell them your name and how old you are. But don't say the other bit about your broken leg.' She said, 'If we don't do this right, they might send us back.' And I knew this was bad, even though I wanted to see mummy and Gertrude again. When the big man with the pen came, I stood as still as still can be.

There were two men. One man had a long thing around his neck and the other one had a piece of chalk. Susi took off my coat and my new cardigan which grandma Hanna had knitted me. It was pale blue with brown stripes at the bottom and it had pretty buttons shaped like flowers. I didn't want to take my dress off but Susi said he needed to hear my chest. It felt very cold and it tickled so I giggled. Then he tried to make me turn around but I remembered what Susi had told me and I stuck my feet very hard on the floor so no one could move me and I made my face look very cross. Then the man laughed at me and I didn't like it but Susi said, 'Don't worry darling,' and lifted me up and put me on her lap. He put the cold thing on my back and smiled again and said 'good' and I understood that word although he said it in a funny way. Then the other man came along and looked at the little white card with my name on it which I was holding very tight, and he took a piece of chalk out of his pocket and put a cross on both our cases.

Susi said I had been a good girl and everything was fine but she didn't move. She sat on the cases and held me very tight. She put her head into my hair and

I could hear her heart going bang, bang, bang and there was a funny sound in her throat like she didn't know how to breathe.

We went to a different big place with lots of children. I could understand some of the grown ups and Susi said those people could speak German. There was a nice woman, she had white hair and she said, 'It won't be hard to find a family for that one, not with those curls and that pretty face.'

And Susi said, 'no we're staying together, she's my cousin.'

It was so cold in that place that we didn't take our coats off not even when we ate our food. They made me take off my clothes to go to bed and I didn't like it. Some food was nice there like the cake and the sandwiches and the square yellow cubes that tasted sweet but some food I couldn't eat at all. Like at breakfast when it was brown and salty and disgusting and the lady said. 'You must eat it, it's very good for you and it's called kippers.' The bad thing was that they wouldn't let me sleep with Susi. I had to sleep in the coldest, coldest room and all the little children were crying. I hugged the little woollen doll with the red dress the lady gave me on the train, but I wanted Susi. When I woke up there was white on the inside of the windows and my fingers felt like they wouldn't move.

Outside there was a long, hard path and when we came out from sleeping in the morning, the children ran along the path to the place where we ate our food. All the children were running and running along that place and I started to run too because I loved running but the lady with the white hair stopped me and pulled at my arm and she said, 'Why are you running like that? What's the matter with your leg?' I remembered that Susi had taught me special words to say when they asked me that, but I couldn't remember them, so I stood very still and I wouldn't move not one tiny little bit until they went to get Susi.

Susi wasn't cross. She told me not to cry and that I hadn't done anything wrong. Then I remembered what I had to say about my broken leg, so I said it and everyone laughed. Then Susi said it again and the woman made a long face and her eyebrows went up in her head.

Every day more and more children came to this place. Sometimes they cried at night. I had a friend called Lotte, she was bigger than me. On one day called Sunday, I put on my new checked dress and my blue cardigan and a lady put a blue ribbon in my hair. Lotte told me that if I was good, some people might choose me and take me with them to live in their house but I knew I wasn't going without Susi because she had told me.

After I had eaten my sandwich, I was sitting down playing with my doll and a man and a woman and a big boy came up to me. The boy had a green cap on his head with a badge on it made of gold and I thought it was lovely. He showed me the badge and I tried to take it but it wouldn't come off the cap. The woman had a horrible thing round her neck. It felt soft to touch but it had the face of an animal with hard eyes in it and on the other end were feet and it made me feel frightened. When she bent over me her face smelt like sweets. The man spoke to me in German although he said the words in a funny way. He said,'Would you like to come with us and you could be a little sister for our son?'

I didn't say anything.

Then he said, 'Come for a little walk with us, there is nice sunshine out there.'

So I went with him into the garden and the boy walked behind me and said, 'quack, quack, quack.'

*

Susi was crying. She sat on a chair and she had big tears on her face, she was sniffing but she didn't blow her nose. There was a different woman all wrapped around in a big white apron and she had white material folded on her head and the material was all hard and her face was hard too. She had a watch on a pin but it was upside down. Susi said, 'You can't take her, I promised her mother I would look after her. I can't let her go away.' She cried and cried and her voice was funny and high.

The woman with the white hair said, 'You can't look after her all by yourself. She has to go to hospital where they'll take care of her.'

I felt scared to see Susi crying and I gave her little pats on her knee but she didn't stop. Her eyes were red and her nose looked very big. She said, 'How long will she be there? Will I be able to see her?'

The woman with the face I didn't like took my hand and the woman with the white hair said, 'She's going to take her now. It's for the best.'

'No. No. No,' Susi cried.

EVA

Norwich and Great Yarmouth

1939 – 1945

Sometimes I was in the hospital for children called Norwich and sometimes I was in another place called Great Yarmouth. They had different smells. There was the smell of the floor when they cleaned it and that smell was always there. There was the smell of boiled cabbage and mince. There was the smell of sick on your nightie or on your sheet and the smell was bad but it was worse when the nurse found out. But the most terrible smell of all was the smell when they took off your plaster cast. It was the smell of wee and blood and yellow sores; a smell that went right up your nose and into your eyes and down your throat. You tried not to breathe when that smell was in your bed.

Susi gave me a shiny little necklace when I had to leave her. She put it round my neck and she said, 'This is yours, it belonged to your grandma Hanna.' And she said, 'Be a brave girl.'

In the hospital, the nurse took the necklace away and she put it in a big tin box with lots of pretty things in it and she never gave it back to me.

Susi said, 'I don't know when I will be able to come to see you, but I will send you letters. She said, 'You are a clever girl and I love you. I hope they will teach you how to read.'

They took all my clothes off and they washed me all over and dried me very hard with a rough towel and when I cried the nurse called me a very naughty girl. She had big scissors in her hand and she cut off all my hair. I saw it all lying on the floor. It was yellow on the floor and it was all curled round.

When the bombs came the nurses carried all the children down the stairs one by one into the huge cellar that was under the ground. There were beds one on top of the other, very high up. When I had the plaster on, the nurses would lift me onto one of the beds that was near to the floor. I would lie in the bed and listen to the loud bangs and hope that the bomb wouldn't fall and make all the children land on top of me. My friend was called Peggy and her bed was next to mine. Sometimes Peggy was very ill and when the bombs fell and we went to the cellar, they left her in the big dark ward all by herself without even the light on.

I didn't cry. If you cried, they would say, 'If you're not a good girl, we'll send you back to Germany. We only have nice English children here who know how to say, The Lord's Prayer.'

Peggy's bed was a long way away from mine but we could talk to each other when the nurse wasn't there. Peggy used to laugh at me and say that I talked funny but she liked me and she was my friend. When I had the big plaster on and I had to lie on my back, which I had to do for a long, long time, Peggy would read to me from her book or make up stories. She taught me how to count and do sums in my head. She would give me a sum and I would tell her the answer and she told me I was very good at sums.

Some nurses would be cross with me when I answered them. They would say, 'Speak properly, we don't want to hear that filthy language. You're in England now.' Mostly I didn't speak except to Peggy. One day, a new nurse came in from a different ward and she was a kind nurse. She asked me lots of questions about where I used to live. She asked me who I came to this country with. I told her I wasn't allowed to say her name and she asked me why.

I said, 'I'm only allowed to say it if I know it in

English.'

And she said, 'Well say it in German and I promise not to tell anyone.'

I said, 'Susi' and she laughed. But I didn't know why it was funny.

Sometimes they would hurt you when they brushed your hair or when they cleaned you and you had sores where the plaster had been. If you cried too loud the nurse would say, 'You naughty girl, if you scream again, I'll throw cold water all over you.'

They would say, 'If you are naughty we will have to give you a punishment.' There were lots of punishments. The teacher would say you could not have your lesson. Or you would have to keep quiet all day and not talk to anyone. Or they would take your book away and you would just have to think stories up in your head. The punishment I hated the most was when they tied up my arms with a white sheet. When they did that, I couldn't move one bit of me.

One day I looked up at the window at the end of the ward and Susi was there. She waved to me and smiled but her face looked sad. I wanted her to come to my bed but she didn't. She waved and waved and she blew a kiss at me. Then she went away. It seemed like she was only there for a little minute. The nice nurse came and said, 'Look what your cousin has bought you' and she gave me a colouring book and some crayons in a little box with green writing. The letters on the box were C R A Y O L A, and I knew all those letters because Peggy had told me. I made the letters into a word, cray-o-la, and Peggy said, 'Clever girl, now you can read.'

In the evening another nurse came and she said,

'You must give those things to me.' But I wouldn't let go of them and I told her they were mine. She said I was the worst girl they'd ever seen and I must give them to her because if I didn't they would have to punish me.

Another nurse came and said, 'You can't keep those, you must give them to us.' But I wouldn't let them go because Susi had given them to me and I didn't want them to disappear into the big box where all the pretty things were.

I held on very tight and I screwed up my face and shouted, 'No!' But she was strong and she pulled them away from me. I cried and cried and I said, 'No, no, no, they're mine.'

'Stop screaming at once,' the nurse said. 'You are a wicked girl and now you are going to have a bad punishment.'

They wheeled my bed into the outside and they said, 'You are bad and now we are going to make you learn your lesson.' And they left me in the dark all night and it was very cold. I could hear things moving about, I could see something shiny and I could see green eyes. I cried for Susi but she wasn't there and I never knew what I had done that was so bad.

The next day they told me it was my birthday and I was five years old, but they didn't give me any cake.

*

Susi wrote me letters and she said she couldn't come to see me because she lived in somewhere called London and that was a very long way away and there was no money. Sometimes Susi sent me a little reading book with pictures but she didn't know I wasn't allowed to keep them.

Sometimes I was in a hospital called Norwich and sometimes I was in Great Yarmouth which had a school. In one hospital there were no visitors at all, and in the other hospital there were only visitors at the window. Sometimes Peggy's mummy came and waved to her from the window and she would wave back. Peggy cried a little bit after her mummy had been and the nurse would say, 'You naughty girl. If you cry, your mother will never come again.'

Susi said I had to stay there because of the plasters. They called it Plaster of Paris and sometimes they called it Frog Plaster. I had to go to Norwich to have the plaster put on and as soon as it was on, I came back again to the hospital called Great Yarmouth. The plaster came right up to under my arms and right down to my ankles. They opened my legs very wide, as wide as they could go and they made my feet stand up in the air and they put the plaster all around them. And there was another bit of plaster to keep my legs apart and that plaster had metal in it so it could not bend. That plaster was called the Plaster Bar. They cut a little hole so I could do wee-wee and number two. It was hard to do number two when I was lying in bed and my tummy hurt me a lot of times.

Sometimes I lay on my back and sometimes I had to lie on my front. The nurses had to lift me over and I was itchy and itchy inside but I couldn't scratch it unless I could hide a knitting needle or a pencil and then I could only get a little way down to scratch. If I lay on my tummy I could read books and if I lay on my back I held the book over my face and my arms were so strong that I could hold the book like that for hours. I could drink and eat lying on my back and usually I didn't spill one drop. When I lay on my tummy they put a pillow under my chest so that I could sit up on my elbows. Or I could turn my head towards Peggy and we would play counting games and guessing games. But one day Peggy wasn't there any more and the nurse told me she had gone to God and I didn't know where that was. I missed her a lot.

When Peggy was there, she used to read me Susi's letters, after the nurses had read them. Peggy said that wasn't nice because you shouldn't read other people's letters unless they said you could. When she sent a letter to her mummy and daddy, the nurses wouldn't let her lick the envelope shut. They said they had to see it first. When Peggy went away, I could read nearly all the words in Susi's letters by myself because Peggy had shown me.

The nurses didn't call me Eva, they called me Dislocated Hips. Every time they had to take the plaster off, I was scared because the man came with a big saw and I thought he would cut through me. But he didn't. When the plaster came off the smell was so terrible that it would make tears come into your eyes. It was the smell like wee-wee only very, very bad and all the other children in the ward said it was horrible and disgusting and made faces. When the plaster came off I could see that there were red bits and yellow bits all on my body which hurt very much. They were itchy and sore. The nice nurse would put cream on it to make it better and the horrible nurse would put cream on it, only she did it rough so it hurt more.

My legs looked so funny as if they didn't belong to me at all. They made me stand in front of the doctors with no clothes on and they would look at my body but not at my face. They would say long words that I didn't understand. I had to lie on a big table and a person came in with a big camera and said, 'Now you must lie very still.'

The doctor would pull my legs and bend them and try to turn them round and it hurt me a lot. They would swing my legs to the side of the bed and say, 'Now you can stand up.' But I didn't know how to do that with legs that were made of jelly.

*

I stopped counting how many plasters I had in all the years I was in hospital. Every time the plaster came off, they said to me, 'Now you must try to walk,' but each time I had forgotten how and I had to learn it all over again.

I only saw Susi six or seven times in all those years. I didn't see her at all for a long, long time, but she sent me a letter every single week even if she had to borrow the money for a stamp. When she did come, she nearly always brought me something, a book or something to wear. One time she brought me a skirt with straps to hold it up and once a pretty dress with a white collar and a matching ribbon. She made them out of old material that had been used for someone else, but they looked like brand new. She got the ideas from an American magazine called *Sears Catalogue* and she was very clever with sewing.

I hardly ever got to wear the clothes she brought

me because the nurse took them away. They told me that it would be better to give these pretty clothes to an English child and I would probably be going back to Germany soon. When I wrote to Susi, I didn't tell her what happened to the clothes, I just told her how much I liked them.

Susi sent me letters and she told me everything, even when she was unhappy. She said she didn't have the money to come and visit me and even if she had, she couldn't have the time from her job. She didn't write about the bombs except the time when the house next to where she was living had its front blown off. She said it was very surprising to see all the stairs and the wallpaper and other people's things and the pots and pans in the kitchen and the clothes in the wardrobe, just like the doll's house she had when she was a little girl.

She had a lot of jobs. She had to earn money so that after the war she could look after me. She had one job where she lived in a house and had to do all the washing and the cleaning and she didn't like it because the man who lived in the house was a horrible man and she had to run away. Then she had to have two different jobs, one in the day and one in the evening. In the evening she cooked meals in a hostel for young people who had come to England on a boat like us and in the day she sewed thousands of pearls and things onto dresses for beautiful women. The women who wore these dresses were very rich and they went to parties where they met the King and Queen of England and the two Princesses. In her letters she would draw me pictures of the dresses. I loved those pictures and sometimes I coloured them in and sometimes I tried to copy them. She said that when the women came to try on their dresses they went into a beautiful room with lots of mirrors and it was all red and gold like a palace, but where she worked downstairs was all bare and hard, like in the story Cinderella. Another job Susi had was for the war effort, and she was making uniforms for the soldiers who were fighting and she liked that job much better.

I wrote her a letter every single week. Susi always said my letters were too short. I would have made them longer but I never had anything interesting to say. Even when the new Matron came and let us write our own letters without anyone else looking at them, and let us keep our things from the box, there was never anything interesting to write. The only interesting thing that ever happened to me was when Susi came to visit, but then she knew about that day because she was there.

Susi said my vocabulary was good but my spelling wasn't. She sent me a list of all the words I had spelt wrong in my last letter and she told me that I needed to learn them because when she had a home of her own, I could come and live with her and go to school. I should write 'beautiful' not 'beutifull'; 'forward' not 'fourwood'; 'drawer' and 'draw' had two different meanings and I should know the difference between 'right and wrong' and 'write and rong'. 'Until' had only one 'l' and 'disappear' had one 's' and two 'p's. She said, spelling was very important. English people decided how clever you were on how well you could spell. She said that when I came to live with her, even though it might take a long, long time to get a home of her own, it was good I spoke English so well, because English people didn't like you to speak German. They liked people who were good at spelling, they liked people who spoke quietly and they liked people who said, 'Would you mind' and 'please could I possibly' and 'I am so very grateful.' I had to remember that it was 'grateful' not 'greatfull'. I knew it didn't matter about me not speaking German because I couldn't remember any of it, and one day when the Matron was in a happy mood she said that if she hadn't known different, she might have thought that I was a nice English girl.

*

In March 1944, for my tenth birthday, I received a special letter from Susi. She told me that she was getting married. She said that she wanted me to come to her wedding and she told me all about the man she was going to marry. His name was Zygmund Friedmann and everyone called him Ziggy. He was twenty-nine years old and Susi was twenty-one, so she thought this was a nice age gap to have. He was from Germany like we were from Austria but he didn't have any family here like she had me. At the beginning of the war he had been a prisoner on the Isle of Man because they told him he was an enemy alien but now he was a Sergeant in the British army in the Pioneer Corps. She sent me a photograph and he was wearing his uniform and she was wearing a dress with a tartan top and a pleated skirt and shiny shoes with high heels and she looked so pretty with her dark hair all curled under. She said on their wedding day, he was going to wear his uniform and she was going to borrow a white dress and I was going to have a new dress and new shoes. Their wedding day was going to be in a synagogue in north London on the last Sunday in May and she was going to write to the Matron to ask if she could come and collect me the week before so that I could be with them.

The man Susi was going to marry put a letter in with hers because he said he wanted to introduce himself to me. He said he was very old compared to me and he thought it would be nice if I called him uncle Ziggy and did I agree this was a good idea? He told me that his English was not so perfect as my cousin's but she was a very good teacher and soon he would learn.

He wrote a long part which I didn't really understand about God and carrying on our religion and his responsibility to bring me up in a certain way, but he wrote a very nice part about how he was really looking forward to meeting me and how I was going to be a pretty bridesmaid.

*

I never made it to the wedding. A month before Susi was due to come to collect me, I felt my hip go again: the left hip, that was always the worst one. I was walking to the schoolroom, because Miss Smith, the teacher, said I could have my lesson, and I just felt it go. There was the usual big, heavy pain and the horrible, familiar, scary feeling. I wanted to lift my leg, but however hard I tried, it just wouldn't go. I tried to cover it up, I was quite good at that. I made myself hide the pain by singing, *Daisy, Daisy, Give Me Your Answer Do*, and counting backwards in my head, and

I walked against the wall so they wouldn't see how I was dragging the left side along with me. It wasn't too hard because the hospital was made up of long, empty corridors and I knew how to hide myself against one side or the other. And when I said my prayers each night with all the other children, I said another special prayer that nobody would find out about my leg.

It worked. It worked right up to the day before Susi was coming to fetch me. I was packed, I'd said goodbye to my friends in the ward and I was ready to leave. The nurses said, 'Good luck dear, we'll miss you,' although I didn't think that would be true. My new friend Hettie in the next bed gave me her special book called *Peeps at the World's Children* which had shiny coloured pictures of children from Iceland and America and Africa all dressed in their national costumes outside their igloos and teepees and adobe huts. Hettie was the only person on the ward who was allowed to keep a book because Matron said she was going to die soon so it was very, very kind of her to give it to me. Mostly the Matron didn't like us to keep our books and if you tried to hide one and she found it, she would tear it up right in front of your eyes.

I was nearly at the schoolroom when the nurse with the hairy face stopped me.

'Eva Shapiro, what do you think you're doing?'

'I'm just going to my lesson with Miss Smith.'

'Stop skulking against the wall like a common thief and come here at once.'

So I knew they'd found me out. They always did.

'They've got your number all right,' one of the nurses said, laughing.

They made me unpack all my things and put me

in the ambulance to go back to the hospital in Norwich. When I woke up from the operation, my leg was in plaster from my ankle to my armpits and I felt so sad. I hated having to lie in bed for months and months never being able to move and with nothing to do. I hated the bed pans which made me constipated. And I hated being scared of the man with the saw who would come and take the plaster off again.

'Now, this isn't like you Eva,' the nurse said. 'You're usually one of our cheerful ones.' I turned my face to the wall and said nothing. I thought of the card I'd drawn for Susi with the picture of a bride and groom and pink roses all around it which was lying in my desk back in the lonely little school room, and I imagined my bridesmaid's dress lying on my new bed in London.

'Cheer up,' they said, 'that's an order.' And when I didn't, they said. 'You're a bad girl to be so miserable, no wonder God has punished you.' And they wheeled me into the bathroom and left me there for a day and a night with nothing to do but stare at the cracked white and green tiled walls, listening to the tap going drip, drip, drip.

I hated having the plaster on but the days after they sawed it off were even worse. It was then the women in blue uniforms told me to do things which were completely impossible.

'Don't be lazy now. Don't start crying, it can't hurt that much. Stand up and hold on to the rail and walk. Start with your right leg and your left leg will just follow.' But I couldn't imagine how anyone could ever walk. It seemed like a magic trick I had seen the conjurer do once when we had a party in the hospital, only I didn't know how to make the spell work.

Of course, I did start to walk again. By the time they told us that the war was over, I was back in the hospital in Great Yarmouth. I couldn't run or skip but I could go pretty quick. I could walk well enough for them to make me do my chores again. I could wash the floor of the ward and do it all over again when they said it wasn't good enough and I could clean the whole row of toilets and never mind about the stinky smell.

We had a big party the day they told us that there was Victory in Europe and no more fighting the enemy. It was the second party there had been in all my time in the hospital and I had the chance to wear my bridesmaid's dress after all, even though it was a bit short for me now. The dress was white and it had puffed sleeves and two rows of red ric-rac on the bottom of the skirt and one row around the neck. Susi told me that she had made the dress from a linen sheet a woman had given to her, after she had made her a skirt and scarf out of an old coat. She said she didn't have to have a coupon for ric-rac because that was called trimmings.

We had sandwiches and cake and green jelly and Tizer to drink and I helped carry the trays around to the children who had to be in bed although some were too poorly to eat. We had a sing song and games and the worst nurse in the whole place came and put a sticky, hairy kiss on my face and said, 'I'll miss you Eva, you've been a good girl here.'

But I wasn't going to miss her. I folded up my dark scratchy dress and the stiff white school apron which smelt of hospital starch and put it on the end of my bed. I packed my few things into my little brown suitcase and I said goodbye to everyone. I didn't really understand very much about what my new life was going to be like, but I knew that I was going to live for ever and ever with Susi and uncle Ziggy and I wasn't going to be frightened any more.

EVA

Compayne Gardens, London

1945

We lived in Compayne Gardens, West Hampstead, London NW6. It was quite near the hostel where Susi used to live with lots of other girls who had come to England like us. They used to go to work in the day and in the evening they cooked the meals in the hostel restaurant. Uncle Ziggy was one of the people who used to come to buy his dinner and that's how they met. One day he was eating goulash with paprika and he said to Susi, 'I could fall in love with a girl who cooks like this.'

She said, '*I* cooked it.'

He laughed and said, 'Then you must be the girl for me.'

The house in Compayne Gardens was very big and white. It had lots and lots of steps: steps to the front door, steps all the way to the top of the house and one more set of steps into the roof where they told me my little room would be. I said that I didn't know we were going to live in such a big house, but Susi laughed. 'I'm afraid you'll have to wait until we're very rich before we have the whole house. Right now, we have just this big room and a little kitchen and we have to share the toilet with Mrs Katz, the old lady downstairs.' She lifted up the long table next to the cooker and showed me that there was a bath underneath it.

Uncle Ziggy said, 'And don't forget Eva's room.' Uncle Ziggy was nice. He had a long, serious face and a moustache but I didn't feel scared of him at all.

It was a Friday, the day I came to live with them. In the evening, Susi lit some candles and we had soup and chicken and a loaf of bread which was plaited like hair, but I was so tired that I couldn't eat anything.

Uncle Ziggy said, 'Don't worry, it will keep until tomorrow.' And Susi took me upstairs and showed me where to put my clothes and the space she had made for my few books. She asked me if my legs hurt today but I said they never really hurt unless my hip went. I began to get into bed and when I was under the sheets, I pressed my hands together to say my prayers.

'Our Father who art in heaven, hallowed be thy...'

'What are you doing?' Susi asked sharply. My heart turned over inside me because Susi sounded like the nurses.

'I have to say it in bed like this, because I can't kneel down very well. Matron said that...'

'Not the kneeling, the prayer. Have you been saying that every night?'

I nodded.

'We don't say that in this house. We are not Christians here, we are Jewish. I will have to get Ziggy to teach you the Shemah.' She sighed and shook her head and I was sorry that I had done something bad when I had only been in the house such a little while. But Susi tucked me up under the soft feather quilt and said, 'It's been too long. I never thought it would take so many years for us to be together,' and she didn't seem cross after all. She began to sing and her voice was so pretty and sweet that I thought I was going to cry. It felt like I had heard the song before because I knew what she was going to sing, even before she sang it, but I didn't think that I could have known it because in the hospital nobody ever sang me a song like that when I went to sleep.

When she had gone, I lay in my bed and it was so quiet. I felt lonely in this little room all on my own.

*

Everything was strange and different. For a long time there were so many things I didn't know. I didn't know how all the things in the house worked. I didn't know you had to go out to the shops to buy food with a ration book and then you had to go home and do things with it on the cooker to make it into something you could eat. I didn't know that you had to make the heat come into the cooker by striking a wooden match with a black, round top against the side of the box. I'd never even seen a match before. I didn't know you could have a bath in the kitchen. I didn't know that a girl my age could sit in the bath on her own and then dry herself without having to scrub so hard that all your skin felt red and sore or that there was some soap which had a really nice smell like flowers. I didn't know that when grown up women like Susi went out, they sat in front of the mirror for a long time and put powder on their face with a soft puff that tickled your nose and spat into a little black box and painted their eyelashes with a brush and their lips with a red stick. I didn't know that a girl my age was supposed to be able to do hard sums with fractions, long division and multiplication because we'd only ever done simple sums and even then, we had to be very good before the teacher would allow any of us to go to the schoolroom.

I didn't know how noisy the world could be. I didn't know that you had to look both ways before you crossed the road. I didn't know how you could be sure a trolley bus or a car wouldn't knock you down when you stepped into the road because even if you did remember to look both ways before you crossed, a car could easily come round the corner very fast. I didn't know that children could shout and run about on the streets outside my bedroom window and that no one told them it was wicked to make such a noise.

There were lots and lots of things I had to learn. I had to learn that on Friday nights when Susi lit the candles she would look very, very sad and that uncle Ziggy and I must be very quiet and not say a single word except a bit later we could say that the soup tasted lovely and so did the chicken. I had to learn that we were Jewish and this meant we were a special people who believed in God but not in Jesus, although uncle Ziggy thought it meant that we should never eat pork or bacon or milk and meat in the same meal and should go to the synagogue more often, and Susi didn't. Uncle Ziggy thought God had saved us all for a reason. Susi thought that God was cruel and she didn't think she had to go to shul every Saturday – a few times a year was enough.

I had to learn so many different things, that every night when I went up to bed I was so tired that I fell asleep straight away and never woke up in the dark, scary night. And even when I woke up, I never had to be afraid that someone would tell me off because Susi was hardly ever cross with me so long as I was a good girl. Sometimes she looked cross, but she never ever said that I was a wicked girl and I would be punished. One day when we were washing up after a meal Susi said to me, 'You used to be so noisy when you were small. You never stopped talking and laughing and now you are such a quiet little thing.' I wasn't sure if she meant it was bad to be so quiet and I just carried on wiping up, hoping that she would tell me some more about when I was little, but she sighed and said nothing.

There were lots of things I didn't know but there were some things I knew right from the beginning. I knew that even if I was scared of people or things, I mustn't cry because people didn't like cry babies. I knew that I had to be a good girl and that if I was good, they would always take care of me and never send me away because when uncle Ziggy wrote to me in the hospital, he said, 'Please God, you will always have a home with us.' I knew that I had to try to walk properly so people wouldn't notice I was different and talk about me. I knew that I had to stand up on the bus and let older people have my seat so that they wouldn't say, 'Oh dear, is she a cripple then?' I knew I had to tell her if the pain came in my hip again and I mustn't pretend it didn't hurt.

I knew that I must never, ever lie to Susi because the truth was very important and, anyway, she would always find out.

*

Susi was shocked to find out that I had read hardly any big books with chapters. Every week she took me to the library at Swiss Cottage and I learned how to read a whole book on my own from start to finish, not just a little bit at a time. When I borrowed a book from the library, I didn't have to be scared that someone would come and take the book away just when I reached a good bit.

The first book I borrowed was *Heidi* and I loved that book so much that I wanted to borrow it every week, but Susi said, no, I must read lots of different books. Clara was like me, she couldn't walk properly but at the end of the book, when she went up onto the mountains, she said, 'I can do it Heidi. Look, I can make proper steps,' and she did. My room was a little bit like Heidi's; it was at the top of the house and it looked out on the sky and the stars.

Uncle Ziggy said that I was behind with my arithmetic but there was nothing wrong with my brain. Every night when he came back from work, even if it was very late, he sat down with me and taught me how to do multiplication and division and fractions and percentages and my times tables and mental arithmetic. He said if I tried my best, I would improve, even if I found it difficult.

The first summer I was in London, the weather was hot and there were no bombs or doodlebugs falling out of the sky. Everyone said that even though the war was over, things weren't easy and they didn't know how long rationing would go on. Uncle Ziggy wasn't in the army any more; he was trying to start a business but he didn't know what that business should be. He wanted to start a restaurant because Susi was such a good cook and he thought that they could have a restaurant that sold continental food, like back home. He said there were lots of people living in Belsize Park and Hampstead and the Finchley Road who would like to come and eat there and they could even have people to play music in the evenings and discussions. I thought a restaurant would be nice because I could help to lay all the tables with nice tablecloths and glasses and things and maybe sometimes I could have a cream pastry if there were any left over at the end of the day. Susi said it would be better to do something in the fashion business because now that the war was over, the ladies were longing for something nice to wear and, anyway, she didn't want to go round smelling of the kitchen, morning, noon and night. I thought a fashion business would be nice too because I could get some bits of material if there were any spare, and maybe I could have the leftover buttons and braid and make some pretty things. Susi said she was going to teach me to sew so that I could help out.

All through the hot summer, I watched the other children walking up and down the street with their mothers or playing with each other. Susi said I shouldn't spend all that time in my room on my own, I should go and play with them, but I didn't know how to do it. In hospital, I hadn't had to go out into the street to make friends, they were just there in the bed next to mine, or along the corridors, or in the schoolroom. All the children there were my friends, even the ones I didn't like so much. If you didn't have friends on your pain days, or in the long quiet evenings, or on the days when you had no letters and the nurses were unkind, then you had nothing. Susi and uncle Ziggy had friends round all the time and they would sit around for hours drinking coffee and eating cake, smoking and talking, talking, talking or listening to music, but their friends were all like them; there was no one my age to play with.

On the evenings that they went out, I used to

get sent downstairs to Mrs Katz and I hated going there, because she asked me lots and lots of questions that I couldn't answer about my family in Vienna and I never knew what to say to her. It was easier when she gave me jobs to do like threading her needles because she couldn't see small things very well, or when she told me stories about the chicken farm in Poland where she had grown up. When I left she always said, 'You're a good girl, darling. I hope life is good to you, it certainly won't be easy.' And she would give me a copper ha'penny. The first time I got two pennies together, I went by myself to Woolworth's, even though I was still scared of the traffic and I bought a bag of toffees for Susi's birthday because they were her favourites. When I gave them to her she said the toffees were a wonderful present and I had always been a sweet girl. She said I had made her happy even though I could see that she had tears in her eyes.

Susi said it was important that I started school as soon as possible. She said that I was going to have the education she was forced to miss. She said the schools in England were good, not the same standard as the schools in Vienna, but still good. I was nearly eleven-and-a-half and the new term was going to start in a few weeks and if she was going to be working in a new business, she couldn't have me under her feet all day. I needed to meet people; I was too quiet and I needed some company my own age. Susi tried to find out about the schools near us but it was hard because schools here were different from those in Vienna. She asked the man in our fruit and vegetable shop at the top of Goldhurst Terrace because he had children of his own and they had been to school near here. He was a nice man although sometimes he made jokes I didn't understand. He looked at Susi and he looked at me and he polished an apple against his apron.

'Well, let's see now. It's all a bit different what with the war and everything. They passed a new act in parliament about education and there's going to be some changes. I expect you'll need to see them up at the Town Hall in Haverstock Hill.' He smiled at me and handed me the shiny apple. 'I don't suppose this little one will be going to any of the schools round here though, will she?'

Susi made that face she made when she was thinking something she wasn't saying.

'I should think they'll be wanting to send her to a school for crippled children what with the way she is and everything. That's what they usually do with children like her. My wife, now she had a cousin...'

But Susi nodded and said 'Thank you' very politely and took my hand firmly, although she didn't need to because I could walk perfectly well on my own.

Everyday I practised my spelling and my vocabulary and my long division and my percentages and how many windows you would need for a house that was twenty feet wide and thirty feet deep and had a window every three feet, and every day, just as uncle Ziggy promised, I could do my sums a little bit better.

Susi went to the library and she asked the librarian who knew everything about schools. There were some elementary schools which took senior pupils and there were schools called central schools and there were others where you had to be clever and pass an exam. Susi wanted me to go to South Hampstead High for Girls, because she had heard that was the best school, but that was one of those where you had to pass an exam so that you could win a scholarship. Susi took me to the Town Hall in Hampstead to see when I could take the exam because she thought that a good education was the most important thing you could have.

The building was big and high and cool, even though it was hot outside. I could hear our feet clatter on the hard, tiled floor. In the room, a man behind the desk was wearing a dark suit with thin white stripes down it.

'Do you speak English?' he asked Susi.

'Yes, I do,' she said quietly but when she spoke I could hear that her voice was different from the people on the street and the man sitting behind the desk. Usually I didn't hear it at all.

'If you would be kind enough to read these,' she said. 'It will explain something of our situation.'

The man gestured for her to sit down and began to look at the papers she had given him. He opened a letter from the hospital and looked at a little white card which I could see had my name and picture on it.

'The letter here states that she has never been in the state school system, despite the fact that she arrived when she was four years old.'

'Well, sir, there was the war and I couldn't take care of her at that time, I didn't have a home for her. But now I am married and we have somewhere to live. My husband and I have been giving her lessons at home. She is a little behind, I think, but she is making good progress. We hope very much that she will be able to sit the examinations for secondary school. We want so much for her to have a good education.'

'The child is not normal though.' There was a hard silence. 'The child cannot walk. She has spent all her school years in hospital and I don't think an ordinary secondary education would be suitable for her.'

'She has had a problem with dislocated hips. It is better now. Please, sir. I am certain that...'

'Madam. The child is a physical defective – physically handicapped, I suppose I should say now – it's hard to keep up with the new terms. In this country we have excellent schools designed for children like her. There is a very good institution in Sussex. She will have fresh air and if she shows the ability, she can learn a trade.'

Susi sat very still in her chair and it was a while before she spoke. When she did, her voice was very quiet. 'I do not want her to go away from London. She needs to stay with us. There is nothing wrong with her, nothing wrong.'

'Well, I don't think we can say that. The child cannot walk.'

Susi's hands were in her lap and she clasped them together. I could see her fingers go into blotches of red and white.

'She walked here, all the way up the steep hill at College Crescent, right up Belsize Avenue. She is a bright girl, she missed a lot of school but she is catching up. Please give her a chance.'

'A child like that needs a different sort of educational provision.' He was talking to her like the doctors in the hospital used to talk to me. 'The best place for her is outside London – specialist medical care. There is a particular institution for crippled girls that comes highly recommended by the inspectors. That is the place she is fit for. I have dealt with many children like this in my time.' He stood up and looked down at us. 'I think I know my job.'

'Please sir,' Susi said even more quietly. 'I don't mean to be rude in any way. We are very grateful to England for taking us in.'

His voice cut right over hers. 'Do you have British citizenship?'

'We are hoping that our naturalisation papers will be through very soon. We want to be good citizens in this country, my husband is an ex-serviceman in the British forces. We just don't want the child sent away any more, I gave her mother that promise. I will take care of any medical matters that might arise. If she could just take the exam like other children – I agree she has problems with the way she walks but there is nothing wrong with her mind.'

The man sat down again. 'You mention her family. How are you related to the child?' Susi seemed to hold her breath for a moment and then she spoke so quickly that her words almost ran into one another.

'She is my cousin. We came to this country without our families. My husband and I are applying to be her legal guardians and to change her surname to Friedmann. We have to apply to Lord Gorrell at the Jewish Committee. At the moment, he is the legal guardian of all the refugee children.'

'And her parents?' Susi looked at him and looked at me and told me to wait outside for a few minutes. It was hard to make out what they were saying but I could hear the pattern of their voices going up and down, up and down. When Susi's voice was louder, the man's became quiet. When he shouted, you could hardly hear her at all. The words went backwards and forwards, backwards and forwards, like the tennis ball the nurses played with in the hospital grounds.

I heard the man huff and puff and the chairs scraping, and I moved away from the door, scared that someone would find me listening like a thief. When Susi came out of the room, her face was as red as fire and her eyes were like two black buttons.

We walked in silence, back down the hill towards Swiss Cottage, but she put her arm round my shoulder and we walked along like that for a while. It felt nice to have her arm around me. When we reached Finchley Road, Susi opened up her purse and held up two big silver coins. 'I think we deserve to give ourselves a treat, don't you?' We turned towards Swiss Cottage until we saw the sign, *New Cosmo Restaurant, Continental Atmosphere and Cuisine.* Inside it was smoky and the waiters spoke to each other in German. We ate bratwurst and sauerkraut and potatoes, and afterwards Susi looked in her purse again and said she had just enough money for me to have a pastry. I chose one which was pastry and meringue and cream all covered in chocolate and it was the most delicious thing I had ever eaten. Susi had a black coffee with sugar and when she finished she put down the little white cup and said, 'You don't get coffee like this in England,' which I thought was funny because we were in England.

*

A few days later the letter came from the Education

Authority and they said I should come and take my examinations in one week's time, but I had to do them all on the same day because everyone else my age had taken them in May and it was August now. Susi spoke English better than uncle Ziggy so he taught me about sums and she taught me writing. Susi helped me to write stories with big sentences to show that I knew the difference between a noun, an adjective and a verb. On the morning of my test, uncle Ziggy lent me his best fountain pen which came all the way from Munich. It was maroon and it had its own little leather case. Susi said I had to take great care of it.

*

The examination room was full of huge tables and chairs and at the front they had put a small school desk and chair for me. There was only one person in that big room, a woman who smiled at me, but not in a way that made you feel happy. It made me think of those times in the hospital when I stood in front of the doctors with no clothes on and everyone looked at me.

There was a paper called the Intelligence Test and one called English and one called Arithmetic. I tried as hard as I could and when I came out of the room my fingers were covered in blue-black ink and my head felt dizzy.

*

When the letter came, Susi opened it and she didn't smile. She told me that I had failed and there would be no scholarship. I was going to the Senior Department of Cricklewood School and I would go by myself on the bus. 'It doesn't matter,' she said. 'I am sure that all the schools in England will teach you well if you work hard and try your best.'

I was sad that I hadn't passed because Susi and uncle Ziggy had tried so hard to help me. I knew that if it had been Susi taking the examinations, she wouldn't have failed. She passed really hard exams when she was young and so had uncle Ziggy. But I was happy because they weren't going to send me away to another horrible place where people shouted at me for no reason and I was going to live with Susi for ever and ever.

*

If getting an education hadn't been so important, I would have happily stayed at home helping Susi while uncle Ziggy went out each day looking for a business to start. There was always lots to do at home. Susi said she didn't know where all the dirt came from and she was sure that London must have more dust than other cities. I helped with the shopping and the cooking, the washing and the ironing. Susi said that in the winter it would be my job to clean out the fireplaces each day and lay them up otherwise we would all die of the cold. She couldn't believe the old-fashioned way English people tried to heat their homes, not like in Vienna where most people had central heating in their flats. She said maybe the English had different blood in their veins.

Susi said there were so many jobs to do, there

weren't enough hours in the day. She had to work to save money so they could start their business. She did alterations on people's clothes; she sewed up quilts in the continental style for people who couldn't get used to the heavy English blankets; she made up curtains.

Sometimes she helped Mrs Schwarz, who made brassieres and corsets when she was behind with her orders. I liked to help when she let me. I sewed on buttons and took out the tacking stitches and sometimes I even did the hems. Every night I tidied all the threads and the needles, pins and thimbles because it was terrible to be wasteful. The job I liked best was helping to make material flowers which would be sewn onto dresses or suit jackets, because the flowers turned out so pretty. This work paid her quite a lot of money. The material arrived in small white boxes; sometimes it would be soft and shiny in lovely colours like pink or gold and sometimes it would be dark wool for suits. My job was to take each flower she had made and fold it carefully in tissue paper to be collected by the man who drove the green and gold van.

Each night when I went to bed, I could hear the treadle on the Singer Sewing Machine in the sitting room below me and it was to this rhythm that I fell asleep.

When uncle Ziggy said that she was doing too much, she always said the same thing. 'We need the money and I can't sit and do nothing all day.' I thought he didn't want to hear the sound of the sewing machine in the evenings because he liked to listen to concerts on the radio. Beethoven was his favourite and he liked Mahler and Mozart. Sometimes he told me stories about when he was young. He told me that when he was my age his grandfather gave him a beautiful violin for a present because he had come top of the class at school, but he had to leave it behind when he came to live in England and now he thought he'd forgotten how to play it. I loved those stories, even if they were sad, but whenever he started Susi would say, 'That's enough Zygmund,' just as if he were still a little boy.

And he would say, 'Ah well Eva, in a different time, perhaps,' and go off and do something else.

*

In September, a few days before I started school, uncle Ziggy said to me, 'This week, you and I are both starting something new.' He had finally got his coupon float and to celebrate we all went to the Dorice in Finchley Road for meat with red cabbage and dumplings. I wasn't exactly sure what a coupon float was but I knew it was something the government gave to help ex-servicemen open a business. Uncle Ziggy could get one because he had been a sergeant in the Royal Pioneer Corps and he had helped the British with prisoners of war from Germany. Their business was going to be fashion and they were going to have a little factory in South London which would make clothes for women. They needed the coupons because otherwise you couldn't buy material to make dresses and suits what with the rationing and everything.

Susi thought up the name – Elite Fashions, which was a good name for it because elite meant the best. I was a bit disappointed that they weren't going to have a restaurant but I thought clothes would be interesting too. There were going to be other people working for them and they would both have to work hard to pay everyone's wages and to buy a house where the bathroom wasn't in the kitchen.

I said, 'Wouldn't it be better if I didn't go to school? I can stay at home and help now there's going to be so much to do. I know how to do the housework and the cooking.'

But uncle Ziggy smiled at me and pinched my cheek and said, 'Don't be scared little one. New things are always frightening.'

EVA

Goldhurst Terrace, London

1949

Brenda and I sat side by side, snuggled under the pink eiderdown in her unheated bedroom, reading *Jane Eyre* together for our end of term exam. Brenda's room was freezing but it was so pretty and feminine, all frills and flowers with wallpaper of trailing pink roses and green vine leaves. Brenda and her mother had chosen everything together. She had a dressing table covered in the same pink and white material as her curtains with a three way gold mirror and a shiny brush and comb set.

Brenda put her book down in disgust. 'Well I think that's a very miserable story, there's hardly any happy bits in it.'

'You don't even know what happens at the end.'

'No, but I've read the beginning and that's enough for me. I don't understand why Jane doesn't keep quiet when her cousins are so horrible to her. It would have made her life much easier if she'd just kept her mouth shut.'

'But that's why it's such a good book. If Jane kept quiet all the time, then it wouldn't have been nearly so interesting. She has to say what's true, even if it gets her into more trouble. That's the kind of person she is. When you read it, you just wish that you could be as brave as her.'

'Well, if I was a homeless orphan, I'd learn to keep my mouth shut. There's no point shouting at adults like that even if they deserve it. It's much safer to just keep quiet. I mean, look where they send her – to that horrible school. Surely she was better off where she was.' She laughed at herself and gave me one of her quick looks to check that she hadn't upset me in any way. She always worried whenever families came up in the conversation. She knew that Susi and uncle Ziggy were my only relatives in this country and they weren't old enough to be my parents. Brenda had tons of relatives in England because her grandparents came over from Poland even before the First War, and all her aunts and uncles and cousins were here. She wouldn't have lasted more than a day away from her home.

'But Jane needed to be sent away from her aunt,' I told her. 'She would never have survived if she hadn't gone to school and met Helen, because everyone needs one true friend.'

Brenda Gold was my best friend, my true friend. We had little quarrels sometimes but she always stuck by me and didn't go off if someone more interesting came along. In school we did everything together. We were in the same form, we sat together in the lunch break, we liked the same film stars and listened to the same music. The other girls sometimes sneered at us and asked if we thought we were twins or something but that was silly because Brenda was long and lanky with dark straight hair and I was short, round and fair and my hair was still as curly as it had been when I was little. Sometimes we joked together and said that if we were a pair of dogs, I would be an overfed miniature poodle and she would be an underfed greyhound.

Brenda wasn't much of a reader. She pushed her copy of the book away and changed to one of her favourite subjects – Susi. Brenda thought Susi was the most beautiful woman she had ever seen. She adored the way Susi looked, her clothes, her hair, her make up, everything. 'She's so glamorous, just like a film star, those gorgeous slim legs in those high heels. She's not one of those silly blonde ones, she's more classy like Olivia de Havilland or Ingrid Bergman, she's even got the foreign accent.' Brenda stood up and walked around the room pretending to be a film star, wiggling her hips. She stopped and turned her eyes up to heaven when she caught sight of herself in the mirror. 'Oh dear,' she said, laughing at herself, 'I'll never make it in the movies.' Of course I thought Brenda was pretty because she was my best friend and the kindest person I had ever met, just like she thought nobody noticed the way I walked, not after they'd got used to it anyway. But she wasn't Susi, that was for sure. Brenda sighed again. 'Tell me about the new clothes.'

'I'll draw them for you if you like.' I tore out the middle pages of my rough book and began to sketch some of the clothes Elite Fashions were making for next spring. 'They're going for a longer look now, very elegant.' I drew a v-necked half sleeve top with a thin gold belt and a long, pleated skirt. 'This gives you a streamlined silhouette. It's supposed to accent your small, slim waistline and make you seem thinner and more graceful.' I giggled. 'Perhaps I should go in for it.' I drew a fitted suit jacket with wide lapels, three quarter sleeves and covered buttons and a front peplum. 'They're going to do this in navy blue, brown or forest green wool crêpe with matching pillbox hat.' I drew a swirling evening dress of glittery rayon worn with long gloves with a bracelet over the gloved wrist and a fur shawl to go with it.

Brenda sighed and twirled around, holding her navy blue pleated gymslip as if it were a ball gown.

'When I'm older I'm going to marry a very rich man and drive to all the best shops in his chauffeur driven Rolls Royce and buy the most expensive clothes and perfume in the world.' She thought about this lovely vision for a moment and laughed. 'Actually, I'll probably be on one of Pop's market stalls selling stockings and cheap nylon socks and end up looking like Ma, but we can all dream.'

I liked Brenda's mum and dad, but no one could say they were glamorous. Her dad was hardly more than five feet, and that was a good few inches above her mum and they were nearly as wide as they were high. Nobody knew how Brenda had grown so tall and skinny and she was always being teased that the stork must have delivered her by mistake. Susi said Brenda's mum was a typical Yiddisher housewife and I think this meant she didn't have a job like Susi. She was always fussing round in the kitchen, baking kiechels and honey cakes, matzo brei and bubbela and feeding everyone until they could hardly move. I hardly ever saw Mr Gold. He left early in the morning and didn't get back till late at night. He always said that he worked all the hours God sent to make a bit of money and every penny he earned, Mrs Gold took straight to Chinacraft to spend on some shmochna or other.

'I didn't live in that dark basement flat in Whitechapel all those years just to put the money in the bank and never enjoy it,' she'd reply.

'Well, I don't make the gelt so you can spend it on things that can break in a minute. Do me a favour and leave a little bit in the bank for a rainy day.'

When I first visited their house, I used to be worried by these arguments, but then they'd both laugh, good-hearted smoky laughs, so I knew they weren't really cross with each other.

Going through the front door of their house in Willesden was like stepping into a different world for me. Every inch was crammed full of bright, pretty things so that there was hardly room to move. Their living room was jam packed with enormous chairs covered with flowery material, red and gold striped curtains, Chinese rugs with blue and pink flowers cut into the pattern, gold mirrors and lots of little tables. Every surface had an ornament or a gilt lamp with a fringed shade, a tinted photograph in a fancy frame or a porcelain figurine. Brenda and Mrs Gold both loved the figurines best. Brenda's favourite was the Balloon Man. He was sitting down on something that looked like the step of a kerb; he wore a black hat and his shiny balloons were red and yellow, green and orange. Mrs Gold gave pride of place to the white and gold Capo-di-Monte figures – the Dancing Maiden and the Boy and Girl on a Swing. Mrs Gold said they looked so real, you felt you could talk to them. She said they could have been in a museum.

When I tried to describe their house to Susi, she told me that their new dining room suite: the glass top table, the sideboard with the curvy legs and feet like a lion's paws, were just reproduction. 'There's not an antique in that house, you could buy the whole lot in an East End warehouse.' She wrinkled her nose and pulled her mouth down in that way she had and I decided not to tell her about the latest addition to their collection, the china Balloon Lady, who was a partner to the Balloon Man. She had a yellow dress and a white apron and lots of coloured balloons. 'I'm not being rude, Eva. They're not educated people, that's all.' She stopped and looked at the expression on my face. 'It's a case of different backgrounds, different tastes. The important thing is that Brenda is a very good friend to you.' She was glad that I had Brenda. She had always worried that I was on my own too much.

Brenda's house was always full of people. Every Friday her mother cooked a big dinner and on Sunday morning she stood at the kitchen stove frying piles and piles of cod and haddock for the aunties, uncles and cousins who would descend on them later that afternoon. The Golds were considered the rich relations of their East End family. Mrs Gold joked that they thought they were coming for a day in the country when they got the train from Liverpool Street to Willesden Green.

They said I was always welcome at their home. 'You're like one of the family, darling. You're always welcome here. Why don't you stay and have supper?'

'I can't stay tonight. I've got to go home now.'

'Will anyone be there?'

I nodded, although it wasn't true.

'Only I don't like to think of you in that big house all on your own. Stay a little bit longer if you like. Nat'll be home from work soon.'

I would have liked a big brother like Nat, with his curly, black hair and huge grin. He was shorter than uncle Ziggy but taller than his dad and very skinny. He told us he did American Air Force exercises every day to make his muscles grow like Mr Universe. Nat was always larking about; he was better at that than being serious. If Brenda asked him a question he was just as likely to make Donald Duck noises with the front of his mouth than speak actual words, and he could do dead ringer impressions of Bob Hope and Jack Benny in an American accent. He was nearly eighteen, a good age for an older brother to be. He treated me just like another kid sister, completely ignoring me most of the time and then turning up with three ha'penny bars of Cadbury's chocolate – I never knew how he got them because there were no sweets in the shops – one for Brenda, one for his mum and one for me.

Mr Gold was nice as well, but I was glad he wasn't always at home.

'Come here, and let me see you. Still got that pretty face?' He'd pinch my cheek and smile at me as if I was a sick puppy. 'Let's have a good look at you. Does it hurt when you walk like that?' He'd watch me walking and shake his head sadly. Brenda and I sometimes joked that he thought my real name was Poorlittleeva, because that's what he always called me. 'Poor little Eva. I'm sure there must be a way to get you fixed. Have you seen a specialist about it?' He thought the doctors could cure anything so long as you saw 'the top man'.

He liked to give me something whenever he saw me, a pair of stockings for Susi or some knee socks, but I knew Susi didn't like me to accept anything from him. Once he gave me a beautiful pair of American silk stockings for her and I could tell she liked them, even though she huffed a bit and said, 'No wonder there's still rationing when there's so much money to be made on the black market.'

'See if Mrs Friedmann will let you come for the second night of Pesach.' Mrs Gold said as I was leaving.

'Nat's starting his National Service and who knows when he'll get leave again.' She sighed as if the weight of the world was on her shoulders.

'Ma, he's not going for months and anyway, the war's over, he's going to Aldershot, not Japan.' Brenda put her arm round her mother's shoulder and put her tall head on hers.

'I know, darling.' She wiped a tear with the corner of her apron. 'Take no notice of your mother, she's just a silly old fool. Still, Evele, ask if you can come. We have a proper kosher do here and I know Nat would like to see you.'

I knew what she meant by a proper kosher do. She didn't approve of the food we had in our house, German sausages and salami; she didn't let Brenda eat with us unless we were having fish or eggs. She didn't approve of anything German at all. Once she asked me if Susi could speak English.

'We always speak English at home,' I answered, surprised.

'Good and I hope she doesn't speak German in the street either.' She turned towards Brenda's red, embarrassed face which was urging her to be quiet.

'What? I'm only saying that I'm glad she isn't one of those who give Jews a bad name. Some of the Continentals can be very pushy. Isn't that right?'

'Ma, please.'

'Honestly, she doesn't let me say anything. I haven't upset you, have I Eva?' And she stood up and gave me a little pat on the arm as she passed me on her way to the kitchen.

*

Brenda hadn't started at Cricklewood School in the first year of the seniors. She didn't come until the beginning of the second year because she'd been living in the East End while her dad saved the money to buy their house in Willesden. Brenda was shy, like me, and a worrier. She worried that people would tease her for her cockney accent and just like me, she worried she wouldn't have any friends in her new school.

My first year there had been completely horrible. Suddenly there was a new list of things I didn't understand, that I couldn't get the hang of. I didn't understand how you made someone want to share your double desk in the classroom, how people fell into groups at break-time, or broke up into pairs and strolled along the school corridor together arm in arm. I didn't know how to ask anyone to wait for me and walk with me to the bus stop on the way home, or how to stop them saying horrible things about me to my face.

Life in the hospital had been so different. There were the nurses and their punishments, and there were the children. We were all in the same boat, and if we could, we helped each other out. There was enough cruelty without us being cruel to each other.

From the very beginning I was marked out. On the first morning, before we'd even met the new teachers, all the first year seniors were marched into the hall for Assembly. I didn't even know what Assembly was and I felt even more nervous when I saw the other girls sitting cross legged in rows on the polished, wooden floor.

'Are you Eva Friedmann?' I looked up and saw someone tall and thin with hair pulled back and metal framed spectacles. At first I thought she must be a teacher but then I saw that she was wearing a school uniform like mine. 'You can't walk properly can you?' It sounded like a question but it wasn't. 'You're to sit separately on this bench here.' She pointed to a long, low, wooden bench arranged along the side of the hall.

All the teachers were sitting up on a high stage and everyone stood up, girls and teachers together, as the Headmistress climbed up the stage stairs. She indicated with her hand that we should sit down again.

'Many of you in front of me today have been in the junior department of Cricklewood School since you were young or since you returned from evacuation. On this first day of a new school year, I would like to welcome all of you who are joining the school for the first time. But in addition to this, I want to draw your attention to one new pupil who is rather different from the rest of you.

'Eva Friedmann, now where are you? Ah, yes, there you are, on the benches. Unfortunately Eva has had to spend all her childhood in hospital and this is her first day at a proper school. When she walks she takes up a lot of *space* and you must all take great care not to bump into her as you move along the corridors. You must give up your seat in the playground if she needs somewhere to sit down. She will not be taking part in physical training or any outdoor games.' The whole school swivelled their heads to stare at me and I felt worse than I ever remembered feeling in the hospital, even though this wasn't supposed to be a punishment.

Perhaps I would have been a misfit even if she hadn't pointed me out like that, but it couldn't have helped.

'Have you always been like that or are you going to get better?' my classmates asked me on that first day and I didn't know how to answer them.

'You're the lame one aren't you?' a teacher said to me on the stairs, and then walked past me without expecting a reply.

'I thought crippled children weren't allowed to come to schools like this,' the prettiest, most popular girl said to me as the class prepared for outdoor games. And then quietly in my ear. 'It must be really horrible being you. I don't know how you can stand it.'

On my own on the bus, or on the walk home, I'd write a story in my head and in this story I would tell Susi what was happening to me. She would come up to school and sort everything out; the other girls would want me to be their friend; teachers would only ask me questions about school work. But I could never find the right words or the right time. It was easier to talk to Susi about my homework or what I was learning in school. Sometimes we would sit together at the kitchen table with a concert or Saturday Night Theatre on the radio in the background whilst I did my homework and she did the book keeping for the business. One day when I was trying to write a composition for English about 'My Favourite Place' I looked up and saw that she had put her pen down on the table and was looking hard at me.

'Do you remember anything about when you were little?' she asked suddenly. 'Do you have any pictures in your head of before we came to this country?'

It was such a long time ago, I didn't think I could

remember anything but when I closed my eyes, I saw a picture of myself on Susi's shoulders and we were running and running along a brown path in a park, with our breath coming out like a stream of white smoke in a bright blue sky.

She looked at me in surprise when I told her. 'Yes, I remember that too. You were three years old then. You had met me from school and we were coming home through the Augarten. You had this big, wicker pram and you hated being in it, so I lifted you out and we ran together.'

I held my breath, willing her to say more, to tell me why we were there and where we were going. But she sighed and looked away from me.

'I'm very pleased with how you're getting on Eva. Keep working hard and you'll do well.' And she closed her books and left the table.

*

I was fifteen and one month and I could leave school at the end of the year or I could stay on and learn shorthand and typing. Brenda had made her mother promise that she wouldn't have to work in the markets with Nat and her dad. She wanted to stay on too. She thought being a secretary was a very good job for girls like us.

We'd been in our new home for a few months. It wasn't like the other houses in the road, great big buildings divided into flats. Ours was a semi-detached house with a front and a back garden of our own. It was the other end of Goldhurst Terrace, nearer to West End Lane.

Sometimes I missed my old room at the top of the stairs in Compayne Gardens. I even missed Mrs Katz calling out to me as I came up the stairs on my way home from school. 'Darlink, can you come and thread me a needle or two? I don't see so good these days,' when really she just wanted a bit of company. But our house was very big; it had a lovely garden with apple and pear trees and most important of all, it was ours.

That's what uncle Ziggy said the day we moved in. 'It's our own home and we bought it with money we earned ourselves in this country. No one is going to take that away from us.'

Susi was proud of it too. She bought a little bit of furniture and made some new curtains out of old dark red velvet that she had bought second hand. She liked old things that were plain and elegant and she liked the floor in our new house which was wooden parquet in a pattern called herringbone. She didn't like flowery or frilly things or things that pretended to be antiques when they were new.

Susi went away a few weeks after we moved. I hated her not being there; I only felt that this big new house was mine if Susi was in it. Brenda and Mrs Gold were worried about me, but when they asked me where she had gone and how long she would be away, I didn't know what to say. Susi had just left, kissed me on the cheek and said, 'Be a good girl and I'll see you very soon.'

'Come and stay with us, darlin. I don't like to think of you in that big house all on your own.' But I preferred to be at home so that I could cook for uncle Ziggy and I needed to keep the house looking nice so that whenever Susi came back she would be pleased with me.

I enjoyed cooking. I often made the evening meal when they had to work late. Sometimes we had a party on Sunday evenings at our house and I always helped with the cooking then. I liked those noisy evenings with all the women beautifully dressed and the men smoking and laughing loudly. We had a special party to celebrate our Naturalisation. Susi saved and saved her coupons and made a big cake with chocolate and dried fruit. I had a legal document to say that I was English now and another one to say that my name was officially Eva Friedmann, not Eva Shapiro.

Susi was famous for her cooking. Her specialities were platters full of little open sandwiches and rolls, decorated with chopped egg and parsley and tiny strips of red pepper, and everyone said they'd never tasted pastries and strudel like hers outside Budapest or Vienna. The people coming would give her some of their coupons and we would spend the whole weekend cooking. She said, 'Those people are our family in this country and that's why I don't mind the work.'

I liked the parties best after I had helped serve the food and cleared away, once the guests had forgotten I was there and I could just sit in the corner and look at all the people and listen to their talk and laughter. The parties were really the only time Susi and uncle Ziggy spoke German at home and I'd learned to understand most of what they said but I didn't always get the men's jokes.

In Domestic Science my teacher Mrs Simmonds taught us how to bake rock cakes, how to lay a table, keep the kitchen ship shape and plan a week's shopping for a family of four, but at home we did things a different way. I followed Susi's way of keeping house. I cooked from her hand written recipe book and I cleaned the kitchen and laid the table in the way she liked. Mrs Simmonds didn't know that there were a lot of things you couldn't buy in Sainsbury's or MacFisheries. You had to go to Ken and Marie's in Goldhurst Terrace for spicy sausages and salami, paprika and pickled herrings, green peppers for stuffing and freshly roasted coffee because they weren't sold in the English shops. Uncle Ziggy liked to go to Rabenstein's the kosher butcher in Fairhazel Gardens but mostly I bought meat in the English butchers – a pound of stewing steak cost eight pence and that made a big goulash or a slow cooked casserole with potatoes. On Friday nights I bought a plaited challah, for four pence. Uncle Ziggy said that my cooking would soon be as good as Susi's and that was a big compliment.

I was so pleased when I heard that Susi was coming back. Uncle Ziggy went to collect her from the airport in our car; we had a black Austin A40 now as well as a new house. 'Can't complain. Mustn't grumble,' uncle Ziggy said proudly when anyone asked him how was business. He learned to drive when he was in the army and Susi was going to learn too. She was going to be the only woman I'd ever met who could drive a car.

As soon as I heard the sound of the engine shutting down in the drive, I ran up the front path and when Susi saw me, she hugged me so hard that it took my breath away. But it was only for a minute. As quickly as she had thrown her arms around me, she let me go again.

'Let me look at you. I feel like I've been away for ever.' She inspected me in the way she inspected the kitchen to make sure Mrs Epstein the new cleaning lady had removed every speck of dust. I looked just like me: plump, flushed, untidy, with fair, frizzy curls poking out of my hair ribbon where smooth waves should have been. Susi looked beautiful. Her hair was dark and shiny, held back with tortoiseshell combs and she wore high heeled pumps and a dark suit with a waisted jacket and fur collar, and a full calf length skirt. But her eyes looked very tired and there was something different about her. It made me uncertain what to say or do.

Susi had been away to collect some things from Vienna and a week after she returned, we drove to the London docks to see them being unloaded from the boat.

'All those boxes from home,' Susi said. 'And I don't even know what's in them. I didn't want to open them up in Mitteldorf, I wanted to keep it until I got home to you. It's a miracle anything was saved, a miracle.'

A few days later, the boxes were delivered to the house. Susi shouted at the delivery men not to be so clumsy and then she apologised and gave them some money for a drink, because the two things Susi hated most were rudeness and unfairness. She said being fair was very important to the English. The men put the boxes and huge packages wrapped in stiff, brown paper in our big front room and we began to unwrap them, the biggest one first.

'Careful, be careful how you take the paper off.

These things are very precious. Oh, my goodness me,' she said, and her voice came out like a prayer. 'Just look at this. Such memories.' She put her hand on the marble top of a glass fronted cabinet. It had a wonderful shiny, fancy pattern down the front. 'This used to belong to my grandparents – my father's parents. That's inlaid mother of pearl.' She ran round the room holding her breath in excitement, like a child. 'These are the Biedermeier chairs we had in the salon,' she said, pulling the thick paper from two dark wooden armchairs covered in faded creamy coloured velvet, with curved legs and arms. She stopped moving and stood like someone playing musical statues. Her hand went over her mouth.

Uncle Ziggy went up and put his arm round her waist. 'Why don't you tell Eva about this?' He removed the paper and unrolled a large rug with a tiny, intricate pattern of deep blue and red. Susi held the soft wool to her face and the dust made her sneeze.

'It was made a long time ago in Persia. When I've beaten the dirt out, you'll really be able to see the beautiful pattern. Don't you think it will look lovely in the sitting room? It will be just right.'

She began to unpack the smaller things. Inside the cabinet, in yellowed newspaper there were two oil paintings. One of the paintings was dull, a glum old man with a beard, but the other one was very pretty. It was a picture of a serious faced farmer and his wife in the countryside and I don't know why but it made me feel warm and happy when I looked at it. Susi smiled at me. 'I felt exactly the same about this picture when I was your age, it was always my favourite.'

The room was now full of cardboard and brown paper and dusty German news print, but when we put it all to one side, we could see that there weren't really so many things. The last few packages were mostly linen wrapped in tissue paper and tied up with faded narrow pink ribbon: table cloths, sheets and pillowcases still white with beautiful embroidered edges.

'Don't untie them, we'll leave them as they are for now,' Susi said, smoothing down the packages. 'Some of these will be yours, when you're older.'

She said, 'when you're older', not 'when you get married', like Mrs Gold always said to Brenda, but I couldn't imagine a time when I would live away from Susi, married or not.

There was only one box left and this seemed to be full of bits and pieces. There was a book with Hebrew and German writing, a pair of candlesticks, a menorah and a little metal Kiddush cup. They looked dark and dirty, but Susi said, 'You wait until we've cleaned them, they'll look beautiful.' And she was right because I went to the kitchen and polished them for her right away and I had never seen silver which shone so bright. She put them inside the glass fronted cupboard and they looked perfect. At the bottom there were some framed photographs. I unwrapped the first one and handed it to Susi to wipe off the dust. It was a picture of a lot of people in old fashioned clothes, sitting in front of the cupboard we now had in our sitting room. There was an old lady in the middle with a girl sitting at her feet, wearing long plaits and a dress with a sailor's collar and white buttons, and standing behind her were two big girls and a lot of smartly dressed men and women. Susi took it from me and looked at it for a long time. Then she opened the palm of her hand and placed it on top of the glass as if to keep it safe, to keep everything in its place. I looked at her looking at this photograph, looking at her hand. I had seen this expression on her face before, but never like this, never so distant and removed from everything. She looked as if something had happened so deep down inside her that what was left on the outside was nothing but a mask – her same, beautiful face, but without any life in it.

*

She was sad for a long time after this. She wasn't cross or bad tempered, she just became very quiet. When she was near me she was always busy and she never asked for anything so I didn't know how to make her happy again. I tried to be very good and helpful, but there wasn't really anything I could do for her.

Then she became sick. She stopped rushing around so much and didn't get up to go to work until much later than usual, if at all. I didn't know what to do. I talked to Brenda about nearly everything in my life, but I had never ever talked to her about Susi, unless it was to tell her about a new hairstyle or outfit.

'Why don't you ask her what's the matter? Maybe it's women's troubles. Ma tells me everything about her women's troubles.'

'I couldn't.'

'Why not?' I couldn't say why not. I just knew I couldn't. She put her arm around me.

'Don't cry now, I'm sure it's not so bad. Why don't you ask your uncle, he's bound to know? He is her husband after all.' The idea of asking uncle Ziggy about Susi's women's troubles was so preposterous that it made me giggle and the tears and the laughter together gave me the hiccups. 'See, if you can laugh about it, it's not so serious after all. He'll probably be pleased to talk to you.'

Of course I couldn't ask him. I could imagine Brenda saying to her father. 'Pop, what's the matter with Ma? She seems to be going up the wall.' But I couldn't talk to uncle Ziggy like that. He was kind to me and patient, but I hadn't had any practice talking to him about private things. Susi was the one who took care of me and he was the one who took care of Susi.

As the weeks went on, I had even less idea. Uncle Ziggy was always kind to me but we were quiet and distant in each other's company. Every morning when he left for work he wished me a good day at school and when he came home at night he was cheerful enough but distracted. After supper, he would put a record on the gramophone and read the newspapers. It was Susi who had made the conversation in our house. Now she was often in bed when I left to go to school and although sometimes she sat with us in the evenings, she didn't eat much and often went upstairs again without saying anything to either of us. Every day, it felt like this big house belonged to me less and less.

One morning, uncle Ziggy came back into the house; he must have forgotten something. I was standing outside their bedroom door. Not doing anything, not moving, just waiting.

'Eva? Shouldn't you have left for school?' In the

silent house, his voice made me jump. He looked at me closely. 'Is anything the matter with you? Are you unwell?' I stood there, my eyes on the floor, unable to speak. When he spoke again, it was more gently. 'Do you want to speak to Susi, are you worried about her?' I nodded, miserably. He put his hand on my head and rubbed my hair like he used to do when I was little, and went into their bedroom, shutting the door behind him.

'Go inside now. She wants to talk to you.'

Susi was sitting at her dressing table in a long, dotted gown. Her face was pale without any make up and her hair was pulled back from her face. She turned to look at me and suddenly I was scared.

'I'm sorry I haven't spoken to you before now,' she said calmly. 'Ziggy said I should but I wanted to wait. Have you been worried that I've been ill?'

I nodded.

'You mustn't think there's anything wrong with me. I haven't been feeling too well but I'm fine now.' She looked at me and smiled suddenly, her face opening up in the old way. 'Do you have any idea what I'm going to tell you? Have a guess.' I knew what she was going to say. Really I had known it all along.

'You're going to send me away aren't you? Do you want me to live somewhere else now that I'm old enough to leave school?' The smile wiped off Susi's face like a clean rag on the floor.

'Eva. Dear God, whatever makes you think that? Why would you think such a terrible thing?'

I held my head down, trying not to cry; I knew Susi would be irritated by my tears.

'Answer me. Tell me why you thought that.'

I hung my head, unable to speak.

'I'll never send you away, never. This is your home for however long you want. Why do you think we would send you away, have we ever been unkind to you?'

'No,' I whispered.

'Well, what on earth makes you think that we would do something like that? Where did you think you would go?' Her voice was half irritation, half sadness.

'Something's wrong though,' I said at last. 'I know it is. I'm supposed to understand, but I don't. When you said you had something to tell me, I just thought that's what it must be.'

She shook her head as if she was trying to clear a cloud of fog and looked at me for a long time.

'It's not bad news Eva. It's good, very good. It has nothing to do with sending you away.' She paused and I held my breath. 'Things have been difficult for me recently – I haven't been able to speak about it but it's nothing bad. I've fallen.'

I looked at her blankly.

'I've fallen pregnant. I'm expecting. There is going to be a baby in the house.'

My tears started then.

'Aren't you happy about it? Be happy. I was waiting until I was sure that everything would be safe, I was so worried that something bad would happen. Bad things have happened – things...'

I wanted to be able to run to her and throw my arms round her, but instead I stood there, unable to speak as usual.

She shook her head at me. 'You are too quiet

Eva. You mustn't hold everything inside you – it's bad for you to do that.'

She turned away from me and began to powder her nose and put on some rouge from a tiny, round box. Through the mirror she said, 'There will be a lot for us to do now to get everything ready for the baby. You will be the greatest help to me Eva, a wonderful helper.'

*

We were going to have a baby in our house and it was the best news I had ever heard. I wished I had been able to tell Susi right away how wonderful it was, instead of crying and thinking of myself, but I was determined to do everything I could to help her. I was going to look after it like Susi looked after me, although of course this baby would have its own mother. I was going to knit lots and lots of things for the new baby. I was a good knitter. In the hospital I spent more time knitting for the nurses than I did on arithmetic, reading and writing all put together. I taught Brenda and we started straight away in white two ply because that was soft for a baby: bootees, hats, shawls and cardigans. Brenda was a quick learner, but she wished she knew whether it was going to be a boy or a girl, so she didn't have to knit everything in boring white.

Susi was better now; she was back at work every day because uncle Ziggy couldn't manage so well without her and I did every little thing I could to help in the house. She was getting really big, although that didn't stop her wearing her high heeled shoes. She hated the maternity dresses other women wore because she said they had no style at all. She designed some clothes and the women in the workshop made them up for her. Uncle Ziggy said she must be the most fashionable pregnant woman in the country.

'What will the baby be to you?' Brenda asked me at one of our knitting sessions.

'What do you mean, what will it be?'

'Will you be its auntie or cousin or sister or what?'

'I don't know. Does it matter?' I lost count of my stitches and had to start all over again.

'No, I don't suppose so. It's just interesting, that's all.'

'I don't think it's that interesting. It will be part of the family. Isn't that enough?'

'Yes. But what exactly is Susi to you, I've never really understood?'

'Well she's – she's my cousin.'

'Well, if Susi is your first cousin, will the baby be like your second cousin?'

'It won't be my second cousin. I don't even know what a second cousin is. It will be more like my little brother or sister.'

'No it can't be that, because Susi's not your mother.'

'Well, it will be my niece or nephew then.'

'No, it can't be that either,' she persisted doggedly, 'because then you and Susi would have to be sisters.'

'For heaven's sake Brenda, does it matter? It will be our baby and it will live in our house and I'm going to be the one to help look after it.'

It was the nearest we had ever come to a proper

argument.

*

That Pesach I did most of the cleaning because uncle Ziggy didn't want Susi to be standing on stools to reach the top cupboards. I took down the special Passover crockery and pots and pans and prepared nearly all the food. It was a lot of work, but I didn't mind doing it. We had Mrs Epstein twice a week but she was old and it was hard for her. 'Oy vay's mir,' she said every time she had to get up from trying to wash the floor. She was Polish and she had been in the camps, so I didn't mind helping her out. It wasn't all that easy for me to get up from the floor myself and I had to hold on to the side of the table to keep steady, but it was a lot easier than it was for poor Mrs Epstein.

On the first Seder in our new home, we had a big party. Our new walnut dining table seated twelve people and so they invited nine of their friends to spend it with us. All the friends were refugees from back home. Some had been in the camps and some had come out before the war started, but they were all like us, people who didn't have much family in England.

Uncle Ziggy was the one who loved Pesach the most. He liked to sit at the head of the table, conducting the service loud and fast in Hebrew and German, dipping his finger in the wine when he recounted the ten plagues, and he had tears in his eyes when he came to the part where he said, 'Next year in Jerusalem'.

After the meal, we had a bit of singing and the

men outdid each other to sing louder and faster and then the talking and arguing would start. If you didn't know better, you might have thought somebody was going to be murdered round that table, or at the very least, leave without ever speaking to the others again. They were arguing about Palestine, again. Next year it really would be possible for Jewish people to go to Jerusalem. Half the table thought that it was the responsibility of those who had survived to emigrate to Israel and build up the new State because it was the only place that Jews would ever be safe from monsters like Hitler, and the other half thought that because the Nazis hadn't managed to kill all the Jews in Europe, we should stay here and be Europeans like our fathers and grandfathers before us.

We just had one Seder but the Golds always had two, a first night and a second night, and I went to spend the second night with them. It was just me and the family because they'd had their big do the night before. Mr Gold said all the Hebrew part very slowly like he couldn't read Hebrew very well and it took ages and ages before we could eat. He didn't sound a bit like uncle Ziggy who sang it all full voiced, at breakneck speed as if he was taking part in a light opera, or like the rabbi in the synagogue at the end of Yom Kippur when everyone was dying to get home and break their fast and he wanted to get the service finished.

Nat was there, rolling his eyes and looking up at the ceiling as his father's voice got slower and slower and quieter and quieter. He made us giggle, Nat. I had to think hard about the nurses in the Norwich hospital in order not to laugh out loud and make a terrible mess of the square of matzo and bitter herbs I was just about to put in my mouth.

Nat didn't want to do his National Service; he didn't want to leave his home comforts and he never wanted to be too far away from his mother.

'First of all, I tried to convince them that I had flat feet,' he told us, weaving his way around the room, knees bent like Charlie Chaplin, trying to avoid bumping into all the side tables and ornaments. 'Then I showed them how my eyesight was very bad.' He squinted and put his arms out, flailing like a man in a pea souper fog. 'The-en. They stripped me off and put their hands on my you-know-where to make me cough and...'

'Nat, please! Young ladies present,' Mrs Gold laughed.

'Stop playing the fool Nat, and do what your mother says,' his father said, giving him a wink. He had rolled up his shirt sleeves and loosened his waistcoat over his expanding belly.

'I think I'll put the kettle on, who's ready for a nice lemon tea?' Mrs Gold heaved herself up from the soft armchair, wagging her finger at her son, smiling fondly at him. He was funny, Nat, but none of us believed his stories. We all knew that in front of the army doctor, Nat would have stood quietly and done what he was told.

'How do you feel about leaving?' I asked. I wasn't as shy with Nat as I was with most people. He looked at me and then down on the floor. Nat was like someone with a stutter who could hardly get a word out in ordinary conversation, but could sing as sweetly as a blackbird. When he was kidding about, he was as fluent as Tommy Handley on *Itma*, but ask him to have a serious conversation and he went shtum.

'I'm trying not to think about it. I expect I'll be able to manage, all the other guys do. And I'm going with Ben from school, we've got nearly the same birthday so perhaps we'll be in the same unit.' He sighed. 'I ought to take you two out somewhere before I leave.' He looked from one to the other, grinning again. 'Now where would you two lovely ladies like to go. Pictures Up West? Dinner dance at the Café Royal? A concert at the Hippodrome? I could ask Ben to make up the foursome, or is Leslie more your type?' He was teasing us as usual, but I could feel my skin begin to tickle and my face go red.

*

Now that we were nearly sixteen, Brenda wanted a boyfriend. According to Brenda everyone our age needed a boyfriend, or at least the promise of one. I didn't, or at least I didn't think I did. I liked my life the way it was – Susi happy again and talking to me about everyday things, the baby due in a month's time, and Brenda and me staying on at school for another year to do shorthand and typing.

'Please come to the Maccabi with me. Please. You'll enjoy it when you're there, I know you will. Everyone goes there, Leslie does.' That was it, of course, Nat's friend Leslie Caplan. Brenda was sweet on him. 'Please, please, please. Just come once, this Sunday. It's just an ordinary evening, not a dance or anything. Please say you'll come with me.'

How could I refuse her? Maybe I would enjoy it; Susi certainly thought it was a good idea. She thought

I should be going out a bit more.

'What are you going to wear? What will I wear?' Brenda asked me every day at school that week. I already had something, the new outfit Susi had given me for Rosh Hashanah. It had a dark, pleated skirt to cover my funny hips.

'This will suit you, Eva, it's very flattering, it's a good length for you, just over the knees,' Susi said, when she gave it to me. I was going to wear it with a white knitted top with a round collar and little pearl buttons. Brenda was hoping for something a lot more glamorous.

'It's a date and you want to look smooth and dreamy,' she read from a copy of the *Sears Catalogue* Susi had brought home. 'Pretty when you walk, heavenly when you dance. A glitter dress for a glamour girl.'

'I thought you said it was going to be an ordinary evening, not a dance or a party.'

'It is. It is. Only it's not going to be easy for someone who looks like me to make a good impression. It's easier for you, you've got a pretty face.' I didn't think that was quite the point, but it was sweet of her to say it.

*

The room where the club was held was bright and bare, chairs stacked against the wall and a few tables. Two or three organised types – a boy with his curly hair damped down and the hint of a moustache, a girl with glasses in a dark tartan dress and a couple of older people were busy arranging the chairs in rows and putting out some papers on a table at the front. There were a few faces I recognised from synagogue and Hebrew classes; Pauline the girl with glasses was one of them, but I felt too shy to talk. Brenda had appeared wearing a short sleeved, pale blue, rayon frock, her arms were covered in goose bumps. 'Do I look alright?' She whispered, her shoulders bent over me.

'You look lovely, aren't you cold?'

She shook her head. She had borrowed her mother's brown leather shoes and the extra height made her nervous.

'It's nice to see you,' the girl with glasses said in a friendly way. 'Come and sit here, the meeting is just beginning.'

The first part of the evening was a meeting with an agenda, young people acting like they were adults. The chairman stood up and said,'Brothers and Sisters, I now call on the secretary of the Entertainment Committee to give us his report.' A tall, thin boy with sticky up hair announced that the next play to be performed by the drama group would be Clifford Odets's *Golden Boy* and auditions would be held at seven o'clock on Wednesday. Someone called for a new nomination for the Social Committee now that Mick Greenberg had left for National Service. 'Brothers and Sisters who have put their names down for the trip to Southend need to pay their one shilling and sixpence today if they don't want to lose their place.'

The friendly girl with the glasses said that the Sunday Ramblers Group was going to start up again and the first trip would be to Epping Forest and it would cost tuppence ha'penny on the 102 bus. The chairman stood again. 'Our debate next week will be:

Communism: is this the end of democracy? Now please can we have volunteers to speak for and against the motion?' Hands went up all over the room.

Then they cleared the tables away and there was table tennis and chess and cards and a play reading group. Brenda and I sat in the corner and chatted to Pauline and it wasn't too bad at all.

We went almost every week after that, even after Jacqueline was born. People liked me because I didn't mind what I did. I took the subs and I typed up the minutes. I poured out the Tizer and made the tea. I bought the biscuits and cakes or made them at home. If there was a job to be done, I was the one they asked to do it.

After a bit, Brenda persuaded me to go to the Saturday night dances too. She was still looking for a tall, handsome boyfriend in general and Leslie Caplan in particular. 'Do you think it's my height that's the problem? Jewish boys are so small, I'm taller than most of them, I'm even taller than my own brother.' I didn't suppose having me for a best friend helped her much either; I wasn't going to be asked to make up a foursome.

*

The dances weren't as bad as I thought. I liked listening to the music and made myself busy helping to put the records on the gramophone and making sure they didn't get scratched, or taking the weekly subs. I liked watching Brenda dance. In the quickstep or the foxtrot, with a tall boy like Leslie, she didn't look gangly any more. Sometimes it could get a bit awkward if a new boy came to the club and asked me to dance but I just made an excuse – I was a bit tired or I was just going to help take the tickets or serve the refreshments. I knew what the look on their face would be if I stood up and walked with them towards the floor. They liked to play cards with me, or have me make the tea. I could be the membership secretary, or the minute taker at meetings. I could run the tombola to raise funds for the club, but it wasn't my place to be anyone's dancing partner. When I absolutely had to move from my quiet chair, I shuffled along with my back against the wall, trying to take up as little space as possible.

At Chanukkah, there was a special dance. Jacqueline was one month old and the sweetest baby with a surprising shock of bright ginger hair. I didn't really want to leave Susi because she looked so tired and the baby was cranky and had to be given gripe water every few hours to stop the wind, but Susi said I should go because I'd bought my ticket. Brenda had finally got her glamorous outfit. It was a crêpe suit, gold, with sequins sewn into the top and a little belt tied in a bow and she had a new pair of flat pumps and a permanent wave. It made her look about thirty. She had begged her mum for it, because Brenda finally had a boyfriend. She'd given up on Leslie and was seeing Bernie, the tall boy with the sticky up hair. They weren't exactly going out together yet, but you could see that they were sweet on each other.

One of the boys who worked in the electric light factory in Neasden had borrowed a mirror ball like out of the dance halls and he'd rigged it up so, instead of the usual glare, the room was filled with magical, dancing lights. As usual, I sat by the record player putting on the Glenn Miller songs: *Don't Sit Under the Apple Tree, Chatanooga Choo Choo, Pennsylvania 6-500.*

'Hi, Eva, where's Brenda? What's she doing leaving you on your own like this?' The familiar voice made me jump. It was Nat, home on leave with a new friend from the army, come to see what his little sister was up to.

'She's over there.' I pointed to the middle of the dance floor.

'Good heavens, who's that? He looks like he's got a horsehair broom on his head.'

'No he doesn't, he's nice.'

'He's not the boyfriend is he?'

'I think so. Nearly.'

'Oy vay. Tse, tse,' he said in a Yiddish accent, imitating the way his mother tutted and shook her head. 'There's no accounting for taste. What happened to Leslie?'

'He never got round to asking her out, so she settled for Bernie.'

'That's his name is it? Yeah, well, I suppose that's Leslie. Ask 'em to dance but don't ask 'em out.' He looked at Brenda again. 'What on earth is she wearing? She's not a bridesmaid or anything is she? I haven't come to a wedding by mistake?'

I giggled. He was different somehow. Still funny, but more confident and grown up.

'Nat, you're talking,' I said bravely.

'I know,' he said, smiling his lopsided grin. 'The army must be making a man of me,' and then he came over all quiet and bit his lip and said nothing. After a minute he asked, 'You okay here for a bit? I'm just going to chat to some old friends. I'll send Ben over to talk to you. Now don't be shy, you'll like him.'

Ben was a good looking boy but it wasn't his friendly smile or nice voice that made my heart pound. I knew from the way he stopped in front of me and just stood there that he was going to ask me to dance and for a moment I couldn't remember what I usually did or what I said when this happened, so when he spoke, I didn't know what else to do but stand up and go towards him like every other girl in the room would have done. And I saw him watching me, and I saw the look on his face as I rocked towards him, and he didn't know what to do, and I didn't know what to do because it was too late to do anything but walk with him into the centre of the room. The music was fast, a foxtrot in double time. He held out his arms awkwardly but as I moved forward to put a hand on his shoulder, he took a step back.

'Oh, I'm sorry.' He brought his watch up to his eyes. 'I didn't realise how late it was, I have to go. Could you tell Nat for me? I'm really sorry.' He scurried away and I was left on my own in the middle of the dance floor, whilst the dancers moved around me in the shifting lights – young people, some a bit awkward, some smooth and in the rhythm, none of them standing still. Only me.

Somehow I made my way back to my seat, grateful for my quiet, dark corner and I made myself not think, not think, not think about anything at all. Nat came and sat by me.

'Would you like to have a dance with me?' He said after a while.

'I don't dance, Nat.'

'Why not?'

'You know why not.'

'I don't, honestly.' This seemed cruel coming from Nat. He had known me since I was twelve years old.

We said nothing, just sat side by side in silence. Nat spoke at last.

'Ben didn't mean to upset you. He had to go, he only had an evening pass, he didn't realise how late it was. We get into terrible trouble if we're late back to camp.'

I took deep breaths in and out, in and out, trying to control myself.

'Come and have a dance with me, please Eva. I know I've got two left feet but I'll try my best.' It was a toss up between doing what he asked or bursting into tears, so I stood up with him. He took my hand and we walked the few steps towards where people were dancing. The song was a slow waltz, a romantic, crooning tune. He was trying to be kind like Brenda always wanted to be, but nobody could take this humiliation away. I had spent my life pretending not to hear what people said about me, and if I couldn't help hearing, then pretending not to mind, but at this moment I had had enough and I just wanted to be on my own and cry like a baby. I put my face against his shoulder, and hid my face in his jacket.

'Look at you you're a good dancer. There's nothing wrong with you at all.'

'Nat, don't.' We moved around the floor for a little while, slowly, slowly and then, unable to bear it any more, I broke away and moved back to my seat. He followed me to my chair and watched me looking straight ahead, determined not to cry.

'Eva, don't be sad.'

I waved my hand at him, unable to speak.

'You could dance if you wanted to. Even if you didn't... I mean... you can dance fine, but if you don't want to it doesn't matter.'

'Oh, Nat...'

'You are the sweetest girl in this whole room. I mean it. Look how good you are to my mum and to Brenda – you don't know how unhappy she was before she found you for a friend – you saved her, you really did, Ma always says that about you. Look at all the things you do for other people. I've been watching you for a long time.'

'That's not the same thing at all.'

'Same as what?'

'Being nice to everyone, being helpful. Good old Eva. It's not the same as someone wanting to dance with me. Someone wanting to take me home.'

'I'd like to take you home.'

'That's because you're my best friend's brother.'

'No it isn't. It's because I like you... I know you won't believe me... I like you Eva, I've liked you for a long time.' He stopped, breathed and started again. 'I'd like to write to you when I go back into the army. I warn you, I'm no Shakespeare – you should see my spelling, but I'll try my best. And you could write back... if you wanted to. Do you want to? I know you're still young, you're not sixteen yet are you, but you've always seemed so grown up to me.'

It was the longest serious thing I had ever heard Nat say. He grinned at me and started to sing in his put-on Yankee accent, '*You are my lucky star. I worship from afar*. There you are, a smile at last. That's more like it.' And he leant towards me and gave me a kiss. Not a brother's kiss, not a friend's kiss, but a beautiful kiss that made something so exciting happen inside me, that I didn't want it to stop. It was my very first kiss from Nat.

EVA

Goldhurst Terrace, London

1953

I was almost nineteen. Nat was my boyfriend, my sweetheart, we'd been courting for three-and-a-half years. For the first couple of years we hardly saw each other – he had another eighteen months in the National Service and I was in my last year at school doing a secretarial course – but we wrote to each other every week.

Hello sweetheart, his letters began. *Are you missing me as much as I'm missing you?* And in the bottom right hand corner he wrote the exact number of days he had left. He hated army life and he hated having to eat pork and rabbit. *You are my sweet girl and I can't wait to get back home and see you again,* he would write. I slept with his letter under my pillow for the whole week and when the next one came, I would tuck it away in the back of my drawer.

I wrote him long, long letters telling him my news. There were two little girls in the house now: Jacqueline, Jackie we called her, was born in 1949. She still had her bright red hair and fair skin but unlike the saying about red heads, she was a calm, controlled little thing who rarely lost her temper. Vivienne was born in 1951, just before Nat left National Service and from the beginning she was the complete opposite, dark hair like Susi's and intense brown eyes. She would stamp her feet and cry when she thought we were teasing her, even before she was two years old. Susi used to call her Sarah Bernhardt and uncle Ziggy said that someone must have left a fuse inside her and if we lit it, she would just go off with a bang.

Susi didn't like being at home all the time. I think she missed going out to work and she worried about the business; she was always asking uncle Ziggy questions about the orders and the figures when we sat down to dinner. I wrote to Nat about what was going on at home, and at the club – I was a secretary now, and I told him about my job at Dunlop and Fines in Old Street in the City. I could tell Nat anything.

One weekend when he was home on leave, he asked me about the years I had spent in the children's hospital. I told him that I had never lost the fear of those dark nights in the hospital, when they left me out in the cold or lying in bed with the frog plasters on, thinking that everyone had forgotten about me and I would have to stay there for ever and ever. He looked at me sadly with his eyes fixed on my face and promised me he would make sure I was never lonely again. Nat was the person I told how I felt when I couldn't get a job, even though they were crying out for secretaries with good shorthand typing and I'd left school top of the class, sixty words per minute in typing, one hundred and twenty in shorthand.

I nearly didn't do the secretarial course at all. The summer before I started, the year I turned fifteen, a girl came into my form room with a message that I was expected in the Headmistress's study. This was terrifying because, as far as I knew, she hadn't given me a second thought since the day she'd picked me out in assembly and announced what a peculiarity I was.

'Sit down, Eva,' she said, looking over my shoulder in the way people did when they wanted to show me they weren't watching the way I walked. Her grey hair was still in its brisk bun but she now wore a startling pair of blue butterfly glasses. 'I've been looking over your marks and you have been doing very well, in fact you've always been one of the brighter ones. A good all-rounder I'd say, good marks in Mathematics as well as English. It's surprising you didn't go to grammar school but I suppose with one thing and another...' Her voice trailed off and now her eyes fluttered irresistibly to my legs. 'It's too late to worry about that now, but I wondered if you had thought of transferring to somewhere like Brondesbury County for Girls in order to do your O Levels and then on to A Level. I'm sure you are up to it academically, although you might need a bit of tuition in languages and science. Now what do you think?'

I was pleased as Punch to be praised like that. It was the first time anyone had really told me I was clever.

'I'm very proud of you,' Susi said distractedly when I told her, spooning food into little Jackie's mouth. 'If you would like to go, you know you'll have our blessing.' But I decided that I wasn't going to transfer to the grammar because Brenda and I had already made our plans.

*

When I left school in 1950, everyone said that getting a job would be a piece of cake what with my speeds and first class reference from school, but each time I turned up for an interview I could tell straight away that they didn't want someone who looked like me in their smart office. 'Does it hurt?' They'd ask. 'Do you have to have a lot of time off work?' 'Will it get better?' It was hard saying no to all their questions and still sound cheerful and polite. They'd tell me about how the lift often broke down and they were sure that would be very difficult for me and they never left me any space to tell them that my school had three floors and no lift and I had no problem there.

'Thank you very much Miss Friedmann. Your speeds I can see are excellent and so is your English. The head of the typing pool will show you out and we'll be in touch.' But I knew I would never hear from them again.

Nat would write and say. 'Just let me know the name and address and I'll give them a good seeing to when I get back to London.' Or 'Anyone who doesn't want you to work for them, doesn't deserve you.'

Uncle Ziggy always said that there was a job for me at Elite Fashions; I could do sewing and maybe a bit of secretarial work, but I so wanted to have a job and money of my own and he didn't try to stop me.

I'd nearly given up when I had my five minute interview with Mr Dunlop at Dunlop and Fines. He looked at my speeds and my reference and he asked me to take a letter in shorthand and read it back to him. 'Excellent my dear,' he said when I'd finished. 'Can you start on Monday?' Other people thought he was a bit odd, but he was a good boss and I liked him. I'd been there two years, and I'd already had two pay rises. The first time I looked in my pay packet and found I had an extra pound, I went straight in and told him.

'It's for you my dear, to show you how much I value your work and your reliability.'

'Is it just for this week or every week?'

I could see him press his lips together trying not to laugh at me and I felt so silly but he just said, 'It's for every week until you deserve another rise. Now you have a good weekend and I'll see you on Monday morning.'

I told Nat about this as well and he wrote back, 'How old is this Mr Dunlop? I hope he's not trying to take you away from me.' And this made me laugh because Mr Dunlop was very podgy and at least sixty years old.

The nature of the company was still a mystery to me. Mrs Bayley, who did the accounts and had been there for donkey's years, didn't seem to know either and neither did Julia who worked for Mr Fines. Sometimes I had to send telegrams using the huge volumes of a special code book which was a way to cut down our costs. These went to Central America confirming our orders for coffee beans but we didn't seem to be a firm that just imported coffee. Sometimes I typed letters to Argentina with samples of all sorts of things: wool and Harris Tweed from Scotland, cloth hats from Ireland, fine cotton shirt material from Lancashire, and then I would have to write back with an invoice, telling them when they might expect our delivery. And sometimes I typed out large orders to Fortnum and Mason for Mr Dunlop's parties which as far as I knew were signed but never sent. Every Friday morning, Mr Dunlop would call me into his office and ask me to put some more coal on the fire – it was always freezing cold and there was no central heating – then with his left hand he would sweep some of the papers from the top of his great, battered, mahogany desk, pull up the legs of his pin striped trousers showing his fine grey silk socks, put his feet up on his desk and dictate his life story to me. So far,

I had typed two hundred pages and we had reached his sixteenth birthday which he was spending in the South of France. Whenever he was about to say something outrageous, he thoughtfully cleared his throat to warn me, but that didn't stop me going bright red as I took it all down. When I wrote about this to Nat he said I should make carbon copies and send them to him so he could sell them to his mates for a fortune.

Every day I longed to have Nat home. I said a prayer for him and slept with his photo under my pillow. I kissed his big soppy grin and the dark curls that sprang out of his forage cap. However much Brylcreem he put on, he could never get his hair to stay down. I tried not to be too hopeful – someone like Nat could have had a hundred girls, but I knew that the place that he had in my heart would never, ever be taken up by someone else.

Even when Nat finished his National Service and came back to London, we were lucky if we saw each other once a fortnight. Each day there was a stall to set up at the different weekly markets around North London and even as far out as Hertfordshire, weekends too, rain or shine. All year round his face and hands were red from being outside in all weathers. He wore black gloves without fingers and a wide cloth belt to hold the money and a big blue French beret so everyone called him Froggy the Onion Seller. He had to go and buy the stock too, socks and silk stockings were still in short supply so he added other bits and pieces when he could and he loved anything from America. He was like an actor working his audience out in the streets of Wembley or Harrow. Mrs Gold said he was good enough to go on the stage.

If he could get off a bit early in the week, he'd come and pick me up from work in his old van and we'd go to Lyon's Corner House for egg and chips and an ice cream. Sometimes, he could get Sunday afternoons off, if his dad did the stall, and then we might go to the pictures where we would snuggle down together in the dark like the other courting couples or go for a walk on Hampstead Heath and try to find a quiet spot for a kiss and cuddle. He was wonderful at kissing, Nat, just wonderful. We could spend hours together, just looking at each other and learning to get closer. I loved being touched by him.

*

Jackie was waiting for me by the door still clean and tidy at the end of the day, with Vivienne by her side, tousled and grubby. 'Hello sweethearts,' I said, bending down to kiss them.

'Eva, Eva,' they said in unison. 'Me, me, kiss me first. No, me. Me.' I kissed them both twice.

'Give her a minute, she's only just walked in the door,' Susi said buttoning up her wide duster coat. I'm so sorry to run out as soon as you come in from work but the concert starts at seven and I promised Ziggy I'd be on time for once. I've left you a bit of supper in a dish on the side, just warm it up for a few minutes. The children have already eaten. Are you sure you don't need anything? We won't be back late.'

'I'll be fine, don't worry.' I took off my heavy coat and hung it in the hall cupboard. 'You just have a good evening.'

'Be good for auntie Eva, and Vivienne, don't make her carry you upstairs, it's too hard for her and you're quite capable of walking on your own.' She turned to me. 'We're at the Wigmore Hall at a concert, the number's in the book if there's an emergency.'

'There won't be.'

Susi stood at the hall mirror, applying face powder and smoothing back her immaculate French pleat. She sighed at her reflection. 'I'm always late these days and I used to be such an organised person.' She pursed her lips together and checked the edge of her lipstick line with her little finger.

'Susi?'

'Hmm?'

'I've asked Nat to come round a bit later. Is that okay?'

'Nat?' She looked at me through the mirror, the girls below the line of her vision. 'Nat?' she repeated distractedly. 'To keep you company, that will be nice. Is Brenda coming too?' She pulled on her leather gloves and clicked her handbag shut.

'I don't think so,' I said as vaguely as I could, but Susi was out of the door, her midnight blue coat sailing behind her. The three of us stood, watching her go. At the end of the drive, she turned.

'We might go out for a bite to eat afterwards. We won't be late though.'

'Just have a good time. We'll all be fine.'

*

The girls played and squabbled in the bath. Vivienne splashed and splashed, she was the mummy fish, protecting her babies from the big boat.

'Don't do that Vivienne, you'll make a mess. Mummy told you that you mustn't make the water come out the bath,' Jackie said seriously.

Vivienne responded by bursting into noisy tears.

'I can do it, I can.'

'No you can't. Auntie Eva, tell her she has to stop.'

I pacified Jackie and kissed Vivienne to stop her crying so loudly. I lifted her from my lap and we walked into the bedroom. She knew that it was hard for me to carry her and walk safely.

'Will you please sing us a lullaby,' Jackie said politely.

'Scarlet Ribbons,' Vivienne shouted.

'No, Jackie can choose because she helped clear up the bathroom,' I said.

'Sing the one about the angels in heaven. The sad one.' It was the song Susi always sang. Sometimes she sang it in English; sometimes there was a bit of German and Yiddish in it too.

Go to sleep my baby go to sleep. When the stars above begin to peep, they're lighting the windows of heaven. Angels watch over you, from the windows of heaven. Mamma's watching you too. Ooh la loo la loo la loo. Ooh la loo la loo la loo. Mamma's watching you too. Vivienne snuggled up on my lap, her damp head against my breast.

'You don't sing it like mummy,' Jackie said. And it was true, no one could sing like Susi.

'She does, she does,' Vivienne said loyally. 'I like it best when auntie Eva sings.' I kissed them both and tucked them safely under the home made quilts Susi and I had sewn together.

'Good night darlings, sleep tight.'

'Hope the bed bugs don't bite.'

*

Nat and I had begun to find ways to be on our own: in his van, very occasionally at home if Susi was out, any quiet corner we could find. I changed my sweater for a blouse which buttoned at the front and went downstairs. I drew the curtains in the living room and turned on the fringed lamp in the corner. There'd been something in Nat's voice when he'd asked if he could come over. I could feel my body getting excited by the thought of him.

His cheek and his kiss were full of the cool night air and as soon as we came into the sitting room, we fell onto the sofa and kissed with our mouths closed and then open, on and on as if we would never stop.

'Happy birthday,' he said as I pulled away to catch my breath. 'Happy Nineteenth.'

'It's not for another week.'

'I know but I couldn't wait.' He pulled a small box from his pocket and handed it to me. Inside was an oval of silver and blue enamel on a long chain. I opened the locket, my fingers clumsy and awkward. There were two little frames and on one side Nat had put a picture of himself in an open necked summer top. 'You can put your picture on the other side. Or one of the girls.'

'It's beautiful,' I said. It was the best present I had ever had. I leaned forward and as I kissed him, he began to undo the little buttons on my blouse, slowly one at a time, looking at me all the time. He put his hands inside and touched my breasts, very slowly. Then he cupped them in his hand and for the first time, bent down to kiss my nipples. I gasped in astonishment and let the hot feeling wash all over me.

'You are so soft. You feel so beautiful.'

'Nat. Nat.'

We kissed and kissed and he touched me and when he moved himself close against me, I could feel that he was big and hard. Nat took my hand and put it on himself and I didn't try to take it away. I felt scared and very, very excited.

'Shall we? Eva. Do you think we could? I want you so much.'

I didn't have any words to tell him what I was feeling. He began to pull my skirt up and his hand went up the inside of my thigh and on to my place and I could feel myself get wet, but I didn't know what it was.

'Nat. I want to, but...' I forced myself to pull away.

'No, I know, you're right,' he said and reluctantly, slightly ashamed, we moved away from each other, his face as red as mine. We sat together for a moment, catching our breath. 'But I want you so much. I don't want it to be like this all the time, we should be together.' My fingers were trembling as I tried to button up my blouse but I wanted him to kiss me again; I wanted it to start and not stop.

'Look Eva, I'm twenty-one. I'm earning good money with my dad. It's hard work but I'm not going to be on the stalls for ever. One day, I'm going to have my own shop and the hours will be better. I'm not going to lead a dog's life like my dad, out in all weathers. Do you believe me?'

'Of course I do.'

'Well let's get married then. I don't see why we shouldn't. We can get engaged now and then married when you're twenty. We could start saving.'

'Don't you think we should wait a bit. Won't everyone think it's happening too quickly?' I hadn't spoken to anyone properly about me and Nat, not even Brenda. She knew that we saw each other from time to time, but I'd never told her the whole story. Best friend and best friend's brother; they just didn't go.

'You silly thing. I've been courting you for three years. Ma and Pop love you, Brenda loves you. They'll be over the moon when they hear.'

I kissed him then. From that first time in the club when I wasn't even sixteen and he told me that I was just like anyone else, and that he'd always liked me, I knew that this was what I wanted.

'I suppose you want me to do it properly.' He knelt at my feet and began to nuzzle his head into my skirt.

'Nat, don't,' I giggled. 'Be serious. Don't do that, you're starting me off again.' I pushed his head away and tried to breathe calmly, to stop myself wanting him so much.

'My darling, lovely Eva. Will you make an honest man out of me and marry me so that we can live together for ever and ever. Amen?'

Of course I was going to marry him. There was nothing I wanted more in the whole wide world. I forced myself to get up and went into the kitchen. I cooled my hot face against the back door while I waited for the kettle to boil. When I came back into the sitting room with Susi's best coffee in the white china jug and some apple strudel, Nat had put a record on the gramophone. He held me tight and we danced around together, laughing. *You make me feel so young*, he sang to me.

'Frank Sinatra, look out, I'm coming to Broadway. Cricklewood Broadway.'

Nat's silly jokes. I loved him and I would always love him and we would be together for ever and ever.

*

Susi always made birthdays special, a big present and a little one, even in the years when we didn't have any money. There was always cake, even if it had to be a tiny one because of the rationing. This year, the little presents came from Jackie and Vivienne.

'I had to get a piece of card like this and cut it out in a circle and then I had to cut out a hole in the middle,' Jackie said, handing me three pompoms made from red knitting wool. 'And that's very hard, because you have to dig the scissors right in and then you get the ball of wool and you have to wind it round and round and...'

'Me now, me now,' clamoured Vivienne, wheedling her little body in front of her sister. 'My card. Mine.' She had made me a card with pictures from her *Robin* comic stuck on haphazardly with flour and water glue.

'They're beautiful, both of them. Thank you.' Jackie turned up her face for a kiss and Vivienne clung round my legs like a little monkey. 'But now I have to go to work because otherwise I'll be late.'

'You don't mind staying in for your birthday, do you? Susi asked, clearing away the breakfast dishes. 'It's just that the girls are so desperate to be part of it and they're too young for dinner in a restaurant.'

'No, I'd rather have it here.' Brenda was coming and Nat too. 'I've got a surprise too.'

When I got in from work, the house was already full of the delicious smell of Susi's cooking. I changed into my new dress, my present from Susi and Ziggy. He thought I should drop the uncle part, now I was so grown up, but it wasn't always easy to remember. My dress was a pretty colour, cornflower blue but it was more or less the same style as all my other clothes, collar and buttons and a pleated skirt. Susi thought that pleated skirts were the most flattering for my figure. When Brenda arrived from her job in the West End, we went straight up to my room. I was in a panic of excitement.

'Brenda, I've got something to tell you.' I blurted out. 'It's about Nat and me. I'm not supposed to say anything yet but...'

'I already know. I've seen it, helped him choose it actually. He met me from work last Thursday, late night closing. It was expensive with that enamelling, but Nat's always been generous. Didn't you like it?'

'Of course I did. It's lovely.' She turned back towards the mirror, with her back to me and busied herself with powder and lipstick.

'Look that must be Nat now,' she said, brushing past me, avoiding my eyes. 'Let's go down shall we?'

Nat shook hands with Ziggy and presented Susi with a pair of nylon stockings as if he was giving her half a pound of milk chocolates, and he kissed Brenda and me. Susi had laid a beautiful table, crystal glasses, candles and our best china and table linen. She'd made my favourite meal: clear soup with noodles; stuffed, baked fish and fried potatoes and, of course, a cake. Brenda who usually loved Susi's cooking, pushed her food round the plate.

'Can I help you to some more Nat?' Susi asked.

'Please, if there's some to spare. It's delicious.'

'And you Brenda, is there anything wrong dear?' Brenda looked uncomfortable. 'Only, it's fish, so it's kosher. There's no need to worry about that.'

'No, I'm fine.'

'Ah well then, I'll bring in the cake,' Susi said, clearing away the table. It was in the best Viennese style with layers and layers of chocolate butter cream, elaborate and perfect as if Susi was trying to make up for all the years when cake had been so hard to come by. They sang me happy birthday, and I blushed.

'I'll bring the coffee in, shall I?' Susi said, getting up again. 'And you girls must go to bed the minute you've finished your cake.' Nat and I looked at each other, uncertain which of us was supposed to speak.

'You say it.' I mouthed.

'I think it's best coming from you,' he signalled back with a strange twist of his head.

'Nat and I have something to say.' I looked at him and he nodded at me reassuringly. 'We wanted to tell you on my birthday.' We both grinned like a pair of Cheshire cats. 'We've decided to get engaged.' There was silence in the room. Complete silence. Even the children stopped, their chocolate covered spoons half way to their mouths.

'When do you plan to get married?' Susi said, in a voice I didn't quite recognise.

'Next year probably, when I'm twenty.'

Brenda said nothing. She looked from me to Nat and back again.

'Have you told your parents yet, Nat?'

'We wanted to tell you first.' I smiled at Brenda, but she wouldn't look at me.

'And where will you live?'

'We'll have to find rooms first of all,' Nat said cheerfully. 'And then we'll save up. I'm a hard worker. I don't want to be on the markets forever, it's a dirty job and the hours are so long. I'd like to have a shop, or a manufacturing business like you.' He looked around the room at the silent faces. 'I'm sorry if we haven't told you in the right way. It's my fault. I only asked Eva last week and I thought it would be good to tell you on her birthday.'

'Well, it is a surprise. We didn't even know you two were serious, but then Eva has always kept things to herself.' My eyes smarted at this injustice and when Susi saw this, she put her hand over mine.

'No harm done,' she said, patting my hand briefly. 'If you are really sure.'

Ziggy stood and held up his glass. 'Well, I think that news is very good. Very good indeed. I think it calls for a glass of brandy and maybe even a cigar. What do you think Nat?' He stood up and walked round the table to pat Nat on the shoulder and kiss my cheek. His good humour shook a little of the silence from the room.

'Thank you very much Mr Friedmann,' Nat said. 'I love her very much, I promise I'll do everything to look after her.' He sounded like something off the Sunday afternoon pictures, but it still made my heart flip to hear him say it in front of Susi and his own sister. Ziggy handed him a cognac in a brandy balloon and poured a little cherry brandy for Susi, Brenda and me.

'To Eva and Nat, may they be as happy together as my beautiful wife and I have been for the last nine years.' He raised his glass to Nat and me and then to Susi. She smiled the ghost of a smile.

'To Eva,' Nat said, and looked at me. Brenda sipped her cherry brandy in silence.

'Girls, it's time for bed.' Susi rose from the table.

'I'll help,' Brenda said. 'You stay here Eva. You stay with Nat.' She stood up without looking at me and followed Susi and the girls out of the room.

'Women, women,' Ziggy said when they had gone, shaking his head. 'You'd think they'd be over the moon, but with women you never can tell.' And seeing my face. 'It's just a surprise that's all. They're both pleased for you, I know they are. It'll be different tomorrow, you'll see.'

*

There was a lot of discussion over the next few weeks. Susi thought Nat's parents should come to our house because it was right to go to the girl's family to talk about a wedding. Mrs Gold wanted us to go to Willesden. There were hints about kosher food and not wanting to go somewhere they wouldn't be comfortable. Brenda and I hadn't talked at all. I didn't know if she was upset with me because I hadn't told her first, or appalled that I was going to marry her brother. Nat said she was just busy at work; he was sure there was nothing to worry about, but I wasn't sure. In the end it was decided that we would go to the Gold's for what they called 'a cup of tea'. I felt nervous and miserable although there was nothing to be unhappy about.

On the evening we had to go, Ziggy came home flustered from work and had to go out again because he'd forgotten to buy the present Susi had specifically asked him to get, a big gold box of Lindt Chocolates, the kind with the drawers and tassels we usually had on Rosh Hashanah. The baby sitter was late and the zip broke on Susi's new outfit. She changed into a full skirted, burgundy dress with a big, black, patent leather belt and insisted on changing her lipstick too. Of course, she looked fantastic, so young compared to Mrs Gold. As a result of all this, our new Rover pulled up outside their house twenty-five minutes late and Mrs Gold was twitching at the net curtains.

'Nat's not here I'm afraid. I had to send him to pick up some stock from the warehouse. It was an emergency, couldn't be helped. He shouldn't be too long. I'm sure we can manage without him for half an hour,' Mr Gold said before we'd even come through the door. He smiled at me, but he didn't pinch my cheek or say, 'How's my little maidele?'

'Your house is lovely,' Susi said in her perfect, accented English as they walked into the sitting room. 'I can see you take great pride in everything, it all looks like new.'

Mrs Gold managed to smile and pout at the same time. 'Feh.' She shook her head from side to side. 'I'm sure your home is lovely too. Brenda tells me that you have modern art.'

'Yes indeed we do,' Ziggy said. He always liked to talk about his little collection. 'I was fortunate to be able to buy a few good pieces before they became too expensive. I even have a drawing by Egon Schiele, a small one of course.'

'Call me a peasant, but I wouldn't pay tuppence for that stuff. Splashing paint all over the canvas, a child could do better. I don't know how they get away with charging for it.' Mr Gold roared at his own joke with a deep smoker's laugh.

Susi looked above their fireplace at the picture of the Chinese lady with the blue and gold face and said nothing.

'Come on, let's sit down and eat something. When my wife tells you it's a cup of tea, she means you won't be able to move for a week.'

The table was full of food: open bridge rolls with little heaps of chopped herring, smoked salmon, hard boiled eggs mashed with butter and cress. There were two kinds of cake, a honey cake and a plain sponge sitting on white paper doilies and the best white and gold bone china tea service was arranged on the sideboard. Mrs Gold sat at one end of the table, Susi at the other. Brenda didn't sit down at all. She handed round the food and served the tea and then stood behind her mother, waiting. The men talked about business and cars, the women about the best places to shop. It was the tip tap of a game of ping pong, not like real talk at all.

'You know Eva,' Mrs Gold said suddenly, turning to me, 'We never knew you had a secretive side to you. We thought after all the times you've been here, you might have been a bit more open with us.'

'Yes, I'm surprised you didn't say anything to me. After all, you're supposed to be my best friend,' Brenda said, her hand on her mother's shoulder.

I blushed deeply and wished Nat was here. 'I'm sorry. We didn't mean to hide anything from you. Nat and me, we only just decided, we haven't been planning it for a long time or anything.'

'Haven't you? Well, we're not at all sure that this whole thing is a good idea.' Mrs Gold turned to Susi. 'I might as well be blunt and get this over and done with. Morry and I are not at all happy with the engagement, this shidduch, this little arrangement they think they've cooked up for themselves.'

Susi's back stiffened. 'And why is that, exactly?'

'Don't get me wrong, we've always liked Eva. We've welcomed her with open arms into this house. No one can say we haven't. There's been many a time when she'd have had to go home to a cold house, no one there, and I always said to her, you stay here, you can eat with us. She could stay whenever she wanted. It's not surprising Nat took pity on her, he's a good boy, a bit of a schlemiel sometimes but kind hearted. He took pity on her.'

'Pity?'

'Yes, it's rachmones, not love. I'm sorry I have to say this. Morry won't do the talking although he feels the same as I do. Nat's got a mishegass in his head that he's got to marry her. But, she's not the one for him, anyone can see that.'

'And what is it that you object to about her?'

'It's not just me but as per usual, I'm the one who has to say it.' She turned to me. 'I know it's not nice for you to hear this dear. Perhaps it would be better if you and Brenda went upstairs for a little while.'

'I'm not a child, Mrs Gold.' I looked at Brenda and for the first time that evening she looked back at me but I couldn't read her expression. I looked at the door, willing Nat to walk through it and make everything okay.

'Well,' she said, sighing deeply, 'If that's the way you want it. As I said, we always thought she was a good girl, even though I can see now that she's got a deceitful side to her, but we have to face the facts, she's not normal is she? Nat needs a woman who can look after him, keep house in the proper way, a family person, balabatisher, someone who can take care of the children.' She shrugged her shoulders and opened out her hands. 'I have to say what I feel, if I don't who will? The truth is, she's not a normal girl, everyone can see that. I don't see how she can make a good wife for our only son.'

'Ma,' Brenda said in an urgent whisper, 'That's enough.'

'Well don't look at me like that. You too Morry, you all agreed with me earlier. I want to be a grandmother, there's nothing wrong with that is there? We don't know if her children would be crippled like her, we don't even know if someone like that can have children. How would she look after them? Look at her, she can hardly walk herself.'

Susi pushed her chair back violently, tipping it onto the floor, and Ziggy stood up next to her, tall and dignified.

'We will not stay here and listen to this,' Ziggy

said. 'Come on Eva, it is better if we leave now, before even worse things are said. There is a lot of ignorance in this house. We would not let you go to people who can say such hurtful things, people who...' He stopped at the sound of the noise in the hall.

'Honest, Pop, what kind of wild goose chase did you send me on? You didn't say it was going to take all night. I had to go all the way to Whitechapel and then they made me...' Nat stopped in the doorway trying to take in the scene: his mother red faced, his father with his head down, issuing little coughs of embarrassment, me in tears, Susi silent with anger. 'What on earth is going on? Eva, what's the matter, what's happened?'

'Your mother has made it clear that she thinks that Eva is not suitable to be your wife, so we are about to leave,' Ziggy said. 'Perhaps you would be good enough to show me where they have put our coats.'

'Ma, what have you said? You promised me you wouldn't do anything. Please, Mrs Friedmann. Please, don't go yet. We'll sort it out. Mr Friedmann, would you like a drink? Eva, you know Ma, she says things she doesn't mean. Brenda, do something to help, get the whisky. Ma, you come and talk to me.' He led his mother into the kitchen and his father busied himself pouring the drinks, shaking his head and making 'tse, tse, tse' noises with his tongue.

'Please, Nat's right, sit down for a little while more.' He picked up Susi's fallen chair and handed her a Du Maurier from a flat blue box. 'Have a cigarette, please, it'll calm your nerves. Don't be offended. My wife, God bless her, she says things and then she's sorry afterwards. Nat'll sort it all out, he's a good boy, he knows what to say to his mother.'

Susi and Ziggy looked at me sitting in my chair, incapable of moving. They looked at each other and then sat down and accepted the whisky.

The others returned after a while like a small procession: Mrs Gold carrying fresh cups and saucers on a tray, a pot of tea and a plate of Bourbon biscuits, Brenda following and Nat, smiling warily. Brenda had obviously been crying, but Mrs Gold looked the same as always, just a bit redder in the face. She sat down with an enormous sigh.

'Sorry if I upset you darling. Nat's given me a right telling off in there, I can tell you. I'm a yachna, I know, I talk too much for my own good but I don't mean any harm, I'm just a silly old thing. You know I've always been fond of you. You've always had a welcome here, like one of the family.'

She turned towards Susi, holding out the biscuits in a peace offering. 'Nat tells me what a capable girl she is around the home, takes care of the house lovely, even does the housework, everything. Helps with the children like she was their own mother, better even. I didn't know that you see. If I'd known that, I wouldn't have said a word. Never mind, it's best out in the open. I don't go in for airs and graces, you have to take me as you find me, but I didn't mean that she isn't a good girl. You're not angry are you darling? Who knows, maybe there's a doctor somewhere who can find a cure, they're always discovering new things.'

'Fay, enough already,' Morry Gold said, his mouth full of crumbs. 'Shah a minute and let someone else speak.' There was silence in the room.

'Eva, what do you want to do?' Susi asked. 'Do

231

you want to go home?' I was incapable of saying or doing anything.

'Ma's sorry she said all those things,' Nat said. 'She's not really against it.'

'Perhaps we should talk about this at a different time, we are all tired now, don't you think so Mr Gold?' Ziggy said formally.

'None of this mister and missus, please, Fay and Morry, Morry and Fay to you, and Susi and Ziggy, is that right?' Mr Gold held out his hand to shake Ziggy's as if he'd just come into the room. 'Don't go yet, there's things to talk about. The young people want to get married, so we'll help them get married. If Nat isn't worried that she's a bit you-know-what, then I'm not worried. He's a good boy, he'll go far. A bit young to get married but never mind. I'm gonna set him up. He can have half the business, or he can start up a couple of stalls on his own, I don't mind. And if you need a bit of a help with the wedding just ask me. You're still a young man yourself, the step father, is that right?'

'Not exactly, but I have undertaken to look after Eva. I can assure you, you will not find me ungenerous when the time comes.'

Mr Gold nodded his head from side to side and kept pouring the whisky. It felt like I would have to sit in that room for ever. The conversation swirled round and round me and even Susi was acting as if all that had happened was a few tactless words.

Fay Gold started on a long story. 'We married in Bethnal Green, Great Garden Synagogue, December 1929. My uncle was a bit of a gambler, not such a bad man, but my mother should never have trusted him with the money. Well there we all were in our finery, the guests hungry, waiting to eat, the soup going cold in the kitchen and the caterer came in and said they wouldn't serve anything until the money had been paid. So my mother and my auntie Rose, may their dear souls rest in peace, had to run down the road, fox stoles, flying and pawn their own wedding rings so we could eat.' She laughed loudly, wiping her eyes. 'And yours? What kind of affair did you have?'

'Just a quiet day,' Susi said. 'Ziggy had a few days leave from the army but Eva couldn't be with us so I had to do without a bridesmaid. We had a few friends, like ourselves and my employer in the hostel gave me away.'

'You had to do it on your own? Without your mother and father?'

'Yes. My parents did not survive.'

Mrs Gold did not allow the silence which usually followed that statement. 'What those Nazi mumzers did to the Jews, terrible, terrible. No one can know what you went through. We just have to thank God our families left Poland when they did.'

Mr Gold tutted and shook his head. 'And Eva's parents as well, they perished too? Both of them?' There was a sharp intake of breath. The bright room suddenly seemed full of ridiculous, garish objects and insubstantial things. Even Mr Gold noticed the change in the atmosphere and it stopped him in his tracks for a moment. 'Terrible things, terrible.' He repeated at last. 'But it could make a little problem with the wedding, if there is no Ketuba, no Jewish marriage certificate. Still, I'm sure the rabbi will know what to do when they go to see him. There must be a way round it.'

'Yes, that could be a problem,' Mrs Gold chipped in. 'We've got a friend, Harry, and when his son wanted to get married, they made a big fuss at the Beth Din. The fiancé's parents had got married in a house, not a synagogue. I don't know why but it meant there was no proper Jewish certificate. They wanted the parents to get married again in the synagogue before they married the children!'

'I'm sure that won't happen,' Mr Gold said, still oblivious to the expression on Susi's and Ziggy's faces. 'Rabbi Levy will know what to do, unless you want them to be married in your shul. You're members of the United Synagogue too, right? They'll find a way of proving that she's a nice Jewish girl.' He laughed. 'You couldn't tell from her face though, could you? She's a real blondie. If you didn't know it, you could never guess that the two of you were related.' He stared admiringly at Susi's Old Testament beauty, her smooth dark hair and eyebrows and her deep brown eyes. 'Now let me get this straight, you're cousins, right? Is that on your mother's side or your father's?' The bright colours of the china objects, the rug, the lampshades spun round me. I put my hand on the table to steady myself.

'My parent's wedding certificate is gone, destroyed along with most of our things. Eva's parent's too, I imagine.' Susi spoke each word like a separate stone falling. 'When the Nazis burned down every synagogue in Vienna and sent our people to the camps, I don't imagine they were thinking about what rabbis in England might want.' She made herself look at Mr Gold. 'I am her legal guardian. I have a certificate signed by Lord Gorrell from the British Parliament, would you like to see that?'

'No, no. No,' he said hurriedly. 'The children can sort it out when they go to shul to talk to the rabbi. Maybe a family picture would do, something like that. Our Rabbi Levy is a good man, I'm sure he'll find a way round the difficulties. Let's not trouble ourselves now.'

*

There were certain truths that were the foundation of my life. Susi and I had left Vienna together when I was four years old and she was sixteen. We were in danger because we were Jewish. Neither of us had any brothers or sisters but her mother and my father were brother and sister and that made us cousins. After the war started, people couldn't get to England like we did: either they weren't allowed to leave or England wouldn't let any more refugees in. A lot of people died in Vienna, but I had Susi. I don't remember ever being told this but then Brenda didn't need to be told that Nat was her brother, and Vivienne had always known that Jackie was her sister. You didn't need to talk about everything because some things were obvious and others were painful and difficult and there was nothing anyone could do to change them. Every living Jew knew what the Nazis had done. People understood that you didn't go poking around in the desolate places of other people's lives, not Fay and Morry Gold, but everyone else we knew. It was rude – more than rude, horribly tactless and cruel to ask people like us about our families, as if you were asking where they went on holiday last year, or how the business was doing. That was why Susi had spoken to Mr Gold like that. That was why she hadn't really answered his questions.

Susi's voice drifted around the car, each phrase separate from the last. 'Those terrible people, to talk about Eva in that way.'

Ziggy drove through the dark streets of north west London, down the Great North Way, turned right onto Finchley Road and then right again into our safe, quiet street.

'Ghastly house, not a single book. Did you see, not a single book,' she continued. 'To ask me those questions in front of everybody. What do they know, people like that?'

Lines had been drawn. Susi had taken against the Golds and she wasn't one to change her mind about people. Fay and Morry Gold didn't want me to marry Nat and to tell the truth, it didn't really surprise me. I didn't believe Nat's mother's apology; I knew she thought that I was the poor crippled girl who wasn't good enough for her boy. More than that, my family were 'Continentals', stuck up Germans, although of course we didn't come from Germany, we came from Austria. We had ideas above our station and were too clever for our own good. And Brenda? She had always been my friend, through all of her dad's teasing and her mother's tactless remarks, but now I couldn't be sure which side of the line Brenda was on.

In the middle there was Nat and me, and I never doubted him. I had seen his face when he looked at me and there was no pity there. He wanted me in exactly the same way I wanted him. My poor, darling

Nat. It was going to be hard for him too. He loved his mum and dad, he loved his sister and he loved me. All Nat ever wanted was for everyone to be happy.

*

For the next few months I went to work every day and took down dictation from Mr Dunlop, I went out with the other secretaries from the office every Friday lunchtime, I helped Susi with Jackie and Vivienne and the house. I went to club meetings every fortnight and typed up the minutes and filled in the membership cards and I saw Nat when I could. And despite the grey cloud on my blue horizon, I was happy. I liked to gossip with the office girls over egg and chips in the café on Old Street near the office. I enjoyed taking down Mr Dunlop's dictation as he recalled his life. I was beginning to doubt that someone who looked so staid and old-fashioned could have had such a racy past but if it was all fantasy that wasn't my business. I liked keeping the office in order and being told that I was the most efficient secretary he'd ever known. I loved listening to Jackie and Vivienne when they told me about their day, and helping Susi at home. I liked seeing my old friends at the club. I had a future to think about.

Nat said he could get round his mum; she had a mouth on her but she didn't mean half of what she said. I missed Brenda of course, I missed her a lot, but there was so much else to do.

Nat and I tried to find places where we could be alone. We sat on the sofa at my house, in his van or, as the weather got better, in the park. We kissed and touched and held each other and talked about what we had been doing since the last time we had been together, but we never talked about that evening at his house. One day, out of the blue, about three weeks after that night, he gave me an engagement ring, a thin platinum band with six little diamonds in a circle and I showed it to Julia and Mrs Bayley in the office and the two new girls we'd taken on, and Mr Dunlop, hearing the squeals, came out to see what was going on and congratulated me and said he'd like to meet the lucky man.

As the summer drew on and the days got longer, people stopped asking when we were going to have an engagement party and wanted to know about the wedding instead. In the office and at club meetings everyone felt they needed details. 'You haven't even fixed a date yet? Well, if you want it near to your birthday, you better get a move on. Nine months sounds like a long way away, but it'll fly by, you'll see.' Only the family didn't ask. Not Mrs Gold, not Brenda, not Susi.

Nat was working hard to build up the business so that he could put down a deposit on a little shop: a haberdashery shop, one that sold stockings and hosiery like on the stall, and all sorts of things. He drove miles every day, as far north as Watford and St Albans where there was good business in the weekly markets, much better than East Street in the Elephant and Castle where his dad still had the old stall.

I didn't know what Brenda was doing these days. I had another friend, Pauline. We'd known each other since the first time Brenda and I went to Maccabi when we were fifteen. Sometimes we met for a coffee before a club meeting in the Dorice next to the swimming pool on Finchley Road. It was good to have someone else to talk to. Pauline was full of good advice.

'Boys are always bad at making plans. The best way to get things done is to let them think they're the boss, but to start the ball rolling yourself. You should make an appointment to see the rabbi and put down a deposit on a hall. I've got two older sisters and one is engaged and one's married, so I know about these things.'

But I wasn't the sort to do something like that.

*

It was one of the last days of summer, coolish under a bright blue sky. Nat and I sat holding hands on a bench in Kenwood watching the girls play together on the steep slope of the grass. It was one of our rare Sunday afternoons together. I took a deep breath.

'Nat. Everyone keeps going on at me about how things get booked up in the spring. They say we might not be able to get a hall, let alone the shul.'

'Who's everyone?' he asked absent mindedly.

'Oh, you know, the girls at work and Pauline. Don't you want to talk about it?'

'Of course I do, sweetheart.' He put his arm round my shoulders. 'If you want to we will. Only just come here for a second because you're gorgeous and I want to eat you up.' He untied my pink, wool scarf and began to make nuzzling animal noises into my neck.

'Nat, stop it,' I giggled. 'Be serious for a second, we have to talk about this sometime.'

He looked at me and smiled, wetting his thumb on my tongue and rubbing it against my lips, taking the words away from me. I bit it gently.

'You are so delicious. Come here at once. Mmmm.' He made a deep growling noise like a dog and pulled me closer towards him and slipped his hand under my jacket.

'Nat, stop it, the girls will see us.'

'You spoil sport. Ah, well. If you don't want to kiss me, I'm going to play in the sand pit.' He jumped up and ran towards the girls, swaying his arm in front of him like a trunk and bellowing elephant noises, so that Jackie and Vivienne shrieked and laughed in fear and joy. The moment was gone and not for the first time. Nat made them turn and wave at me and I smiled at them all in spite of myself, because they were my girls and he was my Nat. I could see that one day he was going to be a wonderful father.

*

I wanted to be married. Not because of the dress and the bridesmaids and all the fancy schmancy business of weddings; the idea of walking up the aisle brought me out in goose bumps and so did the thought of Nat's mother standing under the chupa wearing her mink stole and a voluminous evening gown. I didn't give a fig for the lacy white dress and the bridesmaids and flowers or changing my name to Mrs Gold. I just wanted to be with Nat. I wanted my own little home and a kitchen with Nat sitting in it, while I did the cooking each evening after work, laughing and telling me stories about his day.

I wanted to be with him every morning and every night. I dreamt about us lying in a big bed together with a soft feather quilt and not ever having to stop at the moment we wanted each other most.

Pauline said that I should ring the rabbi and tell him we were planning to get married and then Nat would have to come with me, but it wasn't my nature to do that. When I asked him, he said it was a good idea and he knew it must be hard for me, but at the moment it was impossible for him to get away before nine o'clock in the evening what with the driving back from the markets and picking up new stock for the next day. He promised me that as soon as this busy time was over, we'd make proper plans. When I asked Susi, she said that when we fixed the date she could begin to make her plans; perhaps a little reception at Mrs Lechner's in Broadhurst Gardens would be nice, or a dinner in the synagogue hall.

'Things are a bit slow in the business at the moment, but there's enough to make you a nice wedding when the time comes. You needn't worry, we won't be asking the Golds for any help.'

Nat said that autumn was always a busy time for stockings, what with the weather getting colder, and then as soon as the days started to get shorter, people began to think about Christmas. Women wanted to look a bit more glamorous then and nylon stockings were the ideal present now that rationing was completely over and there was no problem with supplies. When December came, the markets never seemed to close even though it was dark at four o'clock and Nat's hands froze blue in those fingerless gloves. All the stalls stayed open until the customers went home and the inspectors turned a blind eye, because they were getting their bunce. I just had to be patient. It really wasn't very long to wait.

*

For Chanukkah, I sewed little felt dolls for the girls, one for every one of the eight nights and we lit the candles on the menorah together. Susi always made something special for them on the last night: potato latkes and apple fritters fried in oil and we played games.

'Shall we ask Nat to the party?' Jackie asked.

'It's not really a party and he's very busy at the moment, but I'll ask him. It's Sunday, so you never know.'

'Can Brenda come as well?'

'I haven't seen her for ever and ever,' Vivienne said.

'Yes, I know, it does seem like a long time. I'll ring up and ask her. Now come and sit on my lap and we'll make up a little story about your dollies.'

It was nine months since that evening at the Gold's and I'd seen Brenda maybe three or four times.

I was relieved it was her who picked up the phone, not her mother. 'God, it's freezing in this hall, hold on I need to put my coat on, no heating out here. I'd love to come, I haven't been to a Chanukkah party for years. Are you making latkes?' There was such pleasure to hear her sounding so exactly herself, as if nothing had changed. 'Nat's not here at the moment of course. But it should be fine, I'll drag him along if necessary. He's working every single day, it's about time he took at least one evening off.'

*

A week later, Brenda stood on our doorstep, rubbing her gloved hands together, the little astrakhan collar of her coat turned up. No Nat. He'd rung me in the week to say he would try his best to come, but he didn't know what time he'd finish working. I told him that he'd make himself ill if he carried on like this.

'Things get quieter in January, and then I'll be round so much, you'll get sick of the sight of me.'

Brenda kissed me on the cheek, and I laughed at the coldness of her skin.

'Oh, it's lovely and warm in here. Where are the girls? I bought these for them.' She held up two Fry's chocolate bars, red and white with the five different faces of the boys: desperation, pacification, expectation, acclamation, realisation. I was going through the same feelings myself.

After we'd put the girls to bed, Brenda asked if we could have a proper talk. Susi and Ziggy were downstairs, Susi in the kitchen, Ziggy listening to music. We went upstairs together, into my bedroom. I sat on the edge of the bed, hands in my lap and Brenda sat on the dressing table stool. It felt like nothing had changed since we were thirteen years old.

'Eva, you know me, two left feet.' She circled her hand in the air, trying to organise her words. 'I've been planning this all the way here, well ever since you invited me really. I knew what I wanted to say then, now it'll probably come out all wrong.' She closed her eyes and pressed her lips together. When she opened them, she looked straight at me. 'God, this is hard. I've never been any good at this kind of thing, but if one of us doesn't speak, we're going to go on like this for ever. Can we just write off most of 1953 and start again next year? I've been a bit of a cow, haven't I, not keeping in touch and being horrible to you when you phoned? I suppose I was jealous when I first heard that you'd got engaged to Nat. I didn't think that you were going to be first out of the two of us, and to my own brother when I haven't even got a boyfriend. It's not very nice of me, but there you go. And it felt like you'd been lying to me when I was supposed to be your best friend.'

'Oh Bren. I didn't mean it to be like that. I tried to tell you.'

'I can see that now. I know you hadn't been planning behind my back or anything. And then that evening round my house. I know I didn't stick up for you like I should have.' A faint note of self pity crept into her voice. 'The thing is, I've been piggy in the middle and it's a horrible place to be. I've been trying to stick up for you at home but Ma's Ma and I've got to get on with her too. And, you know Nat, anything for a quiet life. And I mean, it wasn't just my mother that evening, was it? I know she was awful, but Susi got on her high horse a bit didn't she?'

'Bren. Don't let's go into all that. Susi was just trying to speak up for me.'

'I know, I know, here I go again. I'm as bad as my mother sometimes. I just want us to start again, to be like we used to be. I've really missed you.' She made a silly doe eyed face at me, and waved a crooked finger in the air. 'Make up, make up, never do it again. If you do you'll get the cane. Remember when we used to do that?' I crooked my finger in hers.

'I'm sorry too. I didn't mean to keep secrets.' We sat for a while not saying anything and from the corner of my eye I could see Brenda make funny, familiar movements with her mouth like a horse chewing hay. She sighed and I knew this had been just the build up.

'Eva?' She started again after a while.

'Yes?' This would be what was really on her mind.

'Nat.'

'Nat?'

'You haven't seen him for a bit, have you? Has he talked to you?'

'What about?'

'About the wedding. Properly about the wedding. Has he told you what my mother's been going on about? He hasn't, has he? I knew it. God, that brother of mine, I could strangle him. He's such a coward sometimes. He hates trouble and he wants everyone to be happy so he does nothing. I knew it would have to be me who told you. It's always me.'

'Bren, what are you talking about?'

'Don't look so worried,' she said, catching sight of the expression on my face. 'It's nothing about your legs or being able to look after any grandchildren or any of that awful stuff Ma came out with. She's got a different bee in her bonnet now.' She made a noise through her mouth like a deflating balloon. 'It shouldn't be me who's telling you this, it's not fair, but someone's got to say it. Ma's got this thing about you only being half Jewish, well not Jewish at all if your mother wasn't.'

'I don't understand. Is she trying to find another reason to break us up?'

'Look, I don't really want to go into that evening again, but d'you remember when Pop asked Susi exactly how you were related because you look so different from her and Susi kind of avoided the question?'

'Your mother thinks I'm not Jewish because I'm fair? That's terrible, Brenda. That's the kind of thing the Nazis used to say about Jewish people.'

'I know, I tried talking to her. I've said to them, people can look different to their family, just because she's shorter than Susi and blonde doesn't mean anything. I mean, look at me. I'm the beanpole in a family of short, round people. I'm the tallest out of the four of us. What does that say about us?'

'What did she say?'

'You know Ma. It's like water off a duck's back. She keeps saying that your father might have married a shiksa, a lot of continentals married out, and if he did, they wouldn't marry you in the United Synagogue. She's just been going on and on and on at Nat to talk to you. And then she went on another tack and started asking about the refugees who came over during the war, how they proved their parents had been married by a rabbi. She rang the Chief Rabbi's Office and spoke to a man at the Beth Din who knows about these things. Eva don't look like that, it's not so bad as all that. It's good really. Susi was wrong when she thought that all the records had been destroyed. This man told Ma there's no problem because they kept the records on every Jewish family in Vienna, right back to the 1820s.'

'How can that be? Susi says they burned down every synagogue in Vienna.'

'It's true, but the records were kept in the... I can't say it in German but it means the Jewish Centre and the Nazis kept it open all through the war. It was never destroyed, they kept a few Jews alive to run it. All the Jewish records are still there.' She pulled a piece of paper out of her pocket with a name and address on it. Israelitische Kultusgemeinde, Seitenstettengasse, Wien. 'Ma says that you can write to them and they will provide you with the evidence you need. You'll be able to prove when your parents were born, where their wedding took place, the names of their parents, everything. That should be enough to keep even my mother quiet. I don't know why Nat hasn't told you this. I know she shouldn't interfere but any rabbi will need to know all this anyway before you can get married. There's nothing to be scared of, is there? Do you want me to do anything? Do you want me to tell Nat I've spoken to you?'

'No, don't say anything. I have to talk to Susi.'

Brenda was right, there was nothing to be afraid of. It was only a matter of asking someone to spell out the plain facts of my life: my mother's name, where she was born, where her parents were married, when she married my father, Susi's uncle. There was only the business of being nineteen years old, just a few months from twenty, and asking these ordinary questions for the first time.

But I could feel the new life I wanted so much begin to close in around me. I was that small child in the hospital in Norwich, wrapped round and round in a white plaster shroud.

*

Every night that week I tried to find a time to talk to Susi, but there was never the right moment. There had always been such a sturdy construction around the things that were unsaid, a closely woven lattice house with a door stitched in so tightly that I didn't know how to find my way in.

And these days, we hardly ever sat down together. When Ziggy came home he was tired and as soon as we'd finished our meal, he would go and read the paper or listen to music on the gramophone. Susi was always busy, rushing here and there. Sometimes she was sharp with the girls and happy to pass them over to me when I came in from work. There was whispering in the dining room and there were the piles of papers and the books from the business that Susi had to work on when the girls were asleep.

'Susi, can I ask you something?' It was the Saturday night before Christmas. I knew that Susi would soon need to get ready to go out. She ignored me for a moment, her mouth moving in the shape of numbers, her pen adding the columns of figures.

'What is it Eva, can it wait? Ziggy has let these get into such a muddle. It's so hard trying to be involved from a distance. If only I could get in every day, the books wouldn't look like this.'

'I have to ask you something.' My voice came out shaky and high and the sound of it made her look up immediately. She put her pen down and looked at me.

'What is it? Sit down.' I had thought about this

moment ever since Brenda's visit. Susi sat absolutely still and listened to me for a long time.

'And what does Nat say about this?' I knew she was stalling. 'Is he happy for his mother to go making havoc with other people's lives?'

'Susi, I have to be able to prove that my mother is Jewish. It's not just Nat's mother who needs to know is it? Other people will need to know too, before we can get married. She found out an address in Vienna. If we write to them, they will be able to give us all the evidence we need.' I unfolded the piece of paper Brenda had given me and handed it to her. Susi's whole body moved as if someone had struck her from behind.

'That woman.' She made a spitting sound of disgust.

'But it's good isn't it? That the records weren't destroyed.'

'And what did they keep them for, while they were busy burning everything else? So that if they'd succeeded, they could boast about how many of us they'd slaughtered?' She stood up awkwardly, knocking the lamp off the table. She put out her hand to right herself. 'I'm sorry, I must go and get ready now. We will talk later.' She walked past me unsteadily like someone on a rolling ship, ignoring the china fragments on the floor. At the door she turned and walked back to me. To my surprise, she kissed me on my forehead, stroking the hair from my face. 'You are a good girl. No one could ever ask for a better girl. We will talk later, I promise. Tomorrow perhaps, not now.' Her voice was tight and constrained and her dark eyes shone with pain.

That night I dreamed that I was in a huge

cavernous place, very cold. So cold that when I breathed, steam came out of my mouth and floated up towards the roof of the building which was made of glass and white metal like the inside of an enormous swimming pool. I was very small and alone, the only child in a great throng of stony faced adults: row after row of them, all holding on tightly to their battered, brown suitcases. The men had long woollen overcoats and Homburg hats and the women wore little felt berets and dark fitted suits with gored skirts. I knew that one of these grown ups was my mother and one was my father and it was a matter of life and death that I found them. I walked slowly past each one and as I went before them they smiled at me inviting me to stop. But their smiles were cold and unkind and I knew that if I let them they would take me away, up the spiral staircases which led right up into the roof and through the sky.

But I had to find my mother. She was somewhere in this building and finding her was the most important thing in the world. I began to run and run between the rows and although I had my dislocated hips, I was running as fast as the wind. I searched and searched but I couldn't find her face anywhere. I knew that if I shouted, 'Mummy, it's Eva here. Eva. Put up your hand and show me where you are,' she would come to me straight away. But however hard I tried, I could not make a sound come out of my mouth.

I woke up and lay in the dark, with the terrible feeling that there was something I had always known and never been able to recognise. I got out of bed and put on my dressing gown and slippers. It was freezing cold. I went into the girls' room and listened. The even, sweet rhythm of their breathing and the sight of their little bodies in their Ladybird pyjamas made me feel calmer.

The light from the electric cooker made a dull glow in the kitchen. Susi was already there pulling hard on a cigarette. The kitchen clock showed three o'clock.

'Couldn't sleep either?'

'No. Shall I make a cup of tea?' I put the kettle on the stove and fussed around with the cups and saucers and the milk for a few minutes, warming my hands on the teapot, waiting.

'You want me to talk to you I expect.' It was a voice I hadn't heard before: low and urgent but at the same time there was mockery in it, an edge that was almost sarcastic. I thought she might have been drinking. She gave another deep pull on her cigarette, stood up wrapping her dressing gown around her, and went to the cupboard for a half bottle of brandy. She poured herself a drink in one of the thick, pressed glass tumblers she kept for the National Health orange juice she gave to the girls, and ran her finger around the rim.

'When you were little, I loved you like you'd love a little sister. I believed I could take care of you, all by myself. You have to understand that I was young myself, a girl; I didn't understand the consequences of what I wanted to do. I didn't know how much more evil there was going to be in the world. I thought we would only be in England for a short time. Or that my parents would soon follow me. That they would bring your mother and the baby. I didn't imagine we'd never see them again.' She lit herself another cigarette and looked straight into my face in a way she had never done before.

'Eva. If at any time you'd asked me I would have told you. I wouldn't have lied. I know that now you think you need to know everything, every little detail, but believe me, there are things best not to know. I've learned that the hard way. What is the point of knowing what those terrible people did to our families? We can't change anything, we can't turn the clocks back. You'll probably look at me now and hate me. You'll think you'd have been better off if I'd left you in Vienna, but if I hadn't got you out of the country, you'd be dead now, just as dead as if you'd been Jewish. The Nazis felt the same about you as they did about me.'

Her voice was dry as dust and she drank down the cold tea in great gulps and poured herself another brandy with a shaking hand. 'I haven't been lying to you all these years. I did what everybody did who had to leave everything behind when they were hardly grown up themselves, I made a new life. I learned to forget about the old one, not forget exactly but not allow the memories to tear me apart day and night. Those years when you were in hospital were terrible for me; even in this country things happened to me I don't talk about. My life was very hard in those early years and I was still young myself, a lot younger than you are now. But even when you were in hospital I felt that I had you in my life. I never neglected you.

'I would have sent you back to Vienna after the war if there had been someone to look after you. I would have done it if I thought it was for the best, but we had no one left, just each other. And I had to think about your health. They told me at one point that you might not walk at all, that you would always have to have treatment for your hips.

'I made a home for you, just like I had promised. You and me and Ziggy, and then the girls. Whatever I did, I always tried my best. My father's last words to me were, be honest and carry with you what you learn. And after they took you away from me and put you in that terrible hospital, I learned that the most important thing was, I must never let you go to strangers.'

I listened and said nothing, only half understanding her words. It was as if she was talking to herself.

'We came out on the Kindertransport. The British Government were letting children in, Jewish children and those in danger from the Nazis. You were in danger because your father was a bastard and he was ashamed that he had a child like you. But your mother loved you and your grandmother and my mother and father, we all loved you. Your father had plans for you to be admitted to a children's clinic run by the Nazis. They had already begun the work to get rid of all the *behinderte* children – backward ones, *the useless eaters*. They called it treatment but children were dying there. Parents left their children in the clinics because they trusted what the doctors said and they never saw them again.

'We were lucky to get the permit to go out, a lot of children didn't. I was brave in those days, I didn't care. I told them in Vienna, I told them that we were cousins because that was the only way I could get you out of Vienna safely.' She showed me the piece of paper I had given her earlier, with the address. 'They kept the details of the children who came out on the Kindertransport in this building, the same place they kept the records of the births and deaths and marriages of all the Jews in Vienna, even while they were murdering them all. It didn't feel like a lie. You were my cousin, even closer, you were like the sister I never had. I put it on the document that you were the daughter of my mother's brother, my uncle Freddi Shapiro, because he didn't have any children, and they were too busy to check up on details like that. That's why you had his surname, my grandmother's name, on your registration card. My uncle had got out, he was already living in America before war broke out. He's still there, everybody's heard of him, even in England. He's the leader of the Freddy Sharp Band, that's what he changed his name to. I thought it was a godsend because I knew that even if you heard his music, you wouldn't recognise the name. They make records, radio shows, big time. He writes to me now and then. He knows you came with me, but not that I pretended he was your father. He's the only one left, he and my older cousin Lori who survived the camps and went to South Africa after the war. We write to each other and promise to visit some day, but we never do.

'I always thought that was when I would tell you all this, when uncle Freddi or Lori came to visit us, but they never have.' She stubbed out her cigarette in the ashtray and immediately lit a new one.

'Your mother was a lovely person, a sweet, good person. That's all I can say. She looked after me when I was a little girl, she was like a nanny and a maid to our family and a good friend to my mother, we all loved her. Your grandmother Hanna too, she worked for my grandmother, she knew our whole family, she was very good to us. She was the one who saved the furniture from Vienna we have here in the house, the clock and the paintings, the cabinet, everything. We cheated the Nazis and took some things to her barn. May God rest her dear soul, she risked her own life more than once.

'Your father was not a good man. I think he must have loved you and your mother once, but the Nazis turned him into an evil person and there is nothing good I can tell you about him. He knew a man, a schoolteacher or something, and they tried to persuade your mother to let them keep you in the clinic, to make you better so they said, but your mother knew that he just wanted to get rid of you. She wasn't fooled by him. She saw what they had written on the form, that you'd never be able to learn anything and you'd be a burden to society, some lies like that, and she wouldn't let you go. She made me promise that if I could find a way to get out, I would take you with me.

'When we left Vienna, it never occurred to me that it would be for ever and ever. I thought my parents would follow me to England, God knows I tried to get them here, but I was just a girl myself. Nobody understood how terrible it was going to be.' She put both hands up over her mouth and sat very still, but there were no tears. 'Your mother was killed in the bombings in 1945 just two weeks before the end of the war. I had a letter from your grandmother in Mitteldorf. She told me that your mother was in Vienna in an underground shelter and the American bombers came over the city. Your grandmother was already an old woman, she couldn't take care of you.

'My parents died – my mother and father of blessed memory, my aunt and uncle, my cousin Klara. All murdered in the camps. And Ziggy's family too: parents, his brother and sister, all of them died. For years after I found out about what had happened to them, until the girls were born, I would wake up in the middle of the night, and the feeling inside me was indescribable, the terrible empty pain of loneliness, even though I had Ziggy. I would climb the stairs into your little room in Compayne Gardens and look at you sleeping and it would comfort me. You were a part of me from Vienna, even though you couldn't remember it, you were the only person in the world who had known me when I was happy.

'When we got on the train to come to England, the last words your mother said to me were, "I hope she'll be brought up like you" and I thought that meant that she wanted you to be brought up as if you were Jewish. If there is a God up there, He must think of you as Jewish otherwise why would we be the ones to live when every one else died? People like the Golds, what do they know? People who can say those kind of things to your face, they're not good people. You are as Jewish as they are. You have been brought up in the religion, you go to shul as much as they do, more. Your uncle Ziggy is a religious person, he is a true believer. So the food we eat isn't always kosher, so what? I can tell you, Hitler didn't care who ate treyf and who didn't when he sent the Jews to the camps.'

Her face took on that hollow, closed-in look I had seen sometimes over the years, when she lit the Sabbath candles and the first time she saw the photograph of her family when it came in the parcel from Vienna. I wanted to put my arms around her and kiss her like I did with Vivienne when she was unhappy or troubled. I wanted to tell her that I understood.

'To go behind our backs like that and ask a rabbi. What kind of people do a thing like that? Without even talking to us.'

We sat together in silence for a long time. Her shoulders began to shake silently and I held her hand. Soon the morning would begin and there would be the noise of Ziggy in the bathroom having his shave and the children squabbling and running downstairs.

I understood it all, I didn't need telling a second time. I was not Jewish, not even half Jewish. I was not Susi's cousin. Her uncle, her mother's brother, the man I had thought was my father was still alive and living in America. A famous man, even I had heard of the Freddy Sharp Dance Band, but he was not my father; he was no relation at all. My father was a Nazi. My mother had been a maid to Susi's family. The words ran round and round in my head, taking all speech from me.

After a while Susi stood up. Her face was pale and drawn. 'I'm going to give you something now. Perhaps I should have given it to you a long time ago, spoken to you about your own family, not allowed you to forget. I don't know any more. I always tried to do the right thing by you.' She came back carrying an old shoe box, the brown cardboard softened with age. I lifted the lid. Inside there was a threadbare, knitted doll with a red dress and a blue hat, a little pale blue cardigan with brown stripes and one remaining flower shaped button, a pack of letters, maybe ten or twelve of them, a thin, gold crucifix wrapped in yellowing tissue paper and a studio portrait. There were three people in the photograph. The woman held a little girl about two years old on her knees, and close by her side stood a round faced child about four years old, her fair, corkscrew curls tied down with a ribbon: me.

'Who is this?' I whispered, pointing to the child in a little corduroy pinafore dress, straight dark hair in a bob and a fringe down to her eyes.

'It's your sister, Gertrude.'

'I have a sister?' I could hardly breathe. 'Where is she now?'

'I never heard anything of her after the war. I always thought she must have died in the bombing with your mother.'

'Why don't you know? Why didn't you bring her to England with me?' Susi looked up at me, startled. I could see her struggling to find the right words.

'You have to understand that l had to accept that there were some things I would never know for sure. It wasn't that I didn't care, but there was no one left to ask. Both our mothers died in the war. Your grandmother died a few years later.' Her voice drifted away. 'She was a sweet baby, Gertrude. I used to look after her sometimes, I fed her and washed her. I helped your mother when things got so difficult. But there was no question of me bringing her here.'

Dregs of grey, winter light began to seep into the kitchen. I stood up to leave and Susi caught my hand as I passed her. 'Don't go into work today. Go back to bed for a little while, you look so pale.'

'No, I'm okay. I'd rather carry on as usual.' I took the box upstairs and put it, unopened, on the shelf in my wardrobe. I was outside myself, moving automatically. I washed and dressed my own body as if I was getting one of the girls ready for school and went downstairs again, dressed in the clothes I wore for work. In the kitchen, Susi had toasted a roll for me and spread it with butter and apricot jam, but I couldn't swallow. I drank a few mouthfuls of strong coffee. Susi, usually so busy and distracted, did not take her eyes off me.

I don't know how I got to work. I remember that there was ice on the ground and I had to be careful that I didn't fall. I waited a long time at the freezing bus-stop at Moorgate and realised that I had left my gloves at home. At work I tried to carry on as usual, but it was impossible to concentrate. Mr Dunlop sent me home before lunch.

'Go home dear, you look terrible. Just take a couple of Aspros and go to bed. Let's hope it's not the flu.' At Old Street roundabout, I found a phone box and pulled out the S-Z telephone directory from the rack. There was nothing there. I put it back and took out the A-K and found what I wanted under B – The Board of Jewish Deputies. Woburn House, Woburn Place, WC1. I took the Northern Line from Old Street Station to King's Cross and changed to the Piccadilly Line. At Russell Square I stopped at a café and bought a cup of tea and a currant bun. The waitress at the counter looked at me with the usual expression, a smile that was three quarters pity.

'Can you manage that alright love?'

'Thank you, I'm fine.' I picked up the tray and walked unevenly to a seat by the steamed up window, my tea half spilt into the saucer. I took the packet of Rothmans out of my bag, the first cigarettes I had ever bought. I peeled back the silver wrapper and tried to shake a cigarette out of the packet imitating Julia in the office. I breathed it in and the hot bitter taste made no difference to me. I felt removed from my body, as if my hands, my face, my heart were not part of me at all; as if I could press this cigarette into my palm and not feel a thing.

The present, the future, my life with Nat, was all I could concentrate on.

I had been brought up as a Jew: I believed in God and Moses and Friday night dinners; in Yom Kippur and Rosh Hashanah and Seder Nights; in Nat and Brenda, the Maccabi Club; in all of Susi's and Ziggy's friends who had managed to escape the Nazis, but I didn't have one real relative in the whole world who was Jewish. Even in my numb state, I knew what a difference this made.

*

Woburn House was an enormous building, and inside it was green paint and dark wood, like a hospital. The man behind the desk looked over his glasses at me as he tried to make some sense of my stammering words.

'So. You want to know whether you can be considered Jewish? We will have to open up a Jewish Status File on you, but we don't do that here. You will need to see someone at the Beth Din.' He looked at my anxious, uncomprehending face. 'Don't worry, you don't have far to go. It's on the floor above. First floor.' He pointed along the corridor. There was a wide staircase, each turn making a different floor and in the centre, a lift with a folding metal door. 'Tell them

I sent you up and take the lift. You look exhausted.'

The man upstairs had the same short grey beard and round, black skullcap perched high on his head and the same unyielding expression, not hostile exactly but uncompromising and vaguely distracted. He took out a form and began to write with a scratchy, black pen. His questions followed no particular order and he wrote and frowned, hardly looking at me at all.

'A refugee? When did you arrive in this country? You should really have brought a member of your family. You will need to bring someone with you when you come back; they should bring all their documents along. Nineteen years old and you want to get married? And the young man's parents, they are members of the United Synagogue? Cricklewood Synagogue and married in Great Garden Synagogue in 1929, but you don't know the exact date? And the people who brought you up were married in West Hampstead Synagogue. Well, that seems in order but you will also have to bring their Ketuba with you when you come back. Now let me go through your situation carefully. It is most unusual, but the war made extraordinary things happen.

You came over on the children's transport from Vienna but you have only just learned that your real parents were not Jewish. But in this country you were brought up by a Jewish family, is that right?'

I nodded.

'Well, if you have been brought up in the orthodox tradition, there shouldn't be a problem. When were you adopted?'

'I'm not adopted exactly, I don't think so anyway. I came over with a family friend who is twelve years older than me. When we left my mother told her that she wanted me to be brought up as Jewish.' Susi's words of last night were like a play script in my brain. 'Susi and Zygmund Friedmann became my legal guardians when I was twelve. I was in hospital for a long time before that. We have a certificate signed by Lord Gorrell.' He looked up suddenly.

'What exactly is the matter with you?'

'I beg your pardon?'

'Is it polio or an inherited condition?'

'Would that make a difference?'

'No, of course not. I just wondered that's all.'

'I was born with congenital dislocated hips.'

'Oh, I see. Is it painful?'

'No, it isn't.'

He shrugged his shoulders. 'Ah, well, let's get on. I need to ask about your upbringing.' He fired a list of questions at me. Do you believe in God? Did you go to Hebrew classes? What do you know about the Jewish festivals? He nodded at each of my answers and to my replies about Jewish Law. Your guardians are members of the United Synagogue in West Hampstead and the Burial Society? Good, that seems fine. And they keep a fully kosher home? I shook my head. They do not work on the Sabbath? They do not drive? You go to synagogue with them every Sabbath and for all the festivals?

Of course Susi and Ziggy did none of these things, but neither did anyone else: not Nat nor Brenda, not Pauline, no one from the club nor any of Susi's friends. Of course there were people who went to synagogue every week, but not the people we knew. We went for bar mitzvahs and weddings and most people dressed up three times a year to go to synagogue for the High Holy Days. Some of them kept kosher at home but ate out in restaurants. Everyone who had a shop or worked in the market had to work on a Saturday, at least in the mornings, and the boys and their dads skipped off to see Spurs play whenever they could. And all of them called themselves Jewish. The man sighed deeply and put his pen down on the desk.

'Look, I'll be honest with you, from what you've told me – the age you came to live with your guardians, the way you have been brought up, we could not certify your Jewish Status and without the certification of the Beth Din you will not be able to marry in an orthodox synagogue. You would have to undergo a lengthy conversion procedure and that won't be easy, it would take three years, minimum. You will need to prove a total commitment to living a full, orthodox Jewish life and from what you tell me that will mean many changes to the way you live now. Changes in the home, and all of this would have to be supervised by the Dayanim. And even if you do undergo conversion, I'm not sure if your fiancé's parents would ever accept you as fully Jewish. There is a lot of prejudice against conversion. And without a Jewish mother... There are people who find that very hard to accept.'

'But how can that be right? I was brought up as Jewish. I am Jewish, I believe in God.'

For the first time, his tone softened. 'I know. I can imagine how it feels from your point of view and I'm sorry for you, my dear. But I don't make the rules. Halachic Law was laid down a long time ago, it's not subject to fashion. Go away and discuss it with your family and with your fiancé. And come back and see me with them.'

I lay in bed that night, thinking about the God I had believed in ever since I came to live with Susi and Uncle Ziggy. A man, definitely a man, stern but kind with a white beard. When I first learned about being Jewish, it comforted me to know that there was someone up in heaven, much bigger than me. Someone who knew where I was and what I was feeling so that I would not be scared and alone. He was there to show us why we were Jewish, the chosen people. We had to carry on the tradition laid down by our forefathers, by Abraham, Isaac and Jacob. We had to keep the traditions alive so that we could pass them on to our children and our children's children.

*

Susi was no more inclined to talk about the past than she'd been for the last fifteen years but she watched me in a new way. Ziggy too. Whenever I was at home, I could feel her eyes follow me around the room. She prepared little treats for me, things she knew I liked. Stuffed peppers, savoury noodles, red cabbage, apple cakes, her own favourites when she was young. For the first time in years, she wiped down the sewing machine in the little room upstairs and decided she wanted to make me something new to wear. We went together to John Barnes to buy the material and she cut the pattern and sewed it all in an afternoon. Not a pleated skirt or an A-line dress but a pair of slacks made of fine corduroy, the colour of milky coffee. They lay flat on my stomach with a concealed side zip, tapering in at the ankles. At the final fitting Susi patted me on the hips, smoothing them into place. She took the pins from her mouth and stood back.

'Very good. It's a modern look. Really, it suits you. And here, a little something from me to go with it.' She handed me a sweater in a bag from D.H. Evans, a cardigan really, chocolate brown with three quarter sleeves and tiny buttons down the front. 'That suits you darling, it brings out your colour. I wish you well to wear it.'

I saved it for Nat on Christmas Day. Christmas wasn't anything special in our house. Ziggy hated it, he wouldn't have a tree in the house, or decorations. 'We don't need them,' he explained to the children. 'We have enough festivals of our own. It's just another day, like a Sunday when we're all home together.' But still, he liked his own traditions. He always prepared a big breakfast for us; he said they called it 'brunch' in America, and there was the annual party at the Kuttners' in Broadhurst Gardens.

This year I came down later than usual to the sound of Beethoven's *Pastorale* symphony which was Ziggy's favourite morning music. There were the delicious smells of coffee and chocolate and Jackie stood at the table, whipping the cream with immense concentration and Vivienne was crying because she wasn't allowed to help. The table was laid with warm brioche, eggs and smoked fish and a porcelain bowl of tangerines. Susi sat with her elbow on the kitchen table, ignoring Vivienne's wails, her thumb and fingers making an arch on her forehead. She looked at me blowing on my coffee, eating nothing and she looked at Ziggy.

At four o'clock when it was already beginning to get dark, I went upstairs. I'd longed to be on my own all day, but Susi was trying so hard and there were the girls who needed my attention and wanted me to play.

I stood in front of the long mirror in my bra and knickers and looked at my body, trying to see myself as Nat saw me. I put on my new trousers, brushed my hair and tied it back in a loose pony tail. The cardigan felt soft against my skin. I undid the first few buttons, looking at myself doing it, and smoothed the fine wool down over my breast, rubbing my nipple softly, thinking of Nat. A little hollow tapping at the door made me jump back into myself.

'Eva my dear, do you have a moment?' Ziggy stood awkwardly at the door, immaculate as ever, even in his black twill trousers and checked shirt, his moustache newly clipped, neat and narrow. 'Ah, your new outfit, turn around and let me see. It suits you very well. You should wear clothes like that more often. Young lady style. I have a little something for you Eva. I found it in a shop and it reminded me of something my sister Herta wore, may her dear soul rest in peace, when she was about the same age as you.' He handed me a little black velvet box and I looked up at him in surprise. 'Open it. See if you like it.' It was a necklace, about a dozen small pearls, evenly spaced on a fine, gold chain. Tears sprang to my eyes.

'Thank you, it's beautiful.'

Ziggy looked at me sadly in his sweet, undemonstrative way. I took a step towards him and reached up to kiss him, smelling the familiar cologne. Briefly, his arm went round my shoulders. 'I want you to know that there has not been one moment when it has not been a pleasure and an honour to have you with us inside our home. You made us a family. You understand?' His voice broke as he spoke.

After they had all gone to the Kuttners' party, I went downstairs and put Frank Sinatra on the record player. Ziggy teased me about my low taste in music, but Nat and I loved Frankie, he was our singer. *You'd Be So Nice To Come Home To,* that was our song. It would be so good to have Nat come through the door every evening; to sit with him in front of the fire on winter nights; to walk in the park when the evenings were still warm. I believed that love would carry us through the horrible time I was having now. I knew I had to tell Nat, I had to tell him everything that I had learned in the past few days, but we would find a way to get through it. It would be hard to wait to get married, but I was only nineteen; a few years were nothing when we had our whole lives in front of us. I would convert, I wanted to. Whatever they said in the Beth Din, I knew that in my heart I was Jewish. I believed in God; that must be enough. I believed more than Nat or Brenda, certainly more than Susi. I didn't care how much work it was, or how long it took. Maybe we could marry in the Liberal Synagogue where it wasn't so difficult, or in the one in Belsize Park where so many of Susi's refugee friends belonged. Love would carry us through this, through everything, because Nat had always loved me for what I was – all of me, without criticism. He would protect me against the things stupid people said to me. He would always be on my side.

When I first began to confide in Nat about my childhood, the childhood in Norwich, the one I remembered, he promised me I would never be lonely again. No one would leave me outside, frightened and cold, unable to tell anyone how I felt. He would love me and take care of me and always make me smile. And I believed him; I trusted him with my whole heart.

*

Nat sat at the kitchen table and listened silently to my long story. I didn't tell him that my mother had been a servant to Susi's family or that my father loved the Nazis but I told him all the rest. Everything. I told him what Susi had said about how my life was in danger and how we'd left the country and everything that the man at the Beth Din had told me. Then I stopped talking and looked at him, at the face that I loved so much.

'Nat?' He looked up at me. I tried to hold his gaze but he looked down at his hands, red and raw from the markets.

'My mother won't like it.'

'I know.'

'I mean she'll really hate it. And my father.'

'I know, but you can explain it all to her. We can make it alright. I'll convert, it's just a formality. I'll be twenty-one or two, you'll be twenty-five, that's still a good age to get married.' He began compulsively gnawing at the skin at the side of his thumb.

'They had a friend in the East End whose son married a shiksa. They sat shiva for him, said the prayers as if he was dead and never spoke to him again. Never even saw his kids.'

'Nat, I'm not a shiksa. I know as much about

268

being Jewish as you do. I went to Hebrew classes.'

'They won't see it that way. I know they won't. It'll be the final nail in the coffin.'

'But it's not like I don't know anything about being Jewish. I can go to shul more often. I'll talk to Susi, we can start to keep kosher properly, I'm sure she'll understand. We already say Kiddush on Fridays and Ziggy would like to be more religious at home, I know he would.'

'It's not the same though is it? Not the same as being born Jewish?'

We sat in silence, my heart banging hard in my chest. Nat chewed and chewed at his nail.

'Nat, do you love me?' He looked up at me then.

'Why are you asking me that? You know I do.'

I moved round the table and sat on his lap. He put his arm round me and touched my cheek. I kissed him, biting his lip, trying to draw him towards me. I undid the buttons on his shirt and opened my cardigan so we were skin against skin. I put my hand on him and felt him get bigger. We were alone, completely alone, in the house and I wanted to be part of him; I wanted him to be part of me.

'Eva, sweetheart. Don't.' He pulled away from me, smoothing down his hair in a gesture I knew so well and began to do up the buttons on his shirt. Desperately, I kissed his mouth, his neck, his ear, but he put his hands on my shoulders and moved me away from him.

'What's the matter?'

'Nothing. I'm sorry, I can't think straight. Maybe it's better if I just go.'

Embarrassed, humiliated, I tried to make myself

tidy.

'Nat?' I asked in a last, pathetic gesture. 'It'll be alright, won't it? You'll talk to your parents so that they understand what we're going to do, and come back and talk to me?'

He looked at me with his sweet face and mouth soft like a girl's and I knew. I knew that I had lost him as surely as if he'd recited it to me like a nursery rhyme. Even with his jokes and songs and funny voices, Nat was no actor.

I shut the door behind him, feeling the last gesture of his fingers on my face, and I threw up in the downstairs cloakroom with the sound of his footsteps on the path behind me. My heart, stomach, guts heaved into that cold, white bowl.

In my room I looked once more at my face in the mirror with the words of a different song spinning round and round and round in my head. Nat was a part of me now and there was nothing I could do about it. I would give up anything to keep him with me. Deep inside I knew that I wasn't going to win this fight. But there he was, locked inside me; I'd got him under my skin.

REBECCA

London

2000

I always knew that grandma Susi hadn't been born in England. You could hear it in her accent and see it in the way she dressed; she was much smarter than any of my friend's grandmothers. You'd never see grandma in a track suit and trainers, however comfortable they were on her aching feet. She used to say that she'd been wearing high heels for so long that her feet had become shaped that way; like a Barbie doll's, permanently tippy-toed.

She had come to this country as a refugee and most of her friends were refugees too. She was born in Vienna, and she had to leave when Austria let the Nazis into the country. We studied that period in school: all about the Holocaust and the concentration camps, but I'd never talked to grandma about it. You couldn't ask her questions like that.

When I was little, I used to spend a lot of time round at grandma's and grandpa's house. Mum and I lived in South London in a council flat and they lived in a huge house in West Hampstead but I used to go there a lot in the school holidays. I liked it round there; it was always warm and comfortable and there was so much space. I could do whatever I liked. Mum said they were a lot easier on me than they were on her when she was a little girl. Grandma Susi and I did things together: cooking and sewing, stuff like that. Grandma was brilliant at sewing. She made perfect, tiny little clothes for my dolls, and party dresses for me, not that I went to a lot of parties. She taught me how to knit and do embroidery. Once I asked her if she could make me an Austrian blouse with lace on it and a full skirt with straps like I'd seen in *Heidi* on the television, and grandma said she'd make me anything

I liked, but not that.

Most weeks, when I was in the infants, grandpa used to come and pick me up after school on Friday and sometimes mum would come too. I loved Friday nights. Auntie Eva would be there and grandma and grandpa; we'd eat lovely food, chicken soup and roast dinner and apple pie or fruit salad and sometimes I'd even stay the night.

Dad didn't come with us. Grandma didn't like my dad at all; she thought he wasn't good enough. He was a plumber and he wasn't Jewish so that was two counts against him. And we lived in a council flat in Lambeth so that was three: south of the river was another country to grandma. Mum thought she was a snob about some things, but I'm not sure she was entirely wrong about my dad because he left when I was seven years old and I've only seen him eight times since then.

After mum and grandma stopped talking to each other there was a long time when I didn't go to their house. Mum says it goes right back to when she was a teenager. Jackie was the older sister and did everything right and mum did everything wrong. She says grandma was forever saying, 'Vivienne, if you want to do something properly, look at how your sister Jacqueline does it.' I could see what mum meant. Grandma Susi often made hurtful remarks, dressed up to sound like compliments.

'Are they new trousers darling? You look lovely in them, but I wouldn't wear trousers with pockets like that if I were you. Plain trousers are more flattering to a behind like yours.' Or 'She was bright your mother. She could have gone to the best university in the country, she had chances I never had, that's for sure. All she had to do was to work hard, but she could never stick at anything.' But I loved her. I suppose everyone loves their grandparents, just like everyone loves their mother.

Auntie Eva once told me that grandma had so much energy that she used up all the oxygen in the house and there wasn't enough left for my poor mother. She said that when mum was little, she was full of determination, full of life; she would concentrate for hours to get things perfect. I can remember mum like that: great gushes of love and energy, big, big tempers when she got angry. And then it just seemed to get sucked out of her.

When she first got ill, everyone thought it was a nervous breakdown because she'd split up with dad and he'd moved to Devon to live with his new girlfriend. One minute he was there and, to me at least, everything seemed fine, and the next minute he practically vanished from our lives. That was the beginning of the time when mum wasn't well and felt tired all the time, sometimes so tired that she could hardly move. She started to see a therapist, at first once a week, then twice, then nearly every day. The therapist said it was grandma who made my mum so ill, because grandma was such a strong person and she was always judging mum. The therapist said that the only way mum would get better would be to stop seeing grandma completely, at least for a time.

For a little while, mum carried on seeing grandpa Ziggy on his own, but he said this hurt grandma even more, so that stopped too. And of course, auntie Jackie took their side and would ring up and make more arguments. The therapist also told mum that it was best for her to keep busy, so she carried on working until she got so ill, she couldn't get out of bed at all.

After this, she saw a doctor at the hospital and he did lots of blood tests and said that her immune system was shot to pieces. She had to rest, conserve her energy, otherwise she'd never get better. So mum had to close down her business and I don't really know how we managed for money. She works now, when she's well enough. She makes things to sell in her friend's shop in Gabriel's Wharf on the South Bank: painted mirrors and frames and things made out of felt, scarves and bags, hats, baby slippers. She does all the embroidery herself. Mum has a lot more good days now, except sometimes things throw her off balance – like if she gets an infection, or something terrible happens, like a death in the family.

Mum never knew that I carried on seeing grandma in the years when they weren't talking to each other. I don't think she did, anyway. When she was too ill to look after me, she used to let me stay at auntie Eva's for a few nights at the weekends or in the holidays. I didn't like leaving her on her own, but I loved going out in auntie Eva's brand new red car. She'd take me to the shopping centre at Brent Cross and there would be this little ritual. After we'd been there about half an hour, auntie Eva would say, 'You've been such a good girl, would you like to have an ice cream?' And we'd go to the café in John Lewis and surprise, surprise, who would be in there but grandma Susi with a cup of coffee and a slice of walnut cake. They didn't have to tell me not to say anything to mum about it, I understood exactly what was going on.

Mum and grandma started talking again after grandpa went into hospital for the last time. When he died, grandma wasn't well for a long time and mum and auntie Eva looked after her together. They'd been married fifty-one years and they'd never had an argument.

'You know, darling,' grandma said to me one day. 'Every day my heart hurts. Every day when I think about him, that's how it feels. A great pain in my heart.' He was eighty-two when he died and they had hardly ever spent one night apart. Grandma kept the big house on for a few more years and sold it when I was thirteen. She'd wanted auntie Eva to move back into the big house with her, but auntie Eva didn't want to leave her own flat.

She wasn't the same after she moved, everyone said so, even auntie Eva and she saw more of grandma than any of us. Her doctor said she had had a 'mini-stroke' and we should expect more of them. Sometimes they were so small that she didn't even know that they'd happened, but they made her disorientated, not her old self. She'd start a sentence and not be able to finish it, or she'd get angry about something and wouldn't be able to explain why. She'd always been a bit bossy, but sometimes there was nothing you could do to make her happy. Other times though, I'd go round and she'd be all chatty and then, if I was lucky, she would have forgotten about the silence she'd always imposed on herself, and tell me stories I'd never heard before.

In November, I went to see grandma to give her a birthday present. I never knew what to buy her. She was fussy and she had very particular tastes, not like auntie Eva, who liked anything you gave her. I'd bought her a silver frame with a photo of myself in it. It was taken in the summer and for once, I was wearing a skirt, so I knew she'd like it. When I arrived, she was sitting on a chair with curved wooden arms that she'd brought with her. She'd made a little corner arrangement like in the old house: a pair of small armchairs, a round table with a fringed tablecloth, a standard lamp with a big shade. The hairdresser had been in the morning so her silver grey hair was perfectly swept back from her face and her nails were immaculately varnished. She had on one of her knitted suits, a navy blue dress with thin white stripes at the top and a matching jacket with gold buttons. But for once, she didn't have any make up on, and her face looked pale and vulnerable.

'You're a lovely girl you know,' she said when she had opened her present. 'Lovely little figure as well, not that I ever get to see much of it. I don't know why you want to cover yourself up like that.' She lifted up the frayed hem of my trousers. 'Look at those gorgeous legs, you should be showing them off. And the shoes.' She shook her head from side to side and rolled her eyes around at the sight of my grubby trainers and we both laughed. 'A woman is not the same as a man. I don't know why you want to dress like one.' She smiled at me. 'You know something? You don't look so different from me when I was your age. I had lovely dark hair like yours, but I wasn't so tall. You want to see a picture of me? Go and look in my wardrobe, the second drawer. You'll see a cardboard box in there. Bring it here and I'll show you something.'

I almost ran into her bedroom, terrified that she'd change her mind, but when I came back she was still smiling. She took the box and put it on the coffee table in front of her. It seemed to be full of bits and pieces: photographs, cards, old envelopes and bits cut out of magazines.

'Look at me here, I was more or less the same age as you are now. If you take away the clothes and the hairstyle, we don't look so different.' She handed me a black and white picture in a faded card frame from a photographer's studio. 'That was the last picture I had taken before I left. And this is the last one I have of my parents. They sent it to me from Vienna. You can't see from this how pretty my mother was. She was always so beautifully dressed, my father too. But they both look so tired here, you can see it in their eyes. Look at what they wrote on the card. In English it means, "We are sending you this picture to keep us in your heart until we see our precious girl again." '

I handed the photograph back and said nothing. I felt that if I sat very still and quiet, she would keep talking.

'I can't believe it when I look at you now. Your age, just a girl. What did I know? And not just myself to think about. I had Eva too. I tricked them into believing that she had had a fall on the ship and there was nothing really wrong with her legs. I knew she would have to pass a medical and I was terrified they would send us both back if they knew she had always been this way.

'I'd never lied before, only that once in the hotel so that I could get the permit for us to leave on the

Kindertransport. My mother always taught me that if I lied I would be found out somehow. In those days, parents were a lot stricter with children, they knew it was their duty to teach you right from wrong. If they didn't who would? But they gave me so much love. Whoever else loves you in your life, you can never replace the love of your mother and father.'

I listened very carefully; I didn't want to lose one bit of these stories.

'You know what I remember most from those first years in England? Fear. Fear of what they were doing to little Eva in that horrible place. Fear of what was happening to my parents. Fear for myself. I knew Eva was scared and lonely in that hospital but I could do nothing. I couldn't even help myself.

'I was too old to be taken in by a family and too young to look after myself. I lost all my education – it was stolen from me. I would have liked to have been a teacher, a teacher of English Literature, but they said, "You are past the school leaving age and there is no guarantor for you." The refugee committee found me a job instead and then they forgot all about me. They sent me to a family in Bayswater, non-Jewish, middle class people. I was supposed to teach their daughter French and German and do a little bit of help in the house and in return, they would let me go to evening classes. That was the agreement.

'The woman of the house, Mrs Parker, she was hardly ever at home, I don't know what she did with herself all day long. The husband was in the house, he was supposed to be sick. Every week my father wrote to me from Vienna. "You must be grateful that these good people have taken you in," but she wasn't a nice person. She was the jealous type. She didn't want me to have the lovely clothes my mother had made for me before I left. She said, "You won't need those foreign clothes, there'll be no money to clean them anyway. I'll give you clothes to work in, that's all you need here. You can keep a skirt and jumper." I didn't see my beautiful clothes again, not for a long time after. She wanted me to alter them so they'd fit her daughter but that was one thing I refused to do.

'I was like a servant in that house. They wanted someone grateful to have a roof over their head but they got me instead. I could see right through them. They put on those English airs and graces, the worst kind of snobs. And their house was filthy, not like houses from home. You wouldn't believe the state of their beds or the bathroom. Nobody cleaned them until I came.

'I was supposed to look after the husband in the day, when she was out, take him up some lunch and tea in the afternoon. That was what they told me before I came. But I had the house to clean and the washing and the ironing and I had to take their little brat to school. So spoilt, she never did anything for herself. And I don't know what happened to teaching her French. She didn't want to learn a thing.

'And him, Mr Parker, he was disgusting. I had to empty his bed pan morning and night when I knew he was quite capable of getting out of bed on his own. "Be a bit more friendly," he said. "Call me Robert." He told me to sit down on the bed and keep him company while he drank his tea. The first time I did what he asked, I didn't realise what he was up to. I sat on the edge of the bed as far away as I could and still he tried to put his hands all over me. After that I wouldn't go near him, but sometimes he'd get out of bed and catch me when I wasn't looking. He'd be at the top of the stairs and try to pin me against the wall. I never knew where he'd be waiting for me, trying to interfere with me. I was only sixteen years old. Sixteen and so innocent.

'I had one saviour, the librarian, Miss Beaton. If I had half an hour off, I'd run to the lending library. She saved books for me every week and she helped me in what I should read: Jane Austen, Charles Dickens, Charlotte Brontë, Thomas Hardy, Arnold Bennett. English Literature, it's a wonderful thing. I buried myself in those stories and I learned to love the English language. Miss Beaton and those books were the one good thing in my life.

'Apart from that, I never told my parents what my life was like. In all the letters I wrote, I never said a word. I couldn't, they had so much trouble themselves. I had to pretend that everything was fine, that I was carrying on with my education, the family was good to me, the child was a pleasure. Every week when I wrote to them I would say what a lovely house it was, how nice to be able to take a walk in Hyde Park on my days off. Right up to the war, I wrote to my parents every week and I had a letter back from each of them. Those letters were the most important thing in my life.'

Grandma took a stack of letters out of the box and ran her fingers across the fragile, tissue paper envelopes with elaborate, old fashioned handwriting in faded black ink.

'As the war came nearer, every letter they sent

me was more desperate than the last. Heartbreaking. Hitler's walls were closing in on them and all the Jewish families still there were desperate to leave Vienna. I thought that if I stayed with the Parkers and didn't tell anyone what was going on, they might find someone who would act as guarantor for my parents. The British government would let you in if you were prepared to do the work the English didn't want to do: servants, cooks, gardeners, that kind of thing. That bastard, Mr Parker. He used to pat the bed and say to me, "You come here and be a good girl to a sick man and I'll write an affidavit for your parents." But I wasn't as stupid as he thought. A man who would try to do that to a girl. You could never trust him to keep his word.

'When Mrs Parker had her friends to tea, they would talk about their women's troubles and all their ailments as if they were at death's door. This private doctor in Harley Street was wonderful, that private doctor was the best in the country and it gave me an idea. In the library, I asked Miss Beaton where you could find out about these doctors and she gave me a book called *Who's Who*. It has the names of all the bigwigs in England. You can find out who the famous doctors are and just at random, I chose one with the most English sounding name, Mr Forbes-Watton, something like that and I made an appointment to see him. I was shaking like a leaf when I got there. His secretary showed me in. He said, "Sit down Miss Rosen and tell me what is the matter." So straight away I said, "I am sorry Sir, but I have come here under false pretences. My parents are Jewish, they are trapped in Vienna which as you know is in Nazi hands. They are in great danger. I have come here to ask you if you would be their sponsor. They need an English person to be financially responsible for them. The government requires a guarantee of one hundred pounds for each of them to pay for their return to Austria when this trouble is over, but I can assure you sir, my parents will never be a burden to you. They will do whatever work is available to them. Anything. They will be more than happy to do it." '

'And this good man, a real Englishman, so cultured and kind, he said to me, "Would your parents be prepared to go to Surrey where I have a house? Can your mother cook, would your father be prepared to act as butler or he could work in the gardens? If so, I will do it." A wonderful man, what they call a righteous gentile. I tried to kiss his hand, but he wouldn't let me. He said, "Chamberlain let your people down and it is the least I can do." I wrote to my parents and told them and they were so proud of me. In the letter they wrote, September 4th 1939, they said, "You are our reason for living and you have saved us."

'Everything was being done to get the papers ready for them to come out. They had their tickets and exit visa, they were almost here. And then the war started and my whole world collapsed.'

For a second I thought grandma had stopped breathing. She closed her eyes and lifted her hands, one fist on top of the other, pressing them tightly together, into her chest.

'Grandma?' She opened her eyes and looked at me.

'Sixteen years old. One month from seventeen. Not so much older than you are now. I know it was wrong but I felt so angry with my parents for sending me away. I understand it now, of course. I can see that it was the most unselfish thing a parent could do, to let their only child go. But that day, when I heard that the war had started, it felt like they had abandoned me – given me up to cold, cruel strangers.

'I went around that house like a crazy person. I didn't speak to anyone, I didn't know what to do with myself. The Parkers acted like nothing much had happened, they expected me to carry on as normal. Like it was nothing that the letters stopped coming and I didn't know what had happened to my mother and father. The British stiff upper lip kind of thing. On the Saturday after the war started I took myself to the synagogue. I'd never been before in England but I knew where it was. I wasn't religious but I wanted to be with people who could understand what I was feeling. A woman sat next to me in the gallery, Mrs Jacobs, I wish I knew what happened to her. She could see at once the state I was in. She asked me to come home and have a meal with her and she wouldn't take no for an answer. She gave me cholent for lunch. You know what that is? It's Jewish food, meat and potatoes and vegetables all cooked overnight in one pot, very low, so you don't have to cook on the Sabbath. And we had fruit compote for dessert, I can taste it now. It was very good to eat that kind of food again.

'She was an ordinary woman, Russian, not rich or clever but a very kind heart. She lived with her mother and her mother only spoke Yiddish, so she just smiled at me and patted my hand. We sat together all afternoon in her little sitting room near Paddington Station and I told her everything. She got it all out of me: my fear about my parents, Mrs Parker taking away all my clothes and no chance to carry on with my education, the husband trying to interfere with me. Everything. The more I told her, the more frightened I became of going back to that house. She said, "What do you think your dear mother and father would do if they were here?" And I told her that they would tell them that good people do not behave like that to a young person from another country and then they would take me away and find me a different place to live. I was hot headed then. And Mrs Jacobs said, "Well, if that is what your parents would do for you, then I must do the same on their behalf."

'We walked round to the Parkers' house. It was a big house with five or six steep steps up to it and Mrs Jacobs was a tiny woman, not even five feet tall I don't think. She marched right in and she gave Mrs Parker such a what for. She told her what a filthy man her husband was and how he should be locked up. She told her if she didn't give back my clothes she would call the British Police Force. She was very brave, like something from a story book and if I hadn't been so scared, I think I would have laughed.

'She took me home with her and made me up a bed on her sofa in that tiny sitting room and the next day, Sunday, she went with me to Bloomsbury House and told them everything. They found me a place in a hostel in Belsize Park run by the Refugee Committee. They'd set it up for working age girls like me with no family here. I made friends there that lasted me all my life and I met my Ziggy. It was a good place to live, because we were all in the same boat. We could share a joke and have a bit of fun, but it wasn't possible to be really happy. The minute you felt happy, you felt guilty for all those who were left behind. And you learned to keep your tears locked up inside you. If one cried, we all cried. It was catching, like yawning. We had to keep working, keep our heartache to ourselves, make the best of things as the English say. I missed my mother especially. When things went wrong, I would imagine myself sitting on her lap with my arms around her neck and tried to think how she would tell me where I had gone wrong and how I should put things right again.

'Mrs Jacobs found me a job with her sister in Knightsbridge. It was a very smart shop where all the gentry used to go for ball gowns for their daughters' coming out parties. Beautiful dresses, such elaborate things, layers and layers of net, beading, thousands of pearls; you wouldn't know a war was on to see the girls in gowns like those. Upstairs it was like a palace, velvet seats and gilt mirrors everywhere, and downstairs where we worked, it was dark and cold. I earned two pounds a week and out of that I had to pay for my board and lodging, fare money and lunches. But I didn't care, I was so pleased to be away from that family.

'Then in 1940 when the bombing started, there was the fear about aliens. I had to go to the police station and then to a tribunal but they decided I was a "friendly alien", Category A. My Ziggy didn't do so well. They decided he was a Category B alien, someone you couldn't quite trust. They sent him to the Isle of Man like a criminal and it nearly broke his heart to be treated like that because you couldn't find anyone who loved England and hated the Germans as much as he did. Later, when things calmed down they let him join the Royal Pioneer Corps, a special regiment for refugees and he was sent to the Forest of Dean to supervise German prisoners-of-war. Now that was what the British would call an irony.

'After the dressmaking, I did war work. That was much better. I felt I was doing my bit, making a contribution to the country which had taken me in. I made uniforms, I did office work, day shifts, night shifts, all kinds of things. When I had time, I helped at the hostel, cooking the evening meals. There was a restaurant there, open to the public, but most of the people who came by for a meal were refugees, trying to find a bit of home. That's how I met Ziggy, on leave from the army. He was on his own in this country. We fell in love straight away. He was very, very good to me, very kind, no one could have had a better husband.'

Grandma stopped talking and I could see her try to focus her eyes on me, as if she had forgotten I was there.

'Half the time, I don't know what I'm talking about. You don't want to hear all this, do you?'

'No, please grandma. I do. Honestly, I do. Show me something else.'

'Show you something else?' She said in her old, irritable voice. 'What do you think this is, a conjurer's box?' And then, relenting, 'Okay, I'll show you something interesting. Look at this.' She pulled out a little booklet marked *Advice to New Arrivals,* published by the German Jewish Aid Committee.

1. Spend your spare time immediately

in learning the English language and its correct pronunciation.

2. Refrain from speaking German in the streets and in public conveyances and in public places such as Restaurants. Talk halting English rather than fluent German and do not talk in a loud voice. Do not read Newspapers in public.

3. Do not criticise any Government regulations, nor the way things are done over here. Do not speak of 'how much better this or that is done in Germany.' It may be true in some matters, but it weighs as nothing against the sympathy and freedom and liberty of England which are now given to you. Never forget that point.

4. Do not join any political organisation, nor take part in any political activities.

5. Do not make yourself conspicuous by speaking loudly, or by your manner or dress. The Englishman greatly dislikes ostentation, loudness of dress or manner. The Englishman attaches very great importance to modesty, understatement in speech rather than overstatement, and quietness of dress and manner. He values good manners far more than he values evidence of wealth. (You will find that he says 'Thank you' for the slightest service – even for a penny 'bus ticket for which he has paid.)

I couldn't help smiling.

'That's enough of that,' grandma said, snatching it away from me and putting it back in the box. 'It might seem funny now but it was serious enough then.'

'What's that? What's that big number?'

'Ah that,' she said, her tone softening a little. She handed me a brown cardboard tag with a number printed on it in big black letters, and a card from Vienna with her photograph, her name, date of birth and the names of her parents: Otto and Sonya Rosen, the great-grandparents I had never even heard mentioned until this conversation.

'That's the identification number they gave me when I came to England with Eva. I was number 112 she was 111. We left on a Saturday night, midnight, from the station in Vienna. The Nazis didn't want anyone to know what was going on. There were hundreds of children on that platform with their parents and the Nazis beating them off. I had to take care of Eva. I was rescuing her, smuggling her out. We thought it would just be for a little while, until we saw our parents again, but that wasn't how it turned out.

'It was so hard not to say goodbye properly, it haunted me for years the fact that I never said a proper goodbye to my father and mother. All through the war, I believed that I would see them again. What was there if you didn't have hope? Even after the war started, I had some letters from them. I could write to them through the Red Cross, twenty-five words, and they could write back. In 1941, I heard from my mother that she and my father had been sent to Theresienstadt, but it didn't seem so terrible. She described it as a resettlement camp in Bohemia, not so far from Vienna; my father had one address there and she had a different one. Right up to 1942, I had a few letters. Then they stopped coming and I didn't know what was happening.

'When the war finished, everyone was dancing in the streets in Piccadilly Circus. People were so happy but all I could think about was finding my parents. Ziggy too, although he wasn't such an optimist as me. I contacted all the Jewish organisations to find out if there was any news of them, but it was too soon. Then, after a few months, a letter that I'd sent to my mother in Theresienstadt was returned. "Deported to Auschwitz, 1943." That's how I knew. Still a part of me could not stop hoping. There were survivors, maybe my mother and father were amongst them. Then I heard from my cousin Lori, her letter was forwarded by one of the refugee organisations. One little miracle in all the tragedy. Somehow, by the skin of her teeth, she had survived, she had escaped the transport. But then the terrible news. Her sister, Klara, my aunt Fanny and my mother had all died in Auschwitz. She was the only one who survived. Her father Georg, she didn't even know where he had perished.

'She was able to tell me that my father had died in Theresienstadt, in 1942, before they went on the transport. He had never recovered from Dachau but she told me that he always spoke of how happy he was that I was safe in England. And one more little miracle. All this time, Lori had kept a letter for me written by my mother.'

Grandma recited it to me from memory.

You gave us so much happiness. I will not see you again, but you must know how much you are loved. Your father and I tried to guide you and now I have faith that you will lead a good and happy life. You have your whole life before you. We bless you and we bless the children and husband you will have.

'There was no funeral, no grave, no mourners, only me. I had been living like an orphan for all those years. I was married to a man my parents would never meet. I had a little home of my own and Eva to take care of. I had to get on with my life. All of us did.'

Grandma closed her eyes and lay still and for a terrible moment, I thought she had died. I kissed her cheek, dry as tissue paper.

'I love you, grandma.'

She patted my hand and gave me a faint smile.

'I know you do, darling. You are a great comfort to me.'

I took her papery hand with perfect pink varnished nails and held it in mine.

'Did you ever tell mummy these stories?'

'I never talked about it after the war. None of us did. I had Jackie and your mother when I was still young, they took up all my time. I had Eva living with us. I ran the business all those years. What time did I have to think about it? You got on with life. Now, after sixty years, I'm telling the story.'

She began to put everything back in the box, carefully, in the order it had come out. I would have loved to have the photograph of her when she was my age, but I couldn't ask for it. She breathed in deeply and then out again, as if she was making herself come back into the world. Then she shook her head.

'Make the tea now darling.' She said in her normal voice. 'Everything is in the kitchen, there's cake in the tin, shop cake but it's still good. Put the box back in the bedroom where you found it, exactly the same place, make sure you don't leave a mess.'

When I returned with the tray, grandma had put on some lipstick and was smoothing her skirt down. She smiled at me, her old self again.

'Sit down with me before you go and tell me how your mother has been this week. She never tells me a thing.'

*

I wasn't sure whether I should tell mum what grandma had told me, but the next time I saw auntie Eva, I talked to her about it. Ever since I'd been twelve or thirteen years old, she'd taken me out for a meal two or three times a year, somewhere really nice. Our favourite place was The People's Palace at the top of the Festival Hall. I liked it because I could sit by the window and look out over the Thames and it was a good place for auntie Eva too, especially when she started using a wheelchair and had to think about the parking and lifts and all that sort of thing.

'You must know what happened to grandma's family.' I said.

'Yes and I'm glad she told you. It's important.'

Auntie Eva liked listening more than talking. She was a good person to talk to because she didn't feel she had to know everything and give you advice like most adults did. She was the one I told about Nick, a boy I really liked who'd dumped me when I least

293

expected it.

'Poor you, that's a horrible thing to happen. You must feel very sad.'

'Yes, I do,' I said simply. I carried on eating my chocolate brownie with praline cream and we were quiet for a minute or two. 'Did that ever happen to you?' I asked her.

'Something like it. I was very much in love with a boy called Nat when I was your age and for a long time after. We were engaged but it didn't work out. It was a very hard time for me.' She pressed her lips together. 'You can't always make life turn out as you want, sometimes you have to learn to live with that.'

'Did you stop seeing him when that happened? That's what I find so hard, having to see Nick at school every day. It just reminds me how much I miss him. I can't bear to see him laughing and talking to other girls.'

'For a long time I didn't see him at all, but now we do, we keep in touch. He's been a very good friend to me.'

Another time, actually it was the last time I saw her on her own, I asked her to tell me about mum and auntie Jackie when they were little, whether there was ever a time when they didn't argue. That was when she told me about her own little sister.

'Gertrude. She was four years old. She died during the war in a hospital where they didn't look after her properly. I only discovered what happened to her a few years ago. I'm trying to sort all the papers and documents I have about her, put them into some kind of order, because I would like to tell you her story. Perhaps when you're a bit older, we'll go through it all together. I don't want to leave it too late.'

'Auntie, you're not old. Nothing's going to happen to you.'

She shook her head and smiled at me.

'Yes I know. I'm going to live for years and years. But while we're on the subject, there are some other things I've sorted out for you. The painting from Vienna of course. I don't want any arguments about it when I'm gone because I've decided it's for you. Susi gave it to me after Nat and I broke up, when I was feeling very sad. She came into my room one day and just hung it on the wall for me. And I've put some things in that blue leather box where I used to keep my earrings. They're not worth a lot but they've been special to me.' And then she said what she always said.

'Don't let's talk about me. This is your time, not mine.'

EVA

Hendon Central

1974

Blame is a big ugly word. How could I blame Susi when she did so much for me? I understood, I forgave her, I tried to anyway. I continued to love her and work to make her happy. But from the moment I discovered that her family were not my family and that she had always known it and I hadn't, a little piece of me, a little triangle in the corner of my heart blamed her for the secret which made life easier for her, not me. I'm not a good person for thinking like this all these years; a better person would have ripped out that corner and thrown it away.

The worst thing is that after I knew her family weren't my family, the house that I loved so much stopped feeling like my home, and started to feel like her house where I happened to live. For a long time afterwards, I felt as if I had lost the one safe place in the whole world. I wanted my history to be the same as hers. I wanted to have been born into the big, confident, Jewish family who had lived in Vienna surrounded by the things I grew up with: the paintings, the Sabbath candlesticks and the menorah, the clock, the mother of pearl cabinet with the glass panels down the front, the velvet covered Biedermeier chairs she was so proud of, the beautiful Persian rug. And if I couldn't have this family for my own, then I wanted to have known my real grandmother who kept these things for Susi all those years. I wanted to have known my own baby sister.

Memory is a funny thing. The psychiatrist she took me to when I stopped being able to leave the house wanted to know why I had chosen to forget the first four years of my life, the time before I came to England. 'Suppressed memory' he called it, as if memory was nothing but an untidy cupboard and if I spent some time sorting it out, my past would appear before me, neat and tidy like a shelf full of ironed knickers. But memory has to be kept alive by other people. The stories people tell you, the photographs, the trinkets and objects of your childhood; these are the things which make up the memory of a child. Memories need to be taken out and looked at from time to time, spoken about by others, revisited, to prove that they are true.

The other thing that bothered the psychiatrist was, why I wasn't angrier. He thought I should be stuffed full of anger: angry with the people in the hospital in Norwich, angry with my mother for abandoning me, angry with Nat. He thought I should be angry with my body for letting me down so badly, not so much angry with the people who stared at me and made unkind remarks every day, but angry with the body itself, for being so abnormal and hard for others to look at. Most important of all, he expected me to be angry with Susi for lying to me all those years.

From time to time, he would stretch out his arms, making a long horizontal line and say, 'There is, after all my dear, so much loss in your life, so much loss. You must not keep it all locked up inside you, you must let it go.'

But where would I let it go to?

Whenever I sat in his large white room in Daleham Gardens and listened to him talking about my anger, I had a vision of a huge lion in Regent's Park Zoo, prowling up and down in his poky cage, knowing that if he roared too loud and too long at his captivity, he would terrify the children, and the next day they would send him somewhere much worse than the zoo, to a place where there were no lions at all, not even the sad ones in their separate cages.

I was Helen Burns, not Jane Eyre. Jane was my fictional heroine and I needed her to be exactly as she was in the story, but I wasn't made like her. I couldn't beat my fists against the door of the red room or rant and rave against all the people who had ever treated me unfairly. At Lowood School, Jane told Helen that if you are struck without a reason, you should hit back very hard so the person knows that they can never strike you again, but what good would that have done? It was better to be like me: a cheerful person, a good listener, someone others liked to be with. My job was not to stamp and rage. It was to fit in with what others needed, to make life easier.

The thing is, Susi never did anything to hurt me, not really. She didn't lie to me, she just didn't tell me the whole truth. Maybe she thought that the truth would hurt me more. In some ways I think she grew to believe, really believe, that the story she told me was true; that we were cousins who grew up side by side in Vienna and the day we stepped off the boat in England was the start of a new life together. In this version of the story, we stood in the waiting hall in the port at Harwich and she was terrified that I wouldn't be given a certificate of good health and we would be sent back to Nazi Germany. There and then, she made the decision that she would always take care of me because I was delicate and damaged and even in England there were people who might mistreat and misunderstand me. I would always need a protector and although she was not fully grown up herself, she would look after me like a big sister, like a little mother.

It took me a long time to understand that Susi needed me too. Not just to look after the girls and take care of the house when she went back into the business, or to help out on Friday nights. In a world where everything she had grown up with had been wiped out, I was the only living part of her childhood: I was her Vienna.

She had had to grow up too fast, I can see that now. When I think now of what Vivienne was like as a sulky teenager, arguing with her mother over every little thing, it's amazing what Susi went through at the same age, alone and without a word of complaint. She had to look forward, not back. All the refugees we knew were the same; the things they left behind were too painful, too big to talk about. They missed the places where they had grown up – Vienna, Budapest, Hamburg, Berlin, and they needed to talk about them. They just removed the people they loved most from their stories. You'd think I might have noticed this, but when people talk with such liveliness, such humour, it doesn't feel like anything is missing. They talked about food all the time: the coffee and cakes, the chocolates, the sausages, the picnics they would have by the lakes. They boasted to each other of their ice skating and skiing holidays; how they had swum the Danube or crossed the Alps wearing only espadrilles and light summer clothes. They talked of the long train rides they took, the trams, how much stricter and harder their education was, the books they had read, the music they listened to, the heat of the summers, the cold of the winters, the elegance of their clothes. I listened fascinated and never heard what was missing: the dark, bottomless hole of the people they loved most, the mothers and fathers, sisters, brothers, grandparents.

As a child I was only interested in what was there; I hadn't learned to look for the spaces, the gaps, the gaping holes where my own early life should have been.

*

When Nat walked out the door on Christmas Day 1953, still doing up his shirt buttons, smoothing his hair, I knew that he loved me as much as he could love anyone and I knew that it was over between us. Like a jilted Miss Havisham waiting for her fiancé to return, I carried on wearing the ring he had given me and didn't speak about it. When people eventually realised what had happened, no one was really surprised. It was not for me to expect the same things from life as ordinary people did. All my life I had been seen as a little oddity, sweet but damaged. I was different, outside of things, dislocated.

I had to learn to ignore the look in other people's eyes. I had to learn to steel myself against their pity.

If I regretted one thing it was that we hadn't made love that last night, properly, until we couldn't tell where one of us ended and the other began. Not because I thought it was a way of holding on to him; I knew that he didn't have the courage to choose between his mother and me, not then. I wanted it for myself, because Nat was the one boy in the whole world who loved me exactly as I was and I wanted to have had the whole of him.

Over and over again I replayed that night with a different ending. I undid his shirt buttons, he undid mine. We went upstairs together and lay on my little bed and slowly, slowly, he touched every part of me and I touched him. He came inside me and I felt him come and he told me that he would love me forever, and wherever he went, whatever he did, I would be there in his heart.

My virginity was no use to me now; I should never have thought it was worth holding on to.

I carried on as usual. Every day, for weeks, I got up, washed, dressed, walked to the station, waited in the cold for the bus to come. I took down Mr Dunlop's dictation and typed his letters. I chatted to the others in the lunch break and sat at my desk and smoked one cigarette after the other. The other secretaries looked at me sadly and said nothing. In the evenings I helped Susi and the girls and went to bed early. I was a machine, a slow moving machine, rocking her way through each day.

In January, Stanley who worked the lift in the office building went off sick and left his son in charge. Everyone knew that the son could never get the knack of stopping it at the right level and we learned to check whether he had parked it too high or too low. But I wasn't thinking about the lift on the morning I walked into it without looking and missed the two inch step that shouldn't have been there. I put out my hand to stop my head from hitting the far wall and crashed awkwardly onto my side. That was the beginning of the broken glass pain of arthritis in my right hip and the time when I began to walk with a stick.

Mr Dunlop put me in a taxi and sent me home

and later, I don't know how much later, a couple of weeks, a few months maybe, Julia packed up my things and sent them home with my last ever pay cheque from Dunlop and Fines.

Even after my hip healed and I was walking again, I didn't want to go out. That was when Susi decided I should see a psychiatrist. I don't know where she found out about him because she didn't really believe in psychiatry. 'Pull yourself together,' was Susi's philosophy on life, put a brave face on things and push it through. Dr Siegel he was called, with a moon shaped face and a sad smile. I went to see him because I didn't have the energy to say no, but like Susi, I couldn't see the point of it. You didn't have to be a psychiatrist to understand why I felt safer staying at home.

*

I stayed in Goldhurst Terrace and for more than a decade I marked time. It took me until I was thirty-four years old before I had a home of my own.

Susi didn't want me to be unhappy and nervous, but there's no doubt that having me at home all the time made life easier for her. Our elderly family doctor encouraged it too.

'She needs rest. Someone like Eva should not have too much excitement,' he said, as if I was a Victorian invalid. 'Perhaps you can find something for her to do here?' Susi was desperate to be back at work. Ziggy's heart was never really in Elite Fashions; he was a dreamer, a musician without a violin. She was the one with the business brain and the eye for fashion.

At first she went in for a couple of hours each day to 'put the books back in order' and ran back again to see that the girls and me were okay. Then she sacked the designer and began to do the drawings herself. She travelled to Milan to look at the fabrics and visited the fashion shows to see what was going on. She looked wonderful again, full skirts and high heels, and a fantastic cocktail outfit she designed for the business, and wore to the New Year's Eve dinner dance at the Cosmo: a white taffeta sleeveless top with lace and sequins and a straight black skirt just below the knees. She had a taste for what was going to be new in fashion; she could smell it in the air.

When the business picked up again and expanded, she brought me home typing and clerical work to do and paid me four shillings an hour, well above the going rate in 1954. It was my pin money, we all joked. I became a housewife without a husband and a second mother to the girls I loved but who were not my own.

I started to go out again when Jackie started school. Nobody knew how hard it was for me. I had to count to ten, a hundred, once even a thousand before I could close the door behind me.

'Why are your eyes closed auntie Eva? What are you saying? I can't hear you.'

'Nothing, darling. I'm just trying to remember something important.' It was me who held on to Jackie's soft little hand for comfort and clung on to Vivienne's pushchair, not the other way round. The relief when we turned the corner of Lyncroft Road and I saw the house again, was beyond words.

Little by little things got better, not perfect but

more manageable. I started back with Maccabi, running a Sunday afternoon junior group for ten to thirteen year olds. It was my old friend Pauline who rang me one day and persuaded me that I was just the person they needed; no one else could do it as well. I learned how to do the shopping without my heart beating out of my chest and I shut the door behind me and went to pick up the girls from school without a second thought. I went to the pictures on Sunday after the club with Pauline and the others, or for a coffee in the Finchley Road or Golders Green.

Once or twice I went out with a boy from the club, friends of friends, a foursome, that kind of thing. There was a kiss and a fumble at the pictures in Kilburn or Swiss Cottage, a bus ride into the West End and tea at Lyons Corner House, maybe even a second or third date. But before it got to the point where I would be invited back to meet his parents, I broke it off.

Everyone thought I was waiting for the right person to come along, but the truth was that I didn't want to love anyone else. I had loved Nat once and I knew that that love would stay with me all my life. He was there, inside my heart and my mind, in every part of me. I didn't set out to make it that way but there was nothing I could do about it. Every morning when I woke up, the first words in my head were, 'Nat, I love you, I love you Nat.' Whatever I was doing – washing, looking after the girls, preparing the dinner, walking in the park, Nat was there with me. I never forgave him for not having the courage to be with me; I hated him for what he had done, but that wasn't the same as not loving him. You don't feel them in the same part of your heart. He was a boy when we met, a weak boy, not sure enough of the life he wanted, too influenced by what others thought. But I could never shake myself free of the idea that we could have had a life together; we could have been happy.

'I don't agree with anything he's done,' Brenda said to me two years after it happened. 'As far as I'm concerned he's been spineless and unkind. But he is my brother, my flesh and blood. I have to stick by him.' Brenda was engaged to a boy from up north and she was getting married in London before she moved to Manchester. 'Please come to the wedding,' she begged me. 'I know it will be hard for you, but I can't get married without you there. Where will I find another friend like you?'

That's where I saw Nat's new girl. She was a skinny little thing, nervous looking. I'd known her years ago at the club.

*

I was welcome and I was loved but I was Eva in the corner of someone else's home. I looked after the house and the girls; I took care of things. On Friday nights Susi and I did the cooking together and then I did the washing up. On their Sunday parties, I slipped away to my corner after the food was served just as I had done when I was a little girl. It suited me this role, and it didn't suit me at all.

I began to plot my escape. Not in a rebellious way; that wasn't my style, but slowly. As the girls became teenagers, I had time on my hands. Ziggy suggested I did some voluntary work; it would be good for me to get out and about a bit more, he said. At first

I visited some of the older people who lived near us, refugees who reminded Ziggy of his own mother and father. I read the German newspapers to them, the words familiar but the meaning only half comprehensible. I wrote letters for them in English and helped them pay their bills. They liked me coming to see them; they patted my cheek and said I was a schaine maidel with a good heart. They trusted me with their secrets.

I thought about getting another job as a secretary, brushing up my typing and shorthand speeds but I wanted a different kind of work. I wanted to work with children, children who hadn't had it easy. At first, I worked as a volunteer, the kind of work you could do if you had no qualifications. I travelled for miles on the single decker Greenline bus, all the way out to a huge mental hospital on the outskirts of London. I did the work no one else wanted to do and I was good at it. The children I saw there were called severely subnormal, ineducable, spastic, mental. I hated the words they used. They were the children no one wanted to touch. I picked them up and cuddled them; I kissed them and sang the songs I had learned from Susi. If you learned to listen to what they were saying, there wasn't a single child who couldn't let you know what they wanted with their bodies or their eyes. When the nurses weren't looking, I went in the cupboard and dressed them in the pretty clothes they saved for Special Visitors Day.

Susi didn't want me to work with lame ducks, being one myself.

'You don't have to work with children like that. I don't see how it can be good for you, that kind of environment. If you want to start working, why not find a secretarial job in a cheerful office, like you used to do? Or you could come into the business full time when the girls have finished school.'

'I want to do something where I can make a difference to these children's lives. It's what I really want to do.'

'But you don't have any proper training. How will you earn a living?' But I had thought through that one. I had already applied for a Home Office grant to do a Diploma in Child Care. It was an eighteen month course at Sidcup College.

'Will they take someone your age? Surely this is for young girls straight from school?'

'I'm thirty-one years old. It's not ancient. I still have thirty years of a working life.'

Susi opened up her palms and raised her eyebrows at me as if to say, I was only asking.

'I can see you've done your homework here. You know I wouldn't stand in your way if that's what you want to do. Education is always a good thing. But where is it? I've never heard of this Sidcup. Is it even in London?'

I laughed. Susi thought anywhere south of Victoria Station was beyond civilisation. 'Susi, it's just the other side of London, near Greenwich.'

'But that's miles away. Where will you live? Eva, darling, you won't be happy so far away.'

'I won't have to stay overnight at first, I can go on the train every day, at least until we start to do our placements.'

Susi sighed deeply.

'If that's what you've decided, you know we'll

support you, but if you're not happy, you can come straight home.'

More than anyone, Susi understood my fear of sleeping in unknown beds in strange houses. But she also had her own reasons for wanting me to stay. Vivienne had turned fourteen and fought with Susi over every little issue. Such passion and rage.

Ziggy would sit in his chair, reading or listening to music and said, 'Just leave her to her own devices. She'll soon learn.'

But Susi couldn't leave her daughter to make her own mistakes, just as Vivienne couldn't leave her mother alone. They said terrible things to each other, things they could never take back.

'You have no idea, do you? Everything has been handed to you on a plate. When I think of the responsibilities I had on my shoulders when I was your age.'

'For God's sake mum, don't start that sob story again. I'm not you, okay. The war's over. It's a different world now, you can't put all your hang ups on me. You think by telling me all that stuff over and over again, I'll feel sorry for you and just do what you want me to do, but you can't make me.'

'Don't you dare speak to me like that. I'm your mother, I'm not going to stand by and let you waste your life. I know what it's like to grow up without a mother's advice and if I see you making mistakes, it's my job to tell you.'

'Well, maybe I'd do better without your advice, have you ever thought of that? Maybe it's easier to live your life if you don't have a mother to tell you that nothing you ever do is right.'

Jackie would look up calmly from her homework. 'Vivienne don't talk to mum like that.'

'Shut up Jackie. Just mind your own business. This has got nothing to do with you.'

'Vivienne you have to put some effort into things, you can't expect everything to be easy, easy, easy. The kind of people you associate with, they're not the kind of people who should be your friends. That terrible boy you brought home last week. The marks you're getting at school. What kind of future will these give you?'

'Shut up mum, I'm not listening. You've told me all this a thousand times before.'

'Well go to your room then, I won't put up with this a minute longer. For as long as you live under my roof you will do as you are told. If I had spoken to my own mother like this...'

'That's right mum, start crying, that's the way to win an argument.'

I would have done anything to stop them causing each other such pain. I hated the cruel way Vivienne spoke to her mother, but I could see that Susi needed to give her some room to make her own mistakes. And secretly, I admired Vivienne's ability to say whatever she thought without fear of the consequences.

*

Susi was wrong about my course. I wasn't even the oldest one there. We were women and girls, mixed ages and backgrounds, and between us we'd done about every job that a woman could do. I enjoyed it from the beginning. I was one of the crowd, accepted for who I was. I don't know if they talked about me behind my back but nobody mentioned my funny walk or the fact that it took me a bit longer to get around.

I liked the long train journey every day and working with the other girls. I already knew a lot of the things we were taught but that didn't matter; it was all interesting to me. We studied basic child care, running a home, crafts, gardening and cookery. We visited schools and residential homes and the county courts where magistrates decided the fate of the children nobody wanted. In the evenings we had classes in catering and crafts and discussions and talks about our day's visits. At first, as I had promised Susi, I travelled in to college every day on the train and back home again to north west London, but the evening classes and the homework began to make the long journey each day impossible.

It was hard to overcome my fear of new places. I had to learn to live with narrow beds and stained, flapping curtains in unfamiliar rooms. I had to cope with the sickening smell of the breakfast eggs frying in lard, the landlady's surprise that they let someone like me work with any kind of children, the slippery lino as I walked up the stairs, the mess someone else might leave in the shared toilet. Each night, after I had written my report on the day's visit and lay dog tired in my narrow bed in a cold, strange room, I had to remind myself that I was not in a hospital in Norwich or Great Yarmouth and nobody was keeping me there against my will. I could get up and leave if I wanted. I could pack my little bag right now and wait for the night bus which would take me back to London. Or I could shut my eyes and bring back my own room at Goldhurst Terrace; the cardboard box from Austria hidden in the back of my wardrobe with the picture of my mother and sister and the little gold cross on its chain. I could recall in a second, Susi, the girls, the sound of Ziggy's music, my chair at the kitchen table, the smell of the breakfast coffee and rolls. They were all just there, waiting for me to return.

In the day, I was in my element and by the time we began our month long placements, I had got used to spending my nights away from home. I began to see what was really going on in the residential homes situated so far outside towns. There were children whose parents couldn't cope with them, who had been sent from home to home, or whose fathers were in prison, orphans, disabled children, all sorts. Poor scraps, no wonder they were difficult. *Abandoned and Relinquished*, that's what they called the ones who had no homes to return to.

In the worst of them it was like stepping back into the hospital wards of my own childhood. The people in charge couldn't recognise the difference between being naughty and being scared, but I understood. I understood how ignorant people used religion as a way to terrify children, and how children cried and shouted and misbehaved when all they really needed was someone to sit with them and hold their hand. I understood it only too well.

My tutor read the essays I wrote and said my evaluations were intelligent and full of insight and awarded me a distinction.

*

After I qualified, I got a job as a matron of a home for maladjusted boys in Seaford, near to the South coast. The head teacher was a wonderful Welshman, a Communist Party member who hated religion and believed that if we gave the boys a sense of responsibility and purpose, their behaviour would improve. He had a disabled wife himself, born with cerebral palsy, and three young children, and he said that if I didn't think my handicap would get in the way of my doing the job, then he didn't either. I didn't really have enough experience for the post, but four matrons had left in the past year and they were ready to take on anyone willing to have a go. I supervised the boys in their leisure time – gardening, table tennis, sport, all kinds of things. I organised the catering, I took care of them when they were sick, I talked to the educational psychologist on her weekly visits and most of all, I tried to be a friend to these difficult, hard to love boys. It was a busy, responsible time for me. I was good at the work and pretended that I wasn't lonely. In the holidays, I went back to Susi and the girls and saw my old friends who were mostly married with their own children. I lay in my bed and dreamt of Nat and the babies we might have had.

Susi carried on hating the idea that I was so far away. She wanted me back in the house and I felt bad about not being there with her, but I had had my taste of freedom and could not go back home, however safe it was, however much I missed her. Jackie had gone to live in Israel. She volunteered to serve in the Six Day War in 1967 when she was nineteen years old and within a few months, she had decided to make Aliyah. There didn't seem much chance of her ever living in

England again. Vivienne had dropped out of school after her O Levels and half the time, we hardly knew where she was. She was as thin as a wax candle, smoking too much, hardly talking to her mother except to argue.

*

One beautiful warm Sussex Sunday, Susi and Ziggy drove down to see me and take me out to lunch. Ziggy had a new car, a pale silver-blue Daimler, and Susi was dressed like Jackie Kennedy, shiny slacks that matched the car, an Italian silk scarf, powder blue, beige and white, and big sunglasses. The boys working in the garden stood up straight to watch her as she stepped out of the car.

We went for lunch in the restaurant of a local hotel: tinned grapefruit cocktail with a glacé cherry, roast beef and Yorkshire pudding, and soggy, burnt roast potatoes. Ziggy lifted his glass of red wine and winced at the taste.

'We have a little proposal for you.' I could tell that Susi had put him up to this by the way he cleared his throat. 'Yes, we have a proposal, long overdue.' He paused and took another tentative sip of the wine. 'Let me explain it to you. Seven or eight years ago we received a sum of money from the German government, *wiedergutmachung,* restitution. It was for Susi's loss of her education and a share of the value of the property her grandparents had owned in Mitteldorf. The flat in Vienna was rented, there was no money for the things they destroyed there. We didn't want the money, we don't need it for ourselves

316

thank God, but Susi decided to take it, thinking of your future.' Susi interrupted him, unable to stay silent any longer.

'There is a sum of money which we want you to have, not a huge sum, but something. We were saving it for when you married, but now we can see that you have already left us, married or not. It will allow you to buy a little flat somewhere, not anything very grand, but somewhere not too far away from us, we hope. And there will be enough for a few pounds to live on each month. You could use it to further your studies or whatever you want. Perhaps you can work a bit less, look after yourself a bit more.'

I looked from one to another, uncertain how to react.

'Of course, whatever you decide to do, you will always be welcome at our home,' Ziggy added. 'You must always think of it as somewhere you are welcome.'

'And Vivienne of course, it will be nice for her to have you nearer to home. She misses you. You are always such a good influence on her.'

*

I didn't leave my job straight away. I was determined to prove that I could stick at it, that I didn't need to go running back to Susi and London. And I couldn't just abandon the boys. They could be wild and difficult, those boys who nobody wanted, but I felt they needed me, especially in the evenings at cocoa time when the teachers and most of the staff had gone and there were just them and me and the fear of the night.

Physically, the work was hard for me. There was so much walking. The grounds were huge and there were long, long corridors and endless flights of stairs for me to climb. All day I had to go from the kitchens to the dormitories, from the garden to the games room, from the sick bay to my own room right at the top of the house. I was using a stick all the time now and it helped to steady me, but often I had to stuff myself full of aspirin before I could even get out of bed in the morning. All my life people had asked me, 'Does it hurt when you walk?' I knew that the way I moved looked ugly and awkward to other people but it hadn't been painful. Now, more and more often, there was a hot, sharp stabbing when I walked as if my joints were full of broken glass.

Eventually I came up to London to see a new orthopaedic doctor in Portland Place.

'It's just wear and tear, I'm afraid,' the doctor said. 'There's not a lot we can do. I can give you something to help to relieve the pain, but that's about all. Eventually you might find it easier to use a wheelchair but that probably won't happen until you're quite a bit older. Other than that it's a case of the old "try to take it easy and put your feet up a bit more." '

I came back to London with mixed feelings. I wanted to be in London, near Susi but not with her, but it was hard to give up my own little kingdom in Sussex. I resigned from my job and found myself a little flat in a new block near to Hendon Central tube station. It had been built in the 1960s, a plain, flat fronted modern block, four storeys high, with eight flats, two on either side of the front entrance with a little shared garden at the back. I chose one on the ground floor, thinking of what the future might hold for me. It had three small square rooms: two bedrooms and a sitting room and a little kitchen with formica fitted cupboards and a pale green bathroom with speckled tiles. I furnished it in a modern style, plain white walls and simple teak furniture, the chairs covered with brown and cream fabric, and a few bright orange cushions to cheer me up. In a little shop in Brent Street, more junk than antique, I bought a frame to hold the photograph of me with my mother and the baby sister I couldn't remember knowing, and placed it on my bedside table.

Little by little, things I loved from the house found their way into my flat – the painting of the farmer and his wife at sunset of course, the big wooden clock, a white linen tablecloth trimmed with antique lace to put on my little table. They sat oddly with the bright, clean things I had chosen for myself.

I did another qualification in Teaching and Training Mentally Handicapped Children. No child was ineducable they had decided in the new Education Act and there was plenty of work for me. I found myself a job in a school in Swiss Cottage, four days a week. I loved my big teenage boys and girls. My job was to help the qualified teachers but really they let me do whatever I wanted. I taught them how to read and write by telling them stories to go with the letters, and drawing pictures to go with the words. We did cooking together and art work and sometimes I took them out on the bus and they learned to pay their fares and count out the change and not care when all the other passengers stared at them and said stupid things. I was asked to join committees. I worked with the parents of these young people and I helped to found an access group. I joined a Progressive synagogue in my own name; I converted and became what I had felt I had always been: Jewish. I helped out; I organised jumble sales and taught at the children's cheder.

Sometimes I still woke in the middle of the night and wondered why I wasn't in my old room in Goldhurst Terrace with Susi and Ziggy down the corridor and all the old familiar things around me. But living alone in my own place changed me. If I was still in the corner of life without a husband and children of my own, at least I was in my own corner.

*

Even after I had my flat, I sometimes stayed over at Susi's on Friday nights and on the Jewish holidays. People still thought of me as the cheerful, pleasant spinster cousin, doing good works with unfortunate children, but I was used to that. I had one or two little romances of my own, but they were nobody else's business. There was Henri, a refugee from Germany, quite a bit older than me. I met him through the synagogue. The wife he had loved had died and he thought I might do instead. He would look after me and I would take care of him; that was the unspoken deal; it would be good for both of us.

He was good looking in a way, a bit pompous and full of himself sometimes, but kind. He had thinning grey hair, swept over, with a low side parting, and he was always well turned out, with immaculate, manicured nails. He would take me out for dinner at a good restaurant, the Cage D'Or at the Cumberland Hotel with its spinning silver hors d'oeuvres trolley, or to concerts at the Wigmore Hall. He bought me presents: a brooch, a silk scarf, a book he thought I would like and told me that I had a pretty face and he could see that I was a good person. He didn't want a fumble in the back row of the pictures, he wanted companionship. Once we went away together to a small country hotel in the Cotswolds. We undressed with the light off and we lay together in the dark, touching but not looking at each other's bodies. He was a considerate lover. Grateful. Neither of us was young; he was in his fifties, fifteen years older than me. I was his chance of a new life.

Then the dreams began again. These dreams always took place somewhere familiar to me from many years ago, although I wasn't a child any more. I was me, an adult, captive in a hospital ward or a classroom from my childhood. For reasons I did not understand, I was unable to tell them that they had made a terrible mistake and I should be free in the outside world, not lying in this tight, narrow hospital bed, or trapped behind this tiny desk. In the dream a group of people from outside would come to visit on a ward round or an inspection, something like that. Nat was with them, walking round, looking at things. When he saw me he would come over and put his hand on my cheek so that I looked up and talked to him. He helped me to get up and move outside. Then we were in a long, quiet corridor, alone, and I was standing against the wall, Nat leaning into me, kissing me and touching me so that all my body woke up to him and I moved into him, knowing that nothing could separate us now.

I would wake up feeling so warm and happy, so loved.

I knew then that I couldn't accept Henri. Even though we were both lonely, I could not share my life with him.

*

I met Nat again at his father's stone setting in 1970, two years after I'd moved into my flat. Brenda had rung me from Manchester and asked me shyly if I would like to come. I'd seen her a few times over the years. She had filled out a bit and her hair was died auburn and arranged in a stiff shampoo and set. She looked plump and matronly, with her same sweet smile.

Nat stood on the men's side of the stark, soulless prayer room in Bushey Cemetery wearing a pork-pie hat, a short car coat and black leather gloves, a prayer book in his hand. I stood on the other side with the women. Even when I tried to concentrate on my prayer book, I could feel him looking over at me.

Outside in the cold, with everyone stamping their feet and shaking each other's hands, he came up to me.

'Hello Eva.'

'Hello, Nat. How are you?'

'I'm okay, can't grumble. I've started up on my own now. I've got a shop in Golders Green, it's doing very well: stockings, lingerie, hats, all kinds of things.'

'So I heard.'

'And you? Someone told me that you moved into your own place.'

'Yes.'

'Station Road, isn't it, the new block up from the station? What's the number exactly?'

'Flat 1, Furness Court.'

He grinned at me like a schoolboy sharing a naughty joke and despite myself I grinned back.

'Are you ever at home on Thursdays, in the afternoon?' he asked quietly.

'Not often. Sometimes.' I stumbled over my words. 'I might be able to change my day off.'

A week later on Thursday afternoon, half day closing at his shop, he rang my doorbell and came back into my life. I was thirty-six years old, and Nat was nearly forty.

He hadn't changed much, more solid in the body, the odd bit of grey in his hair, a lot more confident about his place in the world. Every second Thursday he walked through my door and greeted me shyly and we chatted a little as if we were just getting to know each other. Each week he sat down at my table ready to eat the lunch I had cooked him, politely, humbly, looking at me.

The food remained on the table, going cold.

*

Oh God, being with Nat – making love to him.

Afterwards, his hand still on my breast, mine between his legs, he would prop himself up on one elbow and look at me. 'You know I love you, don't you. You know that really there has only, ever, been you.'

I would put my finger over his lips to stop him talking and slowly, we would start all over again,

323

delaying and delaying the moment when I would watch him walk out of my door to return to his own safe house.

They were happy times for me, these Thursday afternoons; the only times when I was absolutely content in that moment, when I wasn't fretting about what the past might have been or dreaming of a different future.

*

One afternoon, four years after Nat had first come through my door, we were sitting together in my bed, feeding each other chicken liver pâté on strips of toast and slices of honeydew melon. Nat licked the juice off my fingers and gave me his old schoolboy grin. We talked and smiled and ate. It was always afterwards that we talked best. He liked to hear about myself and my work. It was his way of proving that he had never really abandoned me.

'You're wonderful,' Nat said. 'I don't know how you do it, I really don't. I don't know how you have the patience. You've always been a very special person.' He pressed my open palm to his mouth and kissed it.

'It's your fortieth birthday soon isn't it? I'd like to give you something really special, a proper treat.'

'What I'd like you can't give me.'

Nat looked surprised and mortified. I had never been in the habit of asking him for anything.

'I don't mean that. You know that's not what I'm asking.'

'I'm sorry. What would you like? What can I give you?'

324

'A few days together. A whole night. Somewhere we could go out on the streets and walk around together without being scared of being seen.'

'I don't see why not.'

'Really?'

'Yes. As long as we go midweek, I could manage that. We could go in a couple of months. May would be good, there's a trade fair. I could tell Ruby that...'

'Nat, don't.'

I didn't want to know the details. Of course I knew that he had a wife, children, a family that had nothing to do with me. It was hard, very hard, but they weren't my business. I didn't want them in my imagination; I didn't want them in my home.

'Do you have somewhere particular in mind?'

'Would you come with me to Vienna? I've never been, well not since I left as a child and I don't remember anything. It would be good to go with you.'

Nat insisted on paying for everything although I had money enough of my own. He booked a smart hotel overlooking the Stadt Park, a hired car to the airport for me and a rented car in Vienna so that we could explore the countryside. Somehow in the years that had passed, he had become a Mensch, a real grown up man, successful, good looking, even clever. That was the best part of him.

Until we were actually there I never believed it was going to happen. The suitcase I packed was my trousseau, the trip was our honeymoon, our first night was going to be our wedding night. To lie in the dark, all night long, to wake up together in the morning – I could hardly breathe at the thought of the privacy, the space, the wonderful secrecy of this trip.

Like a silly schoolgirl, I went shopping for new clothes to wear for my lover. In Fenwick's in Bond Street I bought a dusky pink negligee trimmed with pale grey lace, long shiny slippery satin which felt gorgeous against my skin. I imagined Nat's hands on it and under it.

The night before we left, I lay in the bath and looked at my plump, uneven body and tried to imagine myself in silk underwear sharing a room and a bathroom with Nat for three nights. I was used to how I looked, but I had never learned to love my body. I had no idea what it would be like to wonder at your beauty every time you looked in the mirror, to be proud when others looked at you. Painfully, I climbed out of the bath and dried myself. I was plump now and there was nothing skinny or elegant about me. My flesh was still firm but my legs were too short, my thighs out of proportion for my legs; my hips were wide and my bottom stuck out. It was ridiculous to behave as if I was some glamorous beauty, a Jean Shrimpton or a Julie Christie. I never had been and I wouldn't be now.

'You're gorgeous to me,' Nat said, whenever I told him how it felt to be me, when he wondered why I had never married. 'You are the best person I know.' And he would look at me as if I really was beautiful to him.

But on our first night in Vienna I lay with my eyes open on the far side of the bed listening to the sound of Nat's soft breathing, 'phe, phe', through his mouth and I couldn't sleep. Even in the morning I didn't want him to touch me. He propped himself up with his elbow and watched me press my stick to the floor to steady myself and walk to the bathroom.

'Eva what's wrong?' he asked when I returned.

'I don't know, I don't understand it myself.' I sat on the edge of the bed and started to cry. He put his arm around me and stroked my cheek, like he would have done if I was a sad child, like he must have done to his own children.

After breakfast, we wandered silently round the city like any pair of tourists on their first sunny day. We stopped for lunch at a restaurant opposite Stephansdom, St Stephen's cathedral. From our table we could see the enormous black and gold Austrian eagle built in to the tiled roof. The sight of it made me shiver.

'They love their churches here, don't they?' Nat said. I looked at the Wiener schnitzel and the mixed salad arranged in four neat segments, unable to eat. 'It says here in the guide book that they bombed it in the last days of the war and that within three years they had completely rebuilt it from the donations people sent in.'

'My mother died in the bombings. And maybe my little sister too.' He looked up at me in surprise.

'I didn't know you had a sister.'

'No, I know you didn't.'

'Why didn't you tell me about her? What was her name?'

'Her picture sits by my bed but you never asked me about it. Her name was Gertrude, she was three years younger than me.' Nat looked at me and said nothing.

The second night too, I lay on my side of the bed and he lay on his. Before dawn, while he slept, I got up and sat by the window in our hotel room and stared at the spongy black shapes of the trees in the park. In the morning I climbed back into bed to feel the warmth of his body but when he tried to touch me, I took his hand away.

Vienna frightened me. I don't know what I had imagined, perhaps a colourful fantasy of young women in dirndl skirts and lace aprons, and men in lederhosen and feathers in their Tyrolean hats. What I found was a place where everything seemed heavy and dark, the men in loden green and grey, the women overdressed and over made up. The huge baroque buildings, beautiful and elegant to the eyes of most tourists were hateful and oppressive to me. Everything made me feel miserable: mothers walking hand in hand with their small fair headed children, the familiar flavours and smells of the food they served us in restaurants – schnitzel, boiled beef with grated fried potatoes, paprika goulash, the smell of the coffee and the huge displays of perfect cakes, the constant, guttural sound of German being spoken everywhere, the impossibility of finding any trace of Jewish life.

I didn't know what I was doing here. It felt wrong to be in Vienna with Nat. If I was here at all, it should have been with Susi. Nat thought I was punishing him for a lifetime of betrayal, but it wasn't that. It was a sickness of the soul that I had caught from being in this city.

*

'Do you feel a bit better?' he asked on our second morning as if I was suffering from a bad cold. We watched the elderly waiter wheel a table into our room.

It was covered with stark white linen, a silver pot of coffee, a basket of rolls and a bowl of fruit. He bowed in an old-fashioned, obsequious way and backed out of the room.

'You hate it here don't you?' Nat said. I made an effort to speak.

'I'm sorry. I don't understand it myself. I can't even say it's bad memories because I don't remember anything about living in Vienna. I feel so unsettled here, like I've dreamt it all, but I can't properly recall the dream.' Nat buttered a roll for me, spreading honey on it, peeling and slicing an apple, removing the green tops from the strawberries.

'I don't want to eat anything. Food won't make it better, I'm not a child.'

'Can I do anything for you? What can I do?'

'Don't keep asking me that, please. It doesn't help.' He looked at me miserably. I sighed and tried again. 'We'll go out in a bit. I'd like to see the house where I used to live, and the park where I used to walk with my mother and Susi. Maybe that will make me feel better.'

'Do you know where?'

'I found a little card wrapped up with some of the linen Susi gave me when I moved. It's like a visiting card, it must have been hers when she was young. I've kept it on me ever since.' I took it out of my purse: *Susi Rosen, stud., Gym., Wien II, Obere Donaustrasse 6, Apt. 4.*

'I think the Gym. part is short for Gymnasium, the secondary school she went to. And the park we used to play in is right near there, the Augarten. I used to walk there with my mother, after we collected

Susi from school. My mother mentioned it in the letters she wrote to me.'

'Why didn't you ever tell me any of this?'

I shrugged my shoulders and he gave me another of his hangdog looks.

'To be honest, I've never known that much myself. Most of what I know I found out that one time when Susi told me the truth about my family, when she had to tell me. I told you it then, on that last day.' Nat began to chew on the side of his thumbnail, a gesture I hadn't seen for years.

'I didn't tell you that my mother and my grandmother worked for Susi's family as maids. I suppose I felt ashamed and I was trying to make sense of it all for myself.'

Even now, I couldn't bring myself to tell Nat about my father.

'That night when Susi told me about my mother, she gave me a little box she'd kept since the war and it had that photo in it and some letters my mother wrote to me. She said that Gertrude used to ask about me, but I'm not sure whether that can be true, she was so little when I left. It used to worry me that I couldn't remember any of this, but a child psychiatrist I met through work a few years ago told me that it wasn't at all unusual because first person memory doesn't start till later. I found that comforting, that I didn't just abandon my own mother and my little sister. I told her about the other psychiatrist I saw in the 1950s after we broke up, the one who told me I had suppressed memory, and she said, all memory is suppressed, it's how it is retrieved that's interesting.'

We sat in silence for a few minutes. I knew that

the way I spoke about these things made it impossible for Nat to ask me to tell him more; I'd learned this trick from Susi a long time ago. He offered me the bread roll again as a peace offering and I accepted it.

Later that morning, we took the tram to Franz-Josef Kai and got off at the wide, grey Donau Canal. We crossed the Canal at Augartenbrücke and walked in silence along Obere Donaustrasse, the Canal and a wide strip of grass on our left, and on our right, big apartment blocks with tired looking shops on the ground floor. At a corner, I stopped in the doorway of a small grocery store and asked directions for number 6. She pointed, without smiling, to the last stretch of the street as it curved away from the Canal, towards the big park. The road was treeless and the big, flat fronted houses made a continuous grey line on both sides. My stick was unstable on the big, square cobbles and my left hip was aching terribly. Nat took my arm through his for support.

We stopped outside number 6. There were three steps up to a huge black door with a brass knocker in the shape of a hand.

'This is it. This is where I lived.'

I stood and looked for a long time, trying to imagine the interior, thirty-six years ago. I could see it like a painting; the kind where the artist wants to tell you a story. The big upstairs rooms were like a Renoir: a bright, dancing picture of the mother-of-pearl cabinet, the velvet covered chairs, the rug and the fine china, with Susi in a pretty party dress with her own laughing family around her. And downstairs, a Rembrandt or a Vermeer: the face of my own mother in her dark little kitchen in the caretaker's flat on the ground floor, chopping potatoes on the table or hanging the clothes in front of the fire, worrying about me and her new baby.

'Do you want to knock and see if they'll let us in to have a look?' Nat asked.

'No, I just wanted to see it.' I took Nat's hand. Gratefully, he kissed the side of my forehead. We walked the few minutes down to the Augarten. It was a large flat park, with immaculate flower borders arranged in separate, neat rows, ordered and regimented with grass so perfect that no one needed the signs to tell you to keep off. We walked around the wide sandy paths and stopped and sat down at a bench.

'I know this place. Susi told me about it once and that was so unlike her. She told me that I used to meet her from school with my mother and walk through this park. This is where we were, I'm sure. We were right here.'

I had the strangest feeling, like a ghost had passed over me. This wasn't a painting I had imagined, it was something real that I had held inside me all these years. I could see a battered old pram, very low to the ground, and I could feel myself pulling up on the sides, desperate to get out of it and run. I was on Susi's shoulders; we were running along very fast and the cold wind was in our faces.

*

The next day, our last full day, we got up early and Nat drove us to Mitteldorf, about fifty kilometres from Vienna. We had first planned it as a wonderful day away from the city. A drive through the country, maybe a picnic, just to see where my family came from. But the atmosphere of the city hung heavy between us, and I could not turn to Nat for comfort and love.

The Austrian countryside was pretty. Long green stripes rolled down the hills, not the patchwork squares of English fields. Nat drove smoothly and efficiently with the map on his lap, unfazed by the unfamiliarity of the roads. It was a fine, late spring morning full of light and warmth. He was wearing a blue summer shirt with short sleeves and I leaned over and smoothed my hand over his forearm. He looked at me and smiled and the silence between us suddenly became companionable again.

It was still morning when we reached the little town, more like a village really, in two parts. The lower part was almost empty with little streets leading off a dull central square, the window boxes of geraniums making the only real colour. The upper part looked prettier with trees and houses built up into the hills. We got out of the car and looked round. On one side of the square there were a few shops and a café and on the others, the Rathaus – the town hall, and several flat fronted stone houses, but there was nothing that looked like the big store that Susi's family used to own. We stopped for a coffee. 'Zwei brauner bitte?' I asked. The waiter smiled and brought us two large cups of coffee.

'Are you visitors?' He asked in an accent that was hard to follow.

'We're from England but my mother's family used to live here,' I said.

'Really? What was your family name?'

'My grandmother was called Hanna and my mother Maria. The surname was Weiss.' I pronounced it hesitantly, not exactly sure that it was correct. 'And my mother's married name was Hofer.' He turned to an old woman standing behind the counter and spoke to her rapidly for a few minutes.

'Ah, you mean Weihs. Yes, my mother knew them. They worked for the owners of the Jew store, before they were kicked out.' Nat, who spoke Yiddish, understood this and bristled. I tried to keep smiling.

'I couldn't see the store. Where is it?'

'Oh it doesn't exist anymore. They knocked it down in the '60s and built those apartments just over there. Can you see?' He pointed across the square at an ugly block of flats.

'I'm afraid I know very little about my family, I grew up in England.' I said, gaining confidence that I could understand him and that he could understand me. Those years of listening to Susi's friends, the only time she and Ziggy had ever spoken German at home, and all the times I had read the German newspapers to those elderly people had taught me more than I realised. 'I know that my grandmother lived in one of the streets near the square with a barn attached where my mother grew up. I have a letter from my mother and she describes it to me, but I don't have an exact address. Do you know who I could ask?' He turned again to the woman.

'My mother will show you if you like,' he said. 'She went to school with your mother and her sister. She knew her quite well. And if you want, they will have their papers at the town hall. You can ask there.'

The old woman wiped her hands on her

enormous white apron and came round from behind the counter. She looked at me in amazement.

'Are you Maria's daughter? The little crippled one?'

'Yes, that must be me.'

She shook her head and made the sign of the cross.

'I didn't think you were alive.' She patted my cheek. 'What is your name?'

'Eva. Eva Friedmann.'

'Eva, that's right. But Friedmann is a Jewish name, isn't it?'

'Yes, it is.' She shook her head again, bewildered at this and indicated for us to follow her. Nat and I walked behind her across the square and down a narrow side road which backed on to the open space of the countryside.

'That's where your mother lived.' It was a low corner house, part sandstone and part rough stone walling. Behind it, on a narrow alley, was a huge, unvarnished door half off its hinges. Nat pushed it open. The place was empty except for a few rusty car parts and some old tools.

'I think this must be where they kept Susi's family things to save them from the Nazis,' I said softly to Nat. 'The things we had in the house, the cabinet with the china in it and the menorah and all that. My clock and the painting.' We both looked and looked into the empty space. I shook my head.

'You know that your aunt still lives in this house?'

'My aunt?'

'Your mother's sister. Frau Danner – Anneliese.

She moved in here with her family sometime in the 1950s when your grandmother was so ill.'

She knocked at the door and called out something I could not understand. A broad woman came to the door, elderly and plain, her hair tied back in a neat bun. They exchanged a few hurried words and my aunt looked at me and gasped.

'This is Maria's daughter? Eva?'

'Yes.'

'I can't believe it.' She crossed herself hurriedly and took my hand. 'Come in, come in. Your husband too.' She pulled me into the sitting room, full of heavy dark furniture and religious icons. 'What a miracle to see you again. We heard after the war that you had gone with the Shapiros' granddaughter to England. Amazing. Did she look after you? Your dear mother missed you so much.' She crossed herself again and wiped the tears from her eyes with her apron. 'And your legs. Did they manage to find a cure for you in England?'

I smiled. 'No, they're still there, just as they were, only longer.' My sarcasm was lost in the translation and I felt ashamed of myself.

'I must go for a minute and find my husband. And you have a cousin, Friedrich, who works as a mechanic, and my grandchildren, but they are in school. And you are just here for today? Wait, wait, I will be back in a minute.'

Nat and I looked at each other, amazed. I had not prepared myself for this.

Soon, despite my protests, there was a meal on the table. Plain boiled beef with strong horseradish sauce and vegetables, beer for Nat, a plain cake, a plate of apples, coffee. I didn't understand everything they said, but if they spoke slowly, I could follow most of it. It was true, they said, my mother had died when the Americans bombed Vienna right at the end of the war, but they were less sure about Gertrude.

'Poor little thing. I know that she was at Steinhof, a very famous hospital in Vienna with a children's clinic. We lost touch a bit during the war. It was very hard for us here because my mother Hanna was...'

'Yes?'

'She was very involved with the Shapiro family and after the war started...well, people were not kind at that time. They were frightened and my mother wouldn't have a word said against the Jews. She was very fond of the family. She even hid furniture and things for them. The Shapiro granddaughter came back to collect them after the war.'

'What was the matter with my sister?'

'I'm not sure. Rickets I think. She wasn't like you, her legs were good when she was little, she walked fine. But there was a lot of rickets during the war because of the food shortage. And your poor mother was living in Vienna in such a damp room.'

'But you don't die of rickets.'

'Well maybe something else. She was sickly as a baby. I remember that she had a lot of bad diarrhoea, and she was small for her age.'

'When did she die?'

'1941, 1942. I think she must have died in the hospital. Perhaps they buried her there. I know that we didn't have a funeral for her here. Your dear grandmother Hanna is buried in the Mitteldorf cemetery with her husband. She'd been ill for a long time. And the first baby. Johann. That was before the war started. They brought him back here to bury him.'

'The first baby? Did I have a brother too?'

'You didn't know? Johann, the first born, named after your father. He died of a fever when he was just a few months old. So sad, your poor mother had so many troubles. Have a piece of cake my dear, you've hardly eaten a thing.'

'Do you have a photograph of him, the baby I mean?'

'I don't, I'm so sorry. But I can find you one of your grandmother if you like.' She went to the heavy sideboard and pulled out an old album. Carefully, she removed a sepia photograph from its paper hinges and handed it to me. It was a studio portrait of my grandmother as a young woman with two pretty girls dressed in Austrian outfits. 'That's your mother Maria on the right. Look at her beautiful plaits. I always envied those.' She laughed. 'You can have it, if you like.' I leaned over and kissed her soft, papery cheek.

'Thank you so much. I'll keep it safe.' There was a pause while I tried to form the next question. 'Do you know anything about my father?'

'Your father?' Involuntarily my aunt screwed up her mouth in disgust. 'I know that he joined the Wehrmacht before the war started and left your mother with you and Gertrude but I don't know what happened to him. I remember that he was furious when he found out that she had sent you away to England but he made some excuse and it was all covered up. I'm sorry to say this but we did not think he was a good man. He was not kind to your mother or to you. But that's enough of the past my dear. Tell

338

us about yourself. Tell us about your life.'

I looked at these kind hearted, fair haired people with their square jaws and it was hard to think of them as my relatives. There was the Virgin Mary on the mantelpiece and the carving of the Crucifixion on the walls. I had grown up a long way away from them. I had learned to love a different God, to have a different life.

We shook hands and kissed as we parted. We exchanged addresses and promised to keep in touch but I felt that neither of us really expected to meet again. My cousin Friedrich took us over to the town hall where, in just a few minutes, a woman found and photocopied the birth and death certificates of Hanna Weihs and Rosa Shapiro, my grandmother and Susi's grandmother. There was a birth certificate for my mother but nothing of her death, nor anything of my sister Gertrude, nor my little brother. Nat drove to the cemetery on the outskirts of town, the Jewish one and the Roman Catholic, separated only by a thin, stone wall. At each office, an efficient clerk was able to tell us the position of the grave. We put a flower on Hanna's grave and a smooth flat stone on Rosa's.

We drove back into town without much speech. It was still early when we got back to the hotel, barely five o'clock but I was exhausted and in pain. I took my shoes off and lay down. Nat lay beside me on the bed and turned on his side, his arm around my waist. He kissed me and slid his hand under my shirt. I lay very still.

'Nat. I'm sorry. Go downstairs and read the paper or something. Just give me a little while. I'll take a couple of Anadin and then I'll come down and we'll have dinner in the hotel. I'll feel better if I have a rest.'

He sighed but did as I asked.

An hour or so later, I got up, put on a dark green, silk shirt and black trousers and went downstairs. The hotel restaurant was plush and ornate. Red velvet seats, heavy white linen tablecloths, the waiters elderly and subservient. All around us were couples: men in heavy dark suits and the women elegantly coiffed, in expensive clothes and jewellery.

'Eva, please talk to me,' Nat said. 'Tell me what's the matter. What have I done?'

'You haven't done anything.'

'But you seem so angry and upset with me. You don't want me near you.'

'Look, Nat. Not everything I feel has to do with you. It may not have occurred to you, but this isn't about you.'

'I know, I know. It was a shock to meet those people today, but you were upset with me before. You haven't been yourself this whole trip.'

'If it's about anything, it's being here, in Vienna. Every time I look at someone over fifty, I think, what were you doing when they rounded up Susi's parents? Were you one of the people who wanted to throw away all the children like me? Every old man I see, I think that could be my father who would rather have had me dead.' I looked over at the row of grey haired waiters, standing ready with their silver trays. 'I keep thinking if I went over there and asked them, what were you doing in Vienna when all that was going on? Which one of them would say, "yes, I helped, I was a Nazi. I believed you should all die, all of you."'

Nat looked at me sadly. 'I'm so sorry, Eva. I

didn't think about how it would make you feel, being here. Maybe we shouldn't have come. We could have gone to Edinburgh or Paris, anywhere but here. I so wanted to make everything nice for you. To make it up to you.'

I looked at him in amazement.

'What do you mean, make it up to me? Did you think that three days away together would make all these years disappear?'

He looked at me with the boyish shame faced expression he had worn twenty years ago.

'You've never talked like this before,' he said quietly. 'I didn't realise you still felt so angry with me.'

'For God's sake Nat!' The staid couple on the next table looked over at me, their eyebrows raised. I took a few deep breaths and tried to lower my voice. 'What are you talking about? Do you think it's all right that we didn't see each other for seventeen years? And now we see each other once a fortnight or so for a few hours before you go back to your cosy life, that's fine too?'

'Eva, don't. You know how much I want to be with you, but I can't. Please try to understand that.'

'I've spent my whole life understanding. That's my job Nat, that's what I do. I understand everything. I make life easier for everyone else.'

'Darling, don't talk like that, please. I'd do anything for you Eva. I'd do anything to be with you.'

'I know you feel that now, when you're with me. But then when you go home, what happens to me then in your heart?'

He looked as if I had hit him.

'I love you. You must know that I love you.'

'You love me and you let me down,' I said and he had to lean forward to hear what I was saying. 'It's always been that way and it always will be.'

I wiped my mouth on the heavy, white linen napkin and folded it neatly on the plate. Nat signed the bill and we left the table in silence, aware that everyone was watching us, watching me, walk out of the restaurant.

Inside the door of our room, he stopped and turned to me, tears running down his face.

'Eva, forgive me. Please forgive me. I know I let you down so badly when you need me. But I can't bear it if you turn away from me.' He took my face in his hands and turned it towards him just like in my dreams of him. My back was against the door and he put his arm round me, and pressed me close. He kissed me and my body moved and responded to him as it had always done.

*

The next morning, Nat packed our cases and went downstairs to pay the bill. On the plane he said, 'Don't be angry with me. I know you told me not to, but I wanted to give you something.' He handed me a little bag with the name of the hotel on it. Inside was an Indian ring, a flat gold band like a wedding ring, inlaid with bright coloured stones: diamond, emerald, ruby. I held it up to the light. It was pretty but designed for a different kind of woman.

'Tell me you love me,' he said. 'Tell me you love me.' I sighed and felt the terrible sadness wash over my soul.

'You know I love you Nat. You know I always will.'

REBECCA

London

2000

Our flat was on the fourth floor of a council estate. Nothing in it was new and nothing matched – 'our hippy palace' mum called it when she was taking the piss out of herself – but it was cosy and bright and the rooms were surprisingly big. Mum loved strong colours: fuchsia pink, cornflower blue, jade green and she filled the flat with stuff she'd picked up in her travelling days or made herself: wicker chairs with velvet cushions, striped Mexican blankets, old saris made into curtains, embroidered cushions, pictures and mirrors in hand painted frames.

Getting to the front door wasn't always good though. When the lifts worked, they stank, and I hated the covered walk-way to our flat because you never knew who you might meet. Most of our neighbours were nice but some of the kids didn't like me any more. They thought I was a posh snob because I didn't go to the local secondary school.

'Don't take any notice, they're stupid but harmless,' Mum said. 'Try to be friendly but if not, just rise above it.' But that didn't take account of what it felt like when I heard three or four lots of footsteps walking in unison behind me as I came home from school.

Grandma Susi had offered to sort us out but mum wouldn't have it.

'We're absolutely fine. You've never been to see us, so you don't know what it's like. You've just got your prejudices about council estates. We have a lot of friends there, it's very friendly and nice.'

Sometimes she'd let grandma pay for new trainers for me or a school trip so I wouldn't miss out, but she'd never take a penny for herself.

Mum was the most honest person in the world. We never had much money but we were never in debt. She always used to say, 'If you can't afford it, it's best not to want it.' I've only ever known her tell one lie and that was because she didn't want me to go to the local secondary school. For once, grandma agreed with her.

'Why don't you let me pay for her to go to a good school, it's what your father would have wanted. You can't sacrifice her education for your silly principles. What would she be learning in a school round where you live?'

Send me to a private school? Of course mum wouldn't hear of it, but she put grandma's address on the form, pretending we were moving to Goldhurst Terrace, so that I could get into Hampstead Comprehensive. She said it was bending the truth, not breaking it – it was still a state school, mixed and all that, but with a more balanced intake. I was only ten at the time; I just did what I was told.

Now grandma had died and auntie Eva had died and suddenly we were going to have money.

'When everything is sorted out, probate and that, we could buy a place of our own, maybe somewhere nearer your school, Kentish Town or Chalk Farm,' Mum said. 'And we can keep auntie Eva's car, I've cleared it with Jackie. Would you like that, to have a car? You could have driving lessons in a year's time. Maybe we'll buy a flat with a little garden in one of those big Victorian houses. Grandma would be pleased, don't you think, that we were finally leaving Lambeth and coming back north of the river.' She smiled that funny smile she had with one corner of her mouth turned up and one eyebrow raised and for a second, she looked the spit of grandma Susi.

Perhaps that was why they didn't get on, mum and grandma, because they were alike in lots of ways. Mum's work for example. Before she got ill, she had her own little fashion business, not classic, old fashioned dresses like grandma's company used to make, but she was still designing and selling clothes. She put herself through art college and started working on her own, buying clothes and material from abroad: India, Thailand, Sri Lanka, Hong Kong. Her company had been called East-meets-West: loose fitting clothes, interesting shapes, the kind of clothes mum liked to wear herself.

Still, mum and grandma got on like a house on fire compared to mum's relationship with her sister. When grandma had sold the house there had been the most terrible arguments between her and auntie Jackie. Mum didn't want to take anything. She told grandma she should sell what she didn't want and spend the money on herself, take a round the world cruise or buy up the whole of Anita's of St John's Wood, her favourite clothes shop.

'Stuffy antiques,' she said to anyone who would listen. Not grandma of course, but anyone else. 'Stuffy antiques, haunted with bad memories.'

Auntie Jackie had different ideas. She flew over and chose all the best pieces, a lot of the china and linen and pictures, and the furniture that was too big for grandma to take with her to the flat. She had them boxed up and sent back to Israel. Mum was absolutely furious, although she kept insisting that she didn't want any of it, nothing at all except a pencil drawing by an Austrian artist that grandpa had loved. I could see this was one of mum's principles that I was never going to understand.

'When I go, just chuck everything out unless you really, really want to keep it for yourself. Don't even think about whether it's worth selling,' mum said then. 'They're such a burden, other people's possessions. At least there'll only be you to inherit it. No money grabbing sister to argue with.'

But this time round, they sorted grandma's flat together without a single cross word and no one even mentioned Israeli politics which was an incredible relief. It was funny to see them getting on, sorting it out, crying together, deciding what to sell and what to keep. Maybe mum had a different idea about keeping things, now that we were going to become property owners ourselves. Or maybe it took two deaths to bring an end to their own little war.

Still, nobody wanted the job of sorting out auntie Eva's things.

'She was so fond of you,' mum said. 'I think she'd like you to decide. Make a list of the things you'd like to keep and we'll give the rest away.'

'What about her electric wheelchair and the new lightweight one she used to put in the car?'

'I'm sure a charity shop would like those.'

'And what about all the things you can't sell?'

'We'll just throw them away.'

'No, I mean her letters and photos and things like that.'

'I don't know love, you decide. You're much more sensible than me. You do this one thing and I promise I'll sort everything else out. Choose what you think we should keep and I'll organise for the rest to be taken away. Promise.'

*

There were three weeks left of my summer holidays and it felt like I'd spent most of it on the underground travelling to the Finchley Road or Hendon Central, doing things I didn't want to do. As usual, Mrs Lampeter's head appeared round her front door, the second she heard my key in the lock.

'Oh, hello. Thought I heard someone. Anything I can do?'

'No thanks, Mrs Lampeter.'

'Come to sort your great-auntie's things out, have you? Need a hand of any sort?'

'No, really. I'll be fine.'

'Oh, well then.' She looked disappointed. 'Let me know if you do.'

The truth was that I had no idea where to start. Our flat was already full of second hand junk and now it was bursting at the seams with grandma's stuff. I didn't see how we could fit in anything more. Mum said we were definitely going to move into somewhere bigger and she never broke her promises, but it could take months, years even. Making decisions was never her strongest point.

It was spooky poking around in someone else's home, someone who couldn't be there to tell you to mind your own business and leave their things alone. I felt lonely and awkward, although being in this empty flat gave me a peculiar sense of freedom, as if I could do anything at all.

I started in the kitchen because that seemed easiest. There were just things in a kitchen, useful, practical things that you either needed or you didn't. More or less everything in auntie Eva's tiny kitchen was in better condition than ours, but there was nothing we couldn't live without. It would be good to have a microwave or a fridge where everything didn't slide down the shelf onto the floor if you tried to put something heavy into it, but it was too much hassle to even think about moving a fridge.

There was stuff in the sitting room that didn't really seem to belong to anyone, like furniture and pictures you might find in a hotel room or an office. I could imagine a presenter from one of those lifestyle programmes going, 'Now that, madam, is an interesting brown sofa with orange cushions, but it doesn't seem to go with this very fine antique side table. And I'm not sure about this teak unit, it has no style at all.' I wrote down some of the things I liked, things that were connected to auntie Eva.

Things to Keep: *Vienna wooden clock, silver menorah, candlesticks, lace tablecloth from the big table, painting of farm scene.*

When I was little, I used to make up stories with auntie Eva about that painting and once, when I was in primary school, I had won a competition for a story of my own.

There was a farmer and his wife and they lived on the edge of a forest. They had a little daughter and she was very adventurous and lively. One day when they were busy working on the farm, the little girl ran into the forest and got lost. The farmer and his wife looked everywhere for her but they could not find her. As the sun began to set they returned to the farm but still she had not returned. The mother and father were very worried about her. Just before the moon came out, their little daughter came home. She was riding on the back of their old cow as if it was a horse. The cow had gone to find her and had brought her home. The mother and the father were so pleased to see her again that they did not tell her off and they gave the cow a special bag of fresh hay. The little girl promised she would never run away again.

Auntie Eva had typed out the story for me and I had copied the painting as best I could. I could remember mixing up the deep green for the grass and purple for the sky. My teacher had framed the story and the drawing in black paper and hung it on the classroom wall. I was so proud of myself.

I had a quick look round auntie Eva's bedroom and tried not to think about the last time I'd been there. The blue leather box she had spoken about was on her dressing table. I took it into the kitchen and unzipped it. At the bottom there were some letters from Austria, tissue paper thin with funny handwriting. And there were five pieces of jewellery: a silver locket with blue enamel, a little chain with pearls evenly spaced along it, and two rings – a dainty, old fashioned one with little diamonds and one I knew mum would love, yellow Indian gold, set with a bright band of coloured stones. It was the last piece that really surprised me: a thin gold cross on a chain. I didn't understand how auntie Eva would have come by this, let alone why she would have put it aside especially for me.

It was the second bedroom that made me realise how long it had been since I'd been on a proper visit to see her. It wasn't my spare bedroom any more with the Peter Rabbit duvet and pillow we'd chosen together in Brent Cross. It was a study now, with a smart, wooden filing cabinet and a matching desk with a new purple iMac right in the middle. Above the desk there was a shelf of framed photographs: mum and auntie Jackie when they were young, me, the cousins, auntie Eva herself – ten or eleven years old, standing outside grandma and grandpa's house with her curly hair held back in a wide hair band and a shy smile on her face. There was one of her at the seaside when she was about eighteen or nineteen, with the arms of a smiling young man tight around her shoulders and I thought that this must have been the boy she was engaged to. The photo that always used to be by her bed was here too but now it was in one of those double frames with a hinge down the middle. On one side was the picture of two little children and their mother which I'd seen before, and on the other side, there was an even older picture, a sepia one with a different mother and two little girls dressed in Heidi costumes with long plaits.

I wrote *photographs* on my list. Whatever mum said about being ruthless, I didn't see how you could throw away someone's photographs.

Tentatively, I opened her filing cabinet, feeling like a house burglar. It was packed full of well organised files, ordinary household things like **Insurance**, **Council Tax**, **Bank Account**. A life divided into clear neat sections. I pulled out the one marked: **Nat**. There were lots of cards and old letters, the kind of cards that have slushy poems printed inside. There were a couple of photographs too, another one taken at the same time as the picture on the shelf – Eva and her boyfriend at the seaside – and a small one like a passport photo of a man in a wide pattern tie and long sideburns. I turned it over: *Nat, 1972*. He was younger then, but I could still see that it was the same man who had been so upset at her funeral, the one who'd shaken my hand and told me what a wonderful person Eva was. I put the file back in the drawer. It didn't seem right to look any further. If I ever had a drawer full of love letters, I wouldn't want somebody else to look through them.

The biggest file was marked: **Gertrude**.

Gertrude, auntie Eva's little sister. These were the things that she had said we would look at together some day. I pulled out a packet of photographs, but they were of things, not people. Two or three showed a very grand yellow ochre building like a town hall or a museum. It had long white windows and balconies, steps surrounded by stone pillars and a huge front door. At the top, laid out in blue stone were the words – *Psychiatrisches Krankenhaus de Stadt Wien.* There was grass all around it and flower beds like in a big park and on the path leading up to it there was an attractive Art Nouveau or maybe Art Deco, I could never remember which was which, clock tower with metalwork in that bluey-green colour that happens when copper meets the weather. The other photographs also showed buildings: most of them white painted stone and honey coloured bricks, two or three storeys high with long, barred windows. There were several of a single doorway, taken from different angles: a green metal porch above the lintel, and hanging from this, framed in the same green colour, was a cube of opaque glass with the number 15 painted in black on all four of its sides. On the back of one of these photographs, auntie Eva had written:

Am Spiegelgrund, Steinhof. Pavilion 15 (Children's Pavilion).

'Reichsausschuss', Committee for the Scientific Evaluation of Severe Hereditary Conditions.

There were photographs of carefully mown lawns and flowerbeds and in one of these pictures, curiously alone in the middle of a field, there was a black marble gravestone with German words engraved in gold. I turned it over and read the translation: *Erected in memory of the victims in the psychiatric clinic of the National Socialist State.* In front of the stone there was a little wreath of artificial flowers and around it there were metal chains arranged in a square, as if someone had tried to make it look bigger and more important.

I went into the kitchen to fetch a chair – auntie Eva must have sat at her desk in her wheelchair. I lifted the file out of the cabinet and opened it flat on the desk. There were newspaper cuttings and all sorts of papers: photocopies, emails, scribbled notes torn from a telephone pad, pages printed out on the computer and a little, yellow school exercise book with lines and margins, full of auntie Eva's neat, round handwriting. But there was no note for me.

I took six or seven pages out of a clear plastic folder. They were copies of photographs of children, old black and white pictures, and a pale blue post-it note stuck on the front – *photographs from hospital records:*

Ludwig Eder. There were three photographs of a boy with a beautiful, sad, intelligent head and the thinnest, thinnest body I had ever seen, as if there was only a layer of skin to cover his bones, no muscles at all.

Stasia Zipfel. Two photographs of a little girl about five years old with dark eyes and straight bobbed hair. One picture sideways on, showed her sitting, her spine slightly curved as if she was bending forward. The other, standing, concentrating so hard on her balance that the fingers of her left hand were splayed out.

Peter Wick. Two pictures. A beautiful, perfect little boy, five or six years old, naked, his arms by his side, his head cocked sideways and in the second photograph of his face, the sweetest, most trusting smile you could ever see.

No. 722, no name, just one large picture. A man or a teenage boy so distressed that he crouched on the floor, his head down, one arm over his face, the other covering his penis.

No name. Two pictures. In one, a laughing baby in a cot with a striped doll. In the other, a picture of her being held by a smiling nurse. There were words typed on the original sheet and auntie Eva had written the translation in pencil: *Children who were killed in Am Spiegelgrund's 'healing and care' clinic.*

Gertrude Hofer. One picture. A little girl maybe three years old, naked on a white sheet, shiny dark hair cut short, her hands in her lap touching each other, her face turned away from the camera, crying hard.

I reached up to the shelf and took down the photograph of the woman with her two little girls, the one that had been by auntie Eva's bed for many years.

The pretty, dark haired girl sitting on her mother's lap was younger but I was sure that it was the same child as the little girl who was crying in the hospital picture. And the second child in this photograph, the one with fair, curly hair and a shy smile standing by her mother's side. It was so unmistakably the face of auntie Eva that I couldn't believe that I had never recognised her.

I flicked through the newspaper cuttings and various letters written in German and took out what looked like a carefully typed school essay.

GERTRUDE HOFER, BORN 11TH JUNE 1937, DIED 26TH SEPTEMBER 1942, VICTIM OF NAZI EUTHANASIA PROGRAMME, AM SPIEGELGRUND, VIENNA.
A REPORT BY EVA FRIEDMANN
Flat 1, Furness Court, Station Road, London NW4
March 2000.

In 1939, before the war started, I left Austria on the Kindertransport and came to London with a family friend. Although the Nazis had not yet fully developed their so-called 'Euthanasia Programme', my mother had very good reason to believe that my life was in danger because I was a disabled child. In fact it was only a few months after I left Vienna that they set up the 'Reichsausschuss', the committee which was to decide which children should be considered as 'not worthy to live'. These were the children who would soon be put to death.

I did not discover that my own sister, Gertrude Hofer, had been murdered in just such a programme until February 1997 when I received a letter and a newspaper cutting from my aunt Anneliese Danner who lives in a small town outside Vienna. The letter she enclosed was as follows (I have translated from the German):

My dear Eva,

By chance I came across this small announcement in the Austrian newspaper yesterday. I thought it might be of some interest to you. As I mentioned when I saw you, I am almost certain that this is where your mother Maria took Gertrude in 1941 when she was four years old. I remember her talking about it when she visited Mitteldorf. Before this Gertrude had been in a different children's clinic, but I do not know where this was. It may be important for you to have information concerning the date of your sister's birth in case you do not know this. I believe it to be June 10th or June 11th 1937. I hope this is of use to you.

I do hope that you will not learn anything that will be of great upset to you. Please let me know what you find out or if I can be of any help to you.

From your aunt,
Anneliese Danner

My aunt accompanied this note with the small newspaper cutting from the Standard, a daily newspaper in Vienna, which again, is roughly translated as follows:

'In the cause of the Euthanasia Programme in the time of the National Socialists, hundreds of children and young people were killed from the area then under the influence of the German Reich in the children's clinic Am Spiegelgrund which is part of the present day psychiatric clinic Baumgartner Hohe in Vienna, commonly known as Steinhof. It is intended to place the preserved brains of these victims which still exist today, in an honorary grave in Vienna.

Therefore the Viennese authority requests the family member who lost their relatives in the children's clinic Am Spiegelgrund in the years 1940-45, to make themselves known by writing before the 14th March 1997, to the Medical Director of the Psychiatric Krankenhaus.'

This began a period of long and painful research for me and I would not have been able to do it without the invaluable help of Waltraud Wick, whose own little brother was also murdered at the children's clinic during the same period.

Am Spiegelgrund was one of thirty or forty child euthanasia clinics set up by the Third Reich to carry out the Nazi policy of 'the eradication of the pathological genotype' or what we would now call the murder of disabled children. Over 700 children died in this clinic in the period 1941 – 45 and it has been proved that Dr Heinrich Schwarz was involved in these killings. After the war Schwarz became one of the wealthiest doctors in Austria, using the brains of these children as the basis for his research. He won many awards and lived in a grace and favour apartment in the grounds at Steinhof. Although the High Court of Vienna ruled that he was involved in the deaths of forty-six children he has continually escaped imprisonment, even up to March 2000 where a trial failed because he was deemed unfit to give evidence.

FACTUAL INFORMATION FROM THE MEDICAL RECORDS:

My sister Gertrude was admitted to Am Spiegelgrund Children's Clinic in the famous Steinhof psychiatric hospital, after a stay in another children's clinic. In March 1941, a public health officer from the first clinic, filled out a medical questionnaire in line with Nazi policy. The conclusion of this report was: 'Strong but small child. Weak musculature, nothing else abnormal discovered. No physical handicap. She is capable of development and education. She is in need of care with regard to the healing of rickets.'

However, when she was admitted to Am Spiegelgrund on 6th June, Dr Schwarz examined her and wrote on his report. 'The child is small and underdeveloped for her age with average condition of nourishment. Diagnosis – Idiotie (idiocy) 1A'.

The medical records also include the following tragic facts:

June – December 1941. Medical charts of around this time show that she is beginning to lose weight. (Weight loss of 4.6 kg during this period.)

3rd October 1941. Dr Schwarz requests the need for further information about the child's family.

25th October 1941. The report on the 'Condition of Biological Inheritance (Racial Purity)' arrives. It includes the information that one child, a son, had died before his first birthday and that a second child, a daughter now living overseas, was born with a physical deformity. It also describes, in some detail, information concerning a cousin of the child's father, Rudolph Hofer who died at the age of six. He is described as 'mentally handicapped (hydroencephalitis)'.

29th October 1941. A page is added to the hospital notes headed 'Decursus Morbi' (Cause of Death).

2nd December 1941. Report states she is unable to stand.

13th January 1942. Records show that Gertrude had now lost another 0.6 kg.

18th May 1942. The report B141 (a report that had to be sent to Berlin for the final decision about the death of a child) is signed by Dr Margaret Hubsch with the diagnosis 'severe mental handicap'.

1st June 1942. Attached to her notes is an extract from the Steinhof hospital records of her father's cousin, Rudolph Hofer.

30th June 1942. From the end of June '42, there is no entry for food in the 'therapy list', not even the bread and coffee or porridge which is all that was entered under food in the previous months.

26th July 1942. Gertrude is moved to Pavilion 15. The notes suggest that she has not understood the change of location. She is suffering from severe whooping cough and is very weak.

5th August 1942. She is given her first dose of Luminal.

11th September 1942. Despite poor health, she is given a pneumoencephalogram. (This is a procedure which involves introducing air into the cavities of the brain to replace cerebrospinal fluid in order to enable an assessment of the size etc. of the brain.)

22nd September 1942. Dr Schwarz reports in own handwriting that the encephalogram has been unsuccessful. He also reports: 'Not made the least development. Physically, notably retarded. Thickness of hairline comes low over the forehead.' He refers again to the relative Rudolph Hofer. There is no evidence that she is being given anything to eat.

23rd September 1942. Whooping cough, lung infection, but no evidence of high temperature. Dr Schwarz in a hand written note, 'took no nourishment, slept all day.'

9th October 1942. A typewritten letter sent to the mother, signed by Dr Schwarz. 'I regret to inform you that the condition of your little daughter Gertrude has worsened. In addition to her poor general condition there has been the development of pneumonia. In view of this, we must expect the worst.' The medical records of this time, however, give no evidence of a fever.

26th October 1942. Time of death recorded as 8am. Hospital records give cause of death as pneumonia, but Nazi central records say she died of idiocy and heart failure. My sister was five years old and at the time of her death she weighed

```
12.6 kg, the weight of an average two
year old child.
```

I thought I was going to be sick. I put my head down on the desk, my heart pounding out of my chest. After a few minutes, I went into the kitchen and poured myself a glass of water. I wanted to put it all straight back in the file and never look at it again, but I knew that, just as it wasn't right for me to look at Nat's letters, I had a responsibility to look at what was here.

One glance at a newspaper cutting with its garish colour photo of rows and rows of numbered jars containing children's brains was enough for me. I picked up the yellow exercise book. On the first double spread, auntie Eva had written **Things I Know** on one side of the page and **Things I Will Never Know** on the other. The **Things I Know** was mostly the stuff I'd just read. Under **Things I will never know**, she'd written:

*1. I know that many parents were impressed by the beautiful grounds and the smart buildings where the clinics were housed and they believed that fresh air and good medical treatment would be good for their children. **BUT**, my mother already had some idea what was going on in these places. So why did she let Gertrude be taken there? Did my father force her when he was on leave from the army; did he take her without her knowledge, or did she believe that because Gertrude was not 'Behinderte', not backwards or disabled, but just had curable diarrhoea and rickets, she, unlike me, would be safe from the harm?*

2. I don't understand why the hospital records keep

referring to a cousin of my father. What did he have to do with this?

She had started writing a number 3, but had crossed it out so heavily, it was impossible to read it and on the next page, she'd written:

FOR GERTRUDE
You were my sister.
We were born of the same womb,
The same mother, the same name.
Johann, Eva, Gertrude Hofer.
Not Shapiro, not Friedmann, not Gold.
Three babies who would never grow up to play
together.
I was the big sister, it was my job to look after
you,
To play with you and teach you things I knew.

Here there were lots more crossings out and then:

While you were hungry, so was I.
But I was the one who escaped.
It shouldn't have been you in that dark, cold
place
With no one to feed you, no one to love you.

After that there was nothing.

I went back to the previous page and looked again. Under the scored biro lines, I could just make out five words:

It should have been me.

*

It took mum and me a long time to piece this all together. Even after she'd had the longest ever phone call to auntie Jackie there were still a lot of things we weren't sure about. It was the names that confused us as much as anything, Hofer and Danner weren't names that we'd ever heard of, and Mum and auntie Jackie didn't think that they were Jewish names. We talked about it all that evening and the next day and the next, round and round trying to make sense of it. It was only when mum had a go at translating the letters from the blue box that we began to have some idea of the truth.

'So that's what she means when she wrote that she came to England with a "family friend". Did you know that grandma Susi and auntie Eva weren't really cousins?' I asked mum.

'It wasn't much talked about when I was growing up. I just assumed they were, because they came out of Vienna together. I knew she'd changed her name to my father's but I always thought that it was because they brought her up. It's hard to remember what I was told, if I was told anything. She was just auntie Eva to us. She was always there when I was growing up, I never really thought about it.'

'Grandma told me once that she had to lie to get auntie Eva out of Vienna but I thought she just meant because of how she walked, so that she would pass the medical. I didn't realise she meant about them not being related.'

'I just can't get any of it straight. This whole thing

about her having a little sister who died like that.'

'I knew that she had a little sister.'

'Did you?' Mum looked at me sharply. 'How?'

'Auntie Eva told me a few months ago when we went out for one of our meals together. She said she was putting all this together so she could show it to me one day.'

'Another dark horse in the family. Why didn't you tell me?'

I shrugged.

'Do you think she ever told grandma what she'd found out about Gertrude?'

'I don't know. It's hard to imagine that she didn't, they were so close. I hope she talked to someone, it must be terrible to discover something like that and have to keep it all to yourself.'

Suddenly there was a hard, painful knot in my throat.

'I don't want to go back to her flat again, mum. I don't want to find out anything else horrible.' Mum put her arms out and I climbed on her lap like I was still a little girl. She smoothed my hair back from my face.

'We'll do it together. We'll do the next bit together.'

*

Mum kept to her word. She said we should give ourselves a treat so we bought a little picnic in one of the takeaway coffee shops: a smoked salmon and cream cheese sandwich for her, an avocado, watercress and pine nut tortilla wrap for me and strawberry smoothies. Mum got out auntie Eva's blue and white striped plates although we didn't really need them, and we sat down together at the kitchen table. When we'd finished, mum went into the study and began to look through the letters and cards that Nat had sent.

'Mum you can't do that. It's private.'

'Well so was the file about Gertrude and we looked at that. She's dead now darling, she's not with us any more. I don't think she'd mind us looking.'

She began to read bits of the letters out loud. 'He must have been on National Service when he wrote these, they all seem to say the same thing. It's sweet though. *Hello sweetheart. Are you missing me as much as I'm missing you? Things are pretty terrible here as usual, but I'll be home in two weeks and I'll be knocking at your door as soon as I get back.* Not exactly Oscar Wilde is it?'

'Mum, honestly. Stop it.'

She made a face at me but put the letter back.

'She told me about Nat.'

Mum raised her eyebrows at me.

'On one of our meals, maybe it was the same one she told me about Gertrude. She said they'd been engaged but it broke up. Did you know him?'

'I must have met him lots of times when I was very young. I remember that grandma and I bumped into him once. He was with a woman, I assumed it was his wife, she had a face like an agitated squirrel.'

'Mu-um,' I giggled, 'that's a terrible thing to say.'

'Well she did. I must have picked up on some kind of atmosphere between him and grandma and I asked who they were. She said the man had been a very good friend of auntie Eva's and that they had been going to get married, but he had decided to marry someone else. I've remembered it because it was about twenty times more information than she usually gave me about anything.' She picked up the picture of Eva and Nat.

'I never thought about Eva as pretty, but when you look at her here, she's lovely. Look at her face, so sweet and happy and she's got a great little body. You know when I was growing up, when friends came to the house for the first time, they always said, "Your mother's beautiful isn't she? What's wrong with your aunt?" Always, as if they were two sides of the same coin. The beautiful one and the one who wasn't quite right. It left its impression on me.' She began to rifle through the rest of the file.

'Do you think you should be doing that, mum?' She ignored me and pulled out a letter from an ordinary looking brown envelope. She read it slowly and when she had finished, she put her hand over her mouth and handed it to me.

May 1974.
Beloved Eva,
As you know, I'm not much of a letter writer but since we returned from Vienna, I felt I must do something. You think I don't care that I've hurt you but it's not true. All these years I've had to live with the fact that I was a terrible coward and that one stupid decision, or should I say one stupid lack of decision so many years ago, changed the course of my life and your life for ever. What can I say in my defence? Nothing really. I made my bed and I must lie in it as the saying goes. You could call me a selfish

mumzer and you'd be right. On the plane you said that after what we have had, you can't imagine us just 'being friends' but please think about it Eva, please don't disappear from my life again. If you tell me you're not going to put up with me any more, I'll probably be getting what I deserve. But it will be hard to live without you, not to make love to you again, not have you listen to my silly problems and give me your sound advice, to not be able to listen to you tell me about your successes in life and confide your problems.

I am writing this in the shop. Everyone else has gone home and I feel a terrible sadness. I know that yet again I'm betraying others by saying this to you now, but you are and have always been the one real love of my life and if I lose you now, all I can say is, thank you darling Eva for all the love you have given me. You are the most beautiful person I know, inside and outside, and I am a better person for having known you.

Your own, Nat.

'That's a real love letter,' Mum sighed and we were both silent.

'I wonder what did happen after that letter,' she said after a while. I looked at the date – May 1974. 'She would have been, how old then, forty?'

'They must have seen each other after he wrote that letter because auntie Eva told me that he was a good friend of hers. And remember at the funeral, the man who came up to us, that must have been Nat.' I looked at the letter again. 'What does he mean mum, when he says, I'm betraying others by writing this, does it mean he was married when he wrote the letter?'

'I think so.'

'What, they went to Vienna when he was married to someone else – that's terrible isn't it?'

'You can't be so quick to blame people. We don't really know what was going on.'

'But he probably had children. How can that be right?'

'I'm not saying it's right, I'm just saying she must have had her reasons. I like to think that we had her wrong all these years, that she had a great, passionate love life. I hope he brought joy into her life. If anyone deserved it, auntie Eva did. It's good to think that she wasn't lonely all the time.'

'I never thought of her being lonely, but she must have been, I suppose. She was always so cheerful whenever I saw her.'

'I once heard her say that, you know, when I told her she didn't have to run around after grandma all the time, not that she could do any running around in the end. She said, "It's my job to make everyone feel happy. I don't mind it." She never complained about anything, but then again, I never really listened to her, not properly listened.' Mum stood up and began pacing nervously round the tiny room, picking things up, putting them down again. 'I hope Nat made her feel happy. I hope he really, really loved her and gave her terrific presents and told her she was beautiful all the time. I hope he wasn't always the selfish bastard he sounds in that letter.' She stopped moving and looked at the floor.

'Mummy, don't. Please.' She began to sob. Terrible throaty noises, slowly at first and then loud, uncontrollable waves of tears like a child at the classroom door who slowly realises that no one, absolutely no one, is coming to collect them.

'What am I going to do now? What am I going to do without my own mother? All these years I've battled with her and now when I feel ready to start again, she's gone. Everyone's gone. All these questions and there's no one left to ask.' She stood in the middle of the room, her hands straight by her sides, tears and snot running down her face. I went to the bathroom and pulled a long strip of toilet paper. When I got back she was sitting on the floor.

'Mum, you okay?'

'I'm just tired. I'm so tired. I don't know what to do with myself.'

I took her by the hand like she was a little girl and led her into the bedroom. She lay down on the bed and I tucked the bedspread round her.

'Have a sleep. I'll carry on sorting out the stuff and I'll bring you a cup of tea in about an hour.'

'Thanks darling, you're the best girl. I'll be okay if I have a rest.' She closed her eyes and rolled away from me.

I went back into the study and started again at the horrible business of throwing away someone else's life. The only way to do it was not to look too carefully at anything, otherwise I felt I had to keep it all. I shoved pay slips into a big, black plastic bag, letters from auntie Jackie and the cousins, my childhood drawings, old bank statements and most of the army letters from Nat. I looked at the collection of cards, thinking I might save a few. One was so big, the corner had been folded over to fit it into the file.

TO MY DARLING WIFE

A terrible, ridiculous picture flew into my mind: sixty-five year old auntie Eva overdressed in an unsuitable, bright, white wedding dress with an artificial flowered veil over her face. Had there actually been a wedding? Was this one more thing we hadn't known about?

Inside, on the right hand was printed the kind of sentimental verse that Nat liked so much and on the left, shakily written over the indentations of the raised drawing of flowers and ribbons on the front cover, was his handwriting.

To My 'Soon-To-Be Wife' from her 'Soon-To-Be Husband'.

I know you'll think I'm jumping the gun and I know it will be quite a while before it happens, but already, this is how I'm thinking of you. 'My Wife'. After all these years of putting up with me, you're going to make this 'old kaka' the happiest man on earth and I hope and pray that I'll be able to make you happy too. As our old friend Frankie used to sing to us. 'You make me feel so young, you make me feel that spring has sprung.' This card is from one very 'happy individual', one very, very happy individual.

With all the love in the world, from your own, Nat.

I brought it in with me when I woke mum up with a cup of tea.

'What do you think it is, mum, some kind of joke?'

'God I hope not. No, I'm sure it isn't. I suppose his wife must have died, I can't imagine he'd divorce her after all those years. Perhaps he'd made a promise that he'd marry her one day. Does it have a date on it?' I looked on the envelope and could just make out the faint postmark: June 30th 2000. 'That's just a few weeks ago. How old would he have been – must be seventy at least?'

'That's disgusting.'

'It isn't disgusting darling. Old people can still love each other.'

'Yuk. Old people kissing.'

Mum laughed. 'You know, you don't dry up entirely when you get past twenty, people can love each other at any age.'

'Wouldn't she have told us if she was actually going to get married? Wouldn't she have wanted us to be there?' Mum shook her head in an I don't know kind of way and blew on her tea.

'Maybe that's what happens after a lifetime of keeping secrets and having them kept from you,' she said. 'You learn to keep everything to yourself and then I suppose it feels almost impossible to talk to other people. She learned it from my mother I suppose, she was always a great one for keeping things to herself.' She coughed a dry cough and when I looked at her I could see the familiar rings of exhaustion around her eyes. She smiled at me weakly and stroked my cheek. 'That's why it's so important that we don't have secrets from each other. I promise you that I'll never keep anything from you that you need to know and you must promise me you'll always talk to me about things, not keep it all inside you.'

*

Mum and I talked once about finding Nat's number

and ringing to tell him what we knew, but we never did. Cowardly really. We were still in our old flat although we'd chosen a place near Tufnell Park Station, the ground floor of a big house with a garden. Mum said we'd probably be moving in the new year.

Grandma Susi's things and now auntie Eva's almost filled our living room: huge cardboard boxes and plastic bags with books and china and tablecloths spilling out of them, the Peter Rabbit duvet I'd retrieved from her cupboard, and one or two of the orange cushions. The only bit of empty floor space was a tiny strip between the television and our sofa. I couldn't imagine how the mixture of all these things was ever going to fit into one flat, even a big one: mum's colourful, shiny, shabby chic, her sequin lampshades and second-hand painted tables, grandma's elegant Viennese rugs and armchairs and Eva's bits and pieces.

Keeping secrets. My old one eyed teddy bear was wearing a threadbare child's cardigan with blue stripes round the bottom that we had found in a box in auntie Eva's wardrobe and the thin gold cross round its neck. Next to him I'd put a raggedy knitted doll in a red dress.

Keeping secrets. Mum said that we would break the family cycle and never, ever have secrets from each other, but there were already lots of things I hadn't talked to her about, not just what auntie Eva had told me. She didn't know how angry I felt with her sometimes, not just irritable and short tempered but really deep down angry and resentful and then ashamed of myself. She didn't know how all the years she was fighting with grandma Susi, auntie Eva had arranged it so that she could carry on seeing me. She didn't know that, technically at least I wasn't a virgin any more and it hadn't been the wonderful, loving experience she'd told me it could be, not at all. It had been a stupid mistake, one of those things where I'd started along a road and didn't know how to get off it in time.

It would just hurt mum if I told her these things. Maybe I'd tell her when I got older; maybe like mum said, you learned how to keep secrets from people you loved and then it grew into a habit you couldn't break. Perhaps I was going to turn out like all of them, keeping things locked inside me until I lost the words that could ever describe how I felt.

I lay on my bed and looked at auntie Eva's painting, propped on my chest of drawers. Mum said it was by a famous Austrian painter and was probably worth a lot of money but I was never, ever going to sell it, however broke I was. It was going to hang at the end of my bed in my new room so that I could look at it as soon as I woke up and however often I moved home, I would always take it with me:

The farmer and his wife with their arms around each other and in front of them their peaceful, fat, white cow. The gorgeous depth of the green grass and the blackened fir trees and in the background, the purple and blue night sky.

ACKNOWLEDGEMENTS

My grateful thanks to the following people who were willing to talk to me about their lives: Ann McFarlane, Elspeth Morrison, Herta Schenk, Henry Kuttner, Olive Kosky, members of the Association of Jewish Refugees at the Paul Balint Centre. Others shared their expertise with me in many different areas: Pauline Ross, Ian Goodyer, Jon Silverman, Keith Simons, Sadie Flank, Vivienne Gay, Fanny Blake, Clare Beaton. I would also like to thank Cathy Bolton of Commonword for her patience and practical advice and my editor Antonia Till.

In Vienna, Norbert Kettner of the Viennese Department of Health allowed me to interview him and Peter Schwarz and Herwig Czech of the Centre for the Documentation of Austrian Resistance gave me invaluable help, responding to my emails and supplying me with photographs, copies of medical forms from the Nazi records and an important article by Wolfgang Neugebauer and Georg Stacher published in the *Journal of Digestive Diseases* in 1999.

In particular I am indebted to Waltraud Haüpl of Vienna who shared her memories and research on her sister Anne-marie Danner who died in Am Spiegelgrund, and on a memorably rainy day, took me round the hospital at Steinhof and showed me Pavilions 15 and 17 where so many children died. The story of Gertrude in this book is closely based on the life and death of Anne-marie.

The characters in this book are fictitious, but Dr Schwarz is based on a real person, Dr Heinrich Gross. Dr Gross was the doctor at Am Spiegelgrund during two periods of the Second World War and is considered responsible for the death of many children in his care. They died through poisoning with Luminal, starvation, being left to freeze on open balconies in the winter and medical experimentation. He has managed to escape prosecution on a number of occasions, most recently in 2000, when he was deemed unfit for trial. It was only in 2002 that he was stripped of the 1st Class Cross for Accomplishment in Science that he was awarded by the Austrian Government in 1975.

The autobiographical writing of disabled people in Great Britain and of those who survived Nazi persecution has been invaluable to me. In particular: *Last Waltz in Vienna: Destruction of a Family* by George Clare, *No Longer Strangers* by Helga Woolf, *Little Grass Orphan Annie* by Annette Saville, *My Heart in a Suitcase* by Anne L. Fox, *Into the Arms of Strangers: Stories of the Kindertransport* by Mark Jonathon Harris and Deborah Oppenheimer, *I Came Alone,* Bertha Leverton and Shmuel Lowenson (Eds.) and *Out of Sight: the Experience of Disability* by Steve Humphries and Pamela Gordon.

This book would not have been written without the financial support of the Sue Napolitano Award, aimed at supporting the work of disabled writers, financed by an Arts Council of England Awards for All lottery grant, the Esmée Fairbairn Charitable Trust and Manchester City Council and administered by Commonword in Manchester.